The Black Sutra

The Black Sutra

By

Walter C. DeBill, Jr.

Edited and with an introduction by

Robert M. Price

Mythos Books LLC.

Poplar Bluff

Missouri

2006

Mythos Books LLC
351 Lake Ridge Road
Poplar Bluff
MO 63901
U. S. A.

www.mythosbooks.com

Published by Mythos Books, LLC 2006

FIRST EDITION

ISBN 0-9789911-1-7

Set in *Silentium Pro I* and *Minion Pro*

Silentium Pro I by Linotype Library
www.linotype.com

Minion Pro by Adobe Systems Incorporated.
www.adobe.com

Typesetting, layout and design by PAW.

CONTENTS

Introduction

Take it from a theologian, albeit admittedly one with Faustian leanings: Satan, like his Master, only seems frightful because of your guilty conscience. Mr. Policeman would be your friend, too, if you weren't doing something illegal. What do politicians always say when their swindles and felonies are captured on the FBI's candid camera? "Entrapment!" Or as Flip Wilson used to say, "The devil made me do it!" Oh did he, now? The biblical character Satan is always the whipping boy for the guilty eager to shift the blame. The character is more ambivalent than malevolent. Take his very name. 'Satan' is Hebrew for 'accuser,' and the Satan stories of the Bible make pretty clear that he is an accuser in the sense of a prosecuting attorney or a security chief. He questions whether supposed loyalists like David, Job, the high priest Joshua, Jesus, Peter, et. al., are really what they're cracked up to be. So he suggests a little sting operation. If they pass it, all the better. If not, it's better to know.

'Devil' means the same thing. It comes from the Greek word *diabolos* (still pretty much the same in Spanish), and this means, literally, 'thrower,' as in 'caster of aspersions' or 'mud-slinger.' But somewhere along the way, in a very few cases, the devil Satan acquires the coloring of evil, a villain instead of a nemesis. And I'd guess this is because the mytheme has by this time been strained too often through a guilty conscience by people who suspect they aren't passing Satan's periodic little stings. He's *their* enemy, all right. But Satan's original character as a Trickster god manages to peep through occasionally, at least in the hands of story-tellers who can see how an ambivalent character presents more possibilities than a flat-out evil one. Witness Mr. Scratch in Stephen Vincent Benet's "The Devil and Daniel Webster."

And while you're at it, witness Walter C. DeBill, Jr. He, too, knows that 'good' and 'evil' tend to look a lot different depending on which side of the mirror you happen to be viewing them from. And perhaps this is what we ought to expect. Because, after all, just look at the progression: Satan, Diabolos, DeBill, Devil. That's a bit too close for comfort, I'd say! Walt DeBill is well represented under the revealing mask of one of the characters in his story "He Who Comes at the Noontime," an eerie stranger, recognized by a stable boy as a demon, who works quite a trick, making a half-dug grave in a drought-parched village fill up with water, from which lush ferns and vines then grow in startling profusion. Life from death, life which is death disguised, and therein lies the sting: who can tell the difference? Who can see that what appears first to be deliverance from death is deliverance unto death, a life more terrible than death, since it is the endurance of an endless dying? And in the case of such a death, the border between black and white again turns an evasive gray. When has one crossed over? Like Zeno's paradox, one is ever, and never, crossing the midpoint.

Long-lived liches: there's another central image, really an allegory of reading, for much of DeBill's fiction. For it appears out of time. Just as Lovecraft (one of his chief inspirations, though DeBill is no imitator) felt himself an outsider, kidnapped by the Yith Race and dropped off in the wrong historical era, there is a feeling of temporal displacement about DeBill's tales. In fact, of double displacement. First, Walt DeBill is a member of that group of writers (including Richard L. Tierney, John S. Glasby, Stefan B. Aletti, and Don Walsh) whom I think of as the 'Lost Generation' of Arkham House writers, the 'Third Lovecraft Circle,' if you will. Just as the original Lovecraft Circle of HPL, Robert E. Howard, Clark Ashton Smith, Frank Belknap Long, Robert Bloch and others were among the early mainstays of Arkham House, and James Wade, Colin Wilson, Brian Lumley, Gary Myers, Ramsey Campbell, and Lin Carter became protégés of August Derleth as the New Lovecraft Circle (as Lin Carter dubbed them), DeBill, Walsh, Tierney, and the others had either just begun to appear in Arkham House books, or debuting in adjacent forums, soon would have. But the untimely passing of August Derleth, as well as vocational and personal changes in the lives of some of these writers, derailed what seemed inevitable. We saw too little of this nascent Third Circle. Until now. A collection of Walt DeBill has been long overdue, a rough beast whose time has come at last.

Like James Wade's horror tales, Walt DeBill's are occasionally marked by their time of writing. The very devices meant to lend them fresh contemporaneity now give them instead a slightly campy quality, a relevance to a vanished time. But, as with reprinted pulp-era tales, this serves only to increase their charm. (Of course, most of them are not in any important sense time-bound).

And this brings us to the second sense in which DeBill's stories warp time: I know of no writer of weird fiction whose stories read more as if they had been taken right from the pages of *Weird Tales* or *Strange Stories*. True, we praise Lovecraft and some others when we claim that their fiction transcends the pulps, but I suspect that is mostly a matter of apologetics aimed at defending their reputation against schoolmarms who think there is something wrong with pulp fiction. Pulp fiction is a genre (or family of genres) unto itself, and one by no means to be sold short. And Walt DeBill manages, like the scholarly researcher into demonology in "Control," to conjure up precisely the old atmosphere. It works because he has noticed the minor notes struck in pulp esthetics, as well as the major ones. For instance, often his characters, lacking novel length in which to grow and develop with psychological verisimilitude, are simple and direct incarnations of their narrative roles, e.g., 'occultists' pure and simple. As such they have the direct one-dimensionality of folktale characters. On the other hand, as in "Memories of a Previous Death," DeBill is easily able to write with realism and cinematic stream-of-consciousness narration. But one often feels while reading DeBill that one can almost see the printed pages breaking up, polarizing into twin columns of a page of *Weird Tales*, that if one flipped back to the copyright page quickly enough, like catching the light inside the refrigerator door, one would see original publication dates in the thirties.

Let me justify my calling Walt DeBill a latter-day Lovecraftian. His use of his Lovecraftian inspiration is both direct and oblique. Clearly, as many other writers, DeBill has been hypnotized by Lovecraft's Cthulhu Mythos. At this point most Mythos fanciers pursue two directions. They usually utilize Lovecraft's own ancient gods and imitate him by creating their own. More than any other, I should say, DeBill has decided to create his own parallel Mythos and stick to it. The resemblance of his own occasionally cited Mlandoth Cycle to Lovecraft's is clear enough to tantalize the reader, make him know what sort of fun to expect, and yet precisely because of the unfamiliarity of the specific names and myths, one experiences anew the chilly fun of discovering (in Sam Moskowitz's phrase) 'horrors unknown.'

And yet DeBill is audacious enough here and there to run a course directly parallel to some Lovecraftian prototype, especially to Lovecraft's most cosmic tale, "The Whisperer in Darkness." Two of DeBill's stories ("Homecoming" and "He Who Comes at the Noontime") borrow significantly from this one by Lovecraft, but the reference to "The Whisperer in Darkness," while implicit, is in both cases so obvious that one quickly realizes the goal is to take the reader back to some narrative nexus in the original story and, like Robert Frost, to take the neglected fork. Suppose that, having heard the dizzying revelations of the pseudo-Akeley, instead of fleeing the farmhouse in terror, Wilmarth had decided to let the Yuggoth beings take him off with them in their journeys? In effect, that is what happens in this pair of DeBill's tales, and with mind-bending results!

Robert M. Price
October, 2005

Prologue: Collector's Item

Outside the window of the airplane the full moon blazed in glorious solitude, dimming the nearby stars and silvering the patches of cloud below. Beneath them the earth was flat and mottled, dark and mysterious. Marlowe Farrell had been lucky to get aboard this night flight. A reservation had been cancelled only after he had called Uncle Morlin and said that he would arrive tomorrow afternoon.

Uncle Morlin was dying, and a solitary death did not appeal to him as had a reclusive life. He had telephoned to demand that his only living relative and heir come to his bedside, with a veiled threat to alter his will if Marlowe did not come. Or perhaps that had been Marlowe's imagination; it was difficult to talk to Uncle Morlin without reading sinister meanings into every sentence. Marlowe's mother had believed her brother to be an evil wizard. His father thought him a nasty charlatan, but was afraid of him anyway.

Morlin Lewis had been born on Midsummer's Eve in the year 1900. A morose and disagreeable child, he was unpopular with both children and adults, and had run away to sea in 1912 on a decrepit sailing vessel bound for India. He was not heard of again until 1938, when he reappeared with a large fortune, the origin of which he never discussed, and four big steamer trunks of bizarre objects and ancient books. These formed the nucleus of the unique collection that Marlowe now stood to inherit. There was a brief round of family visits, during which he seemed bored and ill at ease and let drop that he had spent time in Tibet, Mongolia, Japan, Micronesia and the Near East. He enjoyed dropping the names of faraway places without giving any details of his adventures there. After he purchased a town house in Barrett, Texas and settled down to the life of a scholarly hermit, only Marlowe continued to see him.

Marlowe was a wide-eyed bookish child of eight when he first walked the six blocks to the high narrow brick house on Goliad Street and reached up to the gargoyle knocker in the center of the white six-paneled door. From that time until Marlowe went away to college, Uncle Morlin tolerated him with amused disdain. He allowed him to roam the house freely but let him handle objects or read books only by permission, which was often denied. He answered questions with teasing evasiveness. "Just a trinket from Ulan Bator . . . ," he would say of a golden dagger inlayed with mysterious characters, adding, ". . . if I remember correctly." Or "The natives thought a demon lived in that," of a particularly hideous wooden idol. Or, more than once, "I had to kill a man to get that." He let Marlowe read freely among his phenomenal collection of works on ancient and medieval history, and allowed him access to most of the magical and occult works, usually commenting "Bunk, Marlowe, just more bunk." But by the time Marlowe entered high school the occasional absences of this remark and the titles denied to him had mapped out the areas which Uncle Morlin did not consider to be 'bunk.' They comprised a weird array of antediluvian works in foreign tongues together with their translations, ancient works on yogic practices, histories of cults and secret societies and a small number of magical grimoires. Most of them shared in common a group of names,

1

Mlandoth, Ngyr-Khorath, 'Ymnar and a few others, which Marlowe was unable to learn more about until his college days.

By then the house had grown full and cluttered with gritty dust-laden antiques and exotic objects of art, and the books had overflowed their shelves into untidy heaps. Marlowe was allowed to help move the collection to a sprawling house in the country, full of echoing corridors and dusty, long-unused rooms. Marlowe was surprised to learn that Uncle Morlin had a large amount of chemical and electronic apparatus. He set himself the task of learning these subjects thoroughly. By now he was completely obsessed with the idea of inheriting the collection and acquiring the occult wisdom and power he believed his uncle to possess.

When he went away to college he majored in electronics but also mastered a rich background in other scientific subjects, as well as a broad knowledge of human history. He made every effort to track down the leads to Uncle Merlin's occult interests that he had gleaned in the musty corners of the university's rare book collection. But the results were meager. Little by little reality crept in on him and it became harder to maintain the majestic scope of his interests while completing the course requirements for his degree. After graduation his career as an engineer proved very demanding. The dream of the collection flickered only rarely in the back of his memory. Then, only yesterday afternoon, Morlin had called. And he was dying, and Marlowe was going to have it, the collection, with Uncle Merlin's fortune providing the leisure to use it.

Barrett was a white diamond on the horizon and then a miniature of the starry sky itself as the disorderly ranks and files of tiny lights expanded to cover the earth below. After a rough touch down Marlowe phoned the house and got a hollow voice with cultured diction which seemed taken aback by his unexpectedly early arrival, and promised that a car would be dispatched immediately to pick him up. The conversation was brief and the voice never identified itself.

Marlowe was waiting outside the terminal when the limousine arrived. It had been described to him over the phone and he identified himself and got in before the lumpy-looking driver could emerge. As they passed from lighted suburbs into moonlit countryside the old wonder and fascination of the collection came back like the flood of memories unleashed by a piquant odor. He recalled the five-thousand year old Japanese *dogu* shaped exactly like a man in a space suit, decorated with an irregular pattern very like the symbols in a monograph titled *A Preliminary Analysis of the Micronesian Shards*. Uncle Morlin once mentioned casually that he had identified 'the language of the shards'—had he translated them? And what had he learned from a tongue older than Sumer? He remembered the broken remains of a thing like a candelabrum, which reproduced precisely the eight hundred foot design overlooking the Bay of Pisco on the coast of Peru. It had been covered with an intricate pattern of fine corrosion like the remains of electrical wiring. Had Morlin, with his meters and oscilloscopes, succeeded in reproducing that wiring and discovered what devices belonged in the candle sockets? There was the case of sample jars he had stumbled on, neatly labeled to identify the scrapings from dozens of ceremonial vessels from the prehistoric past. One had contained a mummified human ear. Had Morlin been able to analyze them? Had he left notes on his discoveries or would Marlowe have to duplicate the scholarly efforts of forty years?

They turned off an obscure county road onto a winding driveway through bushy oaks. As they approached the massive two-storied structure it blotted out the moon, leaving the front face of the mansion in darkness except where a few lighted windows shone. At the time his uncle purchased the mansion Marlowe had been too young to be curious about its origin, simply accepting it as another miraculous production of Uncle Morlin. Now he realized that its immense blend of Georgian precision, deep-southern classicism and Texan size must have been the freak of some self-made millionaire, a childhood vision of wealth materialized by success and sold, after death or bankruptcy, for far less than its cost. The lights were scattered randomly, three in the main wing, two in the south addition, one in the north—more light than Marlowe had ever seen here at one time. Morlin had been sparing of light, though he had no need for frugality; he had a sensual love of darkness.

The driver pulled up before the towering main door and led him up the jarring marble steps, opening it without a key. He gestured for Marlowe to enter the small anteroom to the left of the entrance hall. He barely had time to reacquaint himself with the grandfather clock with the two mysterious extra hands that dominated the room before he was joined by a tall cadaverous man dressed in shiny pointed shoes and a dark, conservative, obviously expensive suit. He had a smooth, professionally bland face and if he had worn a flower in his lapel Marlowe would have taken him for an undertaker. But he introduced himself as Niles Ramny, the executor of Morlin's estate—Morlin Lewis had passed away seven hours earlier and been cremated immediately according to his own wishes. Marlowe wondered why he had not been told this over the phone; he could have sworn that the hollow tones of the executor, Mr. Ramny, were the same he had heard over the phone from the airport.

Mr. Ramny was supervising the fulfillment of a few small bequests to museums and needed to oversee the workmen loading the designated objects. It was difficult to get them to come at this hour but the firm of Ramny and Marney believed it best to settle all estate affairs as quickly as possible for the benefit of all, didn't he agree? It would not take long and Marlowe would be comfortable in his uncle's study, which was cleaner and had a well-stocked liquor cabinet. Marlowe had noticed how dusty the room was—after the move from the townhouse, the collection had been kept immaculately clean, though Marlowe had never seen the hired help who must have kept it so. Evidently Uncle Morlin's standards of housekeeping had deteriorated during his final illness.

He followed the tall man through a labyrinth of corridors lined with closed doors to the spacious room where Uncle Morlin had spent most of his time. Ahead he saw a yellow sickle of light where the arched door to Morlin's study stood ajar. A small rat scuttled through it and proceeded down the hall away from them in short erratic dashes. Ramny opened the door and motioned for him to enter, ordering him to make himself comfortable. He closed the door behind him and padded away after the rat.

Morlin's study was a huge square room with a fourteen-foot ceiling. It was lined with bookshelves, many of them glassed in, and closed cabinets. Most of the floor was covered with deep oval carpets of Central Asian pattern. Heavy armchairs stood here and there like guards watching over the books. Marlowe made for the leather-covered swivel chair by the circular table in the center of the room. He sat down and took out his pipe.

A large volume in black letter lay open beside him amidst a scattering of notes in Morlin's tidy script. He picked it up; there was no title on the leather spine but a distant memory identified it as the *Uralte Schrecken* of the Graf von Könnenberg. The open pages felt gritty with dust. He looked around at the thousands upon thousands of books that lined the walls, reaching above the line of light cast by the low-hanging lamps and on to the shadowed levels that had to be reached with a wheeled ladder. They were of all shapes and sizes and colors and degrees of antiquity; many were priceless. They embodied the strange tale that had obsessed his uncle and now himself.

There was a lore that had filtered down through the eons. It was carved in wind-worn stone in the sands of forbidden deserts, it was murmured by preternaturally aged creatures like that known as the Last Harlequin. It was sung in elfin choruses when certain coils of wire were passed through a special apparatus. And the gleanings of the men who sought these things were hoarded in these books, to be suppressed, scoffed at, hidden—or studied with the intensity of religious passion.

It told that Earth has been tenanted not once but many times by thinking creatures, like the crystalline spiders who came from an elliptical galaxy one hundred million years ago to die in peace and beauty on the shores of a halcyon Cretaceous sea. The universe teems with intelligent life. And man was not the first native life form of Earth to evolve intelligence. The alchemy of a certain genetic potential and the proper environment produces intelligence and civilization again and again, and even the amphibious Sanafyil whom the Serpent Men drove back into the sea were not the first. Nor was Sumer the first human civilization. The boreal winds of the Riss glaciation chilled Hezur, the City of Bones, and three hundred millennia passed before the scribes of Ngarathoe wrote of the passing of Hezur.

Among both the native forms of Earth and the visitors from beyond, many were essentially manlike. We seem to fit an evolutionary pattern common throughout the cosmos, variant expressions of a universal life force. The mysterious Dhraion Throl who came from the Small Magellanic Cloud and watched the trilobites play in shallow tidal pools had two arms and two legs and spoke a language difficult but not impossible for men. And the furry hominids who came from a planet of Vega sixty million years ago found the smaller tarsier-like Tamara of the Paleocene forests well on the way toward civilization.

But some were ineffably alien, especially in the earliest times. From the titanic explosion at the beginning of the universe had come radiant Mlandoth and darkling Mril Thorion, the Cosmic Mother: effulgent Mlandoth, knowing no boundaries, no here, no there, in whom galaxies dance with abandon and atoms spy their distant neighbors, Mlandoth, whom few have glimpsed though all life stands before him; beckoning Mril Thorion, creating and destroying in her ceaseless, relentless movement, Mril Thorion, who will whisper to the last dark star at the end of all things. They intertwine forever, pervading all time, all space, with the endless filigree of their movement, and the whorls and eddies of their meeting are the finite life forms we know.

At a time late in the cosmic drama, though remote to us, one such vortex of life had settled in this region of space and soon witnessed resentfully the birth of the sun and her planets: the creature known in ancient echoes as Ngyr-Khorath, the Dream-Death. Soon after the earth formed, the fiery Paighon had settled in her core and the eternal struggle between these two elemental horrors has been the pivotal event in the history of the Earth. It was said that men could communicate with Ngyr-Khorath and his servant 'Ymnar and learn to wield forces beyond the farthest dreams of modern physics, though the way was treacherous.

In contrast to verbal accounts, physical evidence was even more scanty. In the dawn of man Hezur never housed more than fifty thousand of the first true men. And on a time scale of hundreds of thousands of years even stone is a frail legacy. The walls of Belegyr, which felt the icy breath of the glaciers come and go, are no more. There was little danger of discovery by orthodox scientists, digging in known habitation sites or trying to fit new fossils into well-established theories. What archaeologist would dig in the desert of Takla Makan where the tower of Tzechio Tzunnuq lies deep, and what would a paleontologist make of the skull of the serpent-king Tasz who once held court sprawled on a couch of onyx, while his vassals clung casually to the jewel-studded floors and walls and ceilings of the caverns of glittering Gah Khag?

Most were long dead and forgotten by all but a few eccentrics, who pored over curiosities such as the *Amphibian Scrolls* of waterproof parchment which Marlowe saw in a case near him, so ancient and brittle that they could be handled only with special instruments and chemical sprays. Some left remnants: as pathetic as the few dozen rat-like Nireyee who survive in the caverns of the Kun Lun Mountains, preserving the traditions of eighty million years; as horrible as the voracious hundred-foot Ngrambotha whom 'Ymnar created to menace the Dhraion Throl on the shores of Pre-Cambrian seas, and whom a fraction of the current 'sea monster' sightings show to be alive in small numbers. A few of the ancient ones lurk eternally, their power undiminished, though it is difficult to see how one such as Yidhra, the shape-changing mother of all earthly life, could survive unobserved in the overcrowded world of modern man.

The goals of the esoteric few had been diverse. The keenest minds shared a craving for the immortal wisdom handed down from the beginning of time. Of the evil ones, most lusted for the power to wield unknown forces, to rule among one's own race, to influence the paths of destiny. There were the mysterious and much-feared ones known as the Masters of the Life Force, who sought personal immortality, not through a pathetic search for herbs and aphrodisiacs but through control of the deepest principles of existence. Not a few sought some form of mystical union with primal Mlandoth himself; certain arcane sources hinted cryptically that the ultimate fulfillment of life was possible for those who could evade the perils and stand before his face. Marlowe was unsure of his own motivation; perhaps it was akin to the profound, irresistible curiosity about the objects of awe which marks the rare few visionaries of any race.

But the risks were many and terrible; the annals whispered of the physical and psychic mutilations of those who had achieved much but not enough. Even the mere absence of success would be a heavy penalty; Marlowe had no desire to live his life as a bizarre recluse and end it frustrated and alone. Always beneath his enthusiasm lay an undercurrent of nagging skepticism that made him doubt his purpose even as he pursued it. In the course he was choosing, he could fail through his own doubting hesitance as easily as through gullibility. Like Morlin Lewis he had exceptional physical and intellectual courage; unlike his uncle he also had moral scruples. Would he prove ruthless enough to follow Morlin's footsteps into the unknown? He believed that Morlin and many with whom he trafficked were capable of any degree of violence and cruelty in pursuit of their dark goals.

He sat musing for half an hour before he became restless. He got up and moved aimlessly about the room, reading the titles of the books on the shelves. They were interesting but he saw none of Morlin's more prized possessions. The best were either in the cabinets, which were locked, or elsewhere in the house. He resented being pushed aside to cool his heels for so long, with the treasures of the collection so tantalizingly near. Ramny's behavior was altogether fishy. A lawyer working at that time of night? And even the rich could hardly get workmen to turn out in the wee hours. Marlowe got up and quietly stepped to the door. The carpeted hallway outside was softly lit by the sconces his uncle favored. He could near no sound.

He stepped out and went down the hall to his left, silent as a cat on the thick carpet. Where the corridor ended another ran to the right. He walked slowly, listening. Still no sound but the rushing of the wind outside and a cricket somewhere in the house. The hall was lined on both sides with evenly spaced doors, like an abandoned hotel. He couldn't find a light switch, but the glow from the hall outside the study spread some light around the corner. He tried the door to one of the side rooms. It was unlocked. The room was dark but appeared to be full of modern paintings and sculpture. He recognized a little stone figure as a Clark Ashton Smith original. He reached toward it hesitantly, then nervously drew back his hand. He immediately felt foolish; whatever it was, it was his now. He picked it up, grasping it firmly. A sinister thing, it might have been an evil god from some eon-dead pantheon.

He heard a muffled bump far away. He put the figure down softly, closed the door and made his way back past the study. Where the hall ended in that direction a blackened stretch connected with another corridor from which soft light came. It had been so long that he had forgotten his way around the labyrinthine mansion. He crossed the short unlit passage and entered another long tunnel of soft light. He looked into several of the rooms here, waiting for another sound to guide him. His uncle had been one of the greatest collectors in the world, the envy of other occultists the world over. Was his incredible collection being pillaged in the dead of night? One room was crammed with electronic gear, another was dominated by a glass case containing a mummy. Loot from some unrecorded Egyptian tomb? The feet were abnormally large and the ears had a peculiar shape. He strained to hear the faintest sound.

Was his uncle already the victim of latter-day tomb robbers? He opened another door and drew back quickly from a room with chalk marks on the floor and a reek of sulfur. The next room was littered with packing material and crates stenciled A. MacLachlan & Co. with an Indianapolis address. Morlin had been collecting right to the end. Another room was full of big blocks of transparent plastic in which grotesque statues were embedded, ranging in size from a rat-like thing the size of a cocker spaniel to a black anthropoid figure rather larger than a man, all in attitudes of movement. He had seen smaller items like these containing butterflies and seahorses; these must have been enormously expensive replicas of mythical creatures. Or . . . genuine relics of the mystery-laden past, at which books could only hint? Could such things yet survive in the hidden corners of the earth? What ruthless greed could reduce such splendid, living rarities to the status of mere possessions? He shuddered with an intolerable clash of awe and revulsion.

A scraping sound startled him with its nearness. He padded stealthily to the end of the hall, which opened abruptly into a wide landing, now dark, around the well of a circular stairway through which light shone up from below. He remembered now that the broad steps led down to a wide rear door on the lower level at the back of the house, used for deliveries. He tiptoed to the railing.

Below and in front of him three workmen, muffled in bulky coveralls, were struggling with a large packing crate. They had used stout planks to lever it up onto crude wooden rollers and were preparing to roll it diagonally towards the door. Beyond them he could see a pair of dark trouser legs over shiny pointed shoes.

Suddenly something went wrong; the crate lurched, outran the rollers as the workmen hopped aside, crashed onto the floor, first one end, then the other. Two panels of the crate, the one facing Marlowe and the one directly behind it, toppled to the floor, letting the light shine through *the solid block of crystal in which Morlin Lewis stood rigidly in an attitude of panic, like some exotic insect trapped in a bottle, knees flexed, palms outthrust, gape-mouthed, his eyes wide open and undoubtedly alive . . .*

From the Sea

The shop lay down a narrow, cobbled street of narrow, leaning buildings, uniform only in their atmosphere of squalor and decay. The air of antiquity and decadence always appealed strongly to Parker, promising revelations of ancient, curious and even terrible secrets long lost in this obscure and forgotten corner of the old seaport. The shop itself, with its narrow peaked roof and bleary small-paned windows, never failed to fascinate Parker, in spite of the preponderance of used junk and 'pop' trash among the Curios and Antiques advertised by the faded sign outside. The creak of the door and muffled tinkle of the bell always ushered him into a dimly-lit realm of fantasy, a point of contact with exotic places and past ages.

Today Parker walked directly to the back of the store, through the narrow cluttered aisles past the tin toys, dirty-looking bottles, cheap furniture and corroded brass, past the single rack of battered and ragged books to the tables and shelves reserved for the most interesting oddities. An aspiring artist with an unfortunate dilettante mentality, he habitually spent a ridiculously large fraction of his small independent means on fragments of exotic art, in hopes that they would inspire him, and was dependant on lucky finds in dusty corners such as this to be able to afford anything of real interest. This trip, however, seemed doomed to disappointment. There were only new imports, of dubious quality, Kenyan statuettes of teak with obvious saw marks, chipped bookends of Mexican onyx, and worse.

"You seem disappointed, sir."

Parker was startled by the sudden voice behind him. He turned to find a tall, elderly Negro with close-cropped, iron-gray hair peering down at him from a height of at least six-foot four. The cultivated voice sounded out of place coming from above the faded denim shirt, cheap green chino slacks and monstrous brogans. Parker assumed that he was a temporary substitute for the proprietor, a rather colorful black woman of indeterminate age and phenomenal bulk.

"Perhaps you would like to see something different?" He had an incredibly broad nose. "We have something in the back which I think might interest you."

Caught off balance and not quite knowing what to say, Parker followed him silently through a narrow doorway and a maze of scarred furniture. His posture was very erect and he moved as noiselessly as a shark. Eventually they emerged through a low archway into a sort of workshop littered with rusty hand-tools and bits of furniture in the process of being crudely 'reconditioned.' The giant stepped to a tall oak cupboard, withdrew an object and thrust it before Parker on upturned palms.

At first Parker felt let down. The object before him was a flattened triangle of polished stone, obtuse-angled with a convex curve along the thin eight-inch base and swelling gradually to a half-scroll an inch thick at the apex, obviously a stylized representation of a seashell. The stone, however, was more interesting, dark-green striated with black, something like malachite but darker and somehow more lustrous, seeming almost to glow in the dim light of the dusty workroom. There were two narrow ellipses of dark blue inlaid on either side of the half-scroll. The finish was exquisite, and as Parker tilted it searching for scratches or tool-marks he could find absolutely none until he looked along the curved base. Taking it to a window to get better light, he discovered a faint curvilinear design in a band about halt an inch wide which was too unrepetitive and asymmetrical to be anything but writing. Parker was no linguist, but in his search for the exotic in art, literature and history he had seen with an artist's eye examples of almost every form of writing ever used by man and knew that this was not one of them.

"Where did it come from?" asked Parker, trying to conceal his excitement.

"A brother from New Orleans sold it to us last week." The juxtaposition of 'brother' and 'New Orleans' startled Parker with its suggestion of Voodoo cultism and the tall man must have noticed, for he explained, "*You* know, *soul* brother. He said that it came from the sea." His opaque dark-brown eyes seemed to twinkle slightly and Parker felt uncomfortable with the curious mixture of obsequiousness and ebullience.

"From the sea? How do you mean?"

"That's all he said, sir. The price is five dollars."

Parker was surprised at the low price, realizing that his attempt to appear uninterested would not have fooled a child, and suspected that nocturnal abstraction from a private collection and subsequent 'fencing' might be closer to the truth than the 'brother' from New Orleans, but he had the true collector's lack of scruple in such matters and immediately paid.

Hurrying home through the darkening streets with his mysterious prize, Parker immediately began a search through all of his books which might contain examples of obscure alphabets or ideographs, but found nothing resembling the inscription on the stone figure. His collection of books on ancient, prehistoric and ethnic art also failed to help, but an hour at the public library turned up a crude sketch, in an out-of-date archaeology text which resembled it somewhat. There was a footnote referring to a *National Geographic* article and upon looking it up he found a photograph of a very similar artifact.

It had been found in 1932 by a group of zoologists studying wildlife on an uninhabited atoll not far from Rapa in the Tubuai Islands of the Pacific. Carved from a slightly darker green stone and badly weathered, it was of the same shape and proportion with similar elliptical inlays, but the markings along the fan-shaped curve had been nearly obliterated and had been dismissed as a merely decorative pattern. It was quite unlike the art of the Polynesian natives of the region. There were no other signs of human visitation on the atoll. The stone itself presented a mystery, for there was nothing like it known in the Tubuais.

The natives of Rapa and other nearby islands professed to knew nothing about it, but displayed fear at the sight of it. When questioned persistently, they would only hint that it might belong to a legend-ary race said to have inhabited the islands before the coming by canoe of the Polynesians. This race was claimed to possess powerful black magic and to be in league with horrible demons from beneath the sea. The legends told that these beings were annihilated by the Polynesians, aided by the magic of their own gods, but that the sea-demons, the Loita, still lurked beneath the waves, and it would not do to pass near certain atolls in the graceful but frail outrigger canoes, especially by night.

The object itself had been lost on the return voyage, believed to have been carried away by one of the scientists who had apparently fallen overboard during an attack of fever. He had contracted some unknown tropical disease in the islands and been afflicted with delirious fits, horrible nightmares, and hallucinations.

Something in the account stirred a latent memory in the back of Parker's mind. The Loita . . .

"The hideous legend of the Rloedha . . ." The phrase had been dropped casually by Paul Tregennis, a student of occult, legendary, and ancient matters who was so fond of mystical name-dropping that Parker had not in-quired further. Of course the resemblance to 'Loita' might be coincidence, but he resolved to question him as soon as possible.

Returning to his apartment, Parker set the cryptic figure on his bedside table and lay looking at it for half an hour before going to sleep. What was the connection between the blue inlays and the seashell motif? Obviously Parker's prize could not be of similarly ancient origin with the Tubuaian specimen, its condition was too immaculate, but could it be a copy of a better specimen with the writing intact? He finally switched off the light and drifted off to sleep with the moonlight-swathed figure before his eyes.

That night he dreamed of the sea. He seemed to be swimming under water in a dim green world of sinister shapes and eerie, frightening shadows just beyond his range of vision. He felt a strange sensation that something was beckoning him onward toward some unknown goal. As the sea gradually grew clearer and more transparent, he could discern before him the ruins of an undersea city, set on a steep hillside and bedecked with streamers of gently waving seaweed. The low, domed, stone buildings were circular or elliptical and covered with barnacles and a dark green ooze which blotched the walls like climbing ivy. The diffuse green light seemed to originate within the low, arched doorways. There were no windows. As he drew close to the city, the sensation of beckoning became stronger and mere distinct, seeming almost but not quite to resolve itself into words. He became aware of vague, moving shadows among the seaweed and stone, as of some kind of living creatures which he could not quite make out. These shadows caused a mounting feeling of irrational fear. As the shadows began to become more distinct, he awoke with a start to find himself in a cold sweat. The figure on the bedside table had a singularly evil look in the gray morning light.

In spite of its nightmare quality, Parker was pleased with his imaginative dream and felt that he would get more than five dollars' worth of inspiration out of his new treasure. Realizing that he could get nothing out of Tregennis before the evening hours but sleepy surliness, he spent the day painting a sunset of burnished gold over a great white space which he intended to cover with an ocean filled with new mystery.

At shortly after seven o'clock in the evening Parker arrived on foot at the unpainted Victorian relic just beyond the edge of town which Tregennis inhabited alone. Tregennis, his lank form draped with a black silk Chinese robe which contrasted sharply with Parker's threadbare tweed coat and unpressed shirt, led him into a room furnished solely with rugs, cushions, and black-light posters where Parker sat uncomfortably on the floor and sipped green tea, which he loathed.

"The other night you mentioned something about the hideous legend of the Rloedha. I'd like to know more about it."

"Why?" asked Tregennis from the depths of a pile of cushions in the corner. Parker explained about his acquisition, emitting only the dream. There was a long pause before Tregennis spoke, and, though it was hard to tell in the dim light, Parker thought that his dark eyes narrowed.

"The Rloedha," he began in a careful, didactic manner, "according to the *Chronicles of Thrang*, the *Mloeng Texts*, and other sources, were a race which came to earth from the stars before the advent of earth-life. They dwelt in the sea, and built vast stone cities all over the world but centered in the Pacific Ocean. When earth-life began to evolve, they sought to destroy it, aided by their abominable god 'Ymnar.

"There was something about their life-force or metabolism that was incompatible with the presence of earth life. But they were unable to stamp out the new life-forms because they spread so rapidly after reaching the cellular level, and gradually disappeared."

"I guess that lets out my little toy," said Parker in a bantering tone. His blond, blue-eyed boy scout appearance seemed out of place in this room. "It's much too new."

"Not necessarily. Apparently the Rloedha didn't all die out. Some, at least, merely became dormant, and could be aroused under certain conditions. There have been incidents even in historic times which indicated that they were at work. Being unable to travel on land, they worked through human recruits, establishing cults dedicated to the worship of 'Ymnar. There was a secret society dedicated to suppressing them in existence as late as the nineteenth century. Crowley mentioned it in his unpublished notes. At any rate the object you describe was certainly inspired by the legend of the Rloedha. Such objects were well known in Ngarathan times. They are described in detail in the *Chronicles of Thrang*, where they are known as *balthon thlomor*. Their significance is unclear, but they were considered objects of horror."

Parker felt let down. Tregennis' yarn had convinced him that his *balthon thlomor* was a recent production associated with some crackpot occult group. "What about the inscription?" he asked.

"That's a very interesting point. As far as I know, the *Chronicles* don't mention any inscriptions, but I know a man who has seen samples of what he believes to be Rloedhan writing. I could put you in touch with him."

"Please do," said Parker, although he was not at all certain he wanted to get mixed up with any more Rloedhan scholars. He rose to leave.

"I'll talk to him tomorrow and we'll probably drop around to see your new trinket," said Tregennis.

"Thanks," said Parker with a sinking feeling. He was really in for it now. He greatly preferred vague literary references to the occult to real life occultists, who were always incredibly dull.

That night he dreamed again of the city beneath the sea. This time he saw the inhabitants clearly, and started with fear as he recognized the living counterparts of the stone figure. The creatures which floated, hovered, and darted before the low, glowing doorways had fan-like bodies like a ray or devilfish, tapering to a rounded snout with phosphorescent blue eyes at the sides. The long tail seemed to be deep and narrow like that of a crocodile rather than a ray. They swam with the cloak-like body horizontal, flapping the lateral portions and lashing the tail from side to side. He noticed that they had rather manlike arms extending from the ventral surface of the body and even in dream felt amusement at the trite anthropomorphism of his earthbound imagination. But his amusement lessened as he observed how the arms were rooted very close together, and the peculiar praying mantis position in which the arms were held motionless while swimming was not very manlike at all. One particularly close specimen raised both arms toward him as though in greeting, and he must have shrieked in his sleep as the light of a large doorway silhouetted the seven bony talons of each thumbless paw.

The beckoning sensation resolved itself into words, although Parker could not be sure whether he heard them or received them through some form or telepathy. At first he received only strange sounds or sound-impressions which were of no tongue Parker had ever heard. There seemed to be frequent repetitions of the sounds 'bvaazhödhnö gnoortha, bvaazhödhnö gnoortha,' as though this was part of some ritual. Then he became aware that they were trying to communicate with him. They wanted him to do something, and then he would receive some glorious reward. As he strained to comprehend what they wanted of him, the sense of horror and fright mounted to a crescendo and the dream of the city suddenly ended.

This time, however, he did not awaken immediately. When he did finally awake, he felt as though he had had some further strange and restless dream which he could not remember. Upon arising he was amazed to find his feet encrusted with sand and the legs of his pajamas stiff with salt. He must have walked in his sleep down to the nearby beach. He decided the stone must be getting on his nerves, and put it away in a little-used cupboard.

Parker spent the day struggling to put a mysterious, enchanting sea beneath his golden sunset. Every stroke seemed to make the water look more dark, gloomy, and depressing, and when he tried to lighten the color, it became repulsively livid. By evening when Tregennis arrived, it was a relief to put down the brushes.

Tregennis was accompanied by a very small man with an enormous head sparsely covered with kinky reddish hair. He introduced himself as Mr. Braithwaite and demanded with scarcely concealed impatience to see the *balthon thlomor*, which he explained meant sea-stone in the Ngarathan tongue. Parker, however, slightly irritated by Braithwaite's brusque manner, insisted that they be seated and inquired about the origins of the Rloedhan legends.

"Most of what is known comes from the *Chronicles of Thrang*," began Braithwaite in a shrill, nervous voice. "The oldest known copy is on a set of scrolls, apparently dating back to Ngarathoe itself, just after the last glaciation. But much of the material is older, antedating mankind, and some of it is older than all native earth-life. The earlier parts recount how the 'Ithrian race, the original authors of the *Chronicles*, arrived from Betelgeuse and established themselves in Antarctica, which they called Thrang. Somewhat later the Rloedha came to earth from Byldha, which from the Ngarathan star charts must have been Capella, during the Archaeozoic Age about two billion eight hundred thousand years ago. After an unsuccessful eon-long struggle with the Rloedha the 'Ithria emigrated, leaving the documents which became the *Chronicles* to be translated and added to by later races."

"It seems strange that so potent a life-form should be destroyed by primitive earth-life," interjected Parker.

"The *Chronicles* throw no light on that, of course," answered Braithwaite, "since the decline of the Rloedha took place in the interval between the emigration of the 'Ithria and the first translation of the *Chronicles*. But my own speculation is that they were dependant on the presence in the sea of complex organic compounds, possibly amino acids, which the early earth-life would have rapidly scavenged. Likewise there is no explanation for the later outbreaks of Rloedhan activity, but it's possible that some chemical or radioactive effect could alter their metabolism enough to enable them to synthesize the necessary compounds. Actually they don't appear to have been particularly advanced technologically, relying mainly on natural psychic powers and the aid of 'Ymnar."

"Then 'Ymnar was a real creature?" asked Parker.

"Yes. He is written of as actually appearing in battles between the 'Ithria and the Rloedha. He was a protean monstrosity which could change shape, often imitating both the Rloedha and the 'Ithria, and could operate on land."

"Just what was the form of the Rloedha?" asked Parker.

"I don't know," answered Braithwaite, "the *Chronicles* describe them by comparison with marine creatures which linguists have been unable to identify."

Although Parker was rather appalled at the seriousness with which the man seemed to take this wild legendry, there was something about the large pale-blue eyes and the neat, precise movements which was inconsistent with the image of a harmless crank. "Tregennis said you had seen examples of Rloedhan writing," he said.

"I'm not sure. Twelve years ago some shards of a material similar to the shells of mollusks were found in Micronesia with some peculiar carvings on them which appear to be an unknown form of writing. The circumstances of the find suggested that they might have been related to an outbreak of Rloedhan activity there just before the coming of the Europeans. It would be extremely interesting to compare them with the inscription on your stone."

Parker at last went into the bedroom and brought the stone. Braithwaite held it almost reverently.

"There's no doubt about it. Every detail agrees with the description in the *Chronicles*." His excitement was obvious. He tilted it to let the lamp-light catch the inscription and examined it minutely. His eyes first gleamed, then turned opaque as he said, "It certainly resembles the carvings on the Micronesian shards, but I need to make a detailed comparison. Would you accept a hundred dollars for it?"

Parker's jaw dropped slightly, then quickly snapped shut as he passed in half a second from the impulse to accept to the conviction that it must be worth much more.

"Perhaps later on, but for the moment I'm going to keep it," he said casually. He had resolved not to let it out of his sight until it had been appraised by several dealers.

Braithwaite sat motionless, his lips slightly compressed. "Mr. Parker, have you ever heard of the Society of Paighon?"

"No, I haven't."

"We are the oldest secret society in existence. We exist to combat the Rloedha and those whom they serve. We have access to the most advanced scientific equipment and would like very much to submit a *balthon thlomor* to a thorough analysis."

Parker had horrified visions of samples being chipped off and powerful laser beams being applied.

"I want to keep it for now, but you're welcome to copy the inscription."

Braithwaite sensed his growing stubbornness and confided in a careful, expressionless tone, "Mr. Parker, we are very concerned about a current and growing outbreak of the Rloedha. There is evidence that they are multiplying in the sea and recruiting human agents on a large scale. Several of our members have disappeared and others have died in suspicious accidents. We suspect that the *balthon thlomor* are somehow related to recruitment. A member in Liverpool wrote last year that he had located one, but before it could be brought here for examination he and the stone disappeared and the other two members of his group were killed—one in a most horrible fashion. We really need your stone very badly."

"I'm sorry, Mr. Braithwaite, but I want to keep it for a while and have it appraised."

Braithwaite abandoned the effort.

"Very well," he said, rising to leave. Almost as an afterthought he added, "May I come tomorrow and photograph the inscription here?"

Parker readily consented and let Braithwaite and Tregennis out of the apartment with a great sense of relief. He was irritated, excited, highly skeptical and yet impressed. Again he had felt some obscure inhibition against mentioning his dreams.

That night in the dream of the Rloedha the message became clearer. He must bring the proper tribute as part of an initiation rite, and then he would join the creatures for eternity in their shadowy abode of Tchoolmö-Zhr. Rituals would be carried out and strange surgical operations performed, and he would be metamorphosed gradually into a being like themselves, immortal and utterly contemptuous of mankind. They would prepare the earth for the coming reign of 'Ymnar and That Which 'Ymnar Serves. It was when they spoke of the tribute that Parker's fear grew strongest, and as understanding of this grew near, the dream ended in a surge of fear.

He awoke with the acute feeling that there was something wrong. His luminous watch said two o'clock. Then he heard a soft noise at the window. The faint moonlight silhouetted a figure outside, the figure of a small man with an enormous head. Suddenly the figure turned aside and disappeared. Parker could hear the rapid footsteps receding, and had just begun to breathe again when the window was darkened momentarily by a gigantic, stiffly erect figure striding silently and purposefully after the first visitor. Mr. Braithwaite was not the only one on the prowl tonight.

Thoroughly unnerved, Parker turned on the light and checked the window latches. After seven cigarettes and two stiff doses of scotch, he hid the stone under

14

his bed and somehow managed to get back to sleep.

Just before dawn he awoke to find himself at the beach, knee-deep in the low surf and wading out from the shore. The sight of the ocean in the gray dawn light gave him an unreasonable thrill of fear and the ripples of a large school of fish twenty yards farther out sent him into an absolute panic. He ran home through the deserted streets, locked the door and lay panting on the bed.

Badly shaken and confused, Parker found it strangely difficult to collect his thoughts and decide what to do. Later in the morning he went back to the shop to question the tall man, but found that the female owner had returned and would say very little. The man, she said, was a stranger whom she had hired to tend the shop that day while she visited a sick relative. She didn't even know his name. She was obviously frightened and suspicious of Parker's questions and avowed that she wanted no trouble with the police. She claimed she had no knowledge of the object Parker had purchased and would take no responsibility for it. She seemed to think Parker wanted to return it. Parker was sure she was lying about casually leaving a complete stranger in the shop, but was convinced that she knew little about the man and nothing of the sea-stone.

Returning to his apartment, he brooded listlessly until late afternoon when Tregennis arrived in a state of near hysteria. He bore an afternoon paper which recounted the discovery that morning floating beneath a pier of the badly mutilated body of one Algernon Braithwaite. Parker's skin crawled. Tregennis was close-mouthed about his knowledge or suspicions concerning the event, but clearly feared for his own safety and urged Parker to get rid of the *balthon thlomor*.

He left Parker in a state little calmer than his own. The attempted burglary of his apartment the night before with its sudden interruption and the horrifying murder of Braithwaite made it plain that he was involved in some vicious intrigue of sinister cults and secret societies, involved far beyond his ability to cope with the situation. He considered going to the police, but when he realized how bizarre and unsubstantiated his tale of dreams, legends and an untraceable black man was he could not bring himself to do it. And the dreams had become intolerable. Groggy and exhausted though he was, he could not face another night among the abominations of Tchoolmö-Zhr.

His decision to get rid of the *balthon thlomor* was not a product of rational thought. It was a compulsive flight from terror. The sun was setting as he rented a rowboat, rowed out to the deepest part of the harbor and returned the stone to the sea. He felt a great sense of relief, as though he had rid himself of a burden and a threat. He returned home, lay down and fell into a deep, dreamless, restful sleep for the first time in four days.

When he awoke at dawn, the stone from the sea was on the bedside table. His feeling of horror and revulsion was overpowering. He felt the hypnotic power of the accursed figure as an almost physical force. He lay in bed throughout the day, paralyzed by fear. He began to feel the beckoning for the first time with his waking mind. Late in the afternoon it grew stronger, and he began to feel drowsy. Desperately he fought sleep, feeling overwhelmingly that some terrible doom awaited him in the green, shadowy world of his dreams. At last he could keep his eyes open no longer, but drifted off into that realm of terror.

walter c. debill, jnr.

Again he dreamed of the eldritch city. This time its inhabitants filled its watery streets, chanting and welcoming him. They exulted in their victory over his will and mundane fears. Now he would join them forever in weedy Tchoolmö-Zhr, awaiting the reign of great 'Ymnar and the destruction of mankind. But first he must bring the tribute. The tribute! His heart pounded frantically as he sensed the command, and he fought in panic against the powerful hypnotic force of the hellish undersea creatures. But he felt himself losing control as the dream grew vague and his emotions numb.

Later he could remember only isolated snatches and vague sensations of the latter part of his dream. He remembered walking barefoot down paved streets, his wet clothing chilled by the night-breeze. He was hunting something, something he could not identify. He felt horror at the thought of his quest, but had no power to control his actions. It was as though his body and will were controlled by another. He felt unpaved road under his feet, apparently a country lane, and sensed overhanging trees on either side. Still he was hunting. He remembered standing before a house, where a light shone in a single ground-floor window. Here his benumbed willpower seemed to make a resurgence and he remembered a wild churning of emotions before he again succumbed and the dream proceeded to its excruciating, unremembered climax. Of this hideous denouement, he could recall only that it involved such a violent emotional cataclysm that his numbed volition awakened somewhat, and he broke away from the hypnotic force controlling him and fled. He vaguely remembered running homeward through empty streets. There was something in his hand . . .

He awoke in his bed in the eerie light of dawn. He lay there for a full five minutes remembering the dream. His bedclothes were stiff and stained with something dark. His hands were also stained and several of his fingernails were broken off. There was something on the table before the figure from the sea. The outline reminded him of something. He turned on the light. The object was a human heart.

* * *

BEACH SUICIDE LINKED TO TREGENNIS MURDER

Early today police investigating the apparent suicide of artist Charles Parker, found slain on North Beach at 7:30 a.m. this morning, have found grisly evidence in Parker's apartment linked with the savage murder Sunday night of Paul Tregennis. No details were released, but a spokesman for the Police Department stated that there was no doubt that the two atrocities were connected.

Parker's body was found by Clyde Turner of 3412 Hancock Ave. while surfcasting along the beach. Parker had been shot under the chin with a 12 gauge shotgun which was found by the body. Empty shells found at the scene indicated that at least four other shots had been fired, apparently into the sea.

16

Police were puzzled by footprints which indicate that a very large man approached the body, stood watching it for several minutes, and then walked into the surf. A tall, gray-haired Negro male seen in the area is being sought for questioning.

Night Sounds

I hear the stridulation, faint but shrill,
Pricking the warm black stillness of the night.
Of course, it's crickets, nothing more, yet still—
A softer sound beneath stirs subtle fright.
Straining to hear, the jaded ear grows keen
Until the chirping, louder than before,
No longer hides the lilt of some unseen
Night-bird's distant trilling, nothing more.

Or is there? Now, beneath the mindless shriek
Of crickets and night-warblers, my sharp ear,
Grown vast with sound, hears clearly that soft squeak
And can no longer doubt but only fear,
Because from charnel shadows, dank and cool,
There comes the meeping glibber of a ghoul.

Ngyr-Khorath

"'Ig nebna 'yra Ngyr-Khorath, 'odho 'ym khorathna, 'ig snirna 'ym throlna dhrool. 'Ym pane dirai rol 'yin tradhom, sila Ngyr-Khorath 'ym bitha khorath goe phaik kho 'ai mtala. Kho pane dirai thnrana do tradhoi, bitha drail 'id pygon kemna thnrama 'ym krina klam thnrana ny 'my rol 'ym tradhoin. 'Ym 'obro phlar pnyl nyr pa 'yg tlireth dirai gor 'og trakna goe, lyd goe sane 'ig trakna 'aisogyr, 'ig dhrool, 'ith tradhoi, 'Iä, vi ig rol pan, kho by nget pa li gor."

"In the beginning was Ngyr-Khorath, alone and dreaming, in the silence and darkness of the void. And when the sun and planets came, Ngyr-Khorath stirred and his dreams became evil, yet he did not awake. But when life came to the earth, he became mad with the flames of living thought and sought to destroy that life and the sun and the planets. And though the magic of that which came from the stars protects us from his wrath, he lurks ever in tireless rage, in the void, on the planets, yea, even in the sun itself, yet OUTSIDE the realm we see."

—The Texts of Mloeng

The manuscript of Philip X:

I had never intended to reveal the facts concerning the hideous death of the man I shall call Eric Rossbach, but the current widespread use of hallucinogenic drugs and recent developments in research make it imperative that the public be warned. Since my part in concealing his death was quite illegal and I now have a certain professional reputation to protect, I shall use no real names or other information which might lead to my identification. I also think it unwise to identify precisely the experimental drug which brought about the final disaster, but as a partial indication to scientists I will say that it was prepared in good yield from mescaline in seven steps.

It was as a brilliant medical school student that Eric . . .

The unpublished notes of Eric Rossbach:

. . . simple elaboration of Brankovic's hypothesis on brain enzymes can thus be used to correlate the molecular structure of drugs with their psychological properties, and furthermore to predict structures for more powerful drugs than any yet known. The reports on sense-crossing with existing drugs hint at possible stimulation of unknown senses . . .

The diary of Duane Miller:

... can't believe I let Eric talk me into it but when that scrawny little fanatic starts pacing up and down with his hands behind his back and flashing those gooseberry eyes through those steel-rimmed specs my sales-resistance goes to sleep. But logical he is! We can make more progress in six months in secret than in ten years in a lab with all the legal restrictions on drug research. I can see why he wants a clinical psychologist (and after all, I'm the best!) and an organic chemist, though Phil is something of a stuffed shirt, but why he's bringing that crazy hippy pot-head in on the deal ...

Peppy Rogers, rapping, long afterward:

... burn ... burning ...

Phil:

Our laboratory was located in a wild, sparsely inhabited region of low limestone hills, far from the nearest town and secluded in a brushy box canyon. Our progress during the summer was astounding. Eric's theories were verified in every respect. There is no question whatsoever that we were perceiving the solar system through unknown senses, as confirmed by ...

Peppy:

... like, man you can't imagine—we could dig real clear, out past the orbit of Mars—the scene started to kinda fade somewhere in the asteroid belt. There was a smell, like nothing I ever smelled, sweet and weird, we never did figure it out—it was stronger near the planets—but the sound was what really blew my ... turned me on. Chords, man, vast chords over dozens of octaves, textured with eerie rhythms. Every planet, every asteroid had its own tones, they got louder as you got near 'em—you could move your center of consciousness around just by willing it, pretty fast but not instantaneous—and together they made this incredible sound. Underneath the chords there was this real low sound—a low, throbbing monotone, rising and falling in volume. It gave me the creeps right off, kinda like on a bad acid trip, y'know, when you start to worry about something, you can't exactly figure what, and every thing gets real quiet all of a sudden and you hear things you didn't notice before. That was where the trouble started, that real low sound.

Inscription from a canyon in the Takla Makan:

Iä! The Dream-Death!
That which must not be named!
Iä! The Watcher!
That which Was and shall Be
And waits to destroy that which Is!
Iä ... !

Duane:

. . . impression of a vague, generalized hostility, associated with a low, throbbing sound and coming from somewhere near Jupiter. Sounds like an early symptom of paranoia. He says he was on 'speed' for six months—could be a 'flashback'— spontaneous recurrences of the drug experience are well-known, and 'speed' can produce paranoid symptoms, if they're crazy enough to stay on it long.

Phil:

By October we were all abominably familiar with the phenomena emanating from the region near Jupiter. The hideously low, brooding throb; the ill-defined red area in space, somehow both murky and profoundly luminous; the faint tactile sensation, loathsome, clammy, like the skin of an amphibian or reptile; and above all the overwhelming impression that we were the objects of an insane implacable rage.

Duane was the first to notice that the thing was moving toward us . . .

Duane:

It was definitely following my movements this time. As I moved from a point near the moon to the opposite side of the earth, there was a delay while it continued toward my original position; then it began to change course until it was coming straight at me again.

Peppy:

. . . burned out . . . oh god . . .

The last time I took the stuff the thing almost got me. At first I didn't see it anywhere. It was a fantastic high, I was just relaxed and kinda floatin', out by Mars, diggin' the sounds—they were never exactly loud but sorta mind-filling, satisfying— then it was there—sorta materialized right by me, slowly, just a speck of red, then growing—it was never so close before—I moved as fast as I could but it was gaining—the low sound, that throbbing, ghastly, wavering hum was driving me crazy with fear, and this time the touch sensation was real bad, like being smothered in cold, writhing snakes, squeezing tighter as the thing pulled up on me—if the drug hadn't worn off just then . . . I told 'em I was through, no more trips on that stuff. I shoulda split right then—I know too much, man, too much . . .

Phil:

According to Eric's theory, the stronger drug would give us both more mobility and a greater spatial range of perception, enabling us to evade the thing and observe it from a safe distance. He insisted on making the first test himself, in spite of our dependence on his medical knowledge to cope with emergencies.

walter c. debill, jnr.

Eric:

It is amusing to note that the most potent drug in this series has recently been identified as a constituent of the *gryn-tlan* plant, used in the sacramental potion for the rite of the Ultimate Abomination by the infamous cult of Ngyr-Khorath, the mad god of the void!

Phil:

. . . until long after the drug had unquestionably left Eric's system, but he still began screaming hysterically whenever we let the sedative wear off. Finally we tried pentothal. We found that he could answer questions about events prior to the experiment, but direct questions about the drug experience brought only agitation and incoherent replies. We decided to try the hypnotic technique of telling him to relive the experience, starting with the dazed period during the onset of the drug.

Eric Rossbach, transcript of tape:

". . . dizzy . . . don't understand . . . clearing up a little . . . it's working! What a view! Incredible! They'll have to try it themselves to believe it. The planets—I can make out all of them out to Neptune equally well. The perception of distance is completely bizarre this time. I can see the distances between the planets but they all seem somehow equidistant from me, as though viewed from far above, yet each one seems close.

Don't see the thing yet—perhaps it was a spurious side-effect of the weaker drug. There's a diffuse red color all over the solar system. Sight definitely blending into tactile sensation this time. A sort of stickiness, greatest near the sun, weakening in all directions. A furry feeling, in a great spiral pattern perpendicular to the ecliptic plane. And a fainter one, loathsome, clammy—that's it, the thing I can feel it—I hear the sound, too, that maddeningly low, low throbbing sound. That ubiquitous red color is getting stronger everywhere but especially near the sun. There it is! It was hiding inside the sun! Headed straight for me! Incredible speed! Fear rising—can't fight it down—must turn my attention away or go mad with fear . . .

"No eyes! No eyes to shut! Can't shut it out! Must get away . . . can't move . . . like being paralyzed . . .

"God, how it hates, it hates, it rages and hates . . .

". . . drug has to wear off soon, only thing that can save me . . . it can't see me if the drug wears off . . . but soon, it has to be soon, it's coming so fast . . . red everywhere now, but deepest in the eye . . .

"Aaagh! Make it go away! The eye, the hideous blood-red eye . . . !"

Peppy:

. . . fascists always raving about cats burning out their brains on drugs—oh god . . .

Phil:

He had become so agitated that we gave him enough pentothal to knock him out, and he made no other sound until an hour later when the final horror occurred.

The terrible final cataclysm was utterly, awesomely incomprehensible to me at the time, but since then I have read the immemorial legend of Ngyr-Khorath and have some idea what killed Eric, and why others have leapt screaming from upper-story windows after taking impure LSD. The *Books of Thoth* contain certain hints, as do the obscure *Chronicles of Thrang* and the haunting *Texts of Mloeng*, whose preposterous radiocarbon datings have been attributed to some unusual experimental error. But perhaps the most relevant clue is in the *Uralte Schrecken* of the mysterious Graf von Könnenberg, who footnoted his description of the Ultimate Abomination of Ngyr-Khorath thus:

> *"But he who may see may be seen; and the door through which one goes out may let another in."*

The final horror came just after midnight. Duane and I had left Eric alone in his bedroom and were sitting in the living room trying desperately to think of some way to help him. Our hushed and horrified discussion had lapsed into brooding silence when we heard the scream. It began as a high, piercing monotone, held for many seconds at an incredible intensity, then fell slightly only to rise and fall several times in a ghastly ululation, finally trailing off in a choking gurgle. Then silence. We sat paralyzed for a moment, then ran to the bedroom. There was a nauseous stench and we were in time to see two faint wisps of smoke rising from the charred and empty eye sockets, through which we could see the blackened void where the brain of Eric Rossbach had been. He had had a flashback.

In 'Ygiroth

In 'Ygiroth, where once the vile
And hairy things that passed for men
In long forgotten elder times
Did strut in arrogance and bow
To nameless things from outer spheres,
Now only baneful shadows crawl
In 'Ygiroth.

High above him rose the city, deep in a shadowed cleft where the gentle lower slopes of Lerion ended and the jagged, slender spire of her uttermost peak began its long thrust into the hazy sky of Dreamland. Unpeopled and dreaming it had lain through the slow centuries of solitude and decay, and until now no man had come to seek out its dark secrets. Only he, Nylron the Acolyte, had dared follow the sparkling river Skai north to its headwaters in the high valley of Mynanthra between Lerion and craggy Dlareth and then travel the rock-strewn meadows on Lerion's northern shoulder around and upward to where brooding 'Ygiroth slumbered. He tilted the furred brim of his hat to shade his eyes from the setting sun and urged the wiry Bnazic pony on toward the low outer wall.

No one knew where the men of 'Ygiroth had come from or when they came, for the green shadows of Mynanthra had already flickered with their furtive stalking and echoed to their eerie hunting cries when Nylron's ancestors had come from the east forty centuries ago to settle the fertile valley of the Skai and build Ulthar and Nir and Hatheg. Those sturdy tribesmen had instinctively disliked the men of 'Ygiroth, finding them a little too short, a little too hairy, and a little too silent as they crept through the forests. Perhaps if their brow ridges had not jutted so far forward, giving them an unpleasantly beady-eyed look, or if they had cooked the flesh of the buopoth before dining, the men of the Skai valley might have sought peaceful intercourse with them but as it was, none but a few adventurers of dubious repute had ever bothered to learn their coarse whispering language. It was from these ill-regarded and invariably ill-fated individuals that such scraps of lore as were known to the men of the Skai had come.

Not clever were the men of 'Ygiroth, and their stone spears and necklaces of wolves' teeth seemed ludicrously backward to the intelligent and inventive men of the Skai. Very arrogant they were about their skill in hunting the gentle buopoth, though most of their success came from the use of the half-tame kyresh as both hound and steed. This morbid relic of an older time, long extinct in other parts of Dreamland, had a basically equine body which could be ridden by the more intrepid chieftains, a long bloodhound muzzle which could scent prey at great distances, and enormous claws which, together with a mouth full of great irregular fangs, did much more damage in the hunt than the crude spearheads. It did not seem to bother the 'Ygirothians that the vicious and excitable brutes took as great a toll among the hunters as of the hunted—if the hunt succeeded it left fewer to divide the spoils, if it failed, fallen comrades would not be wasted by the hungry.

Even the domestication of this treacherous monstrosity had been beyond the abilities of the 'Ygirothians themselves. They had been taught and aided by a more formidable and sinister being. Their notion of time was so vague that they could not say whether it was ten or ten thousand centuries since the Thing in the Yellow Mask had come to them and taught them to make spears and ride the kyresh and eat fresh-killed meat. And when asked what the Thing demanded in return, they smirked evilly and made crude evasions.

It was the Thing which had made them build 'Ygiroth to honor It and Its unseen brothers, eldritch abnormalities from outer spheres of time and space whose ineffable forms and non-forms could never have been made tolerable to men by any amount of yellow silk or hypnotic incense. It had taught them to place stone upon stone in a remote cleft on Lerion which had been a place of outer evil before men existed, and It had directed the labors of countless terrified generations until the inept beast-men had completed a citadel of horror unmatched in Dreamland (for grim Kadath is not truly contiguous with any space men know or dream of).

Only one man of the Skai had ever been within the walls of 'Ygiroth and returned, and Lothran the Necromancer had said little that could be understood. He had reached Ulthar at sunset, raving hysterically of formless horrors from which he fled, horrors which he refused to name. He had been quieted with a strong dose of poppy gum and left to rest in an upper room of the inn, but in the morning when the elders of Ulthar entered the room in hopes of a more coherent revelation, they found nothing but an open window and a stench of carrion, of lightning and of singed flesh. Nothing, that is, unless one credits the tale whispered by foolish gossips, that old Atal found one of Lothran's boots behind the bed, and that the boot was not empty.

The men of Ulthar and Nir and Hatheg would have been content to leave such unpleasant neighbors alone in their high valley were it not for the disappearance of several of their young maidens each Walpurgis and Yule and of plump specimens of both sexes at odd times throughout the year. The people along the Skai were quick to connect the former with strange lights and drumming in the distant hills and the latter with the footprints in their gardens of short, broad-footed men. Thus from the earliest times small bands of brave men had set out to destroy 'Ygiroth and its inhabitants. Each time, as they approached the shadowy forests of Mynanthra, heavy clouds would gather and they would find themselves ringed with many-colored bolts of lightning. Most turned back at this point; but the survivors among those who did not told of discordant music heard beneath the howling and laughter of the unseen men of 'Ygiroth, of charnel vapors and a distant form draped in yellow silk. Few indeed lived to tell of the sentient whirlwinds that keened and rushed through the murky glades and set upon men like unseen hounds, rending and mangling body and soul.

It was in the reign of King Pnil of Ulthar that the warriors of the Skai had challenged 'Ygiroth for the last time. Every able-bodied man had marched, armed this time with charms and spells of the Elder Ones as well as tools of war. No resistance was met, although the vanguard heard padding feet retreating through Mynanthra and followed fresh claw-marks of the kyresh right up to the gates of the city. Arriving at sunset and not wanting to assault the unknown defenses in the dark, they camped before the walls.

No warrior of the Skai-lands slept during that long night of suspense and brooding menace, none could forget the night-long crescendo of asymmetric rhythms on drums of stretched hide and hollowed bone or the jeering and insinuating voices from the dark crowing of the incomprehensible horror to be unleashed at dawn. As the first saffron rays struck the spire of Lerion silence fell with the force of thunder. For an interminable moment no one breathed, no eye moved from the still shadowed walls of 'Ygiroth. Then began that hideous silent exodus which haunts the legends and fireside tales of Ulthar.

As the first of the men of 'Ygiroth came scrambling over the walls and the gates were flung wide to let out dozens, then hundreds and thousands, all running straight for the ranks of the Skai, it was taken to be a charge, an attempt to overwhelm the besieging forces. But men wondered why they ran in silence, and as the first of them drew near it was seen that they were unarmed. Then as they rushed heedless onto the waiting spears men at last saw their mad, mindless eyes and knew that a terror beyond knowledge or nightmare had come to 'Ygiroth, and that 'Ygiroth was doomed.

When the last beast-man lay crumpled on the gory meadow, the warriors of Ulthar departed in awe, not daring no enter the city and raze it. Since then no man had ventured there, and were it not for the whispers of Lothran the Necromancer perhaps none ever would. But before he vanished Lothran had whispered certain things to the high priest Atal, and in his old age Atal had tried no banish these things from his dreams by writing them down on parchment. Too cleverly had he hidden that parchment, and the priests of Nodens had been unable to find and destroy it despite his incoherent deathbed pleas. And now Nylron the Acolyte had found it and had read things which should never be written down.

Among less mentionable things Nylron had read of the evil secrets taught by the Thing in the Yellow Mask to the priests of 'Ygiroth, secrets they had neither the wits nor the courage no exploit, secrets which could have made them masters of all Dreamland and perhaps even of the waking world. They had merely carved them on the walls the labyrinth beneath their temple in the foul Aklo tongue taught them by the Thing. Unfortunately for Nylron, he was a true scholar of this primordial language, and not without ambition.

The journey had taken him four days; the first along the fertile banks the Skai, whose shady fringe of willows bade him rest and delay; the second through gradually rising hills where spring wildflowers questioned the value of ambition; the third in dark and cool Mynanthra, where a silent buopoth warned that time may stand still; and the fourth, up stony mountain paths where the sky grew inhospitable. As he entered the city black clouds were rolling in from the north and the sun lost sight of Lerion.

He found the city surprisingly well preserved. Few of the buildings had collapsed, the tread of time being shown more subtly by cracked stone, precariously leaning walls and an occasional fallen roof. Only twice were the narrow, tortuous streets blocked with rubble, forcing him to detour through even narrower alleys. He thought of certain rumored corpses, in which decay is said to be unnaturally slow and circumspect. The great beehive-shaped temple was on a high ledge at the rear of city and by the time he had threaded the convoluted streets up to the broad plaza in front of it the first heavy raindrops had splattered on the pavement. He paused only a moment to wonder how the vast dome had survived the centuries of mountain storms and led the pony up the gentle ramp through the only opening, a tall narrow trapezoid topped by a small capstone.

It was quite dark inside, but he kindled a resinous torch and soon saw that the temple was one enormous chamber, cluttered with a gloomy forest of pentagonal columns. At first he saw in them no geometrical arrangement at all, but gradually he perceived an odd asymmetrical regularity which he found disturbing to contemplate. He could barely make out seven large statues of kyresh spaced along the circular wall, some blindfolded, others with staring eyes and open jaws. There was a peculiar sour smell in the air and each step echoed from the dome above. The only natural aisle among the columns led straight back to be rear of the temple and Nylron led the horse, skittish now from the approaching storm, as far as a small stone post of indeterminate purpose. Tethering the horse to the post and removing the heavy pack, he proceeded down the aisle to what appeared to be the main altar. It was a wide irregular heptagon surmounted by a statue of a robed and hooded figure holding a spear in one band and a small figure of a buopoth in the other. Before the statue lay an oval opening and, climbing up on the altar stone, he found stone steps leading downward into the living rock of Lerion.

Downward be went in a huge spiral, circling until he had lost all sense of direction. At last the stairs ended and be found himself in an intricate labyrinth of narrow passageways whose moss-grown walls sloped inward at the top, occasionally opening into substantial low-ceilinged rooms partitioned with arcades of trapezoidal arches. To be certain of finding his way out again Nylron turned always to the right and found himself again spiraling, this time inward.

In the center of the labyrinth was a room almost as large as the temple above and arranged similarly with seven kyresh and a central altar. Before the statue on the altar was a large flat stone, suggesting a covered opening. But what arrested Nylron's attention was the circular wall of the room, for it was completely covered with an inscription in the Aklo tongue.

The uncouth characters of brutish scribes were not easy to read, but Nylron could follow most of them and knew that the rest would yield to patient scholarship in the archives of Ulthar. He read of the feeble gods of earth and how they can be manipulated. He read of the Other Gods who once ruled and shall rule again, of Azathoth, the centripetal impetus of all cosmic chaos, of Yog-Sothoth, the all-pervasive horror which lurks in the inner spheres of existence, of Nyarlathotep, who sometimes shrouds his form in yellow silk and sometimes in mind-blurring illusion. He read of the rewards for their chosen instruments, and hints of what might befall those instruments which failed. And finally he read a terrible passage, carved in immaculate calligraphy on an iridescent plaque harder than Nylron's garnet ring, which told of the joke played by Nyarlathotep on his minions when they summoned him and he declined to come. For he had sent instead his half-brother and other face, a ravenous and by no means sane entity which could radiate intolerable horror like a poisonous vapor.

As he finished this vile postlogue his torch began to flicker wildly and he saw that it had nearly burned out. He thought of the difficult way back through the labyrinth and shuddered. His composure did not improve when, passing the altar, he saw the symbol carved on the flat covering stone and noted the recent disturbance of the moss around it.

The way back proved disconcertingly difficult. At times he almost believed that the arcades and passages had been shifted since his trip inward. Faster and faster he went, frantically exploring multiple branches and dead ends. The padding echoes of his soft-soled boots seemed to conceal more stealthy footsteps and a distant grating of stone on stone. Once he could have sworn he caught a glimpse of yellow silk disappearing into a trapezoidal archway. He found the entrance to the upward spiral just as the torch winked out.

He calmed down somewhat in the spiral shaft and made his way rapidly upward by feeling along the left-hand wall. Total lack of sight raised his other senses to an acute pitch and he could plainly hear the stamping of the horse after each burst of thunder. As he neared the top he could hear the rain itself and feel the dampness in the air. Emerging into the inky blackness of the temple be was unpleasantly aware that the moisture had brought out the odd sour smell much more strongly. He felt his way to the edge of the altar, climbed down, then moved out blindly toward the shuffling and stamping of the horse. He almost tripped over the pack and his reflexively outstretched band touched the smooth hair of the pony's flank. He was patting and stroking it reassuringly when he heard the sound, so incongruous that he took a full second to identify it as the frantic whinny of his horse. What made it incongruous was the fact that it came from outside the temple. At that instant a lightning flash lit up the doorway, silhouetting the gaping jaws of the kyresh and the masked monster that held its reins. He felt its hot fetid breath just before the teeth closed on his head.

Outside in the rain and the dark the horse's hooves clattered madly away through the dead streets of 'Ygiroth.

The History of the Great Race

Dr. Eric von Könnenberg & Dr. Pierre de Hammais

Nothing holds more awe for twentieth century man than the infinite abysses of time and space opened up by modern science; thus, few of the many pre-human races described and hinted at in the Cthulhu and related myth cycles hold more fascination than the Great Race. The Great Race, that conquered both time and space, and roved through both, compiled a unique body of historical knowledge spanning not only the entire history of the planet Earth, but also the histories of other civilizations throughout this and other universes. However, the known sources give only tantalizing hints of a small segment of their own history.

The principal sources of material on the Great Race are the *Pnakotic Manuscripts*, which have been attributed to the Great Race as their surviving records, and the *Celaeno Fragments*, which were collected by Professor Laban Shrewsbury from material located in a library on a planet of the star Celaeno. The origin of this library is mysterious, but is definitely not records left by the Great Race itself. It is often difficult to reconcile these two sources, but a plausible and mutually compatible version can be constructed.

The *Celaeno Fragments* make it clear that the Great Race had existed on at least several different planets of our universe and others billions of years before the recorded history of the planet Earth. Prior to their advent on Earth, approximately 600,000,000 years ago, they inhabited the world known in the *Eltdown Shards* as Yith, and according to the *Pnakotic Manuscripts*, in some unknown bodily form, since their true form was as a free mind, somewhat akin to a shaft of light. Yith is described as dying at the time of their migration, and black and dead by 150,000,000 years ago. Unfortunately, the *Manuscripts* describe Yith's location with an ambiguous word which could place it on the opposite side of our own galaxy, in a distant galaxy, or even in intergalactic space. There are rumors to the effect that Yith exists far beyond the planet Yuggoth (known as Pluto here on Earth), a member of our own solar system, but substantiating evidence is still forthcoming.

They migrated *en masse* to Earth and displaced the minds of a race of rugose cones which had inhabited and ruled the Earth since 1,000,000,000 B.C., and remained in these forms until some time between 150,000,000 years ago, and 50,000 years ago.

At this point the *Celaeno Fragments* and the *Pnakotic Manuscripts* appear to differ. The latter gives the impression that they left the bodies of the cone-shaped race in their mental form, and displaced the minds of the beetle race immediately following mankind on Earth (somewhat after 50,000 A.D.), thus simply not existing for the period of man's sojourn here on Earth. The *Fragments*, however, indicate that they existed elsewhere in time and space during this period. Thus a mutually compatible version must assume that the *Manuscripts* merely neglected to describe this period in the Great Race's history.

Once again, in regards to the Great Race's departure from the planet Earth, the two sources of information differ. According to the *Pnakotic Manuscripts*, the Great Race migrated to the planet Mercury, closer to the aging sun as the Earth cooled and grew closer to its final moment of sustaining intelligent life forms. On Mercury they displaced the minds of a race of bulbous vegetable entities. The *Celaeno Fragments* state that the Great Race first traveled to the planet Jupiter and then later, to the planet of a dark star in the constellation Taurus. They are located there during the present era of their history, but are contemplating their possible return through time and space to Earth because the dark star is dying.

Their departure from the planet Earth may be connected with the wars between the Elder Gods and the Great Old Ones, since the *Fragments* state that this was the cause of their departure. The *Manuscripts* indicate clearly that their departing the bodies of the cone-shaped race was caused by a polypous race, which they had originally driven underground, but the Great Race had grown soft in their security and were threatened with an uprising of the polypous race.

Beyond their tenure of the planet of the dark star, the Great Race's history is completely unknown to us. And most of what we do know of their history is fragmentary. We can only hope that further research can provide more complete and accurate knowledge of the history of this most fascinating of races.

* * * * *

NOTE: For the reader's information, the *Pnakotic Manuscripts* refers to information in "The Shadow Out of Time" by H. P. Lovecraft, and the *Celaeno Fragments* refers to information in "The Shadow Out of Space" by H. P. Lovecraft and August Derleth.

Red-Litten Yoth

Beneath the highest crags of ice-clad stone
  In caverns dimly lit by lambent flame—
  By flickering crimson pools of haunted flame
A mindless thing of evil stalks alone;
  A formless shrieking thing without a face,
  In tireless rage it wanders in that place
Of fire and stone.

A fragment of the thing called Azathoth,
  Torn from inchoate godhood, born in pain,
  In cosmic battle fought with the insane
And mindless nuclear chaos Azathoth,
  Its wailing echoes endlessly through halls
  Of scarlet shadows where blind madness crawls—
Red-litten Yoth.

Blue-Litten K'n-yan

It tells in mouldy books as old as man
       How once SanSu the Dreamer found the glade
       That hides the granite stairway no man made
And trod those crumbling steps down to K'n-yan
       Whose endless labyrinths are filled with mist,
       Blue-lit by noxious fungi, echoing hissed
And whispered words too faint to understand.
He sought to learn the meaning of that dread
       And sinister susurrus, as the pad
And shuffle of his slippers marked his tread
       Through nether caverns elder gods forbade
Until the whispers, fluttering louder, led
To where SanSu, as mists whirled round his head,
Could understand those voices of the dead.

But when he knew just what those whispers said,
SanSu went mad.

Homecoming

May 1, 1946:

Five figures sat around the heavy pentagonal table, contemplating the softly glowing object in the center. A dim and yellowish lamp, hung high behind a lattice of oaken beams, splashed the small rock-walled chamber with a distorted checkerboard. The faces of three, robed and hooded in red, were in shadow. That of the fourth, a tall blond man dressed in ragged khaki, was lit full face. The fifth figure, dressed in a saffron robe with the cowl thrown back, was lit sharply from the right, showing a high cheekbone and oriental eye on one side and blackness on the other. The thin lips barely moved as he spoke.

"You have nothing to fear, Haraldson, the crystalline matrix of the blue ellipsoid before you is capable of holding the patterns of an earthly brain with absolutely no distortion or discomfort. The faceted outer surface is a covering harder than diamond and less brittle, a much more durable vessel than that which your soul presently occupies."

There was silence while the blond man declined to reply. His eyes, fixed on the glowing mass of crystal, showed fear but also rapt fascination, almost eagerness.

"And of course there are less pleasant methods we could use to terminate your investigations," continued the man in yellow. "You are fortunate that we need specimens of terrestrial consciousness for demonstration and study. The smooth red globes on the end facing you function as eyes, and you will see things in the course of your travels which fewer than ten creatures in the history of your planet have seen. There are other sensory organs built into the ellipsoidal portion, each functioning at all times. Speech, however, requires an external device which will be connected only when our friends wish to question you.

"Your body will be maintained in perfect condition here in the caverns, and if your travels should broaden your outlook sufficiently to make you useful to us you may eventually be returned to it.

"We will effect the transfer now through our combined mental force. You will find it entirely painless, the matrix is extremely receptive . . . at times perhaps too receptive."

The figure in khaki began to go limp. The crystalline brain grew brighter, its aquamarine glow pulsating and revealing the hairy surfaces beneath the red hoods, each featureless except for a single orange, unpupilled eye. The saffron robe also went limp, then began to assume firm new contours as Nyarlathotep reverted to his *true* form.

* * *

The Klamath (California) Observer, May 15, 1946:

Searchers have failed to find any trace of Thorwald Haraldson, the eccentric

33

tourist who disappeared on a solitary mountain camping trip near here two weeks ago. Haraldson was a reclusive scholar of folklore and occult practices and is believed by friends to have been searching for a hidden center of cult activity connected with the 'human sacrifice' scandal in Berkeley last year. The Berkeley atrocities were attributed to devotees of 'Nyarlathotep,' the supposed messenger of supernatural monsters from space.

* * *

The thirteenth day of the five-thousand and ninth cycle of Ghlalra:

The table was a solid wedge of green jade, without luster under the three large reddish suns and set in the center of a circular terrace surrounded by lush tropical vegetation. The three figures around it needed no chairs, each standing erect on a single foot like that of a snail. Below a single multifaceted eye each had a fringe of slender tentacles which punctuated the guttural and sibilant conversation with sinuous gestures, often pointing at the glowing crystalline brain in the center of the table. One figure seemed to dominate the conversation, waving its tentacles more wildly than the others and frequently shuddering spasmodically with what might have been laughter. It also extended a tentacle more often to dip into a large bowl of colorless, oily liquid which sat near the brain, and each time it did the level in the bowl fell substantially.

At length the figure turned from the table and glided with surprising speed to a sort of cabinet at the edge of the terrace, its body weaving precariously above its undulating foot. It returned holding a small metallic cylinder. The other figures seemed alarmed at this and waved and croaked in dissuasion, but the swaying slug-thing quickly reached the table and pressed the cylinder between the red eyes of the crystalline brain. The glow of the brain grew to a blinding, frantically pulsating glare while the slug-thing shuddered with drunken mirth.

* * *

The Book of Eibon, circa 100,000 B.C. :

And it is said that the brains of gemstone are sent to the far places of the cosmos and traded by the diverse servants and allies of Nyarlathotep as earthly scholars will trade scrolls and books. Few souls have returned that were not mad, for the friends of Nyarlathotep are not gentle in their questioning.

* * *

Excerpt from a diary, December 17, 1957:

. . . had quite a bit of trouble getting through the rubble in the entrance but the inner caverns were still intact. There was no doubt about what had happened—the spawn of Paighon had broken through from below and the results were not pretty.

The remains of the extraterrestrials were undisturbed and undecayed (immunity to terrestrial bacteria?) and were invariably in attitudes of flight or desperate struggle. We found what was left of Haraldson in the lowest level, where the great fissures had cleft the floor of the caverns and the torrid updrafts made the air almost intolerable. The body had been kept in a tank of some preservative or nutrient solution, long since evaporated to a mottled encrustation. Even the bones were in pretty bad shape. but they had left the ring and the identification bracelet in place and I recognized the crown on the left lower incisor that he acquired after that run-in with the *ghol* things in Bhutan in '44. There was a plaque on the sides of the tank in a debased version of the Yhe script—I couldn't follow all of it and didn't have time to make a copy, but it seemed to recount the abduction of Haraldson. I felt faint when I read of his initial destination. Just before the earth tremors began I found the speech apparatus, the only thing I was able to carry out before the caverns collapsed. The device is exactly as described in the *Book of Eibon* . . .

* * *

An ambiguous region of space-time:

The alien constellations shifted slowly, distorting and recombining in an eerie kaleidoscopic dance that told him he was traveling at some vast multiple of the speed of light. For there were no stars here in the intergalactic void, and he knew that each pinpoint of light was an island universe, a hundred billion suns or more, inconceivably distant.

Perhaps traveling was the wrong word—he knew that travel beyond the speed of light was supposed to be impossible, though he had seen many impossibilities through those red globes. Possibly this was same subtle alteration of spatial relationship quite different from ordinary motion. Certainly the shapeless, many-eyed thing which carried him, inadvertently slopping a pseudopod over one of his eye-globes, and its moronic winged escort all seemed to be quite motionless. The globes were much more sensitive than human eyes and he could see the great bat-things silhouetted against the distant galaxies, frozen in a soaring pose, utterly still. Only the constellations moved in their slow dance.

The excruciatingly acute senses of the crystalline brain had been alternately an ecstatic wonder and a horror; the telepathic faculty in particular had often brought him to the brink of madness. In the vastness of the cosmos few minds were compatible enough for such intimate contact with the frail terrestrial psyche. '. . . perhaps too receptive . . .' the thing had said. Now he was disturbingly aware of the sardonic evil of the man-eyed thing, the noisome idiocy of the huge bat-creatures and worst of all, the faint but growing intimations of those haunters of the void known only as the Lurkers, nebulous, non-material, implacably malignant entities which drift eternally through the abysses and coalesce around travelers. It was their *instability* which unnerved him—one moment a vague unconscious mentality dreaming its own formless nightmares, the next a swirling metamorphosis into a viciously keen intellect, probing his own mind, studying him, trying to find a weak point, a point of entry—then an equally sudden dissolution back to sleeping horror.

walter c. debill, jnr.

Throughout the intergalactic passage the Lurkers had become attentive, their probing, questioning attacks more poignant. But it was not their questions Haraldson feared, it was the *answers* they might give to his own unspoken, involuntary questions. For they were old, older than gods—they had existed before the primordial explosion that began the universe, and knew secrets no human mind could hold . . .

* * *

The Klamath Observer, January 21, 1971:

. . . large fireball in the mountains north of here has stimulated the usual rash of flying saucer reports. Scientists believe it to have been a large meteorite. An air search has failed to locate the site . . .

* * *

Excerpt from a letter, February 26, 1971:

Yes, it is true that we recovered the crystalline vessel in which the mind of Thorwald Haraldson was imprisoned and kidnapped in 1947. There was an identification plaque on the underside identical with the one we found by Haraldson's body in '57. The thing which brought it was destroyed so completely that we couldn't be sure whether it had been a machine or some utterly alien creature from the interstellar abyss—perhaps it had expected some signal from the caverns of the Aqtaba to guide it in safely. It is incredible that the brain withstood the impact—it must consist of some totally unknown form of matter. Of course we had no idea whether the mind within still functioned until we connected it to the speech machine and the thing spoke.

But of those awesome revelations of the gulfs of time, space and entity I shall never speak. I could never have imagined that mere *knowledge* could be so devastating, but of the three who heard that brain speak one has chosen death, another is quite mad, and as for myself, neither my mind nor my body can last another year. The inner moons of Q'in, the hideous insinuations of the living spiral nebula, the horrible past and future of the dark star Nyil-yath Rho—these are not for the minds of men. He had looked upon Azathoth, and yet he lived—how could I say more?

But it was not the nature of those revelations that made us seal the thing in concrete and drop it in the ocean depths, it was their source. From the first we noticed something incomprehensibly odd about his discourse, a bizarre mixture of incoherence and rationality, of hysteria and calm, almost cynical poise. These contrasting aspects would sometimes alternate within a single sentence, and certain arcane statements seemed to express both simultaneously. It was as though his mind had been shattered into fragments which recombined and dissolved with an eerie fluidity. And at last in a moment of unguarded overconfidence that revoltingly amorphous mind said too much and we knew the truth. There had been a

36

fragmentation, an evolution, and an *influence* within that brain; that which was Thorwald Haraldson was no longer sane, and that which was sane was certainly not Thorwald Haraldson. It was the obscene, omniscient, malignant thing which had lurked in the void and entered Thor's mind and fused with it—*the thing that had followed him home.*

What Lurks Among the Dunes

The First Dream:

... she is there ... it is night in the desert, the moon full, preternaturally brilliant, the sky a lucid indigo and soft ... *she* is there, with the things that scurry among the dunes, the brush-topped enigmatic dunes that stretch away in the endless ranks to the leering moon ... her figure flickers as great wings swoop low above her, passing between her exquisite form and the evil, grinning moon ...

* * *

Notebook found in a Packrat's Nest:

When I saw the turnoff I knew it was the way Edward had come. The blacktop turned to leprous concrete, then to a pair of dusty ruts between oceans of hard sand and ragged knee-high clumps of brush, and a barely legible sign proclaimed that 'State Maintenance Ends.'

Edward and I had been aware since infancy of the telepathic link between us, and had accepted it as a natural part of life. It was not until adolescence that we understood that there was anything unusual about it and then our reaction was to carefully conceal it from others, since Edward was already the outgoing, sociable sort who did not want to be thought odd by his friends and I was the reserved introvert, anxious to avoid curiosity and comment. As we grew to manhood, people noted only the sharp contrast between our personalities, remarkable for identical twins, and never sensed the profound bond forged before birth. After our parents' death five years ago, when we were twenty-one, I had used my inheritance for ancient books and a quiet life in the old family house, and he had used his for wandering and adventure. It was not in hope of finding Edward alive that I set out to retrace his route through the Southwest; I knew that he was dead, although the authorities had found nothing but a trail ending abruptly after a stop at a service station in West Texas. The bond had been broken; the images and impressions from Edward's mind had altered suddenly to rare, distorted fragments, often in the form of dreams, quite different from the living sensations I was accustomed to, and I was sure that they came from my own memory, dredged up from subconscious levels which had received them before his death. I suppose I had hoped my telepathic memories might lead me to his remains, and thus settling the mystery of his disappearance ease the empty, unsettled feeling which made it impossible to forget and go on with my life.

But not until I saw that unmapped turnoff from an obscure secondary road did the emotional alarm bell ring in my mind (*'Here*, it was *here*, beware!'). As I proceeded down that bumpy double goat-path, followed by a dust cloud ridiculously large for my little Volks to have kicked up, the alarm abated, but there was left a brooding familiarity with that flat, rocky desert which I had not seen before. As I passed out of sight of the highway the road dipped to ford a dry, chalk-white stream bed, then entered a region where the sand grew dusty and reddish and the little mounds that gathered around the bases of the low, twisted shrubs grew into sizable dunes, topped with flat patches of the brush which prevented their dissolution in the night winds and frequently reaching the height of a man. Among these the road wound a tortuous path on the barren desert floor, reducing visibility so that I didn't see the town until it was less than a mile away.

It had never been a big place. I could see perhaps fifty buildings of adobe or unpainted wood scattered widely to the south of the road on my left, and as I drew near it became apparent that most were in states of extreme dilapidation. I saw no one and was almost convinced that it was a complete ghost town when I saw the hand-operated gas pump with gasoline visible in the glass container at the top. It stood in front of the farthest of three buildings along the right-hand side of the road. As I pulled up I saw white curtains framing the windows at the side ('Beware! Here! Here!') . . .

Reminiscences of Old Buck Allison:

. . . yep, nowadays folks think they know ever'thing about th' desert b'cause they got a map that shows where somebody surveyed 'n built some roads, but ah bet ah c'n show yuh a million acres no white man ever set foot on. An' yew ain't gonna see nothin' in a car—y' drive through makin' all that racket an' th' desert looks dead, not a livin' thing, but get off th' road 'n walk a mile real quiet-like an' you'll see it's jes' teemin' with things scurryin' aroun'.

That's why back in the old days we didn't laugh s'much at those yarns about the Lurkers. The desert was a lot closer to yuh then—now yer in a air-conditioned house or car all th' time. An' there was places out there where a dam' sight more trav'lers went in than came out t'other side. Even as late as when I was a kid there was people settled near where the Lurkers was s 'posed to be that jes' flat disappeared, no trace at all.

It was s'posed t'be some kind of religion among the injuns, Apache and Comanche mostly, not all of 'em but just a few bands who got it from the ancient tribes who was here before 'em. Th' other injuns was as leery of 'em as the whites—most of the whites, that is; toward the last a few groups of whites and Mexicans took up with 'em. They worshipped some kind o' female god called Yee-Tho-Rah, a kind of spirit of the earth with power over all livin' things, a god that gave all life an' in th' end took it away . . .

The Notebook:

. . . parking by the pump and stepping onto the shaded concrete porch, I looked into the clean small-paned windows. I could see a long wooden counter with small racks of bagged potato chips and peanuts, so I entered. There was no one inside. I observed that the merchandise in the little store was sparse, exposing great expanses of bare wall, floor and counter to dominate the long high-ceilinged room, and although I suspected all the edible items were rather stale the place was immaculately clean and neat. After several minutes of oppressive silence I called out and saw a rustling at the curtained door in the rear.

The man who emerged was Mexican, short and slender, very dark, his skin creased from decades of desert sun and wind.

"Yes? May I help you, sir?" (The warning bell again—'Beware!') He seemed surprised to see me.

"I need some gas." I almost asked him to check the oil, but something about his bearing and his threadbare but impeccably clean, freshly-ironed khakis made me hesitate. He had that impressive combination of Spanish dignity and Indian stoicism peculiar to Mexico. I decided to check the engine myself.

"Not much business out here, I suppose. The town doesn't look too lively," I said, trying to start a conversation. But he drew back slightly and looked almost hurt.

"Well, I get a little trade from the men going to the gas wells out in the desert. But not much. Not since the mine closed down. You see the big building over there? Used to be a mercury mine. Dos Piedras was a pretty important town back then. But since it closed down thirty years ago everyone drifted away, except for me and my wife." His English was good, the Mexican lilt very slight. His eyes had a sunken look and his teeth were oddly prominent, as though the lips had shrunk.

"Why don't you move to a better location?" Again the hurt look.

"We got no place to go; no one would buy this place." After a slight pause he added, almost apologetically, "It's all we have."

"Any tourists ever come this way?"

The flash of alarm in the eyes was unmistakable, though his features remained impassive. "No, there's not much to see out here, and the roads aren't too good." I wondered if the resemblance between Edward and myself was noticeable, though Edward had grown a beard that summer and worn his hair much longer than I. I was sure now that he had come this way and had seen this man.

He had filled the tank neatly to within an inch of the top without spilling a drop. I remembered to check the oil and battery, and a plan grew in my mind. I surreptitiously slipped a scrap of paper between the covered part of the wire and the coil. After paying him, I tried to start the engine but of course nothing happened. I got out and fiddled with various wires and tried again.

"Must be a vapor lock. I hope so, anyway. I'll let it sit awhile. If I can't get it started is there any way I could get back to Anderson?" I hadn't seen any kind of vehicle in town.

"We don't have a car. No telephone either." The barren, precarious quality of his existence out here was brought home to me. He looked worried, almost shocked.

"The sun's getting lower," I said. "Maybe it'll start when it gets cooler." His face paled noticeably at this.

"I don't think there are any gas crews out right now. There's a delivery truck tomorrow morning." He almost seemed to be talking to himself. The thought of my staying overnight obviously terrified him.

"Well, maybe it'll start later. Probably a vapor lock. I'll have a look around town while I wait."

He went back into the store while I pretended to tinker some more, and I heard a terse exchange in Spanish, evidently with his wife. I got out a pencil and the little sketch pad upon which this is written and slipped the snub-nosed .38 into my belt under my shirt.

The Second Dream:

. . . night, no moon over the dunes, a million stars . . . flat tire, damn jack wants to sink in the sand . . . something moving out there, darting from dune to dune . . . coyote? Too big . . . is there more than one . . . ?

The Notebook:

. . . the remnants of Dos Piedras were widely spaced and in many places dunes had grown to a height of three or four feet between them. On the eastern border of the town I could see two small rocky hills which had undoubtedly given the town its name, which means 'two rocks' in Spanish. Against one of them stood a wooden structure with a black, gaping entrance which must have been the mine.

Most of the buildings were of brown adobe brick, now crumbled to jagged shells by the occasional desert cloudbursts, but a few of the wooden ones were fairly well intact and I walked slowly toward one which seamed undamaged, with boarded-up windows and a rickety door hanging ajar. There was a wide track in the sand passing by the front of the door, as though something had been dragged, and a scattering of footprints, which made me think that perhaps the gas station man had used it for storage. I glance back toward the station just in time to see a feminine figure step onto the porch.

I could tell that it was a young woman, tall and graceful. As she entered the door she turned and looked toward me for a moment, and, although shimmering heat waves blurred my vision and made it hard to see more than the outline of her face and the dark, enormous eyes, she left an impression of uncanny beauty. Their daughter, I thought. The picture of their barren life out here became doubly poignant.

Looking into the boarded-up building I saw some decrepit furniture and an ancient kerosene lantern. Just inside the door was the bare footprint outlined in sand, of an extremely thin, bony foot. I decided to return and search the building after dark, since I could easily be observed from the windows of the store.

As I set out for a steepled building I took to be a church, I caught flicker of movement out of the corner of my eye—something dark, too large for any animal in that region but too low for a man. I thought perhaps was an illusion caused by the long shadows the sun was beginning to cast; but just before I got to the church I caught another movement off to one side that was unmistakable. There was something darting among the dunes and houses, possibly a man crouching low. It was a relief to enter the church and I kept turned to check the door.

There was a layer of sand on the floor, and I saw many of the bare footprints. Carved into the wall behind the pulpit was a peculiar symbol I had never seen before. I walked down to the gritty aisle to examine it more closely—it looked like this:

Only the combination of alternately peering at that symbol and glancing nervously back at the door could have enabled me to miss the figure on my right until then, and when I saw her I literally jumped and grabbed for the gun. Then in the fraction of a second it took me to raise my eyes from the ankle-length dress the thoughts churned through my mind that, my God, I've almost shot an old woman praying, no, she's asleep, no, she's—the lips were shriveled back to form a terrifying grin, the eyelids sunken and almost closed, no gleam beneath them, the desert air had mummified the flesh to cracked leather. A mummy in an old-fashioned dress and bonnet, dead for years, perhaps decades. There was something horribly wrong in Dos Piedras.

I knew it was time to get out and contact the police and that whoever or whatever I had seen outside was quite possibly stalking me but the conviction had been growing on me that the mine was the one place I absolutely had to search, and after all I was armed. So I decided to risk it.

As I made my way through the dunes I could detect more movement, though I never got a direct look at the thing. By the time I reached the mouth of the mine I was sure there were several of them, on both sides of me and behind.

The boards along the top of the mine entrance were broken and crooked, like monstrous fangs. Again I saw a trail where something had been dragged, this time leading into the mine. It was larger than it had appeared from a distance and I wondered if the bats I had seen circling lived in it. They seemed abnormally large, though there was something about the desert sunset that made it hard to judge distances.

Once inside I felt safe from attack from the rear and relaxed a little. I became aware that my mental alarm bell was ringing frantically. The high-ceilinged wooden superstructure continued for a hundred feet to where a gaping hole angled downward and to the left into the living rock. Past the angle it was very dark and it took awhile for my eyes to adjust enough to be sure of the large light object in front of me, but I didn't really need to see it to be sure. My subconscious mind had already told me that it was Edward's car.

The *Chthonic Revelations* of Thanang Phram:

Of her beginning even the Secret Masters know not, certain is it only that as the life of earth grew, Yidhra grew, and that she was inseparable from that life, its origin and ultimate fate was she, mistress of birth and death. When life was crude and simple, was Yidhra thus, but as life grew to rich complexity and variation so grew Yidhra, appearing in many forms to many races, in ancient Mloeng even taking the form of Woman; for the tablets of Belegyr show her as a fair woman with a basket of fruit on her arm and a fearsome hound at her feet. But it is said that she had indeed one true form, which no living man has seen, though the mad lama of Prithom-Yang claimed to have seen it in a dream, and idle tongues say it was that sight which drove him mad.

Worshipped she was by all manner of sentient things, by uncouth brutes and by high masters of the hidden forces, by the finned horrors of Xilö-Nor and by the great-winged abominations which circle the crags of Ulan Xara. To those who worshipped gave she prosperity and contentment; to those who knew her not she came softly in the dusk and enticed them to strange fates; but to those most favored servitors who gathered under the Sign of Yidhra and did her bidding gave she both life and death, a life that was not life and a death that was not death . . .

The Notebook:

. . . the only thing I could find amiss about the car was a badly torn tire; someone had driven it a long way on a flat. Apparently none of Edward's effects had been stolen. There was no sign of a struggle.

I heard a noise from farther down the shaft, a slithering as of some gigantic serpent. Moving cautiously back toward the entrance and trying to watch both in front and behind I tripped over something, I didn't see what, and fell flat. I hit the ground at the same time as a large flat stone dropped from above. It was large enough to have crushed my skull. I jumped up and pressed my back to the wall, edging toward the entrance. The gun was in my hand and I watched the catwalks and rafters above for any sign of movement. There was none. I hadn't spotted any movement outside either and when I stepped out past the corner of the entrance I thought I was in the clear until the thing that had been waiting there leaped at me and had its leathery hands on my throat.

The hideous grinning rictus and the musty smell of a thing long dead were so overpowering that I almost dropped the gun, but somehow I summoned the presence of mind to jam the barrel into the creature's stomach and fire. The first shot loosened the grip on my throat and the second bowled it over. It seemed very light, though its grip had been immensely strong. When it began to raise itself slowly I ran. There was no blood on the sand.

The thing had looked exactly like the mummy in the church. As I threaded my way among the dunes and adobe ruins I saw several others moving toward me. They seemed to be able to make short darting runs, then lapse into a slow, lethargic state temporarily.

I reached the main road and sprinted for the car, but when I saw the dead thing in the driver's seat turn its head stiffly toward me I stopped, then broke for the boarded-up building I had seen earlier. I sensed that the desert outside the town would offer no refuge by night.

One of them jumped out of a ruined doorway as I dashed inside and I heard it scratching on the door as I slammed down the wooden bar.

The Third Dream:

. . . no, no . . . never . . . I'll never do that . . . power presses in on my mind like a red cloud, numbing, euphoric, but it won't work, it's too late, I've *seen* you . . .

Old Buck Allison:

. . . they just sorta dried up and shrank, like dead bodies do sometimes out there. Durin' th' day they couldn't move, they'd hole up somewhere and lie still as a corpse, but when th' sun started goin' down they begun to come out, them an' th' flyin' things. At first they'd be slow and stiff, then they'd be able to run a little ways before gettin' stiff again. Them that'd been dead th' longest was th' last to start movin', but after dark they could all scuttle aroun' fast as rats.

They didn't need much to eat or drink, but they craved blood and dead flesh anyway, only sparin' them that Yee-Tho-Rah wanted for servants . . .

The Notebook:

. . . I lit the kerosene lantern and checked all the windows and the back door. They were all stoutly boarded up. I could hear them fumbling at the boards from time to time but I seemed to be safe for the time being. I started this manuscript and will attempt to hide it if it looks like I can't hold out until dawn.

Since the moon came up I've been watching through the cracks in the boards. The flying things are horrible—that head like a fanged vulture, those scaly wings. One landed in front of the window where I was watching and stared directly at me for ten minutes. I could swear that the eyes held more intelligence and malice than those of any normal beast.

The attacks of the dead things were sporadic and unorganized until *she* came, but now she seems to be directing them. I've seen her out there, standing on top of a dune, beautiful, her image shimmering in the moonlight. But more than that I *feel* her presence, alluring, beckoning, clouding my mind like a red haze, paralyzing my will. When one of them pried off a board and thrust in a withered hand I sat stupefied and watched it writhe for a full minute before I could pick up a chair and smash that brittle wrist until the severed hand fell to the floor.

Since then I don't trust my mind anymore, I'm hallucinating, it is not Edward's ring on that shriveled finger, the shimmering of that beautiful creature on the dune did *not* stop for an instant to reveal an obscene and gigantic tentacle stretching away to the mine. They are pounding the door with stones now and . . .

R'lyeh

R'lyeh; it sleeps, it sleeps
Beneath the gray-green waves that roll
And roll where once the spawn
Great Cthulhu brought from cosmic hells
Rang bells, clanged cymbals, mocked the futile
Life of Earth until the waves rose up
And bound the god in dim green murk.
He lurks there; stone
And water shroud him as he dreams
Dark dreams, dead dreams, in R'lyeh.

Predator

American Bulletin of Paleontology, Jan. 3, 1968:

. . . most remarkable Eocene fossil of the early mammalian order Creodonta, clearly related to the 34" skull found in Mongolia by Andrews in 1925. The mode of locomotion of this creature remains utterly mysterious; the limbs are atrophied almost as completely as in whales, yet it unquestionably lived on land. The eyes had also atrophied, giving it the aspect of a gigantic mole. The teeth indicate that it was carnivorous . . .

* * *

Diary of Harold Trilling, February 4, 1971:

. . . Sylvia has really picked the most marvelous place for her 'Abbey of Yidhra'— two stories, foot-thick native stone walls, small-paned casement windows—and the location is ideal, in the rocky hills north of town. We're in a little canyon off the main road, surrounded by ancient oaks. The nearest neighbor is a half mile away so we shouldn't get any complaints about the ceremonies—'Yidhra' doesn't go in for noisy rites anyway. I keep telling Sylvia that the term 'Abbey' is inappropriate, signifying a nunnery or monastery rather than the sort of cult center and temple she's established, but she says southern California is so full of 'temples' that we couldn't get anyone to look twice at another one.

I wish I could really believe in Yidhra the way Sylvia does. The beautiful, awesome and terrible earth mother is a magnificent image all right—but I'm afraid having to operate the hidden projectors and slip the hashish into the sacramental wine for so long has permanently dulled my capacity for spiritual belief. I do find the ceremonies very moving but it's not Yidhra I believe in, it's Sylvia. When she throws back her hood in the torchlight, her hair is shimmering gold and her voice is a silver trumpet far away—the robe softens the angularity of her figure and every movement is pure, eternal femininity. Yet in daylight she often seems quite plain and her voice is almost brassy—I think the only time she's really alive is when the torches burn and Yidhra calls. Sometimes when she talks about her mystical experiences in New Mexico and Laos I think she's a bit mad, but it's a beautiful madness. May Yidhra grant that she always have someone like me to handle the practical side of things!

The cellar will be perfect for ceremonies, though we will have to heat it for our pampered middle-aged clientele. Sylvia wants me to break through the wall behind the altar to make an 'Inner Sanctum' from which to make her dramatic entrances, which will be an ungodly amount of work if there's solid rock behind it. I thought I saw some cracks in the mortar there, though, maybe some of the stones are loose . . .

* * *

Mrs. Herbert Wilkerson, August 12, 1971:

. . . meet the Priestess in the Inner Chapel? How thrilling! You must have great confidence in my spiritual development, Mr. Trilling . . .

* * *

American Bulletin of Paleontology, May 8, 1963:

. . . further excavation has only deepened the mystery of the enormous limbless Creodont. The site of the find proves to have been a deep, narrow cave at the time the creature lived, and the original cave floor was littered with the bones of smaller animals. All were marked by the teeth of the Creodont; the majority show some teeth marks of smaller predators, but not to the extent one would expect if the thing were purely a scavenger. And even a scavenger needs some form of locomotion to get to its food . . .

* * *

Harold's Diary. April 4, 1971:

. . . I don't know about her new policy of staying in the Inner Chapel behind the altar all the time, appearing only at the climax of the ceremony. It's certainly dramatic enough and sets up the impressive special visits with her for especially well-heeled devotees, but it throws the entire burden of salesmanship and stage-managing on me. She could at least come out and help before the worshippers arrive. I'd have been better off if we hadn't found that cave behind the wall. The special visits are really effective though, with the heavy wooden door opening behind the heart-shaped altar and then the stone steps leading downward, and of course the advanced worshipper stoned out of her mind. And her seclusion and 'meditation' have put Sylvia in fine form for the ceremonies, pale face and shining eyes, almost ghostly voice, ". . . and the Mother of Darkness shall reign, bringing endless life to her servitors, the Lurkers in the desert, Xothra the Devourer in the earth, the great-winged Y'hath in the sky."

But I wish she would come out sometimes. I feel I hardly know her these days— she's becoming a distant, dreamlike figure to me . . .

* * *

The Secret History of the Mongols, original version, ca. 1240 A.D. :

. . . Bodoncar-munqaq chided Dörben with laughter because the arrow struck the stag in the flank, and the two followed the blood (trail) of the stag on horseback. After a while they saw that a wolf was also following the deer and Dörben prepared to shoot at the wolf. But Bodoncar-munqaq, seeing that the wolf was behaving strangely, said, "See you that the wolf does not slay the stag but drives it as the sheepdog drives the sheep. Let us follow and watch." And Bodoncar-munqaq and Dörben followed at a distance and saw the wolf drive the stag into a narrow canyon (which they had) not seen before. Dismounting, they followed quietly into the canyon and saw the wolf drag the deer alive into a small cave. Shortly the wolf came out of the cave with a still lean (empty) belly.

* * *

Mrs. Wilkerson, August 12, 1971:

. . . down there? I hadn't thought the passage went down so far—it's a natural cave, isn't it? I don't know if I . . .

* * *

Harold's Diary, June 15, 1971:

. . . tired all the time, I sleep practically all of the time that I'm not working on cult affairs or taking care of Sylvia. She hasn't come out for weeks now. I think she's getting rather morbid, but she's still charming. I took Mrs. Arbogast down to see her last night and Sylvia had her laughing and cooing banalities in no time. Sylvia didn't tell me how much she donated after I left them alone but I was too stoned to care about money anyway.

* * *

The Secret History of the Mongols:

. . . afterwards Bodoncar-munqaq and Dörben returned many times to watch the wolf carry animals into the cave and come out without having eaten them, but each time they feared to enter and search the cave, Bodoncar-munqaq saying that he felt a presence as of evil gods.

Finally one day when Dörben had drunk much *araqi* (fermented mare's milk) he pushed Bodoncar-munqaq aside and entered, saying that a beautiful goddess lived in the cave and sang to him sweetly and promised him many things if he would enter and make obeisance. When after many hours Dörben did not come out, Bodoncar-munqaq returned to the camp and summoned many armed warriors, insisting that none who had drunk *araqi* that day should come. It was thus that Bodoncar-munqaq and the others entered the cave and found the . . .

* * *

American Bulletin of Paleontology, June 3, 1969:

. . . shows the most extreme adaptation to extended hibernation ever observed . . .

* * *

Chants from the *Texts of Mloeng*:

> Xothra the Ravenous!
> Xothra the Hidden Devourer!
> That which rests in the earth in its lair of stone
> That which calls . . .

* * *

Harold's Diary, August 12, 1971:

. . . the policeman who came last night about Mrs. Arbogast was really hostile until Sylvia got hold of him and turned on the charm. It seems Mrs. A. disappeared the night of her visit with Sylvia. I really didn't want to take him down there but I was full of hashish and the whole thing threw me into such a panic that I couldn't think of anything to do but let Sylvia handle him. I had a little trouble getting him to go down the stairs behind the altar, something about the atmosphere of the place really bothered him and he acted completely paranoid, but once Sylvia went to work on him he relaxed and didn't give us any trouble at all. In fact, I remember at one point she had him shrieking with laughter, though I can't remember what about—I was so spaced out I could only stand there and giggle.

Tonight I'm taking Mrs. Wilkerson down to see her. Mrs. W.'s a Boston politician's widow and seems a bit touchy and skeptical. I wouldn't pick her for a special visit if she weren't positively dripping with cash. Sylvia will have to be exceptionally impressive because I can't slip the old bag any hash—I think she suspects that the sacramental wine is doped.

* * *

The Lost Book of Herodotus, ca. 445 B.C.:

. . . and Wanderers in this region of the desert are warned to beware of that which is called Xothra; for it is said that ragged beggars appear in the desert and offer the traveler *alkhafar* weed to chew upon, which if taken lulls the mind with pleasant sensations and fancies; whereupon these beggars invite the traveler to visit certain places in the hills where there are beautiful women or jeweled palaces or some other desirable thing. But of those who have taken the weed and gone into the hills, none has ever returned; some few travelers have declined the weed and gone, and of these it is said that one returned; but his tale is not of fair women or of jeweled palaces but of a thing which chilled the blood of those who heard the tale . . .

* * *

walter c. debill, jnr.

Mrs. Wilkerson, August 12, 1971:

. . . what an awful odor! Are you sure there isn't something dead down there . . . ?

* * *

Private correspondence of Dr. Richard Marbridge, August 3, 1971:

. . . think I may have hit on the only possible explanation. It was a predator; it could not go to its prey; therefore, its prey came to it. How could this happen? Not by chance; that would have been too inefficient for survival. Attraction by odor? Think of an animal living most of its life immobile in a narrow cave; the accumulated stench would almost surely *drive off* any other creature. The only explanation is telepathic control.

Now, what form could this control take? It seems clear that the thing not only lured food directly but induced other predators to bring food to it. It is most unlikely that it evolved such a complex ability merely to devour both the gift and the giver at one 'sitting'; it must have actually enslaved other predators, sending then out time and again to fetch prey. But this required letting the slaves roam about freely, possibly at great distances, using their own hunting ability to the fullest extent. I think this required a very subtle form of control, probably some sort of hallucinatory experience acting as an incentive to carry out the thing's wishes. I wonder what sort of hallucination would induce a wolf to bring home the bacon? A nest of warm, cuddly, ravenous little pups? Or perhaps . . .

* * *

Mrs. Wilkerson:

. . . Sylvia!? LET GO OF ME, YOU MANIAC! OH my GOD that THING . . . !!

* * *

Harold's Diary, September 2, 1971:

. . . looks like Mrs. Harris isn't going to show up tonight. Sylvia will be absolutely furious—no 'special visits' (or large donations) since Mrs. Wilkerson last month. I'm almost afraid to go down there and tell her . . .

* * *

Classified Ad, House for Rent, September 22, 1971:

2 story 9 rm native stone, near town on . . .

The Lure of Leng

". . . in that year Duke Gorth of Phaer intrigued with Arlion, captain of the palace guard, to slay the aged king. Prince Bnireth, last heir of the house of Khoralym, fled into the desert lands and of his fate no man knows, though it is rumored that he passed into the land of Leng and was devoured by the evil things that lurk therein. Thus Duke Gorth took the throne and founded the Thirteenth Dynasty of Kadatheron."

—from one of the few inscriptions still legible
on the Brick Cylinders of Kadatheron.

In the first days of flight Bnireth was numb with shock and grief and felt little, and the scattered families of minor gentry who harbored him secretly from the minions of the new king whispered that he looked like a man already dead. But as the weeks passed and the prince traveled farther and farther from Kadatheron a new life stirred in him as sad spring stirs in the corpse-like winter countryside. There was an aching sorrow at the fall of the proud house of Khoralym, but there was also the lifting of a great oppression, for his struggle against the cunning and ruthless Duke's machinations had been long and bitter and he had long known that it was doomed. As the rapidly consolidated power of the new regime drove him beyond the woods and fields he had known in childhood into the open and less civilized steppes he realized regretfully that there would be no returning, for his former subjects and retainers had accepted the harsh new dynasty as inevitable and however fondly they regarded him would riot rally to his cause; but with this realization came a feeling of peace and freedom. A melancholy peace, to he sure, but peace it was; an end to strife.

He adapted easily to the Spartan life of the nomad tribes; the sybaritic luxury of the court had always bored him. The nomads for their part accepted the wanderer with their usual hospitality and quickly grew fond of his quiet courage and laughing love of life. His laughter was rare, but it was the whole-hearted laughter of a child discovering the world. More often, though, he was silent and pensive, gazing moodily toward the eastern horizon whence he had come or the distant mountains to the west where he must someday go, and the nomads named him Xuruk-Ir which means 'Sad Eyes' in the Bnazic tongue.

He rode with many tribes, herding and hunting with them and even fighting in occasional skirmishes with other tribes or with the frontier patrols of King Gorth, but always there came a day when the outer garrisons of the waxing dynasty would come too close, the sinister officers of the king would ride out to inquire about a wanderer of noble mien, and Bnireth's presence would become a danger to his hosts. Then he would ride westward ever deeper into the desert to seek a new haven. It took seven years for King Gorth to bring the whole of the Bnazic desert under his dominion. Thus at one glorious desert sunrise of the seventh year Prince Bnireth bade farewell to the men of the Yorkut clan of the Jirchid tribe and rode out alone to the foothills about forbidden Leng; there was nowhere else for him to go.

As the floor of the desert rose gently between brown rocky mesas of gradually increasing size the land seemed at first to be more pleasant, for a little more rain fell on the eastern wall of Leng than on the Bnazic flatlands and it was slightly greener here, and Bnireth hoped he might encounter desert tribes unknown to the Bnazic peoples. But soon the gnarled and stunted shrubs began to seem less comforting than the barrenness of Bnazia. The squatting toad-like mesas turned black and threatening and he avoided them rather than seeking their cool and concealing shadows as was his usual habit. By the time the broad sandy corridors had dwindled to rock-bound mountain valleys Bnireth knew that no man willingly dwelt in those lands and that he would find no haven this side of Leng. But he also knew that neither the search for human companions nor fear of Gorth's soldiers led him on now; he felt clearly and keenly the lure of Leng, the summons that nomad wise men say beckons to a few fey men of a generation, men who gaze moodily westward until one day they ride off alone and are not heard of again.

When Bnireth emerged from behind a monstrous black crag and saw the vast gray-brown bowl spread out before and below him he had no doubt that had come to Leng. The trail descended tortuously to an undulating moor quite unlike the clean and open desert where one could see a friend or a foe miles away. There was little sand here but an endless sea of leprous stony hills, mottled with clumps of dark green vegetation and riven with gulleys and crevices of unknown depth. He could not judge the size of the plateau at all; the distant horizon seemed to shimmer and wave in spite of the twilight chill and he could not tell whether the forms he saw there were ragged mountains or mirage.

As he wound his way slowly down the slope in the ghastly yellow twilight he saw a flicker of light in the distance. Earlier in his journey this would have gladdened him and he would have sought its source, but none of the tales of Leng mentioned hospitable men. In fact if the stranger tales were given credence the builders of that distant fire might not be men at all. Since he had enough provisions to cross Leng without aid he thought it wiser to thread his way through the hills without coming near it, choosing a low path so that he could not be seen. Yet though his sense of direction was normally good he repeatedly rounded a pile of boulders or topped a low hill to find himself headed straight for that orange gleam, and each time it came closer. At last just as darkness closed in for the night he led his horse up out of a shallow stream bed to find himself in the presence of the fire's attendants.

They were five in number, and they sat in a circle around the fire, seemingly oblivious to Bnireth's arrival. He stood in silence for a time, peering at the indistinct and unmoving features beneath the great black hoods. He saw no gear, no beasts of burden. The thought crossed his mind that they had not noticed him and that he right slip away unseen, but that was absurd; they sat not more than twenty paces before him and his horse had made a great deal of noise scrambling up the slope. Finally he found the silence unbearable and spoke.

"Leng is a lonely place; I've ridden all day through the mountains and seen no one but you."

The figure facing him from beyond the fire raised its head very slightly and replied in an oddly hollow, unresonant voice, "In Leng one meets only those who await him." Bnireth did not like that voice; it made the evening air seem colder.

"Are there no friendly tribesmen with whom a traveler may rest and find provisions?"

The hollow voice answered, "You will find what awaits you," and another, more sibilant and metallic, added, "There is no rest in Leng, Prince Bnireth." And as the night-wind rose he saw a hint of the contours enshrouded by those black robes and, mounting, fled into the night. The stony paths of Leng soon forced him to dismount and lead the pony. For hours they picked their way cautiously in darkness, hounded by the rushing wind and less identifiable rustlings and slitherings. When the gibbous moon rose above the mountains it was sickly and yellow and served more to silhouette the sinister tors and cromlechs on the hills than to illuminate the low paths he trod. He did not like the shadows it cast, many were too long or too curiously shaped and some were not still. Finally the horse fell and lay exhausted and Bnireth lay down beside it and slept. It was a fitful sleep, stirred by a distant baying and dreams of bitter memory.

In the morning he found the bones of his mount picked clean. His supplies were gone; he was afoot and without sustenance in Leng.

It was a long day, lit by an ochreous sun which gave little warmth. Bnireth used the sun to guide him westward, but the jumbled terrain made a straight course impossible and he often looked up to find that he had been walking for some time in the wrong direction. As the day dragged on he was increasingly distracted by the twisted and thorny plants which seemed to reach out and grasp at his legs as he passed and by the peculiar rattlings and scrapings that always seemed to come from somewhere close behind. He looked up less often to check his direction. Eventually, after seeing something emerge from the shadow of a boulder on the path behind him, something quite large which may have had eyes and certainly had teeth, he ceased to check at all. Thus he was not as surprised as he might have been when just at sunset he plodded wearily over the crest of a hill and found himself overlooking the same five figures. The scene was exactly as before; there was nothing to show that they had so much as moved a finger during the long night and day that had passed.

This time Bnireth did not hesitate but stepped immediately up to them. He was hungry and tired but he could not think of food and rest: "Where is the way out of Leng?" he asked. A hooded thing raised its head so that firelight glinted in eyes deep-set behind a rigid mask of porcelain and whispered, "When you are ready we shall lead you to your destination. But for you there is no way out of Leng."

Into the yellow dusk he fled, forgetting hunger and fatigue in his panic fear of the doom ordained for him in Leng. His tortured mind devised a plan; he would follow the mountains, keeping them always on his left until he saw the great crag he had passed as he entered Leng. He was sure he could recognize it even by moonlight. When the twilight failed he rested, waiting for the moon, but did not sleep.

With the rising of the moon he resumed his trek to the east. The hours of rest had not refreshed him, but he was spurred on by his frantic desire to escape from Leng. He heard again the baying that had disturbed his dreams the night before, sometimes distant, sometimes all too near, and each doleful howl made him forget his weary legs and hasten his step. As the moon crept higher above the eastern wall

walter c. debill, jnr.

of Leng he saw erect figures standing on the hilltops around him singly or in pairs; whether they were the howlers in the night he could not tell, but he did not wish to meet them and they too quickened his pace. Toward dawn, though, exhaustion began to outpace fear and when he stumbled into a pit and fell onto soft sand beside a shadowed pool he lay there a while savoring sweet rest in his limbs. But soon he heard small ripples lapping the shore near his hand and looked up to see moonlight reflected in eyes at least half a pace apart; he climbed out of the pit and staggered on. Just before sunrise he fell on a bed of what may have been ivy and again lay resting, but too soon he noticed the slow writhing of the vines and when probing tendrils began to fasten on his arms and legs and throat he felt he should move on. For Prince Bnireth there was indeed no rest in Leng

The sun brought little relief from the terrors of the night. There were still ominous sounds behind the hills and though no figures stood openly on the hilltops he constantly caught flickers of furtive motion with the corner of his eye. He felt thirst, but the water of stagnant pools and clear streams alike proved bitter to the taste and he spat it out. He was faint with hunger, but most of the plants he saw had thorns and the more succulent-looking ones twisted sway from his grasping hand in a way he did not like. He was certain that he had not passed the crag marking the way out of Leng in the moonlight and expected to spot it at any moment, but it did not appear. By evening he crawled as often as he walked and no longer expected to escape from Leng. When at sunset he saw again the fire and the five enigmatic figures it was almost a welcome sight, for no death that awaited him could exceed the agony of life. He summoned all his remaining strength to step with dignity up to the fire and say, "I am ready."

It was not far to the great cliff face where they led him, though it seemed so to Bnireth's fogged and tormented mind. At first he watched his guides or captors closely, trying to discern something of their nature, but after noting that one left more marks in the dust than two feet could account for and that another was dragging some heavy object which left a trail between two rows of three-toed footprints he ceased watching and tried to think of other things. He tried to think of the pleasant days among the Bnazic nomads, but his mind turned ever to Kadatheron, to the house of Khoralym, its heroic beginnings, its long ages of supremacy and splendor which now trickled down to this strange doom in Leng. A shaft of deep blue light caught his attention and he looked up to see a tower on top of the cliff which could only be that elder pharos of evil legend.

Below it gaped a great opening with edges worn smooth like the burrow of some monstrous primeval serpent and into this he was led. It was pitch black within but his companions strode confidently through the darkness and Bnireth followed their scratching and shuffling footsteps. Soon a light appeared in the distance and as they approached it he saw that they had passed into a corridor of polished onyx inlaid with abhorrent symbols which he recognized from the oldest chapters of the *Pnakotic Manuscripts*.

The corridor ended in a vast circular chamber lit by a column of turbulent flame rising from a pit in the center. Its wells were completely lined with niches containing objects his tired eyes could not at first identify. Then he saw that they were dolls, each no higher than a man's knee; dolls dressed in the costumes of all the ages of mankind. As curiosity stimulated him and cleared his vision Bnireth perceived that every race, every kingdom known to man was represented in those niches, as well as many he could not recognize. In the higher tiers the figures grew hairy and brutish, hardly human at all, and in the uppermost niches that he could see with any clarity he thought he saw things with tails and horns and tentacles clothed in strange raiment. Their thousands upon thousands of eyes reflected the yellow flame. But the five denizens of Leng were leading him rapidly toward the pillar of fire in the center and he had not time to ponder the meaning of the dolls. He wondered if he would live to learn about them. They were halfway to the flame now and he saw the great idol behind, its yellow stone obscured by swirling yellow radiance. Or was it stone? He saw the greet yellow-masked head nod toward him, the left arm rise as if in command; the room seemed to grow, his captors to swell until he came barely to their waists, then to their knees; his body grew stiff and with sudden horror Bnireth understood the dolls and knew his fate.

Through the endless years Bnireth stood in his niche, his mind frozen in ceaseless consciousness, watching the high priest not to be described and those who came before him; he watched Arlion after he fell from favor and fled from Kadatheron; centuries later he watched the last king of the house of Gorth meet his doom; he saw Ilathos, a wizard of Lomar who visited the half-buried ruins of Kadatheron in search of elder lore and lost his way on his return; and he is still there, watching.

Where Yidhra Walks

"A hundred April winds disperse her fragrance,
A thousand wet Octobers scour her footprints,
The ruthless years assail the ancient memory of her presence, yet
Where Yidhra walks the hills do not forget."

—Jean Paul LeChat

I

The river was swollen to a mad torrent, the water brown and opaque. I watched a jagged clump of brush sweep by with terrifying speed; three moccasins twined in its sodden branches. The rain had grown heavier for three days while the wind mounted steadily and, though the eye of the hurricane was expected to pass a hundred miles east and the violence of the storm decrease as it moved further inland I knew it would be a week before the river could be crossed here even if the decrepit trestle bridge survived. It was shuddering periodically from the strain of the current and the broken remnants of two of the trestles dangled uselessly.

As I stood on the bank a muddy pickup truck pulled up and two men in ponchos and cowboy hats began blocking the entrance to the bridge with sawhorses. One saw me eyeing the bridge and called out, "Good thing you didn't try it, mister, we already had three people drown today when a bridge washed out over by Iverston."

"Is there another bridge across this river that might still be safe? I hate to go all the way around through Barrett. That's a hundred miles out of my way."

He flashed an unsympathetic smirk, plainly intending to say no, then paused. "Well, there's an old bridge upstream five miles, where the river's not so wide. It's on the old road through Milando." He said it in a tense, subdued voice.

His companion stopped tinkering around the truck and stepped over beside him, "If you go that way I'd recommend you keep movin'. Those folks up around Milando never did like outsiders much, and what this hurricane's doin' to their orchards ain't gonna improve their hospitality." They both chuckled.

I remembered seeing Milando on the map and didn't ask for directions. I glanced in the rearview mirror as I drove off and saw them both watching me curiously from under their dripping hat brims.

I don't know why I was so anxious to avoid a detour and keep driving doggedly through the storm. My cousin in Brownsville wasn't expecting me by any fixed date and even losing a week crossing Texas wouldn't have inconvenienced me particularly. Yet the monotonous downpour lulled me into a mental torpor where thoughtless stubbornness pushed me on, and something about the mysterious raging river demanded that I cross it. And of course the peculiar attitude of the men at the bridge had aroused my curiosity about Milando. So I wound my way five miles north on a pitted blacktop road roughly paralleling the river and clattered across the plank floor of an ancient truss bridge. Less than a mile beyond the river a culvert spanning a tributary creek was under a few inches of water but my little station wagon had a high road clearance for a small car and I decided to risk it. The wheels kept losing traction letting the car slip sideways in sickening lurches, but I made it. I heard a groaning sound and a huge crash behind me and turned to see the culvert tube bounding jerkily downstream. I could no longer go back.

The road was tortuous and narrow as it wormed upward into the labyrinth of limestone hills, alternating gloomy tunnel-like passages overhung by gnarled live oaks with barren stretches below steep cliffs. The striking appearance of the stunted mesquite trees writhing along the cliff tops continually caught my eye in spite of the hazardous driving conditions or I would never have seen the hooded figure against the darkening sky. Somehow I knew that it was a woman, though the hooded rain cape concealed both face and figure. A large dog sat at her feet. I barely had time to wonder what she was doing out there in such abominable weather before I rounded a sudden curve and had my first sight of Milando.

II

Through a lull in the rain I saw the town spread out below me in a wedge-shaped cleft in the hills. The road snaked down a steep hillside and passed along the mouth of the cleft, where the town was perhaps a mile wide. Almost all of the town lay to the left of the load where the streets wandered aimlessly upward to the point of the wedge, nearly level with the surrounding cliffs.

As I entered the town I slowed to a crawl and began searching for a place to get something to eat. It was darkening rapidly and the slope above me was dotted with lighted windows, but every window and doorway along the main street seemed black and deserted. I almost passed the one business still open because the glow at the windows as so dim. The painted sign said 'Saloon-Grocery-Meat Market,' so I parked and mounted the concrete porch, catching a stream of rainwater in my collar from the edge of the overhanging roof. Behind the display windows, which featured pyramids of dusty canned goods and an array of cheap pocket knives, a chest-high partition blocked most of the light and the dingy glass filtered the rest to a sickly yellow. But once I rattled my way through the heavy door it was evident that I had found he center of Milando's night life.

To my left several groups of men sat around heavy circular tables playing dominoes. Through an archway at the rear I could see more tables and dominoes. The bar ran along the right-hand side and behind it the wall was lined with rows of canned and packaged foods rising almost to he ceiling. There was no one behind the bar but as I moved over to it an uncomfortable lull spread through the room and a bald, burly specimen detached himself from one of the games and stepped around to the beer taps in front of me.

"What do you want?" No amenities, no smile.

"Just passing through. Any place in town where I can get a meal?"

"Nope. I'll sell you some of this stuff." His long ape-like arm gestured toward the shelves, apparently indicating some grimy boxes of shotgun shells, while his flat eyes kept me fixed.

"I guess that will have to do."

"Say, which way did you come from?"

"East. The main bridge was about gone and I didn't want to go around through Barrett."

"Well, you're gonna have to go back that way. The low-water crossing west of town's under six feet of water."

"But a culvert washed out behind me not far this side of the river. You mean I'm stuck here for the night?"

The room was silent now. "More than that. Several days, I'd say." Under the bushy brows the eyes had taken on a suspicious cast.

"Plan to check out any old Injun stories?" jeered a beery voice from one of the tables. It seemed to emanate from a set of crooked yellow teeth just below the sharp shadow of a tin lampshade.

The bartender shot a murderous glare in that direction before explaining, "Don't pay no attention to Maynard's warped sense o' humor. He's talking about a fellow name o' Harrison from Barrett, from the university, that came up here lookin' for Indian relics and traces of folklore. Seems this used to be some kind a' medicine place, somethin' to do with a cult called 'Yidhra,' but people around here don't know anything about that. The dam' fool got himself lost up in the hills, never was found. This country's full of caves, deep pools, heavy brush. Well, I got potato chips and stuff like that, sardines—but I don't know where you're gonna stay till the water goes down. No motel or anything   here . . ."

A tall man setting alone at the end of the bar stood up and turned stiffly toward me, "You can stay with us. You're welcome to have dinner. My name's Wilhelm Kramer." The bartender was not pleased and I heard Maynard chuckle nervously.

"Thanks," I said, "that would sure beat sardines and a cold night in my car." Besides, I sensed that the antagonism between him and the others might make him a good source of information about the town. He picked up a heavy rubber raincoat and a canvas fisherman's hat from the jumble of rain gear hung on a set of mounted deer antlers and we left.

In the car he didn't speak except to give terse directions to a rather small unpainted house about halfway up the slope. Crossing the screened-in front porch we entered a neat and cozy living room, warmed by a large radiant heater and the subdued, almost amber light from beneath an opaque cardboard lampshade. From a door at the left emerged a small pale woman who gave me a startled look.

"How do you do, I'm Peter Kovacs," I said, remembering that I hadn't introduced myself to Kramer at the store.

"Mr. Kovacs is staying with us until the creeks go down. The Moreno Creek culvert's washed out and the low-water crossing's under six feet."

Her colorless eyes looked even more startled and after telling us that supper would be ready in a few minutes she disappeared into the kitchen. We hung our coats on hooks by the door and Kramer settled in threadbare but comfortable-looking armchair while I sat on the overstuffed couch. "You seem to be the only one in Milando that cares much for strangers, Mr. Kramer," I said, hoping to draw him out about the town. He smiled.

"Yes, the others are pretty hostile to any kind of outsider." He was about forty, with rugged features just beginning to soften around the sharp lines. "Actually they still think of me as an outsider, though I've been here eighteen years. I'm originally from Iverston . . . met Georgia, that's my wife, at the junior college in Mesquite City and came here to take over her father's business when his health went bad. I sell oil and gas to the farmers on credit. They never did like me." He gave the impression of a normally taciturn man become garrulous under the influence of beer and fresh companionship.

I saw the little goblin faces of three small children peep through the door to a darkened rear hall, then fade away. They seemed to take after the mother.

"Are all the small towns around here this inhospitable?"

"They're all pretty clannish and ingrown, mainly because there's nothing to attract new blood, and tend to peg outsiders as 'city slickers' or beatniks, but Milando's the only one that's downright hostile to *anybody* that wasn't born and raised here. Always was. It was settled right after the Civil War by a bunch that came out together from Georgia. Never did hit it off with the other settlers around here, and then their dealings with the Indians . . ."

His wife appeared in the doorway, looking more alarmed than ever, and announced that the food was ready. We ate in the brightly lit kitchen. The food was as solid and simple as the furniture and there was little conversation. In the light Mrs. Kramer was faintly attractive in a pallid, wistful way, in spite of a prominent nose and weak chin which made her eyes appear to be slightly to the side of her head. I had noticed the same trait in the bartender and guessed that they were related. The children, a girl of about thirteen whom they called Georgie and two younger boys, had inherited it, along with their mother's wispy blond hair and flat, colorless eyes. They were very quiet. Toward the end of the meal Kramer and his wife had a tense exchange concerning a visit the following day from Kramer's mother-in-law. I guessed that she must live somewhere in the hills near town since having the main roads washed out didn't cancel the visit. He evidently disliked her intensely and the atmosphere became so strained that I was not surprised when Mrs. Kramer failed to join us in the living room afterwards.

Kramer brought beer from the refrigerator and I had no trouble getting him back on the history of the town. "The settlers had a hard time at first, most of the land's too rocky to farm, but once they made peace with the Comanche and started raising sheep and fruit trees, apples and peaches, it got to be the most prosperous own in the hills. Probably would've become a big trading center and county seat like Iverston if the other settlers hadn't been so leery of this bunch. Still don't get any business except from right around the town, the old families that came from Georgia."

"Comanche? I didn't know they raided this far east," I said.

"Oh, yes. They were mainly up in the Panhandle, in the flat open country, but they roamed over most of the state when they felt like it. And this area was a medicine place—the center of a special cult of a goddess called Yidhra. Not all of the Comanche belonged, just certain bands. The Tonkawas that lived in the area used to allow 'em free passage to here at certain times in the spring and fall to hold their ceremonies. When the settlers came they cut 'em off, at first, anyway, so the Comanche tried to drive 'em out, but after a while they made some kind of agreement with the old chief they called Snake Eyes to let the Indians come twice a year. I guess they were just tired of fighting, the settlement was pretty poor then and probably not worth fighting about. That caused a lot bad feelings with the other settlements, the Comanche had a pretty fearsome reputation, killin' whites and other Indians was their idea of light recreation, and when they came riding through the hills with their horned buffalo-scalp headdresses and lances and such I guess it was hard to tell a religious pilgrimage from a war party. Anyway, the place became completely isolated. There were even rumors that some of the people here had gone over to the Indian religion. But about that time the place started to prosper and the people didn't care what the neighbors thought." He was slowing down now, his voice getting lower, and I thought he would fall asleep soon.

"Milando's an odd name—sound's Spanish, but I've never heard it before."

"Not Spanish, Indian. Some kind of word they got from the Comanche. They changed the town's name to that in 1887, when some of the original families pulled up and went to California. The town was originally called Kimbrough, after my wife's great-grandfather who led the original move out from Georgia. But when old Kimbrough left with the others in '87 they changed it. Some say they left because they were the only ones who wouldn't go over to the Indian cult. I won't believe that, but it's true that these people know a lot more about that Indian business than they'll tell anybody, even me."

I made a few more attempts to get him to say more about the town's strange history, but he had gone as far as he was willing to for the time being and seemed more and more inclined to brood and let the conversation lapse. I felt uncomfortable in the silence and was too restless to sleep at that early hour so I said I was going back to the store for cigarettes. Before leaving I brought in my overnight bag and was shown into the small rear bedroom, from which Georgie had apparently been evicted for the night, where I would sleep.

I didn't really want to go back to the dingy store with its hostile proprietor and clientele but once in the car I realized that there was nowhere else to go. The rain had become very heavy as the evening progressed and the dirt streets of Milando were in bad enough shape to make driving too risky even if I had been able to see anything. So I crawled down the hill in second gear and parked in front of the gloomy 'Saloon-Grocery-Meat Market.'

This time the domino players ignored my entry. Only the bartender appeared to take notice, giving me a cold smile. "Well, did ol' Willie tell you all about Milando?"

"Just a little," I said. "Interesting place, so isolated and independent. I'd like to know more . . . ," I was concentrating so intently on sounding banal that I didn't notice the sound of the door until I saw the bartender's eyes staring past me and heard the dead silence at the tables. I hesitated a moment before turning, not knowing whether to expect Frankenstein's monster or something worse. When I did turn, I faced the most attractive woman I have ever seen.

I didn't know then what fascinated me about her and I don't know now. She was tall, very slender, even angular but graceful, and from the hooded cape I was certain she was the one I had seen just before entering the town. The long oval face with its short straight nose and almost solemn mouth was pretty, but she was beautiful far beyond any sum of physical attributes. At the time I thought it might be her eyes, they were a luminous gray and very large below a trace of eye shadow which was the only discernable makeup, but since then I have come to believe that some women have a force of soul which casts an irresistible glamour over whatever features they possess.

She gave me a leisurely examination, then addressed the bartender. "I didn't know there was an outsider in town, Ed."

"He just came in tonight, ma'am. The road's washed out, he's staying with Willie Kramer." His voice sounded as though he were standing at attention.

"Well, I hope you enjoy your stay, Mr. . . . ?"

"Kovacs, Peter Kovacs." Her high clear voice affected me hypnotically. "It's an interesting town, I'd like to find out about its history, the Indian cult . . ." I was blurting it out thoughtlessly, my mind unfocused.

She had a silvery little laugh. "You'll find that the people in Milando don't have much to tell. But perhaps you'll learn enough to satisfy your curiosity. 'Where Yidhra walks, the hills do not forget.'" Memory stirred and I placed the enigmatic line from Jean Paul LeChat, the brilliant young New Orleans poet who disappeared in Chad in 1957.

"That's from LeChat, isn't it? I remember wondering what it meant when I read it. I'd never heard of the cult of Yidhra before I came here today."

"I doubt if Mr. LeChat knew much about it either," she said, brushing back the hood from her straight blond hair. "He wrote about more things than he understood."

"And Harrison? Did he understand?"

Her eyes widened and her smile became hard, even cruel. "No, not really. He was intelligent in the purely bookish sense, but not really sensitive. Not equipped to understand the real mysteries of life."

I thought she was eyeing me with increasing interest but she turned abruptly to the bartender and said, "Ed, could I speak to you for a moment, in private?"

After a gruff "Yes, ma'am" they moved toward the archway in the rear. Her walk was fluid, utterly feminine but not exaggerated and I noticed that her high shiny boots were clean, though Milando was a quagmire outside and I hadn't heard a car pull up. Her dismissal of me had been rather imperious and I felt a bit sheepish, the more so because I was left standing there with no one to wait on me. I didn't really need the cigarettes so I left.

Back at the house Kramer sat alone staring into space while a backwoods preacher ranted through the static on an ancient console radio with an illuminated dial. He gave a faint grunt of acknowledgement when I said goodnight, not even turning his head. As soon as I lay down fatigue swept over me like an ocean wave and my mind began to dissolve into fragments of dream. I was vaguely aware of the hissing whispers of the children in the next room, they seemed to have some sort of speech impediment which made it impossible to understand what they said; I remember hearing Kramer's voice over that of the radio preacher, berating his wife about his mother-in-law; last of all before sleep came I remember picturing with abnormal clarity every line and shadow of the woman's face, the woman in the hood.

III

I slept late in the morning and by the time I awoke Kramer had left the house. His wife fixed breakfast for me in spite of my demurrals and apologies, seeming even more flustered and inarticulate in her husband's absence. In the awkward silence I observed her more closely than the night before. There was an almost reptilian suggestion in her features, accented by her slouching round-shouldered carriage and shuffling walk. I wondered how much of her washed-out appearance was due to heredity and how much to a lifetime of small town boredom and narrowness. With more spirit and a little makeup she might have been quite pretty. I thought of the woman in the hood; small town life certainly hadn't stifled *her.* I mentioned the incident to Mrs. Kramer and asked if she knew the woman, but it turned out to be the wrong thing to do. She looked terrified and mumbled something about "Miss Yolanda." I asked if she was an outsider and she said no, she had always lived there but beyond that she claimed to know nothing about her, which was obviously untrue.

Outside the rain had thinned to drizzle and sunlight was starting to break through in patches. I guessed that the center of the storm had passed during the night. I decided to drive out to the low water crossing to see if the water had begun to go down, though I was too curious about Milando to really want to leave yet. The road to the west led around a perpendicular bluff into a long narrow valley. Both sides of the road were lined with groves of apple and peach trees. I saw some fruit on the ground but the storm had apparently done little damage. Farther from the road I caught glimpses of flocks of sheep on the lower slopes of the hills rising to the north and south. At the end of the valley I drove over a low hill and stopped. Ahead of me the road descended into churning brown water, reemerging fifty yards away. Halfway across the creek protruded the top of a concrete post. The painted line marked '4 ½ FT' was just visible above the eddying surface. The rain had stopped and the sun was shining through a hole in the clouds so I got out of the car and walked down to the water's edge. I stood for a while, watching and listening to the rushing stream. When I turned she was there.

She was beside the road at the top of the slope where the trees began, standing in the shade. She was wearing the rain cape with the hood back, the same calf-high boots and short skirt. I resolved not to get rattled this time, the night before I had been tired and off-balance because of the repressed menace of the xenophobic saloon crowd. By daylight she would probably be an intelligent small town girl, perhaps moderately attractive but not exceptional. I started up the hill.

Neither of us spoke until I reached her. By then I felt the same powerful, unexplainable fascination I had in the gloom of the saloon.

"Hello, Mr. Kovacs. It looks as though you'll be with us for a while. There will be more rain." Her voice had an odd distant quality I hadn't noticed before.

"Yes, I'd guess two days at least. Maybe I'll get a chance to find out something about this Yidhra thing, though I got the impression I might be better off digging around in the university library in Barrett than trying to get anything out of the people here. Do you know much about it, Miss . . . ?"

"Call me Yolanda. I guess I know as much about Yidhra as anyone around here.

She's old—the Indians didn't bring the worship of Yidhra with them, they found it here. And the cult existed in the Old World. The men of Sumer knew her. But you wouldn't find out much in any university library. There have been books that told about Yidhra and other hidden things, but man has a habit of avoiding things that make him uncomfortable. In the past books like the *Chronicles of Thrang*, the *Chthonic Revelations* of Thanang Phram, the *Black Sutra* of U Pao, have been denounced, suppressed, burned. In modern times they're disposed of even more simply—the professional scholars merely declare them not authentic. Or just ignore them altogether. Perhaps it's for the best—there are elder things much less benign than Yidhra."

I thought these were rather remarkable statements, though there have been a number of fairly plausible theories about pre-Columbian contact between the Old and New Worlds. But I was more interested in hearing what she had to say than in debating with her and didn't challenge them.

"And is the cult really still carried on in Milando?"

"Yes indeed." She turned and we began ambling side by side down the shady tree line. Almost all of them are in it now. Kramer's not of course. He's an outsider. They take in outsiders from time to time, Yidhra needs them, but Kramer just wasn't right for it."

I smiled, "I suppose the cult couldn't spread very far if they never took in any new members."

"No, but then Yidhra doesn't much care about spreading the cult. She's part of life and death and the earth itself, domination means nothing to her. She takes only what she needs. She was born with life itself on this planet and as life grew she grew, as life changed so she changed. And like all life she must change to live. Milando is small and inbred; to limit the cult, or this branch of it, to these people and their descendants would be stasis, a kind of death."

"You really believe in her, don't you?" I said.

Her smile was politely restrained but her gray eyes, deep set in spite of their size, were laughing at me. "Yidhra isn't a matter of faith, Peter. She's real. She does things. You saw the orchards on your way here; we had fifty mile an hour winds night before last. And the sheep; thousands of sheep will take sick and die from this weather, but none around Milando. Her followers even see her, after a fashion, though the ancient books say that what they see is largely illusion, a protective glamour cast over a far more terrifying reality; only the real *participants* in the cult, the inner circle, those born of Yidhra and those chosen to mingle their blood and seed with her to renew her and bring forth new life, only those see her true form."

The sun was hot where it flickered through the leaves and the sultry soporific smell of wet vegetation became oppressive. I moved into the sunlight onto a high flat rock overlooking the water and she followed.

"I wonder if Jean Paul LeChat saw her," I said as we looked down at the stream.

"Perhaps, in Chad. He was seeking her there—all he had found in New Orleans were old books and third-hand accounts from degenerate pseudo-occultists." As she turned toward me her eyes seemed enormous. "You'll see her I think, Peter."

The spell was broken by a spatter of raindrops in advance of a ragged cloudbank. "I'll have to go now," she said.

"Can I give you a ride?"

"No, thank you, I live in the hills near here. There's a trail." She turned and slipped into an imperceptible opening in the brush. I caught sight of her willowy figure through the trees several times as she flitted up the hillside; then the sky turned gray and I had to run for the car to keep from getting drenched.

IV

When I pulled up in front of the Kramer house and got out of the car I could hear Kramer barking at his wife about the impending visit of his mother-in-law. He had been drinking again and was apparently too engrossed in the squabble to hear me drive up so I overheard some of his taunts before I stepped up on the porch and knocked at the door. At the time I interpreted it as a standard in-law feud—she was a bad influence on the children, she was alienating them from their father, his wife's grandfather should have left with Old Kimbrough instead of staying on and becoming 'the worst of the lot.' I regretted coming back to the house and by the time he opened the door I had made up my mind to get back out as soon as possible, even if it meant driving around aimlessly through the mud or resorting to the saloon.

His wife left the room as I entered and I told Kramer about checking the low-water crossing. When I mentioned running into the young woman I had met in the saloon he looked puzzled and asked her name.

"I didn't get her last name—her first name's Yolanda," I said.

He turned white; it was a while before he spoke. "Look here, Mr. Kovacs—it must be obvious to you by now that there's something pretty strange about this town. You might as well know that the old Indian cult is still very much alive here. They've never let me in on it, but you can't live in a town like this for eighteen years without getting a pretty good idea what's going on. And I think she's at the head of it."

"She seemed harmless enough to me," I said, "imaginative, full of wild ideas but basically a decent girl."

"Girl, Mr. Kovacs?" he chuckled wryly. "When I first saw her, about the time they started to take me for granted and quit worrying about my suspicions, she looked exactly as she does now. That was fifteen years ago."

This disturbed me more than it should have; I had found her age peculiarly hard to judge in the saloon, placing it somewhere between eighteen and twenty-eight, and after talking with her in daylight had inclined toward the lower figure. But then there had been the bartender's rigid deference toward her and the occasional hints of condescension in her attitude toward me; why should it be so upsetting to think of her as in her mid-thirties?

"I think you'd be wise to stay away from her," he went on, "you heard about that student that came here last year—they never found him. There were others before him. She seems to be interested in you. That's a bad sign, Mr. Kovacs. These people are dangerous."

I made some vague promises to be careful and left. The rain was light but steady and I decided to risk a drive around the town. Except for the stretch of road along the foot of the hill Milando consisted of unpaved streets, now soft, slippery and gullied, but somehow I managed to avoid getting stuck. The houses were uniformly low and wooden, with haphazard additions that gave them a rambling look in spite of their generally small size. Considering the alleged prosperity of the town a surprising proportion were shabby and dilapidated, with ragged screens, broken wooden steps and missing windowpanes replaced with cardboard; I wondered if this was an outward-sign of the inhabitants' spiritual and mental degeneracy, of their regression into barbarous superstition. Almost none of the houses were painted, though in the few well-kept specimens like Kramer's the unpainted wood gave an impression of dignity rather than squalor. I found the overall effect depressing and the furtive sullen looks the occupants gave me before pulling down yellowed window shades made me uneasy, so I soon headed down the hill to the saloon. I think I was hoping to run into Yolanda again in spite of Kramer's warning.

Ed, the bartender, greeted me with a nasty smile. "Still with us? I figured you would be, unless you felt like swimming out."

"You were right, looks like two or three more days before I can cross that low-water bridge. You sell beer this time of day?"

"Anytime, the state liquor people don't get up here much and the county law don't care." He handed me a bottle of a popular local brand without offering a choice.

"And I suppose you're the Chief of Police?"

"Naw, that's Maynard. You still interested in the old Indian doings here?"

"Yes, very much."

"Well, I got Harrison's notes here, the student that disappeared. We found 'em in the brush, after Maynard called off the search and the Ranger left. Didn't seem worthwhile to send 'em on."

If the investigator sent by the state had left the search to the local people anything could have happened, anything could have been concealed. Kramer had said these people were dangerous and somehow the bartender's new congeniality was not at all reassuring.

The notes consisted of loose sheets in a cheap accordion folder. I carried them and the beer over to one of the round tables and sat down to examine them. The sheets had been dated and numbered and many pages were missing. The first few pages consisted of accounts, apparently copied from the state archives in Barrett, from early Texas settlers who had spoken to other Indian groups about the devotees of Yidhra, whom they called by many variant names such as Yee-Tho-Rah. The cult had originated somewhere east of the West Texas Plains, among unknown tribes described as tall, hairy and very primitive, and had spread among the Comanche only a few generations before the Europeans appeared. The bands which had adopted the cult had been abhorred by the other Comanche, who seemed to consider them physically repellent as well as dangerous. They occasionally kidnapped members of other bands for some purpose, possibly ritual sacrifice though there were rumors that some of the captives had been found or rescued alive. The Indians were curiously reluctant to speak of these captives but the settlers concluded from various hints that they had been killed by their rescuers because of some physical deformity associated with conversion to the cult. At this point there was a break in the notes where some pages were missing.

The next section was a series of quotes from standard reference works on anthropology and folklore, interspersed with Harrison's own remarks. He seemed to have concluded that Yidhra was a version of the universal figure of the earth mother or goddess of the underworld connected with primitive concepts of prosperity, fertility and death, but that the cult was not directly related to any mentioned in standard sources. Toward the end of this section there were indications that he had unearthed some obscure sources, possibly in a private library, which he thought might contain information on Yidhra and planned to investigate them next. There were a number of parenthetical questions and notes such as: "Related to Mlandoth cycle?", "Try the *Chronicles* on this point", and "c. f. Könnenberg's *U.S.*" Then came a large gap in the page number sequence.

The notes began again during Harrison's investigations in Milando and were plainly fragmentary and incomplete with many individual pages removed. From what remained I gathered that he had never stayed overnight in Milando but made numerous trips from Barrett over a period of about a month. He commented on the reticence of most of the inhabitants, but managed to contact Kramer and two others who told him essentially what Kramer had told me. There was no mention of Yolanda, though one page following a deletion began with the suggestive phrase ". . . she doesn't consider me suitable." There were a few hints that he was correlating the information obtained in Milando with the obscure sources mentioned just before the big gap in the page numbers but there was no explicit or elaborate correlation on the pages present. At first there was much speculation about survival of the cult into the present but toward the end missing pages became more frequent and any references to definite discovery of cult practices must have been systematically removed. On the last page Harrison expressed frustration with the reticence of the townspeople and resolved to go exploring on foot in the hills.

Altogether the notes were less interesting than the fact that they had been shown to me. Last night Ed had been openly offensive and had tried to discourage any interest in Milando; today he affected courtesy if not friendliness and deliberately whetted my curiosity. A decision must have been made, undoubtedly by Yolanda, as to how I would be dealt with and he was no longer worried about me. I was to be led on but not told too much just yet. As I sat smoking a cigarette and sipping the last of my second beer I drew two conclusions, one right and one wrong. The first was that, unlike Harris, I was 'suitable'; I had been chosen to join the cult of Yidhra. The second was that I was therefore in no danger and could proceed boldly to find out what lay in the hills behind Milando.

V

A combination of reason and intuition that told me that what I wanted to know lay over the hill at the top of the cleft. Logically there was the fact that while presumably there were several hundred people involved in the cult I could see no place suitable for a large gathering, no large buildings and nothing resembling a town square. To the north beyond the main road there was a steep rise to sheer cliffs; I had traveled the roads east and west as far as a man could conveniently walk and seen nothing that looked like a gathering place and nothing striking enough to inspire an Indian medicine place. Thus my attention was naturally drawn to the point of the wedge to the south. I had noticed that there was a break in the cliff line there where a shallow brush-choked saddle passed over the crest, but until now the weather and a vague sense of danger had cut off any thought of investigation on foot. But now it was clear that I could learn little more from random conversation and I had, I thought, a kind of immunity from the consequences of prying. I could of course wait for them to initiate me into the cult, but that struck me as a very dangerous course. There had been in Harrison's notes several disquieting suggestions of physical deformity connected with conversion; possibly their rites involved some form of mutilation or worse. I decided to pretend to go along with them, find out as much as possible on my own, and get out of Milando as soon as the water went down.

It was almost four o'clock when I got back to the Kramer house and I wanted to start my hike with as much daylight left as possible. The rain was light, hardly more than a mist, and I was also anxious to take advantage of this. But Kramer insisted that his wife fix a ridiculously early supper because I had missed lunch so I was unable to get away until four thirty. It was a dismal meal, Kramer and I sitting alone at the table with neither of us at all hungry while his wife dutifully rattled pots and pans without speaking to us and the children hissed and whispered in the next room. He made an effort to dissuade me from going out on foot, though I hadn't told him of my plan to go over the hill, but he was too preoccupied with some worry of his own to object strenuously. His wife's presence seemed to inhibit him from referring openly to the danger he had mentioned earlier. Only at the door as I prepared to leave did he give a low-voiced warning. "Don't underestimate these people, Mr. Kovacs. I've been seeing things for years and tried to ignore them, tried not to believe, but I know now that there's something foul going on here. There are things here that have no right to exist in a decent world."

I wore a rain hat, thinking an umbrella would be of no use in heavy brush, and changed to high-topped hiking boots even though I hoped the mud would be less of a problem on higher ground than it was in town. I took a flashlight and extra batteries in case I couldn't get back before dark. There wasn't much chance of slipping out of town unobserved but there were few phone lines in Milando and I hoped the wet weather would delay any organized effort to stop me.

At the top of the cleft a short dirt street, populated only by two apparently deserted shacks, ran parallel to a wall of dense vegetation. I quickly found the narrow well-worn path leading into the brush and through the saddle between the cliffs. At first the trees and bushes were too high to see much but I could tell that the path ran steeply downward. Soon I passed through several rocky spots where the brush thinned and through the light rain I saw the broad green valley into which I was descending, lush and beautiful under the gray overcast. Along the bottom ran an irregular band of darker green which must mark some narrow creek, sunk below the surrounding land by erosion. I passed rapidly down the trail and within a half hour found myself on the edge of a canyon, at least sixty feet deep and perhaps a hundred yards wide. Along the boulder-strewn bottom a racing stream wound among huge oaks and pecan trees. The path turned to the right and followed the canyon rim upstream.

walter c. debill, jnr.

When I saw the pool I knew it was the place, the center of the cult. Eons past an underground river had flowed there, swirling in a whirlpool two hundred yards wide until the cavern roof collapsed leaving a perfectly circular pool. Around the edge slabs of fallen limestone protruded above the surface at crazy angles. Now a waterfall ran over the lip of the crater-like depression and the circle of stone was open on one side where the creek flowed out of the pool into the canyon. The sheer walls were undercut to form a wide sheltered ledge around the water and to the left of the cascade the black mouth of a great cavern, undoubtedly the channel of the ancient underground river, opened onto the ledge. I watched for a while to be sure the place was deserted before searching for a way down to the pool and soon found the steps cut into the rock face. The rain-slick steps had been worn smooth and hollowed almost to a ramp in the center. At the bottom a path led up to the ledge and I followed it around, intending to reach the large cavern. But behind the waterfall I found the mouth of a smaller cave, now sealed with a wooden wall. The heavy door in the center of the wall did not appear to be locked and I stepped quietly up to it. I could hear no sound within and it was fastened from the outside with a simple wooden slide latch. When I slid it back the door swung noiselessly inward. Stepping inside I switched on my flashlight and saw a narrow room extending about thirty feet back into the rock. I closed the door behind me and began to investigate its contents.

The left-hand wall was lined with a row of old-fashioned chests with bowed lids. I tried the first one and found it unlocked. On top were several robes elaborately embroidered with strange designs, but I didn't take them out and examine them closely for fear of leaving signs of my search. On the right were several ceremonial objects of exquisite workmanship, a brazier on a tripod, a four-foot candelabrum and a peculiar thing shaped oddly. This last object was of smooth bronze and mounted on a pedestal. The others were of some alloy resembling gold but lighter in weight and color and chased with intricate designs in which the shape of the bronze object figured prominently. Apparently it was an important symbol in the cult. The remainder of the designs bore no resemblance to the art of the plains Indian, though there were vague suggestions of South and Central American patterns. I saw a table against the rear wall of the room with some papers on it and went to see if I could find some blank paper which I could safely take to copy a sample of the designs. The papers proved to be the missing portions of Harrison's notes, the portions someone had deliberately removed to prevent my learning too much about the cult of Yidhra. There was a chair and a modern propane lamp; I lit the lamp and sat down to read what someone had sought to conceal from me.

One bundle evidently consisted of quotes from the obscure sources Harrison had turned to when the standard reference works failed. The first was headed 'Graf von Könnenberg, *Uralte Schrecken*, nineteenth century treatise on ancient religious cults' and continued, "It is clear that the most ancient gods, the prototypes of all the gods of men, were known and worshipped before men existed; and it is further clear that the most ancient gods all proceed from the one source. That source is Mlandoth, and all gods are but varied manifestations and extensions of the One. But whether Mlandoth is a place, or a conscious entity, or an inconceivable maelstrom of unknown forces and properties outside the perceptible cosmos is not known.

"Certainly Ngyr-Khorath, the mad and monstrous thing which haunted this region before the solar system was formed and haunts it still is but a local eddy of the vastness that is Mlandoth. And is not fabled 'Ymnar, the dark stalker and seducer of all earthly intelligence, merely the arm of Ngyr-Khorath, an organ created in the image of earthly life and consciousness to corrupt that life and lead it to its own destruction?

"And does not even great Yidhra, who was born of and with the life of earth and who through the eons intertwines endlessly with all earthly life forms, teach reverence for Mlandoth?"

The next quote was from the *Black Sutra* of U Pao, which I recognized with a thrill as one of the books Yolanda had mentioned:

"Before death was born, *She* was born; and for untold ages there was life without death, life without birth, life unchanging. But at last death came; birth came; life became mortal and mutable, and thereafter fathers died, sons were born, and never was the son exactly as the father; and the slime became the worm and the worm the serpent, and the serpent became the yeti of the mountain forests and the yeti became man. Of all living things only *She* escaped death, escaped birth. But *She* could not escape change, for all living things must change as the trees of the north must shed their leaves to live in winter and put them on to live in spring. And therefore *She* learned to devour the mortal and mutable creatures, and from their seed to change *Herself*, and to be as all mortal things as *She* willed, and to live forever without birth, without death."

There followed a note not enclosed in quotation marks which I assumed to be Harrison's own comment:

"*U Pao was early Burmese sage—incredibly advanced speculation on evolutionary principles—is it possible that a protean macroorganism could have developed and survived from before the advent of reproduction and individual death? How could it have survived in competition with organisms capable of evolution? References to change in Y. very puzzling.*"

The next fragment was from the *Chronicles of Thrang*:

"Yidhra devoured the octopus and learned to put forth a tentacle; she devoured the bear and learned to clothe herself in fur against the creeping ice of the north; indeed can Yidhra take any shape known to living things. Yet no shape can she take which is truly fair, for she partakes of all foul creatures as well as fair. To her followers she appears in many fair and comely forms, but this is because they see not her true form, but only such visions as she wills them to see. For as the adepts can send their thoughts and visions to one another over great distances so can Yidhra send her thoughts to men and cause them to see only what she wills. Indeed it is by sending her thoughts that Yidhra remains one in soul, for in body she is many, hidden in the jungles of the south, the icy wastes of the north, and the deserts beyond the western sea. Thus it is that though her temples are many, she waits by all, combining bodily with her diverse followers, yet her consciousness is a vast unity."

In the comment following this, Harrison's line of thought became chillingly clear:

"*One of the later additions to the* Chronicles, *probably from pre-Sumerian Ngarathoe just after the last ice age, fragmented organism linked by telepathy would*" *explain ability to manifest herself at cult centers throughout the world—von Könnenberg and Crowley mentioned centers in Laos, New Mexico, Chad, West Texas. Telepathically induced visions could explain appearances in animal and human form. Need for evolutionary adaptation satisfied by absorbing genetic material (nucleic acids?) from organisms that reproduce—could also develop intellectual capabilities in this way."*

I didn't know enough biology to judge the plausibility of this but it was obvious that Harrison had rationalized a possible basis for the physical reality of Yidhra.

The last quotation was difficult and obscure. Harrison apparently saw it in manuscript and was unsure of its origin, though he thought it might be *"a portion of the manuscript Prjevalski found in Kashgar and attributed to the legendary 'mad lama of Prithom-Yang'—Braithwaite's translation?"* In spite of the obscurity of the language and the exotic literary form I began to see a hideous application to the facts and hints I had concerning Milando:

> Yidhra, the Lonely One, craving the life of all things;
> Lonely One, needing the life of the Earth.
> Yidhra, the Goddess, ruling her avatar races;
> Goddess, of vulturine Y'hath of the sky
> Goddess, of Xothra who sleeps in the Earth
> and wakes to devour,
> Goddess, of men in strange places who worship her.
> Yidhra, the Hierophant, teaching her followers mysteries;
> Hierophant, teaching strange tongues of the elder world.
> Yidhra, the Bountiful, making the hills and the meadows green;
> Bountiful, showing the way to the desert springs,
> Bountiful, guarding the flocks and the harvest.
> Yidhra, the Lover, needing the seed of her followers;
> Lover, who must have the seed of all things,
> Lover, who must have the seed of change or die,
> Lover, whose consorts are changed,
> infused with the seed of the past and changed
> to forms not of past nor of present.
> Yidhra, the Mother, bringing forth spawn of the past;
> Mother, of all things that were,
> Mother, of children of past and of present,
> Mother, whose children remember all things
> of their fathers long dead.
> Yidhra, the Life-Giver, bringing long life to her followers;
> Life-Giver, giving the centuries endlessly
> to her children and lovers and worshippers.
> Yidhra, the Restless One, needing the sons of new fathers;
> Restless One, sending her followers forth
> to seek new blood for her endless change,
> Restless One, craving new lovers outside the blood
> of her worshippers

> lest she and her spawn and her followers
>> shrivel and wither in living death.
> Yidhra, the Dream-Witch, clouding the minds of her followers;
> Dream-Witch, hiding her shape in illusion,
> Dream-Witch, cloaking her shape in strange beauty.
> Yidhra, the Shrouder, wreathing the faithless in shadow;
> Shrouder, devouring the errant and hostile ones,
> Shrouder, who hides men forever . . .

The other stack of papers proved to be the missing notes on Harrison's activities in Milando. In one way his experience had been the reverse of mine; the bartender had initially been cautiously encouraging, dropping cryptic hints without giving any definite information, but after Harrison's first encounter with Yolanda Ed and most of the other people in town had tried to shut him out. Even Kramer had been afraid to speak openly of the cult, though Harrison had become convinced that it was active and that Yolanda was the head of it.

I came out of my rapt concentration with the feeling I had heard something through the rush of the waterfall, some barely audible and unidentifiable sound that breathed terror; perhaps it was only my imagination, stimulated by the dark hints I had been reading, but I turned out the lamp and stepped quietly to the door. I opened it a crack and peered into the cavern mouth to the right. It was darkening rapidly but I could detect movement in the shadow. There was a large animal like a hound alternately scampering to the entrance and scuttling back into the cave in a cringing attitude. Then a dark figure seemed to rise up from the floor of the cavern as though emerging from a sunken stairway. I knew I did not want to meet either of those figures and if I waited very long I would have to find my way back in total darkness. The ledge along which I had to return was in shadow and most of the way I would be shielded from view by the waterfall and the fallen slabs of rock along the water's edge. I decided to take the chance.

I ran wherever I was well screened, counting on the waterfall to cover the sound, and made it to the foot of the stair up the cliff without being noticed. On the stairs I was badly exposed, though the trunks and foliage of some of the tallest trees gave some scattered cover, but looking back from the top I could make out the hound and its shadowy master on the ledge and they didn't seem to be in pursuit. I was catching my breath at the top when I heard voices on the trail ahead and ducked into the brush.

Two men I hadn't seen before appeared and posted themselves near the head of the stair. I gathered from the scraps of conversation I could understand that they were part of a search party from town sent to find me. Their mission was to head me off if I tried to descend to the pool. They held the pool in awe and seemed to assume that if I had already gone down I would be 'taken care of.'

I began to make my way as quietly as possible through the rain-soaked brush, moving parallel to the path. The rain was growing heavy as darkness fell and the occasional flashes of lightning did as much to show the way as the dwindling daylight. It was slow going and progress would have been impossible without the frequent outcrops of rock to thin the vegetation. I was able to see the trail and hear voices on it much of the time and soon found that the searchers had spread out over the slope. They were all around me now, passing on both sides.

At one point two men stopped and sat down on a boulder by the trail near me so that I could overhear them clearly.

"... she says he didn't come down there. Must have gone off the trail."

"Don't know why she wants him so bad. He don't seem much different from the other one."

"They say it's somethin' about his mind. The other one wasn't as good—that's why he didn't help much an' she needs fresh blood again so soon. Or we'll all start to shrivel up like the bunch in West Texas. Did Maynard ever tell you about that? He went out there an' saw 'em. Said it was like livin' death."

"Naw, I mostly stay away from Maynard. An' Ed too. I know we're all bound to her, we've all taken the Communion and accepted the eternal life, but I think some of the big shots has had s'much to do with her they're hardly human any more. Anyway they give me the creeps. An' what she did to that Harrison boy! She needed him but she hated him fer not bein' good enough. Course that was the full *Fusion*, not just the Communion. But ain't it about the same thing? She gets a little more like us and we get a little more like her?"

It was a relief when they stopped talking and sat in silence; the horrors of Milando were crowding too close and I had heard enough. I continued up the hill. I had not gone very far when I heard them speak again. I couldn't understand them this time but the tone was one of respect and the answering voice was Yolanda's. I stood close to a big tree trunk to camouflage my outline and waited for her to pass on the trail. It was not completely dark yet and a moment later I could see her slender silhouette stalking up the trail. The hound was following at her heels, dashing from one side of the trail to the other. Then it gave a sort of snorting moan and ran into the brush below me. I could hear it snuffling and crashing through the bushes as it zig-zagged toward me. I stood very still. Suddenly it was charging straight me. I could make out a long muzzle, more like a crocodile than a dog, and it seemed to have a short heavy tail. Just as it rose up and ran on two legs she called to it and it turned aside. I was trembling and it took a while for the phrase she used to sink in. She had said, "Come, Mr. Harrison."

VI

I stood for a while under the dripping tree, trying not to think. There was a cult here, certainly, a dangerous one, but the rest was fantasy. The people of Milando had not seen a primeval abomination that dwelt in these hills, they were victims of mass hallucination or the imposture of the cult leaders. And Yolanda, with a whimsical touch of black humor, had named her dog after a troublesome intruder who had caused a local sensation by disappearing. Or being murdered. The hints of *fusion* and resulting physical degeneracy were ignorant superstition, a man could not exchange genetic material with an eon-old creature and thus become a beast. It was an ordinary hound. A hound that went sometimes on four legs and sometimes on two.

It was pitch-black now and I risked walking on the trail. Once I glimpsed a flashlight beam ahead but I hid in the brush and the searchers passed without spotting me. After I crossed the top of the slope and entered Milando I had to avoid passing near the many lighted windows as well as worrying about exposure in the frequent lightning flashes. Half the town seemed to be out tramping through the rain and several times I passed within thirty yards of people but they either didn't see me or assumed I was one of them. By the time I approached the Kramer house I was wondering whether the search for me could account for all the activity.

I had followed the darkest route rather than the shortest and wound up approaching the house from the east side. I could see light in the kitchen windows and hear Kramer raving in an hysterical rage. I had slipped up next to an old shed on the property next door when I heard someone walk heavily up to the other side of the shed.

"Has he been here?" said a low voice.

"No, didn't they catch him over the hill?"

"No luck. Don't know whether he got lost in the brush or slipped back into town. How long you been watching the house?"

"About twenty minutes. Got the place surrounded. Old Kramer's really out of his mind, threatenin' to kill Miz' Kimbrough an' go out an' tell everybody about Milando an' everythin' else. We'll have to take care of him this time. We're just waitin' on her."

"Where is she?"

"Down at the saloon with Ed. Maynard went to get her, she should be here pretty soon."

I had blundered into a ring of watchers staked out around the house. By luck I hadn't been seen, but in getting away I might not be so lucky. The lightning flashes were coming more often now and though I was hidden from their light by the corner of the shed I would have to pass some long open spaces if I retreated. And I felt I had to warn Kramer that he was in danger, even though the mother-in-law's visit had triggered an explosion I hated to face. But I did not have to make that decision, for a moment later the tension erupted in violence, the gutty boom of a shotgun blast then a woman's scream silenced by another blast. Then a third and I heard small feet running across the porch. Two of the children ran into the circle of window light in front of the house, two more shots and their still forms lay in the rain. While I stood and watched in stunned incomprehension the lights went out all over Milando.

My only thought then was to get away. My car was in front of the house near the corner. With the lights out in the house I might be able to get to it and drive away before anyone could stop me. I moved as quietly as possible to the side of the house. I got there before the next lightning flash. The lightning was from the northwest, to the left and front of the house so that the kitchen side was left in blackness. I moved to the front corner, took off my hat and stood with one eye past the corner until the next flash. Kramer was standing not fifteen feet from the car, holding the shotgun. And stealthy footsteps from behind told me the watchers were moving in next to the house itself. Without thinking I opened the kitchen door next to me and entered the house. The click of the night latch behind me seemed terribly loud.

I stood there only a minute with my heart pounding and the water running off my raincoat onto the floor before I heard Yolanda's voice outside.

"Kramer," she said, "Kramer, you have slain the children of Yidhra." I went to look out the small window over the sink. "You are doomed, Kramer," she said. The lightning was flashing; I could see her hooded silhouette and Kramer fumbling with the gun. He seemed to be trying to raise it and hesitating. "You cannot defy me, Kramer." Then in an extended burst of lightning I saw the hound thing leap at him, and the gun roared. Whatever spell she held over him was broken; he raised the gun high and fired. As the lightning flickered and died away I saw her writhing on the ground, appearing grotesquely shapeless under the sprawling cloak; then she lay still.

I stood petrified. I heard Kramer's heavy tread on the porch, followed by an incongruous sound I could not at first identify. With quiet horror I realized that he was sitting in the rocking chair on the porch, rocking gently, back and forth. He must have been quite mad.

In the long minutes before I began to think again the darkness magnified the sound horribly. The rocking chair creaked. The rain drummed on the roof, it dribbled from the eaves, it spattered into the puddles on the ground, and the rocking chair creaked. I had to get a grip on myself and think of a plan. If I could get to the car perhaps I could get out of town and hide until it was safe to swim across. I tried quietly to open the kitchen door and my stomach knotted in panic; the night latch was of an ancient type that needed a key to be opened from the inside.

The kitchen door was locked and getting past Kramer would be impossible. I could open a window but Kramer would surely hear and come before I could climb out. And besides I was pretty sure someone was out there now. I remembered a back door by the room where I had slept. I would try for that. I began to feel my way toward the door to the living room, moving in slow motion to avoid hitting anything that might make a sound. The lightning through the small window wasn't much help, the light falling mainly on the side of the room away from the door. I was near the door slowly lowering my foot when it touched something soft. Instinct told me what it was before reason could operate and I almost lost my balance as my foot jerked back. I tried to find a way around the corpse and touched it again. I couldn't face the possibility of touching it another time; I would have to risk the flashlight. Kramer was facing the other way and I waited for the lightning before flicking the flashlight for the briefest instant.

The lightning must have been very near, for the thunder followed it closely enough to cover the involuntary sound I made when I saw the thing and knew why Kramer had gone mad and slaughtered his wife and children. It was the mother-in-law, the daughter of Old Kimbrough's son who had been 'the worst of the lot,' the mother of Kramer's wife, the grandmother of those who lay still in the rain. Wearing ample clothing and the wig that lay beside her I suppose she could have passed as fully human though incredibly ugly and deformed, but now there could be no doubt of the alien taint. No fully human being has such wide cheek bones, or such bulging lidless eyes set so far to the side. The ears were vestigial and there was no hair; the back of the head and neck were scaled. The tongue protruded and was perceptibly forked.

I forced myself to step over the thing in the dark. I remember being obsessed with the thought that I might step on the tongue. I was also terrified of bumping into another corpse in the hall between the living room and the rear of the house and moved even more slowly than before. I kept looking back and seeing Kramer silhouetted by the lightning against a window that opened onto the porch.

I hadn't gotten far into the hall when I felt a presence, a numbing sensation both calming and weirdly evil. It reminded me of the enchantment I had felt in Yolanda's presence, but it was different, less warm and human, more savage, more powerful. I realized the rocking chair had stopped. Every nerve was alert as I turned to watch the open door and window. The lightning flickered and in a hideous stop-motion effect I saw the monstrous caped figure move toward Kramer as he whimpered and clicked two firing pins on empty chambers. He shrieked twice as the thing spread its arms wide and shrouded him in the vast folds of its cloak; then he was silent.

I knew I should try to get away but I was incapable of motion as the thing crept slowly across the porch and through the door toward me. It drew itself up six feet in front of me and said, "Hello, Peter", in a voice hauntingly, damnably like Yolanda's, but deeper, hollower, indistinct, with an alien intonation like the children's hissing whispers. I shone the flashlight on the face a full seven feet above the floor—it was her, but larger, with hollow cheeks and sunken, burning eyes and teeth grinning in a rigid travesty of a smile. Kramer's shotgun had shattered the fragment of protean Yidhra that projected the beauty of Yolanda, in its place Yidhra had sent another multiform fragment of herself creeping over the hill, a fragment that had not yet perfected the illusion.

The realization had weakened the spell and I fought for control of my consciousness. For an instant her outline wavered, the face blurred and in mortal fear of what I might see I turned and ran down the hall and into the first bedroom, slamming the door behind me. I found a window in the dark, threw it up and fumbled with the screen latch and in a second was over the sill.

I heard someone running toward me along the side of the house but jumped aside and felt him rush past. Then I ran for the car. I hit the fender running full speed, knocking the wind out of myself, but managed to feel my way to the keyhole, find the key and get in even before I caught my breath. I backed onto the road, slammed it into first and started swerving down the muddy hill. A group of men tried to block the road but when I bore down on them they jumped out of the way. I think I hit one of them. At the bottom of the hill I tried to turn right and slid off into the ditch on the left. It wasn't deep enough to flood the engine but I thought surely I was stuck. I kept spinning the wheels and sliding till the wheels found something solid and pulled me up onto the road. I came out heading to the left and continued that way out of town.

The side roads were fewer in that direction and I kept letting them go by, wanting to get further from town. Before I knew it I was over the hill at the flooded creek. I hit the brakes and nothing happened—they must have gotten soaked in the ditch. The car plowed into the water with a tremendous splash, the engine died and I felt the car being pulled sideways by the current. I felt the car lose contact with the bottom and start floating downstream. Water was leaking in slowly but steadily and when the car rolled over on its side I knew it would soon turn upside down and I would be trapped. I got out of my boots and coat, opened the door above me and climbed out.

There was no question of swimming purposefully in that torrent; I could only struggle to stay afloat and grasp at anything solid I bumped into. Eventually I grabbed something that held me against the current. It was a tree trunk sticking out of a brush jam and I was able to pull myself slowly and painfully to the bank. As I lay panting face down with my feet still in the water I felt the current running from my right to my left. I was on the far side. I had escaped from Milando.

VII

When I walked into Edmondsville at dawn I was suffering from shock, exhaustion and pneumonia and promptly collapsed. I was more or less delirious for a week and said enough to alarm the doctor, who informed the local sheriff, who called in a state lawman. I had been completely incoherent but they gathered that a family named Kramer and someone named Yolanda had died by violence in Milando during the storm.

When I came to my senses they showed me a newspaper article about the tragic death by fire of the Kramer family of Milando, including Mrs. Kramer's mother, Mrs. Elizabeth Kimbrough. After that I pretended to be unable to remember what had happened. I had stayed with a family named Kramer in Milando but could remember nothing else. I knew the truth would be utterly incredible to them and was afraid to concoct some plausibly false version to stimulate an investigation. The people in Milando would refute it somehow and deceive the outside investigators as they had done before. And I would be left in grave danger.

But the authorities would not leave it at that. Though I absolutely refused to go there myself, they went to Milando as soon as the roads were open. I don't know exactly what they were told, but I understand that what finally settled the matter and convinced them I had been hallucinating was an interview with a well-established citizen of Milando, alive and uninjured, a charming young woman named Yolanda Prentiss.

Fragment from the Necronomicon

Iä! The Dark One!
      Him who is not to be named
      But hailed with cryptic
      And horrible titles of Eld.

Iä! Nyarlathotep!
      Bearer of sinister word
      From evil abysses of time
      From gods long forgotten by man.

Iä! The Black Man!
      Creeper in shapes of illusion
      Wearer of scarlet and crimson
      Lurker behind rigid masks
      Bringer of portents of doom.

Iä! The Whisperer!
      Appearing on lurid horizons
      Disquieting presence, a prophet
      Mocking man's zenith off pride
      Foretelling the turn of the wheel
      To carry man back whence he came
      Back to the timeless morass
      Back to the worm.

Iä! Shub-Niggurath!
      Hail the Black Goat of the Woods!
      The Goat with a Thousand Young!
              Whose abominable slithering spawn
              Appear in the dusk of our time.
      First a few, they come furtively slinking
              In dark ways, in unwholesome shadows,
      Then many, fast growing bolder
              A ferment, foul putrefaction
              Corrupting all natural life
              Destroying the dreams of our race
      Till their pitiless hordes overrun us
              Enslaving our last wretched remnant
              While their scarlet-robed Master looks on
              And quivers with ominous laughter
      And shakes with a vast cosmic mirth.

walter c. debill, jnr.

Iä!   The Dark One!
....

Perilous Legacy

The year was 1944. It was a gusty evening in late September and though there was no snow the bitter northeast wind made me hasten down Winthrop Street toward the warmth of Thorwald Haraldson's gambrel-roofed home. Thor's maternal ancestors had built it to shut out the severe Arkham winters, double-planking the walls and limiting the size and number of the small-paned windows, and to the cheery radiance of the fire in the enormous living room fireplace would be added the warm congeniality of the man himself. In spite of his habitual diffidence with strangers and almost reclusive life between his strange travels Thor was the warmest of friends and the best of companions.

I was hoping he could shed some light on a passage in Albertus Magnus' *De lapide philosophorum* which had me stymied and as I stood knocking on the heavy eight-paneled door the brittle leaves of the volume under my arm fluttered alarmingly in the wind. When Thor opened the door his eyes gleamed at the sight of the book and even before greeting me, he said, "That's your priceless unexpurgated Albertus Magnus, isn't it? Treacherous weather to be carrying it around unprotected. How are you, Charles?"

"Cold, curious and confused, in about that order. I think the first problem will go away if you'll just stop coveting my Albertus so energetically and invite me in."

Thor laughed and led the way into the living room to the left. After he served up two scotches we sat down before the fire in the two comfortable armchairs which were the only modern items of furniture in that thoroughly colonial room. Not that Thor lived in the past—I knew that the ground floor rear bedroom was full of electronic equipment hardly known outside of the most secret defense laboratories, and I wouldn't eat anything prepared in his kitchen because it doubled as a very modern chemistry lab—but he loved all things colonial and kept this room uncarpeted and furnished with fine old gateleg tables, corner cupboards and fiddleback chairs, though he had too much good sense and love of comfort to actually sit in the latter.

Having thus provided for the cold he proceeded to unravel my confusion over Albertus without giving me a chance to voice my curiosity about his recent trip to India. While he wrestled with medieval Latin syntax and abstruse alchemical concepts, his hard, gangling figure bounding up out the chair to first one bookshelf and then another, I noticed that something about him bothered me, possibly some minor detail of his appearance that I couldn't quite bring to conscious identification. The straight blond hair streaked with premature gray (he was thirty-five then, I believe), the narrow, slightly aquiline nose, the mild gray eyes with their faraway dreamy look in between twinkles of humor, all seemed the same as ever. Then I spotted it, the broken tooth—the upper left canine. It was only noticeable because of his slightly undershot jaw and short upper lip, but had been enough to detect subliminally. I promptly forgot about it until he finished with my current stumbling blocks in the alchemical text and the conversation lapsed. Then I remembered and asked, "What happened to your tooth, Thor? Souvenir of India?"

He smiled and looked into the fire. "I guess you could call it that. Except that it wasn't exactly in India." And that was how I came to hear about Bhutan, and the *ghol* things . . ."

You know a little about my background, Charles. In 1940 my asthmatic condition improved markedly, leaving me a non-invalid at least most of the time. For the first time since childhood I was capable of an active life. I first tried to enlist in the Army, anyone who could read a newspaper could see that we would be at war within a year, and it was quite a blow when they turned me down because of my medical history. But I soon realized that that left me free to take up another great and no less worthy challenge. During my long years of ill health I had pored over many strange and ancient books and among the jumble of medieval speculation, scraps of forgotten tongues and bizarre myth and legend I thought I had discerned an awesome thread of truth, a cryptic and distorted but hauntingly convincing pattern of malignant evil far older and greater than human tyranny. Perhaps you've heard of the Cthulhu Mythos or the *Necronomicon* of Abdul Alhazred. I was convinced that hideous intelligences had visited the earth billions of years in the past, crossing millions of light years of space, and that they had left their indelible stamp on the course of earth's history. I suspected that hidden cults worked to bring about their return or resurrection. There were hints that primordial sorcerers had wielded forces beyond the known principles of science and left perilous legacies in remote or hidden places.

And now I was free to test the truth of my conclusions. My grandfather had left me a small income, nothing lavish but enough to allow me to experiment with fragments of lost science and to travel the earth in search of survivals. I found them; the ruins of cities older than Ur, experiments that contradict Newton and Einstein but confirm the oldest and most terrible rumors of magic, the bones of things that could not have evolved on this planet . . . but not until I went to Bhutan did I encounter tangible, living evil from across the eons.

I had been studying the *Pnakotic Manuscripts* with their detailed account of Yian-Ho and the surrounding regions in what was once the forbidden plateau of Leng. The suggestions and possibilities for discovery of remnants, of architectural ruins, bas-reliefs and other artwork with narrative content and even of written remains of civilizations older than mankind were absolutely tantalizing. The topographical descriptions were copious and specific and I had constructed a map of the area which lacked only one detail to become a key to fabulous antiquity. That detail was a point of reference to known regions. If I had known the true location of just one landmark in Leng or the regions surrounding it I could have located dozens of lost cities, monasteries, fortresses . . . but I had to wait two years for the final clue.

The clue turned up in 1943. It was a painting in a private collection; according to the owner it had once belonged to the magician Aleister Crowley. Though unsigned it strongly resembled the work of Roerich, who painted so many haunting pictures of Tibet. On the back was written "Shunned monastery 5 miles from Shigatse." It depicted a building of typical Tibetan architecture set on a ledge below a pinnacle whose weathered contours bore a striking resemblance to an entity known in elder lore as Cthulhu. The *Pnakotic Manuscripts* had mentioned such a crag and I lost no time in looking up Shigatse, which was indeed a place in Tibet, obtaining the best available maps of that part of the world and correlating them with my map of Yian-Ho. The correlation was a success; I had found Leng. I decided to go there as soon as possible.

I chose my objective carefully. It was a place far from Yian-Ho itself, one of the southernmost described in the *Manuscripts*, called the Vaults of Pnor. It had been a place of what one might call scholarly endeavor and there was hope of finding written records of that distant era. It had consisted largely of caverns hollowed out of mountain rock and was in an almost uninhabited area of Bhutan north of Dukye Dzong. There more than anywhere else I could expect to find traces of the past without a full-scale archaeological expedition.

With the Pacific war still raging just getting into India was difficult enough. I was only able to manage it because of a friend in the State Department who had disgraced his blue-blooded Massachusetts family by becoming a prominent Democrat. At that time no foreigners were allowed into Bhutan and a clandestine entry by way of Bengal was impractical because of the military activity in that province so I decided on a roundabout route by way of Nepal and Tibet. The *Manuscripts* had described the approach to the Vaults of Pnor from the Tibetan side.

Getting from Calcutta to Nepal proved surprisingly easy; I think the combination of diffidence and impeccable American travel documents convinced the bureaucrats I met that I was some sort of Allied intelligence agent. Outside of Katmandu I escaped from the eye of officialdom and some hospitable Sherpas escorted me to the Tibetan border. The Tibetan leg of the journey was a bit more harrowing; I'll just say that it involved bribing two bandit chieftains and shooting a third. Thus it was that I crossed the pass called Druk-La into Bhutan alone and entered what had once been the Valley of Pnor.

A thousand feet below me lay a narrow mountain vale five miles in length, the yellow-brown of summer grass broken here and there by green cultivated plots. I could make out a few Bhutanese-style houses. Across from me to the east a great peak thrust up to at least twenty thousand feet. In the angle between two spurs glittered the white triangle of a glacier which debouched into the valley, its broad front melting into a web of streams and marshes draining into the narrow river along the valley's center. The glacier worried me, for it had not been mentioned in the *Pnakotic Manuscripts* and I didn't know whether it sealed off the entrance to the mountain halls I sought. But the gateway to the Vaults of Pnor was said to open high up on the mountain and the glacier only reached about eight hundred feet above the valley floor.

The trail winding down to the valley was so exposed that it would have been useless to try to conceal my presence so I made my way down openly, alternately watching the valley below for signs of danger and scanning the mountain before me for any indication of the object of my search. This mountain had once been a major center of the Mi-Go, popularized in half-understood legends as a sort of ape-man but in actuality something far different, far more awesome, for these legends are nothing less than a degenerate memory of an alien race who came to earth from the stars millions of years before men or even ape-men existed. They were a race of winged fungoid crab-things whose knowledge and technology transcended man's wildest imaginings and whose origins transcended Einsteinian space-time. Their interest in this planet was limited; they were primarily interested in obtaining certain metals which they transported elsewhere. But they had a few centers such as the Vaults of Pnor where they studied and experimented with earthly life-forms. Much of their work there was concerned with shoggoths, great protean remnants of an even earlier era whose ability to change shape made them potentially useful. They had originally been the mindless hypnotically controlled slaves of another race but by the time the Mi-Go became interested in them they had developed a primitive but maliciously cunning mentality which made them almost impossible to control.

The attempts to create a more tractable breed of shoggoth involved mindgrafts to produce a consciousness similar enough to that of the Mi-Go to make communication and control possible, but they seem to have involved some interchange of matter because in addition to demi-shoggoths or *ghol*, with some permanent physical characteristics resembling the Mi-Go themselves, the experiments also produced by-products much like the Mi-Go but curiously plastic and having the viciousness of the shoggoth. These were meticulously destroyed after thorough scientific study.

The experiments were never really successful; the things proved to be as impossible to deal with as their amorphous forebears and became extremely dangerous, killing some of their would-be masters and taking over some regions of the Vaults. Eventually the Mi-Go gave up, destroyed as many of them as they could and sealed up the caverns. There the *ghol* lurked alone for eons until men of the race of Atlantis and K'n-yan, the most technologically advanced men who ever lived as well as the most arrogant, reopened the caverns. They had learned of the efforts of the Mi-Go and decided to succeed where the latter had failed. They actually succeeded in gaining control over most of the cavern system and capturing most of the *ghol* things. But after a few centuries of experimentation they too lost control of their creations and following a number of really horrible incidents exterminated them, sealing and abandoning the Vaults of Pnor. They were always reticent about their failures and wrote little about this one, but it seemed likely to me that their departure was rather hurried and that they might have left the bulk of their equipment and possibly their records.

By the time I reached the quaint wooden bridge across the river everyone in the valley must have known of my presence. I made for the largest house in sight intending to make contact with the local headman. I hoped to get some word on the best way up the mountain and any information that might help locate the object of my quest, besides quieting the curiosity of the populace with a cover story. The house was of mudblocks and pine, three-storied in the usual Bhutanese pattern. As I drew near I saw a man standing in front watching my approach. He wore a loose knee-length robe of bright red, gathered at the waist to form big folds which the Bhutanese use as pockets and with a cowl thrown back over the neck. But when I got close enough the face astounded me. It was jowly with bulbous blue eyes beneath receding blond hair and sported a sandy mustache!

"I say, hello there!" he called out in a broad British accent. "A European, I daresay. First I've seen in a year!"

"American, Thorwald Haraldson. I'm amazed to run into a European up this way. Been here a year, you say?"

"Yes, heh heh, Jenkins here, Wilson Jenkins, I'm an anthropologist. Studying Bhutanese customs, you know." He had an irritating habit of bobbing his head two or three times after each sentence. "Don't be put off by the costume—best way to understand the natives is to move right in with them, I always say. All that stuff about 'going native'—ruddy nonsense. Prejudice, that's all it is! Move right in with them, that's the way. Come inside, Haraldson, must be ruddy worn out after that climb down the trail."

I assumed he was a spy. The accent was Hollywood British, I suppose there's a Briton somewhere who talks that way but I've never met one, but beyond eliminating Britain I couldn't guess who he worked for and didn't care. He would assume the same about me. But except in special circumstances cloak-and-dagger types are a peaceful lot with a live and let live attitude, they want to gather information and not be bothered. He would have a hidden transmitter somewhere and report my presence but I didn't expect any trouble. And my cover story could be the truth, or at least half of it. He wouldn't believe it anyway.

The first floor was a barn and storeroom and he led the way to a wooden stairway at the back. "What's your line, Haraldson? Bit out of the way for a Yank, Isn't it?"

"About the same as yours except for the time factor. Archaeology. This was one of the first regions the Bhutias invaded from Tibet and some old Tibetan records indicate your mountain, the one with the glacier, as the site of a ninth century monastery. If there's anything left of it it would be a good missing link between the Tibetan and Bhutanese cultures."

"Monastery? There's one up there all right, been up a couple of times myself, but it's nothing like that old. But perhaps it was built on the site of something older. Anyway, the abbot should know if there are any ruins up there. That is, if you can get in to see him. They're choosy about visitors. Took me months to get the monks to let me come up."

Upstairs in the second story living quarters Jenkins offered to prepare a meal and I assented with unfeigned enthusiasm. He was living entirely on local food featuring the ubiquitous fermented yak butter and was delighted to vary it with tinned meat and chocolate bars from my rucksack. During the meal we fenced with our respective cover stories. He was very professional about it, answering direct questions concisely without volunteering additional details. When cornered on a point that might be checked he would answer forthrightly with eyebrows slightly raised and then thrust his face forward with a bland stare for a fraction of a second as though gauging my reaction. He purported to be from Oxford and I think he must have actually spent some time there. He undoubtedly had a first class European university education. For my part I said I was on extended leave from a large midwestern university and had been in Tibet for some time. The hardest part was faking an intimate knowledge of Tibet, since I had never been there before this trip and had been in none of the cities.

After the meal I sat and rested while he paced around the room, strutting like a little red rooster. When I turned the conversation back to the monastery he was reticent but amicable. At first I was afraid the monastery might be involved in his intelligence operation, a transmitter would be more effective up on a mountain than in the valley. In that case my interest in the place could be dangerous. But he seemed cooperative and made no effort to discourage me other than to mention that the monks who worked garden plots at the foot of the trail might object to my ascent.

It was still early afternoon and feeling recuperated from my hike into the valley I suggested approaching the monks right away about seeing the abbot. He seemed to think it was a good idea and offered to take me to them and help interpret since the local dialect was substantially different from the smattering of spoken Tibetan I knew. I left my pack at the house, for while I hoped eventually to be able to camp up on the mountain while I searched for the Vaults, I thought it would be too pushy to suggest it on first meeting if I got through to the abbot that day. I did take the Webley .45 in its shoulder holster under my bush jacket. I was sure Jenkins had spotted it but it was not uncommon for people to go armed in that part of the world.

The house was near the left-hand side of the glacier and it was only a quarter mile to where the trail began. There were about twenty monks tending rows of vegetables in cowled red robes like Jenkins' and they all gathered round to hear the discussion with their leader. They had wide flat faces and were rather light-skinned for Tibetan stock. I couldn't follow all of the conversation but I gathered that the head monk wanted to consult the abbot before having anything to do with me and Jenkins was pressing him to take me up immediately. He seemed to carry a lot of weight with them. It was curious to watch him speak in another language, there was none of the clowning heartiness and he lost most of the mannerisms I had noticed. At length the head monk gave in. Jenkins assured me that the abbot could converse in classical Tibetan, which was more familiar to me than the colloquial dialects, and the head monk and one other led me to the trail.

It took two hours to reach the monastery. The head monk led the way and the other followed behind me; no one spoke. The way zigzagged up the spur that walled in the left-hand side of the glacier and continued above the glistening ice sheet around the curved bay in which it lay. At the back of the bay narrowed to a high-walled gorge, the original fountainhead of the glacier. Before we entered the defile there was bright sunlight and a humming wind; inside it was shadowed and still, the chill silence became oppressive. We rounded a curve and I saw the monastery.

I was amazed at its size. It was a great rambling structure, four stories high in places, with the typical sloping walls and rows of high narrow windows characteristic of Tibet. A few windows already glowed with soft lamp light. It ended the trail, forming one smooth wall with the cliff below. I was looking hard for pre-Tibetan traces and soon spotted them. There were three small openings in the rock face above me, a little below the highest point of the monastery and about twenty feet from the near wall. The openings were low, wide and arched, unlike anything known in Tibet or Bhutan. But the men of Atlantis and K'n-yan had often shaped their windows and doors that way.

The inside of the monastery was a gloomy labyrinth, as chilly and silent as the trail outside. I lost my sense of direction many times over before we reached the spacious upper-story chamber in which the abbot sat alone. My escort stopped at the door and motioned for me to enter. The abbot sat on a low dais in the lotus pose. His long hooded robe was black. His finely chiseled features did not move perceptibly as he addressed me by name: an impressive demonstration of the telepathic powers common among adepts. He inquired about my quest and I told the same story I had given Jenkins. He questioned me very minutely about the Tibetan manuscripts I cited as sources but this was no problem since I am thoroughly familiar with classical Tibetan literature. All that was necessary to justify my search was to invoke an anecdote in an obscure copy of a known work; text variations are the rule rather than the exception in Tibetan manuscripts.

As the conversation progressed his motionlessness and facial rigidity began to seem sinister, abnormal. When he rose to serve tea from an alcove I was puzzled, I would have expected the abbot of such a large monastery to summon a servant for that task. Once I could have sworn that his arm lengthened as he reached for a cup. I thought of the curiously plastic quality of some offspring of the shoggoth and the Mi-Go, then tried to shrug it off and as he returned to the dais he lit a small oil lamp. He resumed his seat, stretching forth a hand with cup of tea, and I knew that the arrogant scientists of the race of Atlantis and K'n-yan had indeed left a perilous legacy of things less human than otherwise, things combining their own humanity with the protean horror of the shoggoth. For as he reached out his cuff slid back an inch and I saw above the wrist a surface dark gray and pebbled like that of a toad. It was nothing like human skin.

Outwardly I remained calm and tried to think as the interview went on. He maintained that he knew nothing of structures other than the monastery on the mountain and politely discouraged the idea of a search. I was afraid to back down too easily for fear of making him suspicious. The possibility of telepathic powers worried me but he seemed to be probing verbally for details and I guessed that his supernormal perceptions were vague and possibly limited to communication with other monks.

The tea had tasted bitter and I had only pretended to sip at it. As the conversation dragged on it became apparent that he was stalling and I concluded that it was drugged and he was waiting for it to take effect. I pretended to feel drowsy and I wanted to leave in order to get back down to the valley before it was completely dark. He invited me to spend the night in the monastery and I accepted.

He summoned a monk who led me to a small cubicle not much lower down than the abbot's chamber. As soon as the monk was gone I went to the window and found that I was on the side toward the trail, about forty feet above it. I was only one window away from the cliff face though and there was a three-inch projection running along the bottom of the row of windows. I knew the rock was rough enough for climbing. Then I thought of the low arc windows I'd seen in the rock. Sure enough I could make out the nearest one, almost level with my room. I decided to try for it: perhaps I could find out part of what I had come for before climbing down the cliff and escaping down the trail.

I got up quietly and tried to arrange the bedclothes to look like a human figure, then stepped to the window. It was dark night by then but the ribbon of stars along the top of the gorge gave some light and I could see no one below. Inching along the three-inch ledge wasn't too difficult because of the slope of the wall but I still tried to avoid looking down. I stopped for several minutes by the window between my room and the rock wall but heard no sound. Once I reached the cliff it seemed easier, a least there was something to hold on to. When I reached the arched opening I halted again and again heard nothing. I crept over in front of the opening and saw no light inside. I climbed in.

Feeling my way carefully I found that the window was cut about two feet back into the rock. There was a flat floor inside it covered with grit. I wished I had brought a flashlight but a box of matches would have to do. The flare of a match showed a small square room bare of furniture and coated with the dust of centuries. There was a door of what looked like metal. I extinguished the match and made my way to it in darkness.

The door swung noiselessly outward and I began feeling my way in the dark to conserve my supply of matches. I found myself in a narrow passage leading back into the mountain. It led into a network of corridors of increasing complexity. There were many small rooms but all were empty. I was beginning to worry about finding my way back when I noticed the faint blue luminescence in the air. The blue glow of K'n-yan! From there on the glow increased and progress was easy.

Still there was no sound or sign of recent use. There was no dust but that could be a result of the caverns being well sealed from the outer air. The inner parts of the system were lined with the dark metal of the first door. I came out into a circular room a good hundred feet in diameter. Many substantial corridors converged there from the general direction of my approach while the opposite side of the room was featureless except for a huge round-topped door reaching almost to the domed ceiling thirty feet above. It was evidently meant to slide for I could see no hinges and no break in the smooth surface.

Before examining the great door more closely I went around to each of the side passages and listened for signs of activity or pursuit. In one of them I heard a barely audible rustling in the distance but apparently there was no one near.

I turned my attention to the door and soon located a small panel to one side at about chest height, a four-inch elliptical mosaic of gleaming gemstones set flush with the wall. I tried pressing it and it gave slightly. There was a muffled hum and the door began to rise. I pressed again and it stopped. A third push caused the door to close. I opened it again and let it rise just above my head.

Stretching before and below me was a vast azure-litten abyss, illuminated by a ghostly glow emanating from the air itself. I couldn't judge its extent because it was completely filled with a crisscrossing network of golden rods, several inches in diameter and self-luminescent like the air. There seemed to be no pattern to their arrangement, no geometrical design, the rods branched and joined seemingly at random with their infinite ramifications spreading as far as the eye could reach. In places they were interwoven so thickly that a man could not have passed through them but for the most part they were more sparse. A broad staircase descended from the doorway and wound outward into space and along it there was a sort of tunnel which could have passed a large truck, though the golden net crowded right up to its sides. I could see a dozen or so pinpoints of reddish light in the distance in random directions from where I stood but otherwise the abyss was a featureless jumble of blue and gold.

As I walked down the stairway I saw the rods more closely and noticed that they varied in diameter from an inch to almost a foot. On close inspection they proved to be translucent with a shimmering opalescence. A couple of hundred feet down the stairway I reached a place where a dense tangle encroached on the stairway from above, blocking it to about head height. I reached out and touched one three-inch strand very lightly with a finger—it felt extremely sticky and it took a sharp tug to pull free. As I turned to look for the easiest way through my cuff brushed against another bar and stuck fast. I twisted, caught off guard, and my trouser leg hit a low-lying strand and caused me to lurch. I found myself stuck in four places. It was then that I noticed that the reddish lights had moved—they were coming closer and the nearest had resolved itself into a pair of eyes.

I pulled as hard as I could but found myself in an iron grip. As the eyes rushed toward me I saw the outlines of the *ghol* things; the great glowing eyes sat behind a nasty beak, the body was small and round with vestigial wings and numerous tentacles or pseudopodia that lengthened and contracted, lashing furiously even when not grasping the golden web to thrust the beast for-ward at astonishing speed. If anything but khaki had contacted the web I would have gotten to inspect the *ghol* things more closely. As it was the damned cloth refused to tear and I was barely able to reach my clasp knife and hack myself free in time. I ran for the door. From my left one of the creatures moved in to cut me off and when a thicket of web slowed its progress it extended a fifty-foot pseudopod across the stairs. I pulled out the Webley and fired at a red eye—it went out and I heard a monstrous ululating moan like a bass police siren. The pseudopod contracted and I dashed past and pressed the inner panel to open the door. While the door rose with maddening slowness I looked back and saw a new red gleam appear on the thing's head, placed differently from the eye I had shot out. I ducked under the door and started it moving downward.

There was no time to catch my breath, I could hear footsteps scurrying down one of the passages. They couldn't have missed the roar of the *ghol* thing while the door was open. I sprinted up the passage from which I had entered.

After I had made a few turns I slowed down in order not to give away my position by sound. It was a miracle that I was able to move fast even after the blue glow faded to blackness. By luck I found the room through which I had entered after only two or three wrong turns and dead ends.

Outside the night was bitter cold and clear. There were many more lights on in the monastery but still no activity on the trail. The climb down was easier than I had expected and I started off down the mountain.

My eyes were well adjusted to the dark by then and the starlight seemed bright after the outer parts of the Vaults. I made time quickly toward the mouth of the defile. I was only a few hundred yards from the main glacier when I heard the sound of rock falling and looked back. A huge dark shadow was slithering down the side of the mountain from above. The hybrids of the monastery must have controlled other entrances to the caverns through which to release their less human cousins to cut me off. I broke into a run, then stopped when I thought I saw a shadow move on the trail ahead. I caught a glimmer of red and knew there were *ghol* before and behind me.

At the monastery the ice was a good hundred feet below the trail but here the way dipped to within forty feet of it. Probably the trail was impassable during much of the winter. I scrambled down the slope and finding the surface too slippery for running sat down to glissade to the mouth of the defile. Unfortunately the grade was much steeper than I had thought and by the time I got there I was out of control and unable to steer myself to the edge. I hurtled out onto the main glacier at dizzying speed.

I was headed a little to the right of the center of the glacier, which was two hundred feet high where it ended, and would probably come crashing through Jenkins' roof if I couldn't get control of my course. I fought desperately, pounding the ice with my heels and the butt of the Webley to slow myself and steer to the right. I remember spinning on my back several times while the constellations reeled. I made some headway but I could see that I wasn't going to make it. Then I crashed into something solid and lost consciousness.

I awoke to find myself wedged in a narrow crevasse. It was perhaps ten feet to the surface. I couldn't have been out very long or I would have frozen to death. There were no bones broken, just a cut lip and the tooth you noticed. The Webley was gone but I was able to get out my pocket knife and use it unopened to jab the ice and get a little purchase for movement. Afterwards I lay panting for breath on the ice in spite of the deathly cold.

I was near the front of the glacier not far from the right-hand side. The moon was up and I could see no ominous shadows on the mountain but there were moving lights where the trail came out of the gorge. I guessed that the things in the monastery couldn't control the *ghol* well enough to allow them out into the valley and had taken up the pursuit themselves. I made my way carefully to solid rock, found the trail and started down. I had seen no dwellings near the foot of the trail and hoped that the gardener monks went up the mountain at sunset.

I would rather have avoided Jenkins and fled directly but I needed my pack. The house was lit up and my knock brought him to the door.

"Haraldson! Didn't expect to see you tonight, thought you must have decided to stop over at the monastery. Good Lord, what's happened to you? You look as though you'd tangled with a bear."

"I fell on the trail. Or off of it, to be more precise. Nothing serious, I probably look worse than I feel. The lip and a few scratches, that's all. Have you got an extra bed?" I planned to rest a few minutes and then sneak out. After what I'd just been through jumping out a window didn't seem too dangerous.

"He led the way up to the second floor. "Fall, eh? Dangerous business, trying the trail after dark. I'm surprised the monks sent you down alone."

"I guess I was overconfident. They wanted to send someone with me but I talked them out of it." I could tell he was suspicious.

"Well, all's well that ends well, I always say. Bet you could use a spot of grub."

I accepted and tried to appear eager about it, though I actually had no appetite at all. I could use the nourishment before the long night ahead and I hoped it would keep him busy enough to slow down the conversation. I also wanted to keep his eyes off me until I could change into the extra clothes in my pack so he wouldn't see that my old ones were cut rather than torn.

He warmed up some leftover food and had it ready by the time I finished changing. While I ate he brewed tea and asked questions about the monastery. I could sense that he was growing more suspicious of my story but didn't detect any hostility, he gave the impression that whatever had happened was between me and the monks and no concern of his. But I was keeping a close eye on him. He was reaching for something on a lower shelf when the cowl slipped back and I saw the back surface of his neck, dark gray and pebbled like that of a toad. I don't know whether it was instinct or sheer nerves that made me leap at him without delay, but whichever it was I'm grateful for it. He was reaching for a revolver. I grabbed his wrist and we reeled backward, crashing into the table. I smashed his wrist against an upturned table leg and he dropped the gun. There was a rubbery feeling to him and a sinuous strength. I let go of his wrist and hit him across the jaw with my elbow—it felt about like cheese, there were no bones. That stunned him for an instant and I was able to get to the gun. There was no time to point it and fire, I hit him on the head again and again. No bones there either, the head deformed nauseatingly and he began to moan and grope blindly like a demented thing. I picked up my pack and made for the stairs. I looked back once; his head was beginning to resume its shape.

I got to the door, opened it, then slammed it shut again. There were two red eyes and a black beak not ten yards away. There was only one thing to do; I opened it again and fired at first one eye, then the other. I heard again the abominable bass wail of a wounded *ghol* as I ran southward, toward the heart of Bhutan. I stayed east of the river and later looking backward saw from the moving torches that the monks crossed the bridge and looked for me on the trail back into Tibet.

By morning I was far from the valley. Bhutan is sparsely populated and I was able to get almost to the border of Bengal before I was spotted. I played dumb and managed to communicate by gestures that I had come from the direction of Nepal and was lost. The Bhutanese turned me over to the British authorities in Bengal who were extremely suspicious of my story of wandering over from Nepal but let me go after checking with the American State Department. They were probably told that I was possibly a lunatic but definitely not a spy.

The northeast wind rattled the small-paned windows and the dwindling fire flared up briefly. The volume of Albertus lay on the arm of my chair, its obscurities forgotten for the moment.

"That's quite a tale, Thor," I said after a while.

"Yes, I suppose it is," he chuckled. "The trouble is that it lacks a proper ending. You see, nothing's changed. They're still there, as they have been for centuries. The wide-faced monks, the thing with bulbous eyes and a sandy mustache that looks like a man but isn't. And the *ghol* things. In Bhutan."

I said goodbye and went out into the night, under the coldly twinkling eyes of space and eternity.

Heart Attack

The sheriff of Seco County wasn't fat and didn't wear sunglasses. In fact, he looked lean and mean and with his sweat-stained Stetson and slightly scuffed cowboy boots he could have passed for a hard-eyed gunslinger out of Seco City's colorful past. Except that the iron on his hip was a 9mm automatic.

"Well now, Mr. Pearsall," he drawled. "Bein' that the old courthouse is public property we don't try to keep people out. But it's in pretty bad shape, so you'll have to sign a waiver for any personal injuries caused by the condition of the building. And the custodian will have to go with you. You'll have to pay the county five dollars for his time."

"No problem," countered Pearsall. "I can take it off my income tax even if I don't sell the article." Peculiar, he thought. He had done dozens of pieces on historical sites for the big Dallas and Houston papers, and the authorities had either let him roam at will or told him to go to hell. As a rake-off, five dollars wasn't much in a part of the state where an out-of-towner can get whacked a hundred bucks for a loud muffler; just enough to discourage idle curiosity, without driving anyone with a serious interest in the building to prowl around surreptitiously. The sheriff looked intelligent behind the practiced solemnity of the elected lawman.

Pearsall got into his battered Volks and followed the gleaming patrol car through what was left of the old town. It was a half-deserted shell now, a dusty crazy-quilt of weed-grown vacant lots and half ruined frame houses, with only three or four families between it and ghost town status. But in the 1880's it had been a booming trade center, growing like a weed, noisy, free-spending and as wild as anything the west ever produced. From the Seco County courthouse a tough lawman and a hanging judge had tried to hold the line for law and order against the rowdiest bunch in Texas. Its lower floor had been the usual site for the infamous Seco City Duel—a quasi-legal institution in which two irreconcilable enemies fought to the death with knives, in the dark. The theory was that it was better than exposing innocent bystanders to the hazards of a gunfight. But it had not stopped the gunplay. Eventually a stray bullet had killed the town. The son of a powerful rancher had been the victim and the grieving father had given the railroad a free right of way across his land on condition that Seco City be bypassed. And the town had shriveled and died.

The sheriff pulled up next to a rusty pickup truck in the front yard of an inhabited shack a hundred yards from the courthouse. After telling Pearsall to wait outside he went in. Pearsall thought it odd that he didn't call out first and edged closer to the unpainted building. He could barely make out soft voices inside and understood nothing but a fragment in the sheriff's voice, ". . . don't want to make him any more curious than he already is. Just show him around a little, make it dull as hell and get him out before dark."

Pearsall was back out by the cars when the sheriff emerged with a stoop-shouldered Mexican-American of middle height and age.

"Mr. Pearsall, this is Armando Campos, he's in charge of the building and can show you around. 'Mando, let him see anything he wants and take pictures, but watch out for the stairs and the bad places in the floor."

As the sheriff drove off, the taciturn Armando led the way to the courthouse. Pearsall stopped twice to take exterior shots in the late afternoon light. Pictures were all he really needed; he had already researched the place thoroughly in the historical archives in Barrett. The courthouse was oblong, about sixty feet by forty, built of limestone blocks. A wooden walk or balcony ran the length of the upper story. An outside wooden staircase at the far end and two large doorways opening onto it were the only entrances to the building. The lower floor had no doors, only a row of small and high windows with bars. He noticed that the unbarred upper windows still had the dingy glass intact; either Seco City and the surrounding countryside had a shortage of children, rocks and baseballs, or kids were afraid of the place. He recalled a vacant warehouse from his childhood in St. Louis whose windows were similarly inviolable; it was said to be haunted.

The building had looked sturdy enough from a distance, but when they started up the stairway its age became apparent. Both men stepped gingerly, gauging every creak and groan of ancient wood before venturing the next step. The glutinous slow motion and preternatural hush got on Pearsall's nerves at first, till he began to think professionally. He decided to build the article around the creepy aspect of the place; invent a few local ghost stories, specters of condemned men in dusty cells, of gory victims of the Seco City Duel.

The first heavy oaken door was unlocked. As Pearsall passed into the gloomy corridor he noticed that the lock was hopelessly rusted. A door on the left with the word Sheriff carved in it opened on a small office, now bare of furniture. Armando muttered "sheriff's office" unnecessarily and offered no further comment, but Pearsall could picture stubby Tom Hagerman sitting at his desk sipping corn from a jug till the regular Saturday night row came to a boil. He had kept his desk facing the door in modern executive fashion, though he appears to have had tactical reasons in mind. When Charlie Fishbeck, just back from a cattle drive, dropped in waving his .44 horse pistol to discuss the hanging of his younger brother during his absence, Hagerman raised a sawed-off shotgun from his lap and disemboweled him.

The other door on the left was marked Judge; a fine old roll-top desk remained. Judge Marlin Greene had favored bottled whiskey, a luxury in those days, and like many frontier judges had been able to put away a quart and still maintain an impressive dignity. He had been a firm believer in capital punishment and must have sat at that desk many times hearing curses from the cells below.

Pearsall shook his head and refocused his eyes. The images were so intense, it took an effort to detach his imagination from them. The reality of the place was so much more vivid than the dry words in the archives.

They skipped the courtroom door opposite the judge's chambers and proceeded to the door at the end of the hall. Armando produced a large old-fashioned key and opened it to reveal a steep staircase leading downward. Three right angled turns led to a flagstoned floor. Below the walls were lined with cells, leaving a central rectangle. The tiny cells looked grim in the waning light; he knew they had been inhabited mainly by drunks sleeping off a bender and men waiting to die. The floor of the center space was darkly stained here and there. Probably coffee or soup, he mused, but of course it would be blood in the article. Though it was a hot day he felt cold, and the floor had an intolerable gritty feel. He had to pull himself away, but he was glad to leave.

After the lower floor the large courtroom upstairs seemed bright and almost cheerful. The raised judge's bench, the low railing separating it from the spectators and most of the spectators' benches were still in place and, skirting the center of the floor which Armando declared to be unsafe, Pearsall took flash pictures from several angles. The sun was rapidly going down by now and Armando pestered him to hurry. Pearsall had no objection.

As he headed out of town, he saw an unilluminated tavern sign over a row of pickups and decided on a beer to wash down the courthouse dust before driving to San Antonio. Inside the place was by no means crowded, though the clientele still probably exceeded the population of Seco City. They were unusually quiet for a country tavern crowd, and Pearsall had the bar to himself. As he drank alone he considered trying to strike up a conversation and digging for local legends and ghost stories about the courthouse but rejected the idea. He had more material than he could use from his library research before coming to town and besides he had developed a distaste for the place. Let the dead rest, he thought.

Outside an habitual glance around the car told him that something was wrong. The camera was sitting in the middle of the back seat, but the flash attachment was missing. He cursed softly. He had left it in the courtroom, of course. Would Armando charge him another five bucks? The courthouse was only five blocks away and the doors were unlocked. He got a flashlight out of the glove compartment and started walking down a dark deserted street. He dreaded going back to the place, yet felt a dreamy attraction to its brooding shadow-world.

The two men stepped out of the tavern and paused by the little Volkswagon. The tall one said, "I thought about gettin' one of them once, they're supposed to be cheap to run."

"Yeah, but you can't get anybody to work on 'em around here," said the short one. "Besides, they don't have enough clearance for the potholes in the dirt roads. Say, look at that camera, sittin' right out in the open like that. Wouldn't dare leave it lyin' around like that in the city. Expensive one, with that big ol' flashbulb thing stickin' up."

II

There was no moon, and he didn't want to use the flashlight during the five block walk to the courthouse. He went very slowly at first, letting his eyes get accustomed to the dark. There were no occupied houses between him and the courthouse and the street was spotted with weeds here and there; he wasn't worried about attracting attention. He stopped a block away and watched for activity. The shadowy bulk of the courthouse loomed indistinctly against the deeper blackness beyond. Farther on there was a yellow glimmer from Armando's house, but no movement anywhere. Moving his eyes he could make out the foot of the stairway on his right with his peripheral vision. He advanced cautiously, still not using the flashlight.

He paused again at the foot of the stairs, listening hard for any sound beneath the whir of cicadas and crickets but there was nothing. As he crept up the stairs his footsteps sounded terribly loud; the creak of the unlocked door was alarming. He peered intently toward Armando's house before entering but still nothing stirred. He felt his way along the wall to the courtroom door. Once inside he tried to remember where he had left the flash attachment. He flicked the light on and off in different directions. On the third blink he saw it plainly on one of the spectators' benches. He groped his way forward in the dark to where he thought it lay and felt for it, finding only dusty surfaces of wood. He was about to try the light again when the first squeak of rotten wood alarmed him. The floor sagged, gave way. A sickening fall through black space ending in a stony jolt.

Armando jerked erect in his chair. Had he heard something? He wasn't sure. What did it sound like? He couldn't remember. The sound hung in the back of his mind, just out of reach, like the memory of a dream. The thought faded and he lowered his eyes to his magazine.

Pearsall raised himself up on one arm, feeling the cold gritty flagstones under his palm. Inky blackness surrounded him, stifled his eyes. He knew he was in the center space between the cells. Dazed as though recovering consciousness, he didn't think he had been out cold. A ringing in his ears blurred his sense of place. He sat still and tried to think. He had had the flashlight in his hand when he fell, it was probably on the floor somewhere. He tried to remember whether Armando had locked the door at the top of the stairwell. If so, he would just have to make enough noise to rouse him, if the splintering floor hadn't already. He felt hot and sweaty and hideously cold at the same time—brain concussion, maybe.

The ringing went away and left a residue of sound, distant, as though blown on the wind. Voices, laughter—had the tavern livened up that much? He thought he heard a gunshot, far away. He strained to hear more distinctly. He became aware of the breathing in the room. Slow, hard, controlled—someone trying not to be heard. He involuntarily softened his own panting breath. Slowly, with infinite care, he pulled himself to his feet, trying not to make a sound. He could hear the other men now, there were two of them.

He inched backwards till his back felt the bars of a cell. There was a sudden patter crossing from his left to his right. Not rats, human feet, bare feet. Then an answering patter far to his left. A sliding sound, someone brushing the bars of a cell opposite him.

A long slow breath not five feet to his left; his hair rose. Someone holding his breath and creeping. He turned toward it and started to back away along the line of cells. The faintest possible movement of air touched his right arm and he smelled sweat, not his own. He froze. There was a muffled groan from in front of him, then more pattering. The raw smell of blood wafted across the room.

He turned; he tried to move steadily toward the opposite end of the room, listening hard. The thumping of his own heart was a distraction now, louder and louder. He froze again, holding his breath, at a minute rustle behind him. Then the searing pain entered below his left shoulder blade and thrust in and upward and he screamed and gurgled.

* * *

"Heart attack," said Armando. "Not a mark on him."

"Dammit," said the sheriff.

"To hell with the Historical Society, we got to get this place torn down," said Armando. "It ain't safe."

"You're right," said the sheriff. "But they ain't gonna like it. Anyhow were gonna do ourselves a favor, and carry him back to his car, and say we found him there. Otherwise the whole thing will come out and we'll have every spook chaser in the country on our necks."

"Yeah," said Armando, "I don't know why people with weak hearts got to go messin' around places like this. He's the fifth one in two years."

The Horror from Yith

Guozar Aldecoa's wiry and slightly bowed legs carried him through the rugged Idaho wilderness at a remarkable pace, constantly threatening to outdistance his two charges. It is a point of pride among the Basques to be able to travel rocky or thickly forested terrain faster than any man and most sheep and Guozar had no intention of letting the two men keep up easily. The tall one, Laszlo, was keeping up well enough though breathing hard, but the heavy-set Dunaway was already gasping for breath; they would have to stop to let him rest soon.

They were crazy anyway, paying him so much money to rush thirty miles into the woods after the young man with the long hair and the mustache. Evans-Douglas himself had paid him almost as much as he would have made for the summer following the sheep herd up into the mountains, and Laszlo had doubled that to hire Guozar to lead him to the remote cabin where Evans-Douglas was staying. And for a much easier trip at that, since Lazlo's rented Jeep had been able to get within ten miles of the cabin. Alone Guozar could have made the whole round trip in a day and he cursed Laszlo for making him carry the heavy pack, but for that much money who could argue? Laszlo finally called a halt at the edge of an open meadow. Dunaway collapsed at the foot of a tree, his red hair dripping sweat, while Laszlo and Guozar sat at the edge of the shade looking out over the pale yellow-green grass at the landscape beyond. Yes, Laszlo had kept up the pace pretty well for a city man, thought Guozar. He was a tall, thin man with black hair and pale skin and a thin face like a wolf. Guozar noticed that he was systematically scanning the scene in front of them with a practiced movement of the eyes, barely moving his head. Maybe he wasn't a city man after all.

"Which way from here?" asked Laszlo, not turning his head.

"We go down the slope and cross that creek there, then up into the woods on the other side and around that hill. There's a ridge on the other side. We follow that two, three miles, then cross the valley below the ridge. Maybe five miles altogether." Guozar noticed that his eyes had stopped moving and followed his line of sight to where three vultures circled a spot below and to their left.

Laszlo stood up and said, "Let's go see what those birds have while Phil catches his breath," then strode off without waiting reply. Guozar hopped up and followed. The broad-bladed grass was knee high and made a whistling sound against their jeans, otherwise, the dry meadow was oppressively silent. They couldn't see the elk until they were right on top of it. It was stiff and swollen, dead for several days. The flies were buzzing around it and Guozar stood fifteen feet away and just thought about something else.

"What killed it, Guozar?" asked the tall man quietly.

"I don't know, "he answered casually. "Maybe wolf, maybe cougar, maybe even bear, the old grizzly do crazy things sometimes. Maybe just die." He was thinking about cold beer and wishing he hadn't left his rifle up with the packs.

"Use your eyes," said Laszlo impatiently. "What killed it?"

Startled by the affront, Guozar moved closer and looked at the thing. Not wolves—the vultures had been at it, but otherwise it was not eaten. Not bear—the throat was torn out very roughly, too ragged even for wolf or cougar. There were peculiar punctures in the side. The head was crushed out of shape as though it had been run over by a truck. He didn't like it.

Laszlo was moving in a wide circle around the carcass, looking at the ground. Finally, he met the little Basque's eyes with a flinty stare. "You know these mountains as well as any man alive, Guozar. Ever see anything like that before?" He spoke with a low even tone.

Guozar shook his head. Laszlo motioned to him and Guozar stepped to where he stood in the tall grass. A large jagged stone lay at his feet, one side black with clotted blood. He could see wisps of elk hair. Near it was a stick, probably the trunk of a young sapling. One end was broken to form a sharp point; it was stained with blood.

Laszlo turned abruptly and stalked off up the slope. When they reached Dunaway all he said was, "Dead elk," but for an instant there was a suspicious look in the heavy man's eyes. As they fastened the packs, Guozar noticed that they both unconsciously checked the pistols on their belts. He had thought they were foolish to carry them; lots of tourists liked to do that in the woods for no reason, but now he wondered. They knew something they weren't telling him. He hefted his battered .30-30 nervously as they started down to the creek.

The part of the creek bed in front of them was lined with a dense growth of trees, impenetrable to the eye. A hundred yards from the edge of the copse Guozar suddenly stopped still.

"Did you see it, too?" asked Laszlo.

"Yes—bear, big one," said Guozar. "Better to go around, I think, but to the left the creek is too deep, and up there to the right the rocks are very rough. But safer, I think."

"Probably so, but we're in a hurry. With two .44's and a .30-30 we can probably stop a bear if we have to. Let's go as far to the right as we can without getting into the big boulders and cross there."

They moved a quietly as they could, watching the trees intently. Guozar was worried. It had been big and dark alright, but it hadn't moved like a bear. Or anything else. They were a good two hundred yards from where they had seen the movement when they turned and made their way through a jumble of rocks and scrubby trees to the water. They had gotten across the slippery stones of the creek bed when they heard a whir and clatter and instinctively ducked for cover behind the boulders lining the stream. The heard the sound again and this time all of them saw the crude flint-tipped arrow glance off the rocks. Then the air was full of them.

The shucked off their packs and Laszlo and Dunaway began firing sporadically at the shadowy forms flitting from tree to tree, while Guozar held his fire and wished he hadn't been too stingy to buy another box of cartridges. Who could have foreseen being attacked by legend? For the things in the trees were furry and huge and ran on two legs, and though he had never heard of the *oh-mah* shooting arrows, he knew they must be the dreaded beast-men of the mountains that the old prospectors and Indians spoke of in hushed tones. Suddenly a monstrously long black arm reached around his waist from behind and lifted him high in the air, squeezing him till he couldn't breathe. He saw Laszlo below him holding the pistol with two hands, aiming at an unbelievably high angle and then the report and muzzle blast of the .44 magnum blotted out his mind. When his senses returned he was kneeling on the ground by the dead monster and Laszlo was already behind him firing again. There was no time to examine the thing; its kindred were making a suicidal charge and Guozar grabbed up his rifle. Many of the beasts staggered and turned back or fell under the withering fire, but still others came on. When Guozar felt the hammer fall on an empty chamber, one was leaping over the rock in front of him. He ducked, letting it pass over him and, to the amazement of Laszlo and Dunaway, grabbed the rifle by the barrel and began swinging at the thing. When the stock broke, he jabbed at it with the pointed remnant. Again the roar of a .44 Magnum rattled his brain and the beast ran howling back into the woods.

For several minutes they watched the woods intently waiting for a second charge, but there was no further movement and no sound. Laszlo was the first to turn and walk over to the monstrosity that had grabbed Guozar. The others followed, nervously glancing back at the trees. The thing stretched out on the ground was a full ten feet in height. It was quite man-like in form, though the arms were proportionately longer than a man's. The huge feet were those of a man except for a weird double-jointed big toe, with nothing like the thumb-like opposed toe of an ape. It was clad all over in long black fur with a scattering of grizzled tips and wore no clothing.

Laszlo's bullet had made a mess of one eye, but other the bestial features were intact. The coarse hair on a curiously pointed head and extremely low forehead led down to sort of upswept bang over heavy beetling brow ridges. The nose was broad and flat, the mouth incredibly wide with no external lips. The death grimace showed long fangs like the fighting canines of a bull gorilla.

"God, what is it?" whispered Dunaway. "Some kind of missing link?"

"Possibly. It could be an evolutionary holdover, a 'living fossil' of a stage ancestral to us, but I doubt it. It's a hominid of course; with those feet it's no closer to an ape than we are, but look at those huge grinding molars—there's been nothing like that in our direct line. And the only other hominid line known to have existed parallel with and distinct from ours, the paranthropoids of over half a million years ago, had teeth like that. But that's only a guess. Have you noticed the eye? It has a vertical pupil like a cat. It's kind have been nocturnal for a long time. Which makes it all the more curious that they should attack us in the daytime."

Guozar bent to look at the eye; it was as Laszlo had said. "You know much about the *oh-mah* Mr. Laszlo. Where did you learn of such things? I have heard many times of the legends of the beast-men, but have never seen them before."

Laszlo smiled. "I, too, have heard the tales, though I've never been to this part of the country before. There are men who have studied the stories of the *oh-mah*, the bigfoot, the *sasquatch* of Canada, and have concluded that they are more than legend. I work for one of them."

"Did they send you here to find them?" asked Guozar.

"No. Right now, finding Dr. Christopher Evans-Douglas is more important. I think it's safe now, we must go on." He said it with such quiet authority that Guozar shouldered his pack along with the others and walked for half an hour before questioning the decision in his mind and realizing that, in fact, it was a crazy thing to do. Why not go back to town and get help, more guns and men, to rescue the young man? But by then he would have felt foolish to bring it up and besides, he had recovered fully from the terrifying encounter and was avid for adventure. He knew he was on the edge of deep mysteries, the most fascinating and exciting events of his life. His dark eyes gleamed and his short legs led them into the hills with resolute energy.

* * *

The banded oval of Ogntlach's giant fifth planet cast razor-sharp shadows among the uneven crags of its own barren seventh satellite. The sphere animated by Dr. Christopher Evan-Douglas drifted aimlessly in and out of its light, basking in imagined warmth. It was an illusion, of course, since the temperature sensors of the sphere could be adjusted to keep the subjective sensation within comfortable limits, but he had felt cold ever since he had fled with the remnants of the Great Race to this airless ball of rock from which Ogntlach appeared so small and heatless. He adjusted the sensors to feel like a warm spring day and relished the illusion of being warmed by the light of the great planet.

He often wandered alone outside the underground complex in which the four thousand-odd survivors of the attack had taken refuge. The atmosphere there was morbid; most of those who survived seemed totally demoralized by the disaster, particularly the loss of the archives. Whenever a plan was suggested to further the recovery of the Race, they declared that it could not be carried out because this or that item of information had been lost in the archives. Fully a fourth of the original group had by an effort of will neutralized their own thought patterns and simply ceased to exist, leaving an uninhabited sphere floating uncontrolled through the tunnels of the colony like the Flying Dutchman of earthly legend. He suspected that the majority of casualties on Yith had come about in this way; in fact, the calamity was in a sense self-inflicted, for if their superstitious fear had not prevented them from studying the danger the from the polypus things, they would have been easily capable of foreseeing what was to come and taking measures to save themselves as they had done numerous times in the distant past.

But not all of the survivors were useless pedants crumpled in despair. At least five hundred of them seemed to be more resilient and had begun activities, over the objections of the others, designed to assure long-term survival and the recreation the Race's consummate accomplishments. It would be wrong to call them leaders, for they were looked on by the others as insubordinate and almost criminal, but certainly they had taken the lead in everything that Evans-Douglas considered constructive. They were the ones who in the face of the attack had rallied to the few available space ships and rounded up as many of the Great Race as they could hold and remembered the long abandoned catacombs on this satellite. Unfortunately, they did not in general come from the ranks of the old leadership of Yith and so had been unable to take control of the group. It was fortunate for Evans-Douglas that the surviving leaders had not regained composure enough to assert their authority before landing here, otherwise they would never have permitted the pilots to remain in dangerously low orbits above Yith picking up individual survivors.

Since establishing themselves here they had begun laboriously rebuilding the basic tools and instruments of their incredible technology using only their own memories and the data stored in the memory shells of the spheres, though to his amazement all the older leaders could think to do with them was to initiate a preposterous project of analyzing the minerals of the rocky moon to 'replace the data lost in the archives.' To the horror of the others, the 'rebels' as he had come to think of them, had devised a way to operate uninhabited spheres by remote control and transmit sensory images back to the satellite and by sending them out from spaceships, kept in high orbits, to explore the inner planets and find out what they could about the situation. A sphere would cruise on a planet's surface, relaying impressions to someone on the satellite as though he were actually in the exploring sphere, until the hydra-things or their winged black minions spotted and destroyed it. These proxy encounters with the polyps were so terrifying that even among the rebels, few could stand them and several had committed self-annihilation during the early attempts.

Evans-Douglas lacked the superstitious obsession of the Great Race and proved of great value as an observer, but even he felt the terror of the polyps keenly. He had begun to have groggy spells, sometimes seeing dimly the cabin in Idaho and feeling the sensations of his own body, and hoped that the shock of the encounters was loosening the grip the sphere seemed to have on his mind. He was very much afraid of the effects of prolonged absence on his body. Another effect of his spying activities was that he was becoming increasingly isolated from the Great Race members. They valued his ability to observe the polyps at length, but he reminded them of what was to them the ultimate horror and he began to notice them avoiding him; purely social contacts almost ceased and conversations would break up when he entered a room. He had become very lonely. He turned the sphere back toward the entrance to the tunnels and thought of the green earth.

* * *

Dunaway was the last to emerge from the thick stand of aspen and approach the edge of the precipice. After leaving the creek where they had been attacked, Guozar had led them up the opposite slope into a heavy growth of pine which cut out the sun and Dunaway had lost all sense of direction as they wound their way through the trees following no discernable path. The little guide had apparently been navigating by the gradient of the slope, for they had consistently climbed slightly to their left. At last they had reached the spine of the ridge, lined with shattered rock and twisted junipers, and crossed to the left into a maze of aspens rustling in the late afternoon breeze. The slope was more gradual on the down slope and they soon broke out of the trees at the edge of a two hundred foot sheer drop.

Below was a narrow valley, floored with the dusty gray-green of sagebrush, stippled with yellow wildflowers and cleft by a swath of willow bushes along a marshy creek. At the opposite side where the valley floor began to rise again was a small square cabin, built of heavy squared logs. It was right at the edge of the trees. Following Laszlo's lead, Dunaway and the guide dropped their packs and stopped a while to watch for signs of activity. Grateful for the chance to rest, Dunaway sat down and, in spite of the eerie circumstances, found himself admiring the beauty of the scene. He had spent his entire life in big cities before being recruited by the mysterious Laszlo for the even more mysterious organization he represented, and he found the beauty of this glorious wilderness overwhelming even though it did conceal ten-foot ape-men and what Laszlo called 'possibly the greatest danger in the brief history of the human race.'

There was no smoke from the cabin and no movement anywhere in the valley, but Laszlo still waited a full half hour, scanning the trees behind the cabin with binoculars, before giving the word to shoulder the packs. Guozar led them a quarter mile along the cliff to where the descent was only slightly more gradual and picked out a zig-zag downward path which Dunaway found more terrifying than the encounter with the sub-men. He wondered if Basques have an admixture of goat blood.

Laszlo insisted that they hurry across the valley so that they could get into the cabin if they were attacked, but it took a while to force their way through the six-foot willow growth and Dunaway sank knee deep in the mud several times, arriving far behind the others and out of breath. He found the two standing by modern casement window set in the very old wall next to the door. Guozar's eyes were wide. Looking over their shoulders Dunaway could see a motionless figure slumped in a chair before a fireplace. Laszlo tried the door, found it unlocked and stepped inside. Guozar crossed himself as he stepped over the threshold.

The figure in the chair was a short slender young man with very long dark brown hair. He had a full mustache and a growth of stubble all over his face. A moth-eaten army blanket lay askew across his body.

"Dead?" croaked Guozar, crossing himself again.

"No," said Laszlo. He had raised one eyelid of the still form.

"But he does not breathe!"

"He's breathing, but so slowly that you can't see it."

"Ah," said Guozar, his eyes growing even wider, but with excitement rather than fear. "I have seen something like that before. In Bilbao, before I come to this country. *La Bruja*, what you say . . . ?"

"Witch," said Dunaway.

"Yes, a witch, she sleep like that without breathing and her soul fly out and see things." Dunaway and Laszlo gave him a peculiar look, then looked at each other.

"I'll try to wake him up," said Laszlo as he rummaged through his pack. He extracted a small black case. Inside were a hypodermic needle and a small bottle with a rubber gasket in the top. He prepared an injection of the pale blue fluid and administered it to Evans-Douglas. There was no visible effect.

"It will take a while to act—I don't know how long. In any case, he won't be able to leave before morning. We'll stay here and take turns watching him during the night. He may be disoriented and confused or even violent when he wakes up."

Evans-Douglas had left a neat pile of firewood just outside the door and they soon had a fire going in the fireplace under a pot of jerky stew. They watched warily for signs of the sub-men through the windows at the front and sides of the cabin, but there was none on the side toward the woods. After eating, Laszlo took the first watch. He admonished the others to wake him immediately if Evans-Douglas showed any sign of waking.

The little Basque promptly preempted the canvas camp bed and was soon breathing deeply and regularly. Still Dunaway was surprised when Laszlo began to speak openly about their mission.

"He seems to be in good physical shape, the retinal reflex is normal, no signs of decomposition on the skin, and his beard's been growing. There have been cases of mind travel lasting even longer than this without danger, though it's unusual."

Dunaway looked suspiciously at Guozar, but Laszlo just smiled. Dunaway shrugged. "You know, I've never been properly filled in on what it's all about. We got on the plane in a hurry and after we landed we were busy making the arrangements and rounding up Guozar."

"You know about Grodek's surveillance operation with the mediums, I suppose," began the tall man. "He has a way of using hypnosis to channel their trance into a sort of selective telepathic receptivity. Every few days he stages a sort of séance with one of them and they try to pick up unusual thoughts or psychic activity concerned with those outside or similar things. Of course, that's a pretty crude description. I doubt if Grodek himself knows exactly what happens. He's more interested in ferreting out dangers and evils than in figuring out the scientific basis of the techniques he uses.

"Anyway, about two months ago one of the mediums hit on something. A case of mind travel or astral projection. The subject was in contact with Yith."

"Isn't that the planet from which the Great Race came?" interjected Dunaway. "I thought they had fled to earth from there in the face of some horrible peril."

"True, but the race that drove them out eventually weakened and some of the Great Race reestablished themselves there, using artificial bodies and driving their enemies into the interior of the planet. They apparently seized the subject, trapping his mind on Yith. This made it extremely difficult for Grodek's mediums to make contact with him and after that, the information they got was fragmentary and difficult to interpret. Only a week ago Grodek put together enough facts and impression to guess that it was someone associated with the college in Caldwell, faculty, rather than a student, who had been making serious studies in the occult. A contact in Caldwell pinned it down to a young professor, Dr. Christopher Evans-Douglas, who gone up to a cabin in the mountains for the summer. After that, Grodek put us on the first plane out."

"Did he tell you about the beast-men? Where do they come in?"

"He's mentioned them to me in the past. Besides plenty of modern encounters are on record, there are references to them the ancient books you saw at Grodek's place in Providence. Apparently, they've been in the Western Hemisphere much longer than the Indians, and in the past they had traffic with those outside. But since the Indians, and then the Europeans, came, they've sunk to a very low cultural level. I'm very surprised to see them using bows, or even traveling in something larger than family groups. Grodek didn't even mention them during the briefing."

"I see. Then that wasn't part of the great danger you mentioned?" asked Dunaway.

Laszlo's eyes narrowed and he glanced sidelong at Guozar, who was forgetting to breathe deep. "No," he said, "the danger concerns what happens to Evans-Douglas' body while he's out of it."

* * *

It was night on Ogntlach's airless second planet, but its moons, small but very low, illuminated the scene in shades from gray to ivory. The sentient sphere through which Dr. Christopher Evans-Douglas watched, hidden in the shadowed rubble of a basalt tower probably destroyed by earthquake, for there was no weathering here to weaken the structures scattered over the undulating plain.

Before him were six of the polypus beings. Above the obscenely bulbous bodies three appendages curved outward and down to the five-toed feet. The creatures were capable of levitation and apparently touched the ground mainly for sensory purposes, but now five of them stood in a ring with all three feet firmly planted. Perhaps they wished to conserve whatever form of energy was involved in levitation for the task at hand. The sixth creature floated in the center of the ring, its appendages spread out horizontally above the body and jerking spasmodically. Its body had begun to expand and contract in an uncanny rhythm, as did the others, and Evans-Douglas was reminded of certain rituals and chants in the elder lore he had studied. Now the thing in the center of the ring began to alternately fade and congeal, its double shadow in the dust below almost disappearing, then growing dark again. Then it was no longer there.

His visual sensors on the antennae had both been turned toward the teleportation ceremony. Since there was no air to carry sound and the sphere was a few inches above the stone, he had no warning that the huge trapdoor below and behind him was slowly opening or that a five-toed tentacle was reaching out, until the sphere was crushed.

Abruptly he was back in his own sphere in the catacombs with a group of the Great Race applying electrodes to revive him. The debriefing was strained and formal, even though those present were anxious to hear his account. This was the first time the polyps had been observed teleporting, though some had already surmised their means of space travel. They had known for long that the uprising had begun on the second planet. It had been the last citadel of the polyps in the ancient war and they had never really been conquered there, merely discouraged from carrying on extensive activities on the surface. Eventually, the Great Race in their decadence had ceased to keep watch there and finally the polyps had become active again. They had made contact with their own kind who had survived beneath the surface of Yith and multiplied in secret until they could overrun the Great Race and rule the system of Ogntlach again, as they had billions of years before.

The Great Race survivors had given up on any immediate counterattack and were attempting to build the metempsychosis apparatus that would enable them to reach groups of their own race in other periods of time. There were great technical difficulties owing to the crudity of the equipment available. In particular, they had to carry out the exchanges with periods in which the subject had not already been alive, which was difficult and called for great precision because most of them had traveled extensively in time. A principle they called 'the law of conservation of consciousness' made it impossible for the mind to exist twice during the same time interval.

Fascinated though he was with the events here, he wished desperately that he could return to his own body. During the rest period (for mental and emotional rejuvenation; the spheres were immune to physical fatigue) he had had a vague dream of the cabin in which other people seemed to be there talking. He had no idea how his body would appear to others, it might even be in a cataleptic state resembling death.

Another sphere drifted in through the low entrance and a conversation began in the mental symbolism of the language of the Great Race. He could not follow it all, but gathered that seven more spheres had been found floating lifeless in the tunnels. He moved unobtrusively to the entrance and thence toward his resting chamber. At times like this they showed diffidence bordering on hostility—perhaps they hated having the weakness in their Race shown to an outsider.

* * *

Laszlo was wide awake an instant after Guozar touched his arm. Guozar pointed silently to Evans-Douglas, who was moving in short spasms. Laszlo bent over him and felt his pulse—it was detectable and he was visibly breathing. The movements were becoming fewer and less violent. Laszlo looked at his watch and began to prepare a second injection. The pale blue fluid brought on a second flurry of motion, but after a few minutes the young man again lay still, though he continued to breathe audibly.

Guozar rekindled the fire and put on coffee. While outside the forest shaded from black to gray to gray-green, the two carried on a low-toned conversation which did not wake the snoring Dunaway. Guozar was going to be a problem; it had been Laszlo's intention to say that Evans-Douglas was recovering from an attack of a rare cataleptic condition, but he had had to arouse Guozar suspicions when he needed his expertise concerning the concerning the elk, and the appearance of the sub-men had blown the whole thing. It would be impossible to keep him quiet. He would have to play it by ear, Laszlo thought.

Guozar had an endless store of Indian legends and prospectors' tales concerning the *oh-mah* and Laszlo countered with stories of more recent sightings. Guozar was fascinated with Laszlo's accounts of the similar *sisemite* of Mexico and Guatemala and of the 'abominable snowmen' of the Himalayas, which were new to him. Eventually the conversation worked around to the mysterious Grodek. Laszlo explained that there were many ancient evils alive in hidden places, things in which men no longer believed and so had forgotten how to combat; Grodek's people fought these things, secretly. Guozar's eyes gleamed. Laszlo stressed the need for secrecy, so that ignorant and unbelieving officials would not charge in blindly and stir up a hornet's nest they could not put down. This seemed to strike the right note; the little mountain man's respect for constituted authority was, to put it mildly, lukewarm.

An hour after daybreak Evans-Douglas stirred again, but did not awaken. Dunaway woke up and started breakfast while Laszlo thought hard about what to do. There was no way to hasten Evans-Douglas' recovery. Grodek had given very specific instructions about the use of the blue fluid and said it would be dangerous to increase the dosage or frequency. The effects were unpredictable; he might come out of the coma at any time or the injections might fail altogether to bring him to complete consciousness, in which case he would have to be brought to Providence where other methods could be tried. Carrying him out would be difficult, but another night in the cabin would probably be dangerous. If the sub-men attacked again, the cabin with its blind side toward the trees could not be well defended; their position would be hopeless against a night attack using fire. Getting him up the cliff opposite the cabin would be the hardest part; when Guozar agreed that it could be done, the decision was made.

It took an hour to get him to the top on a stretcher made from saplings and a blanket, with Dunaway guarding the top of the trail with both pistols and the more sure-footed pair carrying. Making their way through the dense forest with their burden was slow and fatiguing. Just before noon they reached the grassy slope overlooking the place where they had been attacked. The temptation to rest and eat was great, but when careful surveillance found no sign of the sub-men, Laszlo insisted they push on across the creek. They waded across at the point where they had fought and found that the creatures had returned to carry away their dead.

They had reached the top of the far slope and were catching their breath before the plunge into forest gloom, when Guozar froze wide-eyed and pointed upward toward the north where the creek ran out of a jumble of boulders on the shoulder of a great crag. There, standing on and among the rocks like solemn black sentinels, were a score of the sub-men, spears and bows at their sides, watching, motionless and enigmatic. Through the binoculars Laszlo could see the breeze riffling their fur, the glint of yellow eyes staring intently, but they did not move. Aching for revenge but afraid to attack? Relieved to see the intruders pass out of their territory? There was no way to tell and no choice but to move on.

The long afternoon trek was a delirium of speckled shadows and excruciating fatigue even for the hardy Laszlo. It was almost completely dark by the time they reached the jeep and he decided that it would be too risky to drive out at night. He felt confident that the sub-men would not attack since it was plain that the group was leaving. They made camp and ate a cold supper, all being too tired to cook and too hungry to wait for the fire to burn down. Guozar took the first watch, Dunaway the second and Laszlo the third. Laszlo repeated with heavy emphasis his order to awaken him immediately if Evans-Douglas showed any signs of awakening, warning the other two again that he could conceivably become violent; then he lay down and was asleep in seconds.

* * *

Again Dr. Christopher Evans-Douglas gazed upon the great Jovian planet around which the Great Race remnant orbited. This time he was not on the surface, but in a special observation room almost never used by the members of the Great Race themselves. The equipment in the room was connected to visual sensing devices on the surface. The images were not displayed on screens, but brought to electrical connections that transmitted them directly into the spheres, giving the sensation of seeing with one's own eyes. He often came here to relax.

He was becoming more hopeful about returning to earth. During the past twenty-four hours he had had increasingly strong sensations of being back in his own body. At first it had been the old feeling of sitting in the chair before the fireplace, with the impression that others were moving about the room. Then it had been a distinct feeling of lying on his back. But the hold of the sphere on his mind seemed very strong. Each time the impressions had come and begun to grow clearer, he had felt a powerful counterinfluence arise as though some other mind were jamming his mental reception. It was a little like the sensation when one is in a light doze and a dream begins, then when one tries to seize it, it vanishes and one awakes. He guessed that the spheres had some sort of monitor that interfered when the enclosed mind slipping away.

He disconnected himself from the viewing circuit and swiveled his antennae. Five of the Great Race spheres had entered the room. They carried devices he recognized as being used in the process for deactivating the spheres. He reached out for telepathic contact and touched a wall of violent hatred mingled with fear—he could not break through to communicate. He tried to move away, but found that they were jamming his motion and antigravity controls. He was helpless. An indescribable feeling of mental dissolution began to grow, together with hazy sensations of his own body on earth. Then the interference he had noticed before cut in and his mind went murky as though in deepest, unrememberable dream.

* * *

The whole thing must have been horribly quiet. It was Dunaway's last thrashing kick that hit the tin coffee cup and woke Laszlo. By the time Laszlo was wide awake and scrabbling over his pack, Dunaway was quite dead and the savage thing with glassy eyes and bared teeth had released his crushed windpipe and turned on Laszlo with a gurgling snarl. It was crouching to spring when Laszlo found the small metal box and flicked the toggle switch even before getting it out of the pack. The needle of a small meter on the top of the box twitched, then held steady and the killer shot upright with arms outstretched and howled a wailing crescendo scream, then fell prostrate. Guozar was awake and staring as Laszlo examined Dunaway then turned grimly to the other form and turned it over. The features of Dr. Christopher Evans-Douglas had lost the savage grimace and were again recognizable; he was at last coming out of his long sleep.

* * *

Kazimerz Grodek's study was paneled with dark walnut and soundproofed, not only to keep irritating noises out but to keep confidential conversations in. In addition to the soundproofing, the walls contained steel mesh, grounded to keep electromagnetic radiation both in and out, and a number of curious objects on the walls were talismans to keep out less definable influences. It was the only place in the world where Janos Laszlo let himself be completely off guard.

Grodek was a short, very heavy man with close-cropped steel-gray hair and colorless eyes behind rimless glasses. He might have been any age between forty and seventy. He rarely moved except for the oddly opaque eyes and the agile mind and it was not in a spirit of subordination that Laszlo served the brandy and lit cigars; it was his role to move and Grodek's sit behind the great mahogany desk and think.

"It was my fault," said Laszlo. "I should have told him more or guarded Evans-Douglas myself, or tied him up." He spoke in Hungarian.

"Nonsense, Janos. You must sleep like anyone else. You could not tie him up without making Guozar suspicious. You told him enough; he was careless. He was a good man, but careless men do not last long with me. And you could not have been sure."

"Even after the elk?" said Laszlo. "I knew from that that some savage thing was at work, something that killed blindly with no purpose but destruction. I knew it was not the beast-men; they had flint-tipped weapons. It seemed more likely they were out to stop the menace at large in their territory."

"You could only guess, Janos, only suspect. I, myself, am quite surprised that the polyps were able to infiltrate his mind without the Great Race detecting it immediately. From what he says, he must have killed quite a few of them during his blackouts before they found him out and attacked him. They thought the deserted spheres were suicides."

"The device you gave me was very effective in driving the polyp mind out of Evans-Douglas' body. Why didn't the Great Race use the same principle to shield their entire colony?"

"It isn't suitable for large-scale use, and besides, they probably didn't think of it. You see, the Great Race, themselves, are immune to that form of possession. They are more conscious than we. They have a personal unconscious composed of repressed memories, otherwise the disastrous blindness about anything concerning the polyps would not have been possible, but their collective unconscious complex of instincts and archetypal conceptions of which they are unaware is much smaller and simpler than ours. And it is only through these deep unconscious levels that the polyps can operate. They are much too alien to take over the entire nervous system to operate the body directly as the Great Race can. Perhaps there are creatures in the dimensional manifold from whence they once came which they could control directly, but in our continuum they must be more subtle. They touch only the deepest instincts and desires, stimulate an uncontrollable impulse toward some end, and let the subject's own mind contrive means. In this case the results were crude; the 'end' was simply destruction of any living things at hand, and Evans-Douglas' conscious faculties were never brought into play. But they are capable of doing much better. In some cases they have caused highly developed intellects to work quite cleverly toward specific goals. There was a secret society in Damascus in ninth century which attempted to investigate the polyp remnant within the earth; one of the members managed to systematically infect almost the entire membership with smallpox before he himself died of it. He died raving about cleansing the world of Allah's enemies, completely unaware that he had been used the polypus horror. Imagine what they could do with a nuclear physicist."

"You mean that in a way it *was* Evans-Douglas, himself, who killed Dunaway?"

"Yes—he was the polyps' agent in both body and mind, though the fully conscious part of his mind was apparently never involved. But I don't think we should explain that to him just yet. He is still quite shaken at the thought of the polyps using his body alone to kill. By the way, I'm glad you brought him here. Besides being the best way to keep him quiet about his experiences, he may prove very useful, with his mathematical and scientific training. He's already worked out a hypothesis about how to make contact with Yith possible in contradiction to the known laws of relativity. And even Guozar may be of use to us."

"Well," said Laszlo with a slight chuckle, "there wasn't much else I could do. He's a natural conspirator and will be silent now that he's joined us, but if I hadn't brought him into the organization, he'd soon tell everyone in Idaho about what happened. And in his own way he's as formidable a recruit as Evans-Douglas. He's a marvelous woodsman, tough as nails. He knows English, Spanish, French, and Basque. And he's quite intelligent, though uneducated."

"Yes, I think we'll find plenty of use for him, I'm sure, now that the polyps are again active on earth; we'll be needing a woodsman's skills, among other things, to find out what they're up to."

"I take it you've heard from La Rue in Australia—he should have reached the ruins of the Great Race's city there and reported by now."

"I am certain the polypus things are active because I have *not* heard from La Rue," said Grodek. "He disappeared without a trace, during a gigantic windstorm."

A Movement in the Grass

Below me high grass mottled with sagebrush covered the floor of the valley, except for the bare rocky patch where Petersen lay dead beneath the cold gray sky. For him the adventure was over; for me the worst was yet to come. The valley was about two miles wide at that point, lined with long parallel cliffs. At that time the high rocks seemed a haven of safety, and I sat high up in the jumble of boulders at the valley's head, my attention focused on the dull gray-green of the valley floor, watching with hideous expectancy for any sign of movement in the grass.

In a sense the adventure had begun a hundred and twenty-two years before, in a murderous surprise attack on a small band of Comanche in the Texas Panhandle. They had been camped along a stream at the bottom of a deep sheer-walled canyon, hundreds of feet below the vast grassy plain called the Llano Estacado, in a spot which had always been safe from intrusion. They had not posted lookouts, for few white men knew anything of the interior of the Llano Estacado. But those few were among the buffalo hunters from Adobe Walls, Texans who carried out the raid. They crept down into the canyon before sunrise and attacked the straggling line of teepees in the sleepy dawn light, destroying the entire band before they could get to their mounts. Petersen's great-grandfather Jacob had taken part in the raid and as a souvenir had taken a Comanche medicine bundle from a bullet-pierced teepee. The small rawhide pouch, decorated with an intricate design in beads and horsehair, had contained a rude stone pipe, the mummified ear of a fox and four rough greenish stones which had excited no curiosity among the unlettered frontiersmen. But Jacob's descendant was educated in geology and the ancient keepsakes were uncut emeralds.

They were the size of robin's eggs and flawed. But the lanky blond geologist knew that there would be more where they came from. Emeralds were plentiful in South America but rare on the northern continent, and the geology of the area where they had been taken was all wrong for them. The idea of an unknown lode in the western United States intrigued him, though his family was now wealthy. He had them cut and polished and thought little more about them until he showed them to me during a spring break visit to his home.

"Mike, wherever they came from, it sure wasn't any part of Texas," he said, "or any other part of the Comanche country." His geological reasoning had stopped there, and he probably never would have come any closer the source of the stones if it hadn't been for me. But my family was by no means wealthy and the green fire before me glittered with dreams of wealth, of freedom from drudgery.

I was working in Barrett and taking some courses in ancient Indo-European languages at the university there, and it didn't take me long to find out that they had a huge amount of information about the Comanche buried in their archives. The first thing I found out was that the sacred articles kept in medicine pouches were greatly revered as sources of magical power and were traded, bought and sold, won in battle and passed on from generation to generation for centuries. The Comanche might well have gotten the stones from another tribe and they could originally have come from just about anywhere. Next I delved into Comanche folklore. Most of this had been written down after the Comanche were settled on the reservation in Oklahoma, and was not too detailed or reliable. But I did find a few references to some kind of magic pebbles. The green color wasn't mentioned but the tales definitely referred to a single collection of stones, not to any widespread custom; apparently they were unique. The number of stones was given as anything from four to seven, but then the accounts were second-hand versions by people who had probably never seen them; the pouches were very private affairs and it would be most unusual far anyone but the owner to see the contents. The only clue to their origin was the recurrent statement that they had come from the north.

There were an awful lot of Indians north of the Texas plains, all of them sharing the great Plains Indian culture with the medicine pouch custom. I had no idea where to start until I learned that the Comanche were an offshoot of the Shoshone or Snake tribe centered in Wyoming. Their languages were very similar, almost dialects, and they appeared to have diverged in recent times, certainly after the white men brought the horse. I reasoned that if the stones were highly treasured they probably stayed in the hands of blood relations, i.e., they originated with the Shoshone peoples and came south with their Comanche descendants. But there wasn't much information on the Shoshone in Barrett, so further progress had to await a trip to Wyoming.

The chance came a year later, when I was able to combine a camping trip in the Grand Teton area with three days of research at the college in Laramie. I found a mountain of material on the Shoshone there, and was barely able to scratch the surface. Sheer luck uncovered a reference to the stones. An old reservation Indian had told an anthropology student an ancient tale, heard in his childhood, of the 'serpent stones,' a much-valued medicine relic. They had been given to a brave long ago, in the primordial past. Lost in the desert, he had stumbled on the hidden valley of the serpent god Ayi'ig; the resemblance of the name to the Yig of the Cthulhu Mythos was striking. In fact, I was struck many times by resemblances between Comanche and Shoshone lore and both the Cthulhu Mythos and the even more obscure Mlandoth cycle. I resolved to investigate this when I returned to Barrett. According to the Shoshone tale the location of the valley of Ayi'ig was mysterious, a remote and unknown place of horror revealed only to rare wanderers destined to play a role in events of supernatural importance, or fated to be devoured by the serpent god and his minions. This time the general direction of the origin of the stones was said to be southwest. Remembering my experience with the Comanche I looked into the origins of the Shoshones and found that they were indeed close relatives of the Ute to the south.

I learned that the place to go to learn about Ute legends was the college library in Boulder, Colorado but by then my time and money had run out and I had to return to Barrett. The university there has a fine but little known collection of books bearing on magic, the occult and both the Cthulhu and Mlandoth myth cycles. It is rather difficult of access, a result of bureaucratic incompetence rather than deliberate policy, but I had long ago found effective, though illegal, methods of getting at the books I wanted. I don't read the ancient tongues of the original volumes but there were enough English and German translations to provide me with most of the background available on Yig and the related aspects of both cycles.

Among the primordial horrors known as the Old Ones, Yig stands out as even more archaic, formless and abysmally evil than Yog-Sothoth or Cthulhu. The latter have utterly alien but highly developed intelligences; in Yig there is only a primal bestiality abhorrent even to the other Old Ones. A local manifestation of that inchoate principal of matter and life known only as the Great Mother of the Old Ones, he is often associated with repulsive lower forms of life, most often snakes, though in the *Book of Eibon* there is an appalling tale of swarms of rats acting as though directed by a single common will. It is not clear whether Yig himself has corporeal form, but certainly he has spawned many corporeal horrors in the form of snake gods and the Central American flying serpent, Quetzalcoatl.

Ayi'ig is one of the numerous spawn of Yig which are mentioned by name, and in fact I found parallel accounts in two diverse sources. The fragmentary German translation of the *Pnakotic Manuscripts* in the Barrett library mentioned 'Aeg' as the daughter of Yig and 'Yeethra,' the Yidhra of the Mlandoth cycle and the Yee-Tho-Rah of the Comanche. Aeg was the primary object of worship of a civilization far to the east until it collapsed following an undescribed catastrophe referred to cryptically as 'The Revenge of Yog-Sothoth,' leaving the survivors in a state of barbarous degeneracy.

I found the other account entirely by accident, not in an ancient tome but in the current issue of an archaeological journal. It was a controversial translation of a recently discovered series of tablets from Crete in Linear B, the archaic Mycenaean Greek records of the pirates who superseded the Minoan sea-kings. If the translation was correct the Mycenaean aristocracy in Minos and Pylos had inherited from the Minoan a secret cult which served the sea-demon Cthulhu, Yig and his spawn and others in opposition to Yog-Sothoth as well as to the Indo-European Zeus and the Olympian pantheon. There are indications that this cult aroused the enmity of the rest of the Mycenaean world and was related to the frantic defensive preparations going on in Pylos shortly before its destruction, as documented in other tablets. The lost civilization far to the east was also mentioned, this time described as beyond the sea, east of a place-name which could possibly be a rendering of the Chinese 'Shang.'

I found enough catalog information on the Ute data in Boulder to convince me that I was going to find the source of the emeralds eventually. I had mixed feelings about handling Petersen; he had no real claim to the emerald lode, but as a friend he had set me on the track and been involved from the start. I considered leaving him out of it and going alone but it would be rough country of a kind in which he was experienced and I wasn't, and besides I had no money for a suitable vehicle or even for the camping equipment. But I knew that if I waited until I had enough information to make it look like a real business proposition instead of a wild adventure, he would turn serious and drive a hard bargain on dividing the profits. He was like that. So I put it to him casually, in a spirit of fun, before I went to Boulder. Sure, we'd go get those emeralds, if I could work out the location. Sure, we could go anywhere in his good ol' Jeep. No problem. Even be room for a good supply of beer. A fifty-fifty split? Naturally! If I could work out the location. And so it was settled.

110

Back in Boulder, again the mass of material was great but again luck was with me. There were many items referring to the snake god Ayi'ig and his hidden valley but only one saying anything about the location. You won't find the stained and brittle document there that gave me key; I stole it. Actually it only narrowed it down to a certain part of the Four Corners region, and mentioned two landmarks which could only be identified when seen from a certain angle. To the pre-Columbian Indians, roaming the vast desert on foot, dependent on hard-to-find roots and berries and rare springs or seasonal creeks for sustenance, the location would have remained a hopeless mystery, had any them wished to find such a place of terror. But with the aid of detailed topographical maps I was able to narrow it down to four possibilities. We found nothing at the first two; at the third Petersen died.

II.

Petersen's body was a scrap of flotsam in an ocean of dusty grass, framed by the long rows of black forbidding cliffs that stretched away toward the point where a blurred red sun penetrated the clouds near a preternaturally distant horizon. The infinite gray vault of high clouds was oppressive. I feared the waning of the light.

We had arrived at about four o'clock after driving since dawn through the most barren of badlands. By the time we set up the big tent on a flat shelf a little above the valley and prepared and ate a meal, we felt tired. We decided to rest a bit before beginning our explorations and lay down on our folding cots on each side of the tent. Petersen soon fell into a fitful doze, but I found myself unable to drop off. It was getting chilly and we had both ends of the tent closed. I felt an uneasiness, even more than the combination of fatigue and excitement could account for. The sense of oppression went beyond physical fatigue. At length I got up very quietly and went out to sit in one of the canvas chairs, placing it so that the tent would give shelter from the slowly rising wind. I sat facing the valley; the alien desolation of the landscape made the camp seem like an island of comfort and secure humanity. Had this once been the site of an antediluvian city, perhaps on the shore of a great inland sea, a city now erased by disaster and relentless time? There was a disturbing regularity to the arrangement of low hummocks dotting the valley floor, and barely visible straight lines of darker color through the sagebrush and grass where the remains of walls or streets might have altered the soil.

Lying and sitting had rejuvenated me enough to feel restless. It never occurred to me to descend into that morbid sea of grass. I took a rifle from the Jeep with the idea of using the telescopic sight to look around and made my way up the cold rock mass behind the camp.

It was rough going, and it took me at least half an hour to reach a comfortable ledge a hundred feet above the tent. When I looked around I was surprised to see Petersen moving down into the grass. He was carrying the shotgun we had brought along, in hopes of bagging some rabbit or birds to fill out our canned and dehydrated supplies. He held it upright across his chest and advanced slowly, step by step, like a stalking hunter.

I stared hard at the area around him, trying to spot what he was hunting. I saw a movement in front of him and to his left, a movement in the grass. He stopped and seemed to be looking in that direction but didn't lower the gun. I was reluctant to point the rifle in his direction to see with the scope. There were ripples on each side and behind him. He was surrounded by whatever it was. I thought it might be a herd of javelina.

He was out on a flat open rocky space. Now I could see the little twitches in the grass all around him, but still no trace of their cause. I saw him lower the gun, pointing it toward the grass, and step back as though horrified at what he saw. He whirled as though he heard something behind him and fired into the grass. Then a great dark serpentine form, as big around as his arm, swept up out of the grass behind him and wrapped itself around his neck, dragging him to the ground.

He dropped the shotgun and began grappling with the thing. I opened the bolt of the rifle and a cartridge popped out. There was no real possibility of hitting the creature and a good one of shooting Petersen. I jacked all of the shells out of the magazine before I pointed the scope down there. Even through the scope I couldn't make out any details. It had to be some kind of enormous snake as large or larger than the boa constrictor of the tropics. I couldn't see the head. The body was dark brown on top with lighter markings on the underside. Another one of the serpent things thrust out of the grass and grabbed his legs. They were pulling him from each end. Petersen stopped writhing.

I stuck a cartridge back in the gun and took careful aim and fired at one of the things holding his feet. The recoil disturbed the scope and I couldn't see for sure whether I hit it or not but it flopped spastically, releasing Petersen's leg and thrashing around for a moment before disappearing into the grass. The one wrapped around his neck let go and disappeared too.

I sat there shaking and perspiring. I must have been pale. I opened the bolt and twisted the magnification on the scope to full and looked at Petersen. I was sure he was dead. There was no sign of breathing and his mouth was open. His eyes stared blankly at the sky. There were indistinct red marks all around his throat; I'm pretty sure there was blood there.

III.

> "And the people of the region refused to guide me through the valley because of the rare and curious serpents said to dwell there, which they call the Servants of Aega. These giant snakes, ten times the length of a man, are said to hunt in packs, stalking the unwary traveler and surrounding him. They do not bite like poisonous vipers but choke and strangle and tear their victims limb from limb, carrying off the remains to their foul master Aega, whom no man has seen . . ."
>
> —The Lost Book of Herodotus

I sat stunned for half an hour, just staring at that dusty morass of brittle vegetation, watching for the slightest flicker of motion. I scanned every inch of that silent valley. I looked down to the mouth where it opened into a vast plain stretching away to the high plateau which rose sheer almost fifty miles in the distance. I looked both with my naked eye and with the scope on the rifle, which I loaded completely. I saw nothing I could be sure of, but once I thought I saw the slightest flicker of motion in the swath where the Jeep had crushed down the grass on the way in. Then a sinuous length of dark brown appeared and disappeared between clumps of sage between me and the camp; I knew I was cut off.

I looked around me for a way to escape. I was on a steep rocky slope that continued for hundreds of yards in both directions. I felt a creeping sense of terror, making it hard to think, though it didn't make sense to think of a snake waiting for darkness and pursuing me up the slope; snakes just don't do that. But then snakes don't hunt in packs or silently stalk a man through the grass. And snakes of that size and description just didn't exist in North America. The only chance I could think of to get into a safer position would be to climb higher. I knew snakes have very limited vision—perhaps I could get out of sight. Above me the steep slope ended in a sheer rock wall only twenty feet higher up. I looked off to the right; a hundred yards in that direction there was a pile of fallen rock that I could use to climb to the top. I tried moving that way, but I hadn't gone far when ahead of me, half way up the slope I saw a waving arc of brown pass between two rocks. They were cutting me off. I turned and moved back the other way, moving carefully and watching in both directions. They were good at keeping out of sight but I was pretty sure there were none in front of me. I looked back once and saw a black pointed streak sticking out from behind a rock and wriggling. I kept on moving. The line of the cliffs swept backward after a hundred yards and I couldn't see what lay around the curve. It couldn't be worse than my present position; there wasn't any sense in waiting for the things to come get me. I worked my way up to the bottom of the cliff and scrambled around the edge as fast as I could, keeping an eye out for the things.

I kept looking back at them. They kept to cover and never came completely out in the open, but I saw dark spots moving here and there. The whole pack seemed to be following me, surrounding me in a semicircle and blocking every route of escape except the one I was taking. There were at least six of them, and probably seven or eight.

As I followed the curve of the cliff around to my left I found myself entering a narrow gorge which cut back into the rock mass for about a hundred yards. The floor of the rock slanted back into the canyon in a long thin triangle, as though it had been formed by a watercourse eons before the strata had tilted into their present position. It was washed clean of loose rubble; probably water still flowed out of the canyon at times. As I started moving down into the floor of the gorge and went farther back, I could see a dark opening, very round and smooth; I guessed it was once the exit of an underground river. The cave mouth didn't look too wide, and I thought perhaps I could block the entrance with rocks and hope that the things would eventually get tired of waiting for me to come out. I reached the floor of the gorge and ran up to the entrance.

Looking back I saw that none of the things had appeared in the gorge yet, though they couldn't be far behind. It was surprisingly light in the cave, even though no direct light shone into it. There were a lot of water-worn cobbles lying around, probably not enough to completely close the entrance but enough for a substantial barrier. I started grabbing them, keeping a close watch for rattlesnakes which, though much smaller, could be deadly in this isolated place. We had antivenin but it was back in the Jeep.

Outside the things were now coming into the canyon quite openly. There were eight of them now, and they moved about half way up the gorge and stopped, rising up and swaying like king cobras. The gray light of the sky was behind them so that I couldn't see much more than I could before, except that they were monstrously long, fifty or sixty feet at least, and the eight of them practically filled the gorge. They raised the front part of their bodies fifteen feet off the ground and swayed. They still seemed to taper to a point in front; I couldn't make out the heads at all. The markings on the underside appeared to be double rows of lighter-colored circles. I thought of firing at them but they were keeping their distance and I had only four rounds left. I had to tear myself away from the hypnotic terror that tried to keep me frozen before them, and keep working on the barrier.

I needed to find more stones. Twenty feet in the passage constricted slightly and angled to the left, widening. Past the bend it grew lighter and led gently downward to a dark smooth surface which proved to be water. As my eyes grew accustomed to the dim gray light, I saw a perfectly circular pool, sixty yards across. The light diffused from a small round hole high above in the ceiling of the grotto. I could see green and orange mosses and lichens blotching the boulders at rock walls that lined the pool for most of its circumference. On my side the floor of the passage entrance broadened to form a smooth beach broken only by two black rock masses extending into the water. A ripple broke the surface half way out; I thought of a pebble falling from the sky hole.

Fatigue caught up with me. I lurched against the rock mass on my right. The mass was not rock; it had a disgusting rubbery texture. It began to squirm.

The water began to slop wildly against the shore and something round and rough and very large broke the surface, rising till it was a huge dome, three feet, six feet, twelve feet above the water with immense gleaming eyes just above the water line; the eyes fixed me and I felt an infinite malevolence and rage like a half-heard voice in a dream, powerful yet inarticulate. It was a barrage of telepathic fury, I was hardly able to make myself move as the thing lurched out of the water; it moved in the manner of a snail, creeping on a scalloped skirt of muscle from which great finger-like organs projected at intervals, two of which had been resting out of the water on the bank. In a flash of comprehension I remembered a finely wrought bowl of gold from Mycenaean Pylos, decorated with an octopus. The thing coming at me was exactly like a gigantic octopus, but with the tentacles outside, cut off at the skirt. Of course! The eight 'serpents' outside, separated from the body but controlled by the same telepathic power that tried to root me to the floor before the oncoming devourer!

In the next fraction of a second a flood of thought rushed through my brain. To run would be hopeless, I would be trapped between the monster of the pool and the serpent-tentacles. A few rifle bullets could do little damage to such a massive thing, especially through a tough thick skin...Shooting at the eyes would be a hopeless task in the dim light and with a weirdly lurching target. What I needed was a bomb—I thought of the concussion from the muzzle blast of a high powered rifle combined with the shock wave from a supersonic bullet. The plan was conceived and executed before I could feel any fear. I ran toward the thing, dashed up onto the writhing apron of rubbery muscle and jammed the muzzle of the rifle between its eyes and fired.

I was splattered with foul-smelling fragments of pulpy tissue and then thrown wide by a violent convulsion. I could hear a ghastly whooshing roar from the thing, echoing from the walls and water. I scuttled back into the passage without trying to retrieve the gun. I expected to encounter a probing tentacle at each step but I didn't. When I reached the barrier of stones I could see that the tentacles were flailing about on the ground in a disorganized array. I guessed that I had stunned the brain, but very likely it would recover quickly. I scrambled over the barrier. The threshing forms completely blocked the canyon so I ran to the canyon wall and scrabbled up ten feet or so as quickly as a desperate rat. At that height the surface was rough enough to find finger- and toeholds and work past them.

As I came abreast of them I looked around and saw great curving loops sweeping over me. They were still waving randomly but were now raising up in the cobra pose again. The brain was starting to recover. I felt the rush of air several times as tentacles swept close to me. I was almost past them when one grabbed my arm and yanked me into the air, swinging me in a dizzy arc twenty feet above the wriggling mass below. I landed on a cushion of twitching muscle where two of the things intertwined on the ground. The landing should have stunned me but didn't and the one that was holding me let loose. I ran frantically out of the canyon and through the sagebrush to the Jeep.

As I started the engine I saw one of the serpent-things reach out of the canyon and sway tentatively as though sniffing the air. They must have had some kind of sense organs, probably a form of extra-sensory perception relayed telepathically to the brain.

I couldn't bear to leave Petersen there. I pulled up by the body and got out to load it into the vehicle. I found that my left arm, the one gripped by the tentacle, was useless, but I managed to get him into the back seat. I looked back and saw the things pouring out of the canyon in a very purposeful way as I roared away into the desert.

IV.

The heavy-set balding man carried the two mugs of beer carefully from the bar to the dimly lit booth where his red-bearded acquaintance waited with his elbows on the table. He set the mugs down tenderly, seated himself and took a long swallow before he spoke.

"Yes, I had heard that Mike Hourihan told some kind of wild tale about what happened to him in the desert. But I really don't think you can cite it as serious evidence for the reality of these mythical creatures. After all, he was incarcerated in a mental hospital at the time of his death, and they were keeping him under heavy sedation most of the time. He had lost an arm from a peculiar injury which had gone untreated while he walked out of the desert after his vehicle ran out of fuel. It was amputated by a country doctor whose home he wandered up to. If you're determined to quote him in your book the most it rates is a footnote, or perhaps an appendix."

The bearded man smiled defensively. "True, he was crazy all right, at least at the end. But the events surrounding his trip were verifiable and there was something very, very fishy about his death. The official story was that he got out of his room and committed suicide, hanged himself from a tree on the hospital grounds."

"Yes, that's what I heard too. Seems natural enough."

The bearded man sipped his beer and stared into space for a moment. "But I managed to talk to one of the attendants who was familiar with the case. They're not supposed to talk of course, but they get paid minimum wage and a pitcher of beer will buy a lot of conversation.

"It seems that at first he was sane enough, they committed him mainly for observation because he was suffering from shock and had told this weird story about a giant octopus in the middle of the desert. But they figured it for delirium rather than mental illness and sure enough, he seemed to make rapid progress and stopped telling tales.

"But after a couple of months in the hospital he apparently suffered a relapse. He started having nightmares and waking up the whole wing and raving things like, 'They're coming after me!' and 'The call! I hear the call, I can't fight it!' Tried to get away a couple of times too. That's when they started to keep him doped up."

"Crazy as a bedbug," said the fat man.

The man with the beard ignored this and went on. "On the night he died there was a mix-up with the medication. A patient across the hall got a double dose, slept for eighteen hours straight, and Hourihan got none. He woke up about 3 a. m. and tore the screen off his window. Broke three of the legs off a chair punching a four-inch hole in it and then just ripped the whole thing out, shearing off all the bolts."

"Strength of a madman," muttered the heavy man.

"They found him under a tree with a big overhanging branch. The autopsy showed that he died of strangulation. But they never found the rope or sheet he must have used. And they never explained the circular marks on his neck."

"A footnote," said the heavy man, "or perhaps an appendix."

The Oldest Dreamer

The starry purple sky of early evening
    Engulfed the flickering campfire's feeble warmth and glow
Where, robed against the desert night-wind's keening,
      We seven dreamers told of worlds that we had known
      That only haunted star-flown dreamers ever know
While round us all a desert on a dying world lay dreaming.

I heard of azure-litten hells where demons
    With eyes of opal sang to unseen elder things;
And told of spiral galaxies where eons
      Before the dawn of mind great flocks with shimmering wings
      Traced enigmatic symbols in the void to bring
Strange blessing from mad gods throughout the cryptic astral seasons.

The night grew deep as one by one each dreamer
    Told of beauty and of terror and of cosmic awe
Till only one remained, the oldest dreamer,
      Who sat in silence, speaking not of what he saw
In dreams, beyond the rim.

He sat there wearing silence like a veil
    Remembering awesome things too strange for waking thought
Until a rash young dreamer from a pale
      And raw new world too young for fear or caution sought
      To draw him into reminiscence. Then I caught
A look I could not fathom in his ancient eyes
And he began this tale.

* * *

Yes, once I flew the interstellar gulfs in dream
And saw such wonders with the dreamer's cosmic eye
As waking souls could never bear to comprehend.
I saw a scorching orb so near its giant sun
That through its crumbling hills ran streams of molten bronze
And when a slug-like thing with horns of glinting stone
Slid down to drink, a grayish mound beside the stream
Stretched out a tentacle with claws and rent its prey
Until the viscid blood mixed with the torrid flood
And rose in clouds of crimson vapor. Once I saw
Beneath a blue-green oval star a giant world
Whose frigid seas rose up in hyaline waves while far

Below there lurked a thing of crystal longer than
The rivers of this dying world. I watched it swim
In solitude until it rolled upon its back
And as it stared at me I felt a keen desire
To plummet to those lucid waves and feel the cool
Refreshing seas of Yilla all around me and
To join great Yorith in those depths; but then I fled.
There was a small and airless moon whose leprous crags
Thrust out like grasping talons toward a sky half-filled
With radiance where a silver globe hung silently
Encircled by diaphanous rings of gold. I knew
That there could be no life among those airless peaks
And so I wandered carelessly among the vales
Until a web of shadowed forces swept me down
Into the hollow planet's fearful labyrinth
Unto the hideous core, where in the centuries
Before I woke up screaming I had learned too well
The hateful wisdom of the dwarfish Lloervs who delve
In Xithor's bowels, and how they use the captured souls
Of Dreamers. And one night when sleep had born me far
Among the galaxies I found a twilight world
Lit by a double sunset; in the east the sky
Was scarlet fire and saffron while the western clouds
Shone balefully with flames of green and indigo.
The stars came out in thousands, each one brighter than
The gibbous moon you see above this desert world,
And in the starlit silence flew my dreaming soul
Until I found the portal of an empty fane
A thousand cubits high. I stood outside that door
And wondered who had lit the lambent torch within
Until the outer shadows stirred and then I gasped
At what had come to pray. But finally there came
A night when dream and nightmare passed beyond the bounds
Of human soul's endurance. It began with flight
Beyond a score of sparkling galaxies to where
A clustered group of island universes drifted
Slowly through the nighted gulf in solemn splendor;
In one pool of stars I saw a glowing cloud,
An emerald vapor lit by seven swimming suns
Enshrouded by its lucent folds. I watched it move
For countless centuries in what I took for aimless
Roiling till it formed the semblance of an eye
And, waking, spoke a word I knew. I flew in panic
To the outer void between the galaxies
Where phantasms of eldritch consciousness could never
Follow; only blackness, without entity.

But as I gazed back at the clustered galaxies
That wandered lazily through endless time end space,
Like monstrous silvery fishes in an ebon sea,
I saw that theirs could be no random, mindless flight;
Those glittering legions formed the dreaded sign of Koth.
I strove for wakening that would not come, my flight
Grew wilder than the swiftest ever known before
In half-remembered dream. The teeming universe
Streamed by my staring eyes until the galaxies
Of all dimensioned time and space receded far
Behind me, looking back I saw their myriads swarming
Inward to a single gleaming point of blue;
Then it winked out. I was alone in outer darkness.
For a time or for a space or for eternity
I rested in oblivion, knowing peace.
But when the dark began to grow, its black grew blacker,
Spaceless space grew thick, and timeless time grew long
With pregnant waiting; then the outer darkness spoke.
There are no words to tell the nature of that voice;
It was the deep reverberation of the waves
Whose clang and throb and weaving rhythms form the cosmos
Of existence on the surface of the Dark Abyss.
No tongue of speaking creatures bore those words,
No mind of sentient entity their message wrought,
And yet I understood their meaning all to well
And what they told of life and black infinitude
And why the words were spoken and *by whom* . . .

Since then

I shun the darkling gulfs and dream of nothing save
A campfire in a desert on a dying world.

* * *

I sat and listened to the night-wind's keening
     Until a worldly dawning bore me from that place
But one day in the waking world I saw again
     The oldest dreamer's lined and shadow-haunted face;
     They said he was a poet who had dreamed of space
And written tales of wonder till some horror stilled his pen
And brought an end to dreaming.

The Barrett Horror

I.

In the void he slept alone; as the primordial dust clouds gathered he drowsed and dreamed; when the sun and the planets were formed he woke to frightful consciousness and that consciousness was Ngyr-Khorath. And the living things that walked the earth were never alone and unnoticed, for he watched them with implacable wrath. He waits and probes for weakness in the forces that guard us; where his all-destroying wholeness cannot enter comes his emissary and extension, the shadowy thing of many shapes which is 'Ymnar. And where the forces weaken, the evil of Ngyr-Khorath filters through the veil to destroy, to slay, to seize men's very minds . . .

—*Gualterus Vasconium*

1.   Excerpt from *The Truth Behind the Barrett Horror*:
       The First Victim.

It was a tribute to the state of law and order in Barrett, Texas that Barbara Koehler and Lisa Eckhart were walking up Crockett Avenue at all. The street is narrow and poorly lit and at 1:05 a. m. it was quite deserted. From the Travis Theater, where they were employed as usherettes they could have reached Miss Eckhart's car almost as quickly by walking down brightly lit Broad Street, turning right along well-patrolled Cañon Avenue, then doubling back a hundred yards up First Street to the parking lot. But street crime is not yet common in Barrett, and the girls thought nothing of climbing a steep and blackened side street to save two minutes. A block and a half up Crockett in front of Stern's Jewelry Store, Miss Koehler stopped to retie the lace of her left shoe. They both disliked the high heels they were required to wear at the theater and always changed shoes before going home. The habit undoubtedly saved Miss Koehler's life and possibly Miss Eckhart's.

As Miss Koehler knelt, Miss Eckhart turned and saw the man behind her in the shadowy doorway. Afterward the newspaper accounts used the hackneyed word 'crouched,' but in her interview with the police she was more specific. He was squatting with his elbows on his knees. He was resting flat on his heels. She is quite certain about this point because she saw the man shift onto the balls of his feet in order to spring at Miss Koehler. He covered the full nine feet between them with one leap, landing with his fingernails on her shoulder blades and his teeth on the right side of her neck. The teeth inflicted superficial wounds, by which the police surgeon identified the assailant as an adult male of below average size. Contrary to some of the more sensational reports the teeth were in no way abnormal, and though some accounts have described the man as snarling, both Miss Koehler and

Miss Eckhart agree that he made no sound.

As Barbara jumped to her feet his fingernails raked her back, making deep scratches and tearing the top of her low-cut blouse. He made no effort to grab the handbag slung over her left shoulder. She began to run west, up the hill, while Lisa ran north across the street then east toward the lights of Broad Street. The assailant followed Miss Koehler. He seemed to have trouble finding his feet; in fact the whole incident suggests clumsiness and lack of coordination. All accounts of the Barrett horror have stressed the progressive brutality and gruesomeness of the crimes, yet none has pointed out the equally obvious progression from crude brutishness to diabolically skillful butchery. Miss Koehler's escape was almost comic. She angled out between two parking meters into the street; the fiend of Barrett ran into the first meter full tilt and went sprawling onto the pavement. She doubled back down the hill after her friend. By the time they reached Broad Street and found a police car the man had disappeared.

In most large cities the abortive attack on Barbara Koehler would have attracted little notice. The police would have classified it as an attempted mugging and the newspapers would have given it at best a few lines just ahead of the sports page. But in Barrett the story was assigned to page one. After the two women were interviewed, the story was expanded to a column and a half and the Barrett Horror began.

2.   Howard Grey:
       August 25.

The 5:30 bus arrived early that day and Carl's assistant wasn't there to meet me yet, so I bought a Barrett paper and sat down to wait. The waiting room was dirty and smelled of old cigarette butts, and the paper was as interesting as the directions on a can of soup. I noticed a story about an attack on two women the night before but didn't read it, not then. I was too preoccupied with my irritation at Carl, it was so like him to insist that I come halfway across the country to help him and not even come to meet me himself. And of course there was no real 'Barrett Horror' yet, just a trumped-up newspaper version of an attempted street robbery. When the assistant arrived he proved to be a thin pale wolf-faced youth of less than medium height, though still taller than Carl. After introducing himself as Johnny Venable he lapsed into monosyllables. He wore jeans and walked with a sort of drugstore cowboy swagger. I found him amusing because I had predicted to myself what sort of assistant Carl would have and had been dead right: Carl wasn't comfortable around tall men (my own six-two annoyed him terribly), no one with any personality could avoid clashes or tolerate his domineering for very long, and he wouldn't want anyone intelligent enough to understand the implications and hazards of what he was doing. In fact, he was so secretive that I had no clear idea what he was up to, other than that it involved proof of a real basis for the Mlandoth myths.

Johnny was silent after we got into Carl's dusty station wagon. The seedy downtown area just north of the river was small, but in rush hour traffic it still took too long to get out of it. The streets hadn't been improved much since the violent frontier times when the scattered limestone and yellow brick relics were new. I didn't like Barrett, having left it in disgrace after a ruined academic career, and opined that the area had gone steadily downhill since the Texans took it away from the Comanche and Tonkawa. It must have been beautiful before that, with the broad Colorado River winding placidly out of the hill country into the lush coastal plain. It looked better after we crossed the bridge and turned west along the river bank into an area of old tree-shaded homes on spacious grounds. But I still would have voted to give it back to the Indians, or even to the Cretaceous ichthyosaurs who swam above while the seas deposited the stone of the hills.

As the river broadened into an arm of lake Bowie the homes grew larger and the lush yards grew into good-sized estates. The road curved inland along a low bluff while the land below us on the right became a flat alluvial plain bordering the lake, thickly forested. Finally we descended through a cut in the bluff, drove about a mile through the trees to the edge of the lake and pulled up in front of a fine old two-and-a-half-story Victorian relic facing the water. Carl had certainly found the seclusion he wanted; on this side of the lake there wasn't another house in sight.

Johnny led me through the oval-paned door and deposited me in the living room to the left while he went to get Carl. I sat down in a plush armchair and saw a cloud of dust motes catch the lamplight.

"Good to see you, Howard," said Carl as he charged through the door. "Glad you could come." His short barrel-chested figure and pop-eyed look had a way of dominating a room. He was twenty-eight and looked younger with his hair down over his collar. "I suppose you haven't eaten?"

"No, but that can wait. What's this project I've come seven hundred miles to assist you with?"

"As you will. Have some coffee, anyway." It was unlike him to be solicitous of guests; he was amusing himself by teasing my curiosity. The project must be really good.

"Coffee will be fine, thanks. Black." I tried not to give him any satisfaction. While he was out of the room a tall girl with stringy blond hair and a tie-dyed shift wandered into the room and murmured, "Hello." Carl reappeared with the coffee and introduced her as Cindy Blankenship. She had vacant blue eyes and a full figure, going soft but not fat yet.

"She's a telepathic sensitive. Johnny's an electrician." He mused, hoping I would ask the obvious question, then went on. "I was using mechanical hypnosis to enhance extrasensory faculties. At first I used simple rotating discs with geometrical patterns on them. Then I added a strobe light. Never a trance state, just strong suggestion while fully conscious. I soon found that I could get impressive scores identifying symbols on cards, good enough to rule out luck anyway. I had rented a house by a small college in West Texas and hired a series of students to help me test myself, and of course I tested them too. That's how I discovered Cindy.

"Her first tests were amazing, nearly eighty per cent correct in tests where random chance would account for only twenty. After a while she dropped down to about forty, probably from the boredom of repetition. But I could raise her scores again temporarily by changing details of the routine to put some novelty in them without altering the twenty per cent random probability.

"In the course of devising minor novelties I discovered that some figures on the rotating wheel got much better results than others. Symmetrical figures worked best, especially with slow rotation. A basic four-point symmetry seemed to be important. I also found that the frequency of the strobe light was important and guessed that synchronizing the light with the subject's brain waves might prove interesting.

"The breakthrough came when I used a simplified version of an ancient Indian mandala, a symbol of mystical completeness. The first day she scored one hundred per cent, even reporting details of the appearance of the cards accurately. I had been building a device to deal the cards mechanically so that she could call them before I saw them and tested it for the first time that day; she couldn't call the cards unless I saw them. It was telepathy rather than ESP.

"The next day was a crashing disappointment. She began with some mediocre scores, complaining of a vague feeling of uneasiness and apprehension. She mentioned a sort of blue-green mist which seemed to interpose itself between her mind and the cards. Eventually her scores dropped to random chance. I tried the tests myself; I saw the same mist and felt the same creepy sensation.

"At that point something rang a bell in my memory. I recalled something from the *Chronicles of Thrang* about the use of moving symbols and lights for magical purposes. I had a Xerox copy of Braithwaite's partial translation with me and soon found what I was after. It was a technique obscure, even to the wizards of ancient Ngarathoe who had written that portion of the *Chronicles*, a method of unknown origin which had been tried only by a few ill-regarded men of those eon-distant times. It involved a ritual with a large complex design on a rotating table, a converted potter's wheel no doubt, which was moved in a peculiar rhythm. There were colored candles placed at certain points of the design, and it was necessary to keep them in a flickering condition; the rate of the flickering was said to be of critical importance. It all fitted in beautifully with what I was doing.

"But the exciting thing was the purpose of the ritual. The object was communication with a being not of this earth. I know you're familiar with the Mlandoth myth cycle, Howard. You know of Ngyr-Khorath, the evil non-material entity that inhabited this region of space before the solar system was formed and hated all matter and life. Consciousness was not its natural state, however, and after the coming of the planets it was slow to awaken. By the time Earth life had evolved sufficiently to arouse it to action, the creature known as Paighon had come from the great galaxy in Andromeda and established itself deep within the earth. Paighon was able to keep Ngyr-Khorath at bay and protect the planets and the evolving life forms of earth. But Ngyr-Khorath lurks eternally in the void, seeking to penetrate the mysterious forces controlled by Paighon and his spawn.

"Unable to break in by main force, he resorted to subversion, contacting aberrant individuals on earth and persuading them to work for his end. Direct communication was difficult and hazardous owing to the alien nature of Ngyr-Khorath's consciousness and life force, but from time to time it was achieved."

My eyebrows went up.

"I thought direct contact was supposed to be impossible," I said, "and the attempt extremely dangerous. I know von Könnenberg said so in his *Uralte Schrecken*."

"So he did, and so do most of the more recent works that touch on the Mlandoth cycle. But they're just parroting old legends. The oldest source, the *Chronicles*, says clearly that it was done." He was very deliberate and consciously relaxed, his bright button eyes level and steady like a chess master making a decisive move. He had known that this would be the crux, inducing me to accept the risk of exposing a human mind to an awesomely potent alien sentience. "Dangerous, yes, but possible," he went on. "That's where you come in, Howard. We are near the greatest breakthrough in the history of human knowledge. There's no doubt that we can do it. And will. We have the mandala the Ngarathans used. We aren't certain of the pattern of motion, but we're experimenting and getting close; and Johnny's built a device to synchronize both the lights and the mandala movement with the subject's brainwaves, something the Ngarathans could never have managed. But the passage in the *Chronicles* that discusses the details, and the results and dangers, isn't available in translation. They have a copy of the original here at the university, and we need you to translate it. Or we continue to work in the dark, and risk the consequences."

Checkmate; I almost laughed. He knew how much a brilliant success in Barrett would mean to me, and he had crafted the perfect appeal to reckless curiosity, caution and my love of elder lore.

"Count me in," I said. "Where do I start?"

"You might want to go over the material I've collected on Ngyr-Khorath in English, it's all upstairs. I think I have just about everything that's been translated. It will give you something to do while Johnny gets the equipment set up for the test run tonight. If the brainwave synchronization works, we can program the motion and alter the mandala to correspond to anything new that you come up with, and I'd like for you to see what we've done before you start translating. That way you'll have a better idea what to look for. But first let's have some food."

The food turned out to be cold sandwiches and canned soup prepared by Cindy. I tried not to imagine the condition of the kitchen, she didn't look like the fastidious type. While we ate, Carl monopolized the conversation with an ostentatious technical harangue with Johnny, who replied with his usual monosyllables; I suppose he didn't want to give me a chance to bring up the subject of hazards. I wolfed down the food as quickly as I could and followed Carl's directions to the upstairs bedroom that had been prepared for me. The reading material he had gathered on Ngyr-Khorath was arranged neatly on a table by the window.

I skipped all of the modern secondary sources on mythology and the occult. I was familiar with most of them and they contained only rehashes of the material in von Könnenberg. His *Uralte Schrecken* was there in the 1903 English version, but Carl had also obtained a priceless copy of the 1832 German original, which he couldn't read. I picked up the latter.

Through the ponderous Teutonic sentences I followed the primordial horror of the thing of neither matter nor energy as we know them, a vortex of primal life force itself, one of an inconceivable number born of the struggle or interaction between Mlandoth and the Cosmic Mother at the beginning of time. Alone it slept in darkness and empty space until the sun and the Earth coalesced. The new presence of concentrated matter was an irritant, but the thing had been slow to wake. By the time it was sufficiently aroused to react a life form potent enough to hold it at bay had settled within the now cooling Earth. After the Earth's crust hardened, intelligent space-wandering races came to colonize the new world and the telepathic babble of conscious thought intensified his irritation to cosmic rage.

It was unclear whether domination and control were satisfactory substitutes for destruction of the intruding life, or whether they were intended as preliminaries to ultimate annihilation. In any event Ngyr-Khorath began to make contact with the races inhabiting the Earth and attempted to recruit them to serve his ends. Direct contact, whether physical or telepathic, proved unworkable, resulting in physical or at least psychic destruction. The life force of Ngyr-Khorath was too destructive, his consciousness too hideously alien. Thus he created a sort of organ or projection or fragment of himself in the image of the chemical life forms typical of Earthlike planets throughout the universe, the entity known in elder lore as 'Ymnar.

'Ymnar appeared to earthly creatures in a form similar to their own, though capable of changing his shape to resemble almost anything. This latter ability caused von Könnenberg, and others before him, to speculate that 'Ymnar's material form might be merely illusion. The mind of 'Ymnar was sufficiently Earth-like to employ speech and other methods of symbolic communication, thus insulating the Earth-creatures from the maelstrom of Ngyr-Khorath's sentience. By promising power, knowledge or whatever a race or creature most craved, or by subtly stirring powerful emotions of awe, fear or megalomaniacal lust he drew individuals and even entire races into the service of Ngyr-Khorath. Just before the evolution of life native to Earth, he had succeeded in controlling life upon the surface through an oceanic race called the Rloedha, who succeeded in destroying or driving off all other races present at that time.

But the Rloedhan race eventually proved to be an inadequate tool. Von Könnenberg and his predecessors didn't have the scientific knowledge to describe what happened clearly, but I guessed that the Rloedha were dependent on the complex organic substances which theoretically existed in the oceans before the evolution of native Earth life. These substances were, in fact, the material from which Earth life evolved, but once terrestrial organisms began to reproduce, they multiplied and scavenged all organic substances present in the seas. The terrestrial microorganisms mutated and developed the ability to synthesize what they needed from mineral substances. The complex Rloedha could not. They became dormant or died, though there have been hints that they could revive under certain circumstances.

As the native life of Earth grew complex and sentient, 'Ymnar attempted to corrupt it. But von Könnenberg's accounts of this were unreliable, being based on faulty translations of ancient human texts. Fortunately Carl had a copy of Braithwaite's excellent unpublished translation of the *Texts of Mloeng*. I didn't get to read in it that night, because just then Johnny knocked and announced that the equipment was ready for a test. His eyes were more alive than before and he had a sly half smile as though at some private joke; I found out this was his standard expression when he had done something clever with the equipment.

While I was reading I had heard sounds in the room below me, so I wasn't surprised when he led me there. It was a room about twenty feet square, papered in a dark old-fashioned pattern and fitted with heavy black curtains, even in the only window overlooking the lake. The only pieces of furniture were four chairs, the spindly kind with padded seats and curved armrests, spaced evenly around the wheel in the center. Carl and Cindy were sitting in two adjacent chairs talking in low voices and ignored me at first, while Johnny fiddled with the knobs on a rack of heavy electrical parts next to the empty chair to Cindy's left. She was worried about the green mist with its feeling of mounting terror and Carl was reassuring her, trying to keep her calm.

The wheel was a wooden disc three feet wide, lying flat like a table. There were electrical cords running from under it to Johnny's apparatus. It was painted black with a design in white, in general outline a curved swastika like two S's crossed, but formed of much intertwining filigree. Within each curved arm was a different letter of the Ngarathan alphabet. I thought this odd because the Ngarathans generally used older prehuman glyphs in their ritual magic. Set in the center of each letter and passing through to the underside of the wheel was a black tube surmounted by a small colored bulb, red, green, blue and yellow at the four arms of the design.

After a few minutes Johnny declared the apparatus ready and Carl placed a narrow band around Cindy's head. To it were attached two small electrodes which pressed against her temples and a bundle of very thin wires which hung down over the back of her chair and ran over to the equipment rack. Johnny sat down in the chair next to the rack where he could reach the knobs. Carl asked me to turn out the overhead light at the switch by the door. After an instant of darkness the small colored bulbs on the mandala came on with a steady glow. Carl got up and took the chair opposite Cindy, leaving me the chair to her right. He explained that formerly, with only three people present, he had sat next to her for symmetry, but with four he preferred to be able to watch her face without turning his head.

He told everyone to relax and watch the lights; we were to clear our minds and think of nothing else. Cindy would try to describe her sensations as well as she could without disturbing her concentration; otherwise only Carl would speak, giving Johnny instructions if necessary and questioning Cindy. I thought he sounded pompous. I was staring fixedly at the red light in front of me and had lost track of what he was saying when I heard the click of a toggle switch and the lights began to flicker; another click and they began to move.

They moved in a bizarre compound pattern, moving back and forth with an asymmetrical rhythm, gradually drifting around clockwise. I found my eyes had a tendency to follow the red bulb around. We watched in silence for what seemed like hours before I first saw the green mist. Though awareness came suddenly, I had the feeling it had grown gradually in my mind. It reminded me more than anything else of the retinal images that persist after looking at a bright light, except that it didn't move with my eyes. With it came a feeling of profound dread, welling up in me like a wave of nausea; at the time I thought this might be imaginary, brought on by Carl's prior description. The color was very intense and lucid, a deep blue-green. It was in the mind, overlaying the scene before me and when I concentrated on it the room vanished momentarily. It grew more vivid when I stared at the red light, most intense when the red light was near me. It also seemed to fade in and out as the rate of flickering varied slightly, presumably getting stronger when Cindy's brain wave frequency was near my own. I had been aware of it for about five minutes when

Cindy began to speak of it.

She was terrified and rather incoherent, but it was clear that we were seeing the same thing. The patch of color was roughly circular with ill-defined edges and had grown until it filled the whole field of mental view. Both Cindy and I saw detail in it near the end, faint dark markings and tiny bright specks with an impression of swirling motion. Carl said later that he did not see this, though the circle of green was plain. Johnny never saw any of it.

I saw the red spot in the center before Cindy did. At first I wasn't sure of it. I thought it might be a persistent retinal image of the red bulb. Carl asked Cindy if there was any sense of direction associated with the cloud and she said it seemed to be coming from her right; about that time she became almost hysterical and raved of an 'eye of flame' rushing toward her. Carl was trying to calm her when the lights went out. Johnny said "damn," followed by a steady stream of equally unimaginative obscenities as he moved to the overhead light switch and turned to check out the equipment.

Carl was trying to get Cindy calmed down and apparently didn't think it wise to question her then about what she had seen. I had a headache and could see that there would be no more tests that night, so after being ignored for fifteen minutes I slipped out the door and went up to bed.

II.

> *But while there are many good passes through these mountains travelers usually follow the river around them, though it is a week's journey longer, because of the terrible men who dwell there, who are called the Katheroi. These men were once as Greeks, but fell under the spell of a strange god of the sky whom they call Gir-Chorath. It is said that they call upon him with strange rites, and that when the stars are right his spirit comes down upon them and they become as savages and even as wild beasts and know not their own souls . . .*

—The Lost Book of Herodotus

1.   The Second Victim.

The sun was not quite above the horizon as Juan Morales walked to work along River Street at 6:00 a. m. on August 26. Though there was a light mist from the river, he could see clearly as far as the bridge ahead and to his left. The maze of warehouses, rail spurs and alleys on his right between River Street and Cañon Avenue was not noted for neatness, and a large dark object of indeterminate shape on that side of the street would not have attracted his attention. But the area on his left between the street and the water was maintained as a public park with well-cropped grass and a scattering of small trees, and the object was quite noticeable. Still, he would probably not have bothered to investigate it if he had not been early for work at the Cunningham Furniture Warehouse. He stopped, lit a cigarette and walked down the grassy embankment.

He had not recognized the shape of the object because the body of Jeannette Hagerty lay on its side facing away toward the river with the knees drawn up in front, and her head had been smashed almost flat. As the cigarette dropped from his nerveless fingers and he stepped back, he was unaware that his left heel, as the subsequent police investigation showed, kicked the murder weapon; the blood-clotted enigma which makes the case one of the most bizarre in the annals of crime. It was a flint hand-axe of Middle Acheulean pattern, a weapon common a quarter of a million years ago.

It is a sinister thing. Some of the more optimistic experts believe that the hand-axe was an innocuous general-purpose tool, but one cannot but suspect that in the dawn of man it was often used for exactly the sort of operation performed on Miss Hagerty.

The Barrett specimen is a flat piece of flint, an inch thick, five inches long, in profile shaped like a rather pointed egg. Viewed edge-on the sharp cutting edges are curved in an S-twist, a characteristic of the Middle Acheulean style. It had been fashioned with great skill using what archaeologists call the cylinder hammer technique, in which thin flakes are struck off with a round object of wood or bone. Stripping off the weathered outer surface had exposed the unweathered inner part of the flint, leading a geologist from the university to conclude that it had been shaped within a day of the murder; perhaps only hours before.

The police did not accept blindly the theory of an irrational murder by a complete stranger. They explored Jeannette's personal background meticulously for motives. She was twenty years old, a short girl with auburn hair and a well-padded but attractive figure. She had come to Barrett two years earlier as a university student, dropping out after two semesters. She had remained in Barrett, circulating in the 'hippy' community and holding a series of waitress jobs. The Barrett police, who are recruited primarily from the rural 'redneck' class, had a field day harassing the various 'longhairs' she had known, without turning up anything of interest. The night of the murder she had been at Armadillo Heaven, a rock club with a light show and no liquor license. There had been an argument with her current boyfriend (subsequently cleared by a polygraph test) and she had left alone at 1:15 a. m.

The most direct route from Armadillo Heaven to her seedy one-room apartment ran along Cañon Avenue. It is hardly a cheerful street in the small hours, but reasonably well lit and certainly more inviting than the blackened warehouse district which lay on her right. There is no evidence to indicate why she turned down some gloomy side street and headed for the river. It is unlikely that she was lured by curiosity; anything unusual in the shadows would probably have scared her off. And to chase her that way her pursuer would have had to come from her left, exposing himself to the lights of Cañon Avenue. Possibly she simply decided to cut over for a walk along the river.

By the time she was halfway to River Street she was running. The testimony of Ernest Freeman has been largely discounted; he admits that he was sleeping off a half gallon of wine in an alley that night, and that he only half roused from a drunken stupor. But his account is consistent with the known facts. He saw a woman running through the murk toward the river. He says she made no sound. I find this credible because she knew there was little chance of summoning help in this neighborhood, and she needed all of her breath; she was running for her life. Freeman saw the thing behind her as a moving shadow, sometimes running erect, sometimes in a crouching lope, at times apparently descending on all fours, freeman sat against a wall, sweating and wondering in the dark for a while before passing out again. And on the grassy river bank Jeannette Hagerty died, horribly.

The police formed no conclusions about the killer's route of escape. He had to have been drenched with blood and it is hard to believe that he could have been behaving normally immediately after the bloody debacle. Yet the warehouse quarter is bounded on three sides by wide, well-lit streets where cars and pedestrians pass every few minutes throughout the night. It is of course *possible* that he escaped this way, but it is not likely. The police first assumed that he must have remained in the district or on the fringes of it and searched literally every inch. They found nothing suspicious. In particular they found no bloodstains; not a single one. I think this makes it almost certain that he never even crossed River Street.

A few hundred yards west of where Jeannette Hagerty died is the main bridge across the river. There is a pedestrian walk across it; a blood-soaked maniac would surely have been seen crossing it, but he could have come from that way before the murder. And he could have swum back. On the south bank opposite the park is a wide divided road lit by vapor lamps. But west of the bridge is an older residential area where the bank is quite dark, and there are no obstacles to a man making his way along it. It is unfortunate that the police never examined the south bank of the river.

    2.   Interlude:
              A Half-Awakening.

. . . a dream, a nightmare, so clear, yet swiftly fading . . . must hold it, hold the dream . . . Fading . . . won't remember . . .

    3.   Howard Grey,
              August 26.

It was almost noon when I woke up. I went to the window and stood looking out over the lake, waiting for the fog to clear out of my brain. I felt washed out, fatigued by the long trip (I can never sleep on a bus) and the high-tension excitement of the night before. I dressed and went down to the kitchen, which was even worse than I expected. I settled for toast and coffee.

Afterwards I found Johnny in the mandala room working on the electrical apparatus. He said Carl was out buying parts. The stupid smirk he wore told me he had found the trouble and we would be able to test again that night. There was no sign of Cindy; later Carl told me she never got up before two in the afternoon.

I was on my third cup of coffee when Carl showed up. He looked more excited and smug than ever. After carrying some cartons in to Johnny, he cornered me with an incomprehensible explanation of the problem with the equipment. I doubt if he understood what he was saying much better than I did; my mind kept wandering. I am not normally an imaginative person but somehow all the bustle and keen excitement seemed far away and hollow; it was like watching people playing a game on a ship about to strike an iceberg. I broke away and went upstairs to tackle the books again.

I picked up the *Texts of Mloeng*. Though scorned by the professional scholars of the academic community, the work has been well-authenticated by more open-minded investigators. Mloeng was a realm in what is now Asia Minor, populated by men of the Neanderthal race who called themselves the Wafakhar. Mloeng was the name given it by its destroyers, the Ngarathans; its own people had no name for the nation.

With knowledge obtained from 'Ymnar, they built a civilization which was supreme in its time. They seem to have been a naturally unambitious and non-aggressive people, and 'Ymnar was unable to induce the race as a whole to use the magical technology he gave them against other Earth life or against Paighon and his subterranean spawn. Knowledge and contact with 'Ymnar were rigorously limited to a small hierarchy of sorcerer-priests.

This situation led a few abnormally ambitious individuals outside the hierarchy to attempt to communicate directly with Ngyr-Khorath. Quite possibly 'Ymnar instigated this for his own obscure reasons, connected with his dissatisfaction with the unambitious hierarchs. The accounts of these attempts were disappointingly sketchy, but the priests of Mloeng seemed to assume that controlled communication was indeed possible and that, if successful, would lead to great and dangerous power. But it was never successfully achieved; those who attempted it generally went mad. One aspirant is said to have been consumed with supernatural flame.

The rigid centralization of power and knowledge, concentrated in the hands of a small priesthood eventually led to the Wafakhar's downfall. Shortly after the last ice age, Mloeng was attacked by a less advanced non-Neanderthal people from the east. The barbaric ancestors of the Ngarathans, known in the *Texts* as 'the Naked Scourge,' were at first routed by eerie forces which they personified as gods and demons, but they soon learned that they could easily defeat the Wafakhar in battle as long as they avoided a direct confrontation with a high priest.

In a millennium-long war of attrition, recorded with great pathos in the *Texts*, the great Wafakhar empire eroded and shrank to the very walls of Belegyr, its capital city. The *Texts of Mloeng* end at that point, for of the Wafakhar, none survived to tell of the city's fall.

When the Ngarathans became civilized enough to keep historical records, they added their accounts to a composite work known as the *Chronicles of Thrang*, whose earliest portions came down from fabulous prehuman antiquity. The massive text is extant in the Ngarathan language, but no complete translation has ever been made into a modern tongue. Carl didn't have a copy but I had seen the chapters dealing with earliest Ngarathan history, and I knew that the doom of Belegyr was mentioned but not described. That chapter consists of oral traditions written down centuries after the events, but even that is not enough to explain its vagueness; evidently the end of Belegyr was too horrible even for the bloodthirsty Ngarathans. The one thing that is certain is that Belegyr was destroyed from within. Possibly 'Ymnar turned against the Wafakhar in favor of more promising pupils.

Eventually the Ngarathans learned much about the gods of Mlandoth from the

Texts of Mloeng and the prehuman portions of the *Chronicles of Thrang*, but while individuals often dealt with 'Ymnar and learned much from him, he never succeeded in bringing the whole of Ngarathoe under his sway. Throughout its long and turbulent history political power and organization above the city-state level remained militaristic rather than the theocratic and while the constantly warring nobles, kings and emperors courted the powerful wizards as allies, no wizard ever controlled any large group of people.

The wizards for their part never developed any scientific understanding of the powers derived from ancient wisdom and unholy intercourse with things from the void, and never tried to reduce their potent resources to techniques usable by other than advanced mystical adepts. If they had, the subsequent history of the planet might have been radically different; a Ngarathoe united in the service of Ngyr-Khorath could well have been the terminal chapter.

I knew most of this from previous reading; all Carl had of the voluminous *Chronicles* was a Xerox copy of a fragment typed in English. I don't know who translated it, but it wasn't Braithwaite, though he was known to have been working on a translation of the *Chronicles* when was murdered in New England, because the text had been rendered into rather awkward English and Braithwaite would never have done that. There were also some grammatical twists that had an un-Ngarathan look even in translation, and made me suspect faulty interpretation. I guessed Carl had been hoaxed into paying an exorbitant price for an amateurish piece of work.

This excerpt was much more explicit about the phenomenon of contact than the *Texts* had been. After the fall of Belegyr the tribal wise men of the Ngarathans captured and learned to read the *Texts of Mloeng* and also obtained, from some unknown source, the already existing portions of the *Chronicles of Thrang*. Within a few generations the traditional sages became powerful wizards, vying for supremacy in occult power. 'Ymnar was present and furtively active, but the wizards of Ngarathoe were aware of his destructive goals and dealt with him cautiously; for his part 'Ymnar cunningly limited the power and knowledge he passed on. Bargaining with 'Ymnar came to be known as tricky and dangerous business; it may have been the ultimate source of our own folklore of 'deals with the devil.'

Thus 'Ymnar never achieved the power he sought and no wizard was ever entirely satisfied with the knowledge and power he obtained. A few of the most ambitious ones seized upon the legend or rumor that direct contact with Ngyr-Khorath could infuse one with miraculous power. There was a method handed down from Mloeng involving an alkaloid herb, but this led only to hideous death. Later however another method began to spread slowly among the secretive sorcerers, leaving a trail of terror and madness among those who dared to attempt it; the method of the *dlith pygon* or 'wheel of flame.'

The *Chronicles of Thrang* recounted many tales of these attempts. Some aspirants simply went raving mad, babbling of a menacing blood-red eye; some were found dead with looks of monstrous fear frozen on their features; a few perished in flame (not surprising if they wore loose robes near candles) and Ngaph the Sinister was found in his tower in Balthon Throl with his eyes and brain burned away. But apparently a few had made some sort of contact and remained alive and sane, at least in a relative sense. Of these the scribes of Ngarathoe had written with horror.

They gave no details, but it was clear that they had become a menace and been destroyed, usually assassinated by servants or close colleagues. Oenokh the Star-Mad 'was set upon in the night by Tliretha his mistress and murdered, his body torn limb from limb and left to the jackals.'

However, I was suspicious of the entire passage discussing these attempts; it intermittently lapsed into language much smoother than most of the rendition as though the translator had made deletions and improvised to provide continuity.

Carl's useful resources pretty well ended there. It was still early in the afternoon, so I decided to have a go at the university library. Carl loaned me the key to the station wagon. I took an attaché case full of writing materials and stopped off for a sandwich along the way. The former proved optimistic and the latter providential; the Texas educational establishment wasn't going to yield up its treasures in an hour.

The campus was a hodge-podge of concrete boxes, each in a different 'style' and jammed together into a sort of intellectual slum. The students too were polyglot, scruffy hippies beside fanatic-looking engineers with calculators hanging from their belts, well on their way to their first ulcer. There was no unified personality to the place, no tradition, probably no coherent policy or control. The thought of their formidable collection of occult and antediluvian volumes, windows on lost eons and keys to outer forces, made me think of a hydrogen bomb in the hands of savages.

I began in the tower building, a twenty-five story dungeon topped by a ridiculous pseudo-classical thing which, it turned out, contained an out-of-tune carillon. The main library was there and a card file reassured me that one of the seven existing copies of the *Chronicles of Thrang* was there. It and the other two million books were, however, defended by an effeminate young man with a nasal voice who briefed me on the special problems of non-student non-Texas resident scholars who wished access to it. I visited five buildings, spent three hours in anterooms waiting for interviews with various undesirables, told an ingenious variety of lies, filled out thirteen forms and posted over ninety dollars in deposits before I got back to him. He had one last bureaucratic quibble; I was grimly pursuing the most awesome book in existence, to use its ancient knowledge for an experiment which could lead to hideous disaster or the greatest revelation in several millennia, and this limp-wristed dolt was babbling about a 'Building-Use Fee.' I was considering throttling him when he finally gave in. I could see the book. Tomorrow. The library was closing for the day. I had to laugh; Carl's weird household was beginning to seem a haven of sanity.

Back at the house I opened the oval-paned door and was confronted with a reek of burning insulation. In the mandala room Johnny was no longer smirking, he was perspiring and his eyes were bulging as he frantically switched wires and prodded things with the probes of a little meter. Carl was in a state of righteous indignation and started simultaneously lecturing me on the perfidy of electrical parts dealers, one of whom had given him the wrong transformer or a defective one, and giving technical advice, which just made Johnny's eyes bulge more.

I retreated to the kitchen and made a sandwich. There was a newspaper on the table: I suppose Carl had picked it up. The death of Jeannette Hagerty was all over the front page. While I ate and read in the living room Cindy wandered in and asked if I wanted to go swimming. I started to demur for lack of a suit but I remembered a pair of walking shorts in my suitcase and it had been miserably hot all day. After I changed she led the way to a pretty little cove a few hundred yards down the shoreline. When she took off her robe it turned out she didn't believe in suits. I was embarrassed at my own inhibition.

The lake water was just cool enough to feel better than the summer air and I floated and did lazy breast strokes. The cove was a semicircle in a little limestone outcrop detached from the main cliffs by the road. There were nodules of gray flint in the tan walls of the cove and a scattering of black fragments where one of them had been smashed.

After a while we both sent ashore and stretched out on a flat shelf of rock there to dry out. I lay facing out across the lake looking at the twinkling lights of the houseboats and apartment houses along the far shore, mainly to avoid embarrassing myself by staring at Cindy. It was 8:30 and getting dark and we soon went in. I had a headache, probably sinus this time from the murky lake water. I could hear Johnny and Carl tinkering with the equipment in the mandala room, and judged from the tones of their voices that they weren't making much progress, so I went upstairs and to bed.

III.

1.   The Third Victim.

The afternoon paper for August 26 carried a very detailed account of the Hagerty murder. It caused a great stir in town, many chain bolts were purchased and quite a bit of pistol ammunition, letters were written to the editor of the paper and to the chief of police. And the downtown area was absolutely deserted on the night of August 26-27. But there was no hysteria, as yet no one suspected that most terrifying of all criminals, the psychotic who kills at random till he is stopped.

While the downtown area was empty except for an unusual number of patrol cars there was no effect at all on the region west of it. There, along where a steep hill rose from the edge of the lake, the area was heavily populated, brightly lit and often very busy at all hours of the day and night. This was an area where most of the old homes had been bought out long ago. There were now modern apartment buildings, big old houses converted into rentals and a few houses owned by the very wealthy who could afford to live both right on the water and practically downtown. In past times the residences bad been built all the way down to the river and many houses stood partly on pilings extending out over the water. The more picturesque of these had survived and been renovated. One of them was owned by a prominent state senator and throughout that summer it was inhabited by his daughter and three friends. It was Friday night and they were having a party.

Houses of that vintage are much sought after these days because they were designed to be comfortable without air conditioning. The senator's house was fitted with window units but they were not in use that night; all windows and doors were open to let in the night air. It was the only house built entirely on stilts above the water and had to be reached by a fifty foot walkway. It was painted dark green and flanked on both sides by private marinas. The dark color may have been important to the occurrence that night, as we shall see.

The house was a small specimen, high and narrow, from the turn of the century when gingerbread and long covered porches were fashionable. This one had a porch running around three sides of the ground floor, one running the width of the second floor lake side and three smaller unconnected balconies on the dormered third floor where the murder took place.

It was a very lively party of wealthy students from the fraternity-sorority set and the first floor of the building was crowded and brightly lit, including the first floor porch, from six in the evening on. Guests swam in the water off the house, in a few cases fully clothed. Not far away the lake bottom dropped off rapidly, but it was only six feet deep around the house. The second floor, reached by a staircase in the center of the house, contained the only bathroom and several spare bedrooms which were used for coats, and perhaps romance, that night. There was no constant crowd on the second floor but there was constant traffic up and down the stairs. It is absolutely impossible that anyone not a member of the party could have passed that way unnoticed. The third floor was all bedrooms; the bedroom on the northeast corner, facing the shore and one marina, was used by Mary Ann Morse, who was destined to be the third victim of the fiend of Barrett.

By a little after twelve o'clock Mary Ann had overindulged in frozen Daiquiris and had gone up to her room to lay down. About 1:30 a. m. she was seen coming out into the hall and heading for the bathroom. By 4 a. m. twenty-one-year-old Rodney Weinberger had had enough of the party and went up to the second floor, where he had left his sport coat earlier. The party had quieted down to isolated and desultory conversations and he heard the ceiling creak above him in Mary Ann's room. He glanced upward. There was a spreading stain on the paper on the ceiling, dark red. He immediately thought of red wine.

There bad been a lot of it at the party. But the thing was still somehow disturbing. He went quietly out into the hall; he heard the floor creak again. He went upstairs to see if Mary Ann was sick.

He saw no one on the stairs or in the third floor hallway. There was a light on in Mary Ann's room and the door was ajar. He looked in and saw what lay on the bed, then rushed down the hall to the screen door which opened onto the small balcony overlooking the water. He was certain that the screen door was unlatched at that time. When he leaned over the rail of the balcony, very, very sick, he says he saw nothing in the water below. But remember that it was very dark, except for bright spots where the lights from the house and the other buildings illuminated the water. As soon as he was able to control his stomach he went back down stairs and called the police.

The remains of Mary Ann Morse lay face up on the bed. The throat had been cut and the coroner considered this to be the cause of death. It must have happened very quickly, because no one heard a scream. The abdomen had been partly opened and most of the organs of the abdominal cavity carefully removed. Certain organs were missing. The murder weapon lay on the bed beside the victim's right leg, half in a pool of clotted blood. It was a carefully made flint knife with a straight sharp edge on one side, and a deliberately flattened surface on the other, by which finger pressure could be exerted comfortably. It was only about three inches long. It was not polished but it had been very carefully chipped into shape and was still quite sharp, even after the sustained use that night.

The blood spot had dripped down onto the floor after the bed itself had become soaked. The dissection must have taken some time. Is it possible that Mary Ann was still alive at the time Rodney heard the floor creak from below? There were people standing near the stairs on the second floor at the time Rodney went up, and it is also impossible that anyone came back down by this route. The creaking floor was undoubtedly the movement of the murderer. It is quite certain that he escaped from the building in the few seconds between the time Rodney heard the creaking and the time he got to the top of the stairs. Later the comings and goings of all of the guests at the party were fully accounted for. The unofficial police opinion was that one of them was the murderer because they cannot believe that anyone could get in and out of the house unseen. However, it is inconceivable that the murderer could avoid being splashed with blood from head to toe, and it is also inconceivable that anyone could have descended the stairs in that condition without being noticed. There were no bathrooms on the third floor, and no way for anyone to get clean even if there were time. There was, however, a drainpipe from the rain gutter which rises up the side of the building next to the third floor balcony, the only one which the first floor porch does not reach.

This writer has seen it. It is not particularly strong, but experiments show that it is possible for a man to climb such a pipe if he does it slowly, carefully and smoothly with no sudden or jerky movements, and with no force exerted away from the wall. The pipe goes directly down to within a foot of where the water level was that night, and rises up the wall between the window to Mary Ann's room on the right and the balcony on the left. The window screen was latched when the police arrived. In addition there were no tracks or blood at the window. The balcony passes about five feet from the drain pipe. It would not be too difficult for a reasonably athletic person to get from the pipe to the balcony but I believe it would take the strength of a madman to climb the thing silently in the dark.

But no one could have descended the pipe between the time Rodney heard the floor creak above him in Mary Ann's room and the time he went out on the balcony. He would surely have seen anyone climbing down at that time. The police reject the idea that anyone escaped this way on the grounds that if he had jumped, the splash would have been too noisy and would have been heard and if he had dived into six feet of water he would have broken his neck. However, it is possible to dive this way.

I believe that someone swam up to the house in the dark, on the side toward the balcony where there was no stairs, and saw the light in Mary Ann's room. He climbed the pipe gently, with the strength and stealth of a hunting animal. Perhaps he reached out silently to the window to see if it could be opened. Then he reached out the other way, grasped the railing of the balcony and climbed over in silence and entered. I think this must have happened while Mary Ann was down stairs in the second floor bathroom around 1:30, and that he was waiting behind the door when she returned. This is the only way to explain the lack of any scream. At 4 o'clock, having finished his work, he heard Rodney coming up the stairs, padded out into the hallway and onto the balcony and dove into the water, parting the water cleanly and curving to miss the muddy bottom and swimming away as silently as he had come. Terror spread through the city of Barrett.

2.   Interlude:
              A Realization.

. . . real, the dreams were real . . . I killed them . . . can't stop, they'll catch me sooner or later . . . but now I have the power, to terrify, to kill . . . no one suspects, they are stupid, foolish little creatures . . . He comes, so terrible, so beautiful, I am he . . . He stirs the ancient feelings . . . the flints, must hide the flints where I made the knife . . . will I remember this time? . . . will I remember?

3.   Howard Grey:
              August 27.

I slept very late that morning and woke up tired. Carl and Cindy were still asleep when I got downstairs and Johnny was smirking again. I headed out for the library and picked up breakfast and a newspaper along the way. The murder was all over the front page.

Even with classes not in session I had to park a mile away. It was a long walk to the tower library in the stifling summer heat and it did nothing for my concentration.

The books of interest to me were all in a special section of the rare book card index. The selection shown in the index was tempting but I started directly with their copy of the *Chronicles of Thrang*. I filled out a card and asked to see it. I also requested the inadequate but helpful dictionary compiled by Laszlo from Braithwaite's notes. I had brought Carl's copy of Braithwaite's partial translation with me. After a forty-five minute wait they brought me the dictionary and a clumsily bound photocopy of the *Chronicles* and informed me that I would have to read them in a special corner of the reading room and that I would not be allowed to make any Xeroxes from them.

There was no identifying information on the *Chronicles* but I recognized the copy Flannery brought back from Greenland in 1912. I carried the books into the reading room, a high-ceilinged cavern of reinforced concrete made to look like stone. The drafty air conditioning felt good after the heat outside.

There was of course no translation or footnotes or concordance with the copy, so I had to try to remember or guess the order of things in the huge book and translate a couple of sentences on a page to see where I was. The earliest non-human portions were the most difficult to read. The book had been originated by the 'Ithria, a shadowy race about which little can be deduced. They arrived on earth three billion years ago, the first material race to do so. Their time-sense was so different from ours that it is difficult to extract their meaning even through the literal parallel inscriptions of their successors, the Dhraion Throl. Prefacing the history of their own tenure on Earth was a distillation of cosmic lore handed down from race to race from the beginning of life in the universe.

Indeed sentience had been present at the primal explosion which began the universe, for it had separated from a former unity with the dark Yidh Nak or 'Mother of Space' from radiant Mlandoth and their struggle to reunite created innumerable vortices of matter, energy, life force, and other more subtle quantities in all combinations to fill the cosmos with immortal things alive and, in many cases, sentient. One of these was Ngyr-Khorath.

Alone in empty space his condition resembled sleep, but long before the arrival of the 'Ithria the dust of space had swarmed together to form the solar system, and the nuclear force-creature Paighon had settled here, and Ngyr-Khorath was awake with an infinitely patient and horrible rage. The exact conditions of their struggle and their effect on life on Earth were too difficult for even the 'Ithria to comprehend. But they came to know of the sinister *presence* that came in the night when the planets lay in certain positions before the stars, and seized certain among them and killed them in fearful ways or sent them ravaging like mad beasts that must be destroyed.

The Dhraion Throl were a small dark-skinned anthropomorphic race who arrived half a billion years after the emigration of the 'Ithria. With their intense passion for knowledge they found and deciphered the copies of the *Chronicles* carefully stored in Antarctica by the 'Ithria and built their own Earthly annals on it. Near the end of the Pre-Cambrian Age they developed a limited ability to travel in time, and mapped the history of the Earth forward through the Paleozoic as far as the time when a race of crystalline spider-like creatures came from a distant galaxy.

They communicated with patterns of color running through their legs and left records in long narrow hieroglyphs. They wrote of many eerie presences on Earth, strange descendents of the struggle between Paighon and Ngyr-Khorath like the *Ta Svani* or Black Eddies which were bound to one place but could seep into the soul of one who came near and seize control of him for malignant purposes. But above all, they feared Ngyr-Khorath himself, who periodically corrupted a few of their number and sent them murderously berserk.

The next additions to the *Chronicles* were made eighty million years later in Australia, by men who had been adopted by a race from a passing interstellar planet, Wu'unaya, first as pets and then as servants. When their mentors left they had already produced a few dozen men capable of founding a civilization and preserving the ability to read the records unearthed by the aliens in Antarctica. It is not known how the document traveled to Asia Minor where it appears among the Ngarathans long after the demise of the Australian Ngkuliibong civilization.

The Ngarathans were one among many civilizations which flourished in the wake of the last ice age, before a dark age of unknown cause descended on the Earth: they wrote of their battles with the agile horsemen of Mong, their intercourse with the evil men of Hsia to the east and the mysterious empire of Qam to the south, the terrors of the African rat-masters of Ppkung and the wonders of distant cities like Stera, Sperap, Dera . . . relics of far older cultures. Their portion of the *Chronicles* is much easier to read, and I soon spotted the passage containing the anecdote about Oenokh the Star-Mad.

I immediately saw the error that had been made in Carl's bootleg translation. Oenokh had not been set upon by Tliretha, he had set upon or attacked her. Where

Carl's copy said 'torn limb from limb' the text here used a verb which means 'separated' or 'cut,' as with a knife. Concerning Oenokh's behavior the scribe had used a peculiar phrase, translating literally as 'ancient force' which meant something like animal instinct, suggesting that Oenokh had been overcome by atavistic impulse.

A horrible thought began to grow in my mind.

I continued to turn the pages looking for the mandala diagram. There it was, identical with the one in Carl's copy. When I looked at the text I spotted another error. The translator of Carl's copy had translated the word *ploatna* as 'rotating,' indicating that the disc should rotate. This was a likely mistake because it had the form of a gerund, but was just an emphatic form of the word *plo,* 'round,' sometimes used to mean 'circular.' So the wheel should not rotate. The letters of the Ngarathan syllabary at four points of the diagram were also there as in Carl's copy with no explanation in the text. They were 'a, ba, dy, and 'e. I thought a minute. Of course—'alan, band, dy, 'egor—north, south, east and west. The wheel should not rotate but should be properly aligned with the four points of the compass. The red candle should go at the north.

And here were two sentences completely omitted from Carl's copy. The first said: 'Only in the north is the way opened.' The second said that the persons sitting at the other points feel only the fear of Ngyr-Khorath and for them the way remains closed. Johnny was going to be very disappointed. It must have been a lot of work to make the wheel do its little crabwise rhythmic dance, around the circle.

It had taken me several hours to get this far and I must have been getting tired because I suddenly felt dizzy looking at the mandala. I looked up to see a very tall man in a dark suit and tie standing by my side.

"Good afternoon," he said. "I noticed you looking at the *Chronicles of Thrang.* I was curious, Ngarathan scholars are extremely rare." He had very fair skin with dark eyes and hair and high brows. It was a comic book face, very simple and smooth and striking, all straight lines and bold contrasts. I felt a little flustered. I hadn't anticipated being accosted like this and had no cover story prepared. I tried to think fast.

"Yes," I said. "I got interested in it years ago in college, and learned it gradually over time. I think it's a marvelous addition to human folklore and legend."

"It's a pleasure to meet a fellow enthusiast. How do you do, my name is Theodore Ramny. I see you are reading at the page where the *dlith pygon* is described."

"Yes, it and the stories surrounding it interest me very much. It seems to me to bear a close resemblance to the sort of mandala that appears in Indian and early Indo-Aryan symbolism, and was discussed in such a fascinating way by Jung."

He started translating at sight from the page in front of me in an odd toneless voice, the inflections as neat and precise as those of a ham actor. I felt myself getting dizzier, I had been sitting down too long and still hadn't recuperated from the long bus ride.

At this point the librarian descended upon us like an effeminate hornet and shushed us, adding that the library would close in five minutes. Ramny suggested that we go to the campus coffee shop together. On the way we talked about the Ngarathan language and the *Chronicles.* He said he had the Trieste copy, which is less complete but more legible than the one in the library, and invited me to his home to consult it.

When we arrived at the coffee shop we found that it was closed because classes were not in session and the coffee shop was keeping short hours. He offered to drive me to his house and then drop me back by my car later. He led me out of the building and removed a thing that looked like a transistor radio from his coat pocket and pressed a button. We strolled to the curb at the large street that bordered the campus. I was amazed to see a long black limousine with a liveried chauffeur pull up in front of us. The car was long and low and quiet and I lost track of the route as the chauffeur whisked us out of the university area with its old run-down houses converted to rooms for students through the suburbs and then on up toward the top of one of the hills that crowd in on three sides of the city.

Ramny was still making conversation, talking about various manuscripts of the *Chronicles* very accurately. I was still feeling dizzy at times and still groping with the connection between the mandala and Ngyr-Khorath, Oenokh and atavism, flint knives and Mary Ann Morse. As we climbed the hill the houses showed more custom architecture and more money. They were arranged from bottom to top in a hierarchy of wealth.

The house we pulled up in front of was at the top. It was not enormous, but the brick and ivy look and the terrace and the heavy paneled door and the circular driveway all said 'rich.' There were two lithe guard dogs slinking around in the shrubbery. Ramny led me inside and turned left off a corridor into a room with ceilings twelve feet high with bookshelves almost to the top. There was something wrong about the room. It took me a moment to put my finger on it; there were no knick knacks sitting around anywhere, no cherished oddments sitting on the bookshelves, no pictures, no ash trays. It was an impersonal room.

Ramny brought the book immediately and I was amazed to see that it was the original manuscript found in Trieste. I had assumed he would have some sort of copy. He got the book from a locked cabinet full of books and scrolls. I would give much to know exactly what was in that cabinet. Of course I had to handle the incredibly old document before me with the utmost care and it took a long time to find anything in it. No one knows what the material is, it seems to be some sort of fiber other than ordinary wood pulp or papyrus that lasts longer. As I searched Ramny was talking about the danger of attempting to contact Ngyr-Khorath with the *dlith pygon*.

"Altogether, it would seem much better to deal with 'Ymnar," he said.

I tried to play dumb.

"It doesn't make sense," I said. "Why all the rigmarole? If Ngyr-Khorath wants Earth creatures to deal with 'Ymnar, why answer the summons of the *dlith pygon* ritual?"

He smiled slightly.

"You see, Ngyr-Khorath's mind works at a vastly slower rate than ours and is much greater and less unified. Only the specialized fragment of it that is 'Ymnar can operate at approximately our pace. The fire wheel and other direct methods attract the psychic center of Ngyr-Khorath's consciousness in a sort of reflex or tropism much more rapidly than he can reach what we would consider a reasoned decision.

And while theoretically this sudden invasion of primal life force could result in union, in practice it always . . . ," he hesitated slightly, ". . . works out badly."

"Yes, but how is one to find 'Ymnar?" I said. "There is no explanation in any of the books."

"That's true. Perhaps he will come to you," he said. His dark eyes were bright and still.

"And isn't he supposed to be pretty tricky to deal with? I'd probably get outsmarted."

"I think that's just a matter of misunderstanding. Ngyr-Khorath wants only union with sentient life, he rejects only chaotic and destructively fragmented sentiences."

I didn't like his tone. He was beginning to sound like some kind of fanatic devil-worshipper. I found the mandala in his copy much more easily than I had in the library. I knew about where it came in the text and when I searched that portion the pages came open to that page of their own accord, as though that had been the last page consulted by other hands. The passage was in better shape than in the library, more legible. Undoubtedly the way was to be opened at the north. Who had been sitting north at Carl's? I have a poor sense of direction and had no idea how things had been oriented there.

"Yes, but don't men want to preserve their own identity and freedom?"

"Their fate is to be enslaved by their own kind anyway." He abruptly changed the subject. "Where are you staying? The hotels here are dreadful."

"I have friends here who are putting me up," I said.

"Fellow scholars? I didn't know of anyone who knew of Mlandoth here."

"My cousin." Could he be pumping me? "My cousin Carl knows something of it, but he's hardly a scholar." True enough.

"Does he live near the university library? It's so hard to park in that area."

I saw no reason to lie, but felt reluctant to tell him more. I made some vague reference to the lake and started avoiding all specifics about the household. I was feeling dizzy again and at times his face seemed to blur or fade, leaving only the phosphorescent depths of his eyes. I caught myself staring fixedly. He returned to the subject of 'Ymnar.

"But the direct methods," he said, "with the wheel of fire or the oil of the black lotus, are much more dangerous. You read of Oenokh the Star-Mad. Ngyr-Khorath seized his brain and body and, operating through the ancient savage instincts, caused him to run amok in his own household and cut his mistress Tliretha to pieces with a ceremonial knife."

I needed to break away and get out of there.

"I realize it's all very dangerous," I said, "and I take it seriously enough not to try to do anything like that. I really must go now, Carl will be looking for me and they will have supper prepared." Fat chance.

"My chauffeur can drive you," he said. "You don't mind if I don't accompany you?"

He led me out past the guard dogs and the luxuriantly planted foliage, and instructed the chauffeur to drop me off where he had picked us up. As we wound our way down the hill, I had a magnificent view of the city below. The sun had set behind us and the lights were coming on all over the big buildings in the downtown area and the sprawl of suburbs to the north. On my right to the south the broad dark river swelled into Lake Bowie. I tried to make out Carl's house along the far curve but the shore was blurred by a mystical haze in the dusk. Was it my imagination or was there a green glow in the eastern sky where Jupiter would soon rise? There were strange flashes going on in my mind, where instantaneously the city would recede and grow dim and the great glowing green cloud in the east, in the sky or in my mind, would grow more prominent. I never saw the red spot though. Who was Ramny? If he spelled it R-A-M-N-Y it would be an anagram of 'Ymnar . . .

Was that the original Trieste copy? I mused about what we were doing and my adventure with Ramny, and what I had found out about the method of the wheel of fire. Who had sat north? There was the lake shore—I couldn't quite figure it out. The line of the shore was erratic. That was when I first accepted the fact of a connection between what we were doing and the killings. I felt a sense of dread.

IV.

1.   The Fourth Victim.

North of the shoreline where Mary Ann Morse died, a hill rises precipitously from the water. The top of the hill is an extensive plateau of shady streets, magnificent old oaks and old but well-kept houses built shortly after the turn of the twentieth century. They are generally quite large, and in many an extra room or two is rented out to a student. Some have had additional rooms built on just for this purpose. Twenty-year-old Sheila Koch lived in such a room. The Barker house at 4111 Goliad Street was a three story frame structure clad in white clapboards. Rentals had long been the sole source of income for the last of the Barkers, seventy-year-old Miss Emma, and on the night Sheila died no fewer than nine students had rooms there.

In the 1920's a garage had been added along the left side of the house, sixty feet down the straight driveway from the street. In 1953 Miss Emma had another rent room built over it. It was a small but pleasant room, with windows on three sides and a private entrance via an exterior stairway at the back, out of sight of the street. At two a . m. on the morning of August 28 the windows were glowing. Sheila was drinking black coffee and cramming for a rescheduled final exam, which she had postponed in her summer Spanish course. No doubt she got up and walked around the room from time to time to stretch.

One can usually find students walking the sidewalks at any time of day or night. The killer's approach to the Barker house is a mystery only if one assumes, as the police and the people of Barrett did, that he had the same brutish appearance and behavior that terrified Barbara Koehler three days before. But I have pointed out the progression from crude savagery to more sophisticated violence. It is reasonable to suppose that as he approached the Barker house he appeared quite normal and simply walked down the sidewalk.

He may have been seen. George Pollock, a student, was walking down Goliad Street on his way to an all-night hamburger stand at about ten minutes to two. He passed a man in the shadowy stretch just south of the Barker house. The man was walking slowly and normally, and all George remembers is that the man was taller walter c. debill, jnr.

than he and was carrying a small shapeless bundle under his left arm. George is five-foot six. As George continued down the street the man reached the driveway leading to Sheila's room. Perhaps Sheila was moving about the room; he would have seen the silhouette of a woman pass by her window.

... is she alone? ... wait a while and see ... oh yes, they'll catch me soon, but not now, not now ... catch me when you can ... how can they catch a god? ... there she is again ... no sound, surely she's alone ... Jupiter burns, it burns, and the green storm is upon me, the eye fills me with power! ... have to send them something to chew on, I'll write a letter to the police—maybe I'll even send them a little souvenir, perhaps an ear ...

"Who's there?"

"Police, ma'am. Just like to ask you a few Questions."

The physical evidence tells us much more about the murderer's actions here than in the previous killings. He grabbed Sheila from the front, just inside the door, placing a hand over her mouth and bruising her lips. They scuffled, disarranging the little throw rug in front of the door. He turned her around without allowing her to make a sound loud enough to arouse the inhabitants of the house, three of whom were awake. He cut her throat from the rear, holding the knife in his right hand and cutting from left to right, and held her up until her violent twitching had ceased. The knife was at least six inches long and extremely sharp; it could not possibly have been made of stone.

He then lay the body down gently (no loud thump was heard in the main house) and calmly stepped to the wash basin and cleansed his hands. He would have gotten some blood on his clothes during the killing, but not necessarily very much. Next he returned to the landing outside the door and picked up the bundle George Pollock had noticed. It was a cheap white laboratory smock.

He closed the door, put it on, and carried the body to the bed. After cutting off the blood-soaked clothing completely, he began a systematic dissection resembling standard autopsy procedures. He opened the abdomen and thorax with what is called a butterfly incision, and in the hour and a half before he was interrupted he emptied the body cavity almost completely, laying the organs neatly on the bed, the small table, and the desk.

The ovaries were never found. The cuts were all very neat and carefully executed except for the rather clumsy removal of both ears. These were also never found.

At 3:30 a. m. he heard someone climbing the outside stair. Ann Elroy, a roomer in the main house and a friend of Sheila's, had been up reading and, hearing movement in Sheila's room, had come around to suggest stepping out for fresh air and coffee. She heard indistinct sounds from within the room as she knocked softly several times and called Sheila's name.

At the first sound on the stairs the killer froze. Then he leaned forward and quickly removed the ears. We may speculate that he placed them in a small plastic bag brought for the purpose. Then he calmly removed the blood-spattered smock and dropped it across Sheila's feet. The window at the rear of the room was already up. He unhooked the screen, lifted it off its hinges, and drew it into the room. He stepped up onto the windowsill and jumped out.

Ann heard the thud as he hit the ground, making indentations in the lawn and smearing the grass with traces of blood. She felt fear; she called Sheila's name twice more, while the killer walked between the houses behind the Barker place. Then she leaned out to the left over the railing, peered through the side window and screamed.

Sixty feet away the killer carefully wiped his shoes on the grass before stepping onto the sidewalk. Four feet from the place where he wiped his feet, a tiny blood stain on the concrete tells us that he headed toward the lake.

2.   Howard Grey:
           August 28.

I was going to say "What the hell is all this racket at 5 a. m. when I'm trying to sleep?" when I stalked into the mandala room, but I didn't because I could see right off that Johnny was dead. He was lying on his back with one hand in the electrical apparatus; his eyes were bulging and his mouth was drawn into a ghoulish rictus. Carl's eyes were bulging too, and his mouth was open: he was standing over Johnny with his pasty face sweating profusely. He looked up at me, "He's dead, he's dead . . ." he said. "What are we going to do? He was fooling with the equipment . . ." I could smell burnt insulation mingled with burnt flesh. Carl started pacing around the room, he wasn't exactly wringing his hands but he didn't know what to do with them. "My god, if we call in the police . . . what could they charge us with? It was an accident, an accident . . . but we'd have to explain the equipment . . . the publicity . . . laughing stock . . ."

I sat down in my usual chair by the mandala. The wheel was sitting askew with the Ngarathan letter for north pointing at Johnny.

"Maybe we could cover it up," I said. Carl's eyes turned to me with a look of panicky hope.

"Cover it up?" he said.

"If we got rid of the body is there anyone who would look for him?"

"No, I don't think so, but then we really would be guilty of a   serious . . . committing a felony. What could we do with him?"

"You've got a whole goddamn lake within fifty feet of here," I said. "Are you sure no one would look for him?"

Carl put his hands on his head. I suppose he was trying to think. "No, he has a mother in . . . somewhere in town, but he hasn't been in contact with her since he met me. It's too dangerous," he said. He really was wringing his hands now, off and on. He stepped over and pulled back the curtains in the bay window and looked out at the lights of Barrett. "No, it's too dangerous. We'd be committing a *felony* . . . God, they'll search the house . . . What have we got? . . . . I think Cindy's got some grass. Where the hell is she? She went swimming a couple of hours ago."

3.   The Fifth Victim.

The skin of Cindy Blankenship showed that she had left the water only a few minutes before she died. She lay on a large bath towel on a flat rock by the water. Did she feel death in the black water under the starry void? Did she shiver in the night-wind? The lapping of the low ripples against the rock masked the sound of someone swimming up in the dark. Someone with a knife.

The cove in which her remains were found is lined with limestone slabs dotted with flint. It is undoubtedly the place where the weapons used on Jeannette Hagerty and Mary Ann Morse were manufactured. It lies at a point on the shoreline almost exactly opposite the house where Mary Ann died and, further inland, the Barker house.

The dissection of Cindy Blankenship was even more thorough than that of Sheila Koch, as though the killer were improving with practice. He used a stag-handled hunting knife, freshly honed to razor sharpness. The remnants were laid out neatly, diagrammatically, as one might pin the parts of a laboratory frog to a board. No organ was wholly missing, but several were damaged; the fiend of Barrett had indulged in cannibalism.

4.   Howard Grey:
       August 28 (continued).

"It might work," said Carl. "It just might work. But we don't have a boat. How could we get him out into the deep water?"

I stepped over to the window and looked out. A low clinging mist was curling up from the water, making the scattered lights of Barrett twinkle and dance. I could see Jupiter going down in the west.

"We weight him down with chains, bricks, anything heavy that we can tie to him," I said. "Do you have anything like that here?"

"I've got the snow chains I used out in West Texas," he said. He was calming down a little, looking at Johnny again. Poor Carl, the flamboyant one, the man of action. "Then we need something to float him out into the water—an inner tube, an inflatable raft, anything like that."

"I think Cindy's got an air mattress," he said. Jupiter going down in the west to my left . . . north. North would be across the lake toward Barrett, the way I was looking. My chair. I had been sitting north, of course. And I remembered Carl saying Johnny had sat there the night before I came, the night of the first attack, before the god came so near.

"I think she's got one," he said. "I saw her using an air mattress to sunbathe out in the water."

What a fat little neck you have, Carl.

"Would that be enough?" he said. "I didn't know you could swim so well." Jupiter in the west. I could see the green glow. "Afterwards, of course, we should clean everything up and leave quickly. We'll be hard to trace if he . . . he comes up. I'll get my lab coat."

I don't think you'll be wanting to use it, Carl. It's all bloody now.

I turned away from the window and walked slowly toward the wheel.

"We have to make sure there are no police boats around when we do it," I said. "I saw a few lights here and there on the water."

He stepped nervously over to the window and looked hard.

. . . I remember . . . the dreams were real . . . I killed them . . . when did I know? . . .
my mind, like a jigsaw puzzle, waiting for the last piece . . . I remember it all now . . .
the gaps, the puzzling dreams I couldn't quite remember, the dizziness, the disoriented
feeling, the headaches . . . and I remember the savage thing growing within me,
growing, leering, hating . . . making the killing tools in the ancient ways . . . I
remember them all, the rage, the blood, the ecstasy . . . then planning more and more,
knowing it all . . . the last ones, I knew then . . . in the little room up the stairs . . . I
was ONE . . . Howard and the savage thing and HE . . . I am HE now . . . I know the
microscopic room where the little man-thing looks out the window . . . I know the
hateful blue globe and the hateful yellow moon and the hideous roiling sun and the
cold soft space which they befoul which is HOME and the infinite void beyond which
cold and soft and empty but is not HOME and I know the microscopic room where
the little man thing . . .

I moved in quietly behind him. I had the knife in a scabbard in my belt behind
me.

V.   Excerpt from *The Truth Behind the Barrett Horror:*
        Epilogue.

The house by the lake was very old, the wood very dry. It burned completely to the
ground before the first fire truck arrived. In the confusion it was assumed to have
been deserted. No one even looked for bodies in the smoldering ash until the
remains of Cindy Blankenship were discovered. After that the ashes of the house
were sifted carefully, though the fire had been thorough that almost nothing was
found except the tell-tale odor of kerosene and the two charred bodies. There was
enough left of one to identify him as the Carl Thurlough who had leased the house,
and to determine that his throat had been cut to the bone. The other, presumed by
the police to be the fiend of Barrett, was never identified and the cause of death
never determined. In height, build, sex, and age he fit the description given by
Barbara Koehler.

The police theorize that he parked Thurlough's station wagon in the downtown
area, walked to the Barker house, then, probably because his clothes were stained
with blood, was afraid to go back to the brightly lit area where the station wagon
was parked. They believe that he started the fire and, either accidentally or
suicidally, was overcome by smoke.

But nothing is really known of the group in the old house. Could there have been
a third man? The station wagon was parked just two blocks from the bus station.

He Who Comes in the Noontime

I. The Coming of the Demon

Bernardo had been scratching at the hard desert soil with a pick and a shovel all morning and the top of the grave was now level with his eyes. This cursed desert was hard as stone, even the twisted mesquite beside the grave could penetrate no more than a few feet with its roots and lived stunted for lack of water. Since the spring had stopped the earth around the village had grown almost too hard to till. If water did not appear soon the entire village would scatter or face death from starvation.

He rested on his shovel and watched the stranger approaching from the east. Bernardo had watched the distant figure all morning, making an ant's progress across the sun-washed waste, until he disappeared in the midday heat mirage. Now he reappeared out of the formless shimmer and would soon arrive. Bernardo could see that he was very tall and wore dark clothing and a dark wide-brimmed hat. A Spanish gentleman, neither a priest nor a soldier. A little trade, perhaps a silver piece for Señor Vargas the trader and saloon-keeper. The horse was wildly spirited, dancing from side to side and tossing its head, raising such a plume of dust that Bernardo had thought a train of wagons was coming. It had an evil look, jittering mindlessly in the noonday heat. Bernardo traded the shovel for the pick and scratched the desert some more in front of his broad splayed feet.

He listened as the clopping unmistakably approached the side of the grave and stopped. Bernardo rose and looked at the stranger. He was impossibly tall and thin, with deep-set yellow eyes in the shade of the hat brim, deep and disturbing, reaching into the depths of hell. He was too frightening to look at directly; after the first moments Bernardo hardly saw a face at all.

And such a horse! Violent red-rimmed eyes tossing and rolling, muscles twitching beneath the glistening sable coat.

"Hard work," said a deep melodious voice in the Indian dialect of the village. Bernardo assented vigorously and cursed the desert and the dead spring, then ran out of words in mid-sentence and stared at those startling eyes.

"You shall have water," said the deep voice with the quality of an echo. The sun was squarely behind the stranger's head, dazzling Bernardo's eyes. He felt a cold sensation at his feet. The grave was filling up with water! It seeped out of the ground. Bernardo scrambled out on the side away from the horse and knelt staring at the stranger in terrified bewilderment. He stood up and backed away, his eyes darting from the filling grave to the stran-ger's yellow eyes to the horse and back to the grave again. His eyes opened, his mouth formed a large circle. He turned and ran.

He must tell Fray Marcos. He ran straight for the whitewashed chapel with the cross on top, his flapping sandals making little puffs of dust. He stopped. Perhaps it would be better to tell Bartolomeo, the *curandero*. This magic might have more to do with the ancient Indian religion than with the faith of Fray Marcos. But then his wife Aurelia would surely be angry with him if he did not tell her first. He looked from the church door to the door of his house and back again and licked his lips. Fray Marcos solved his problem by stepping out of the chapel. He was almost as tall as the stranger but not so dark, his lean ascetic face neatly mustachioed and bearded. "Water!" squeaked Bernardo, "Water in the grave! The stranger made water flow in the grave!" Fray Marcos's eyebrows came together in instant disapproval.

"Nonsense!" he said. "Miracles belong to the Lord!" and strode toward the grave with Bernardo shuffling worriedly behind.

The stranger had dismounted, his mount stood very still.

The priest's fierce disapproving eyes probed suspiciously at the bubbling water and at the lean figure standing beside the earthen rectangle. He did not flinch from looking directly at that face; he saw the features as lean and regular, more Indian than Spanish, the yellow eyes cat-like and luminous, unwavering and unblinking.

A shrill female voice yelled "Bernardo, you fool! Have you not finished the grave yet?" Bernardo's stout wife Aurelia popped out of the adobe house next to the church. It was one of the few dwellings in the village that was whitewashed like the chapel. "What are you doing, you lazy good-for-nothing?" she said, shaking her head back and forth and making her long pigtails fly. She stomped toward the group at the graveside, menacing Bernardo with her broom.

Curious faces emerged from the houses within easy earshot of the chapel and the grave, where those Indians most touched by Spain lived. Bernardo saw Juan the bricklayer, round and solid with his long mustaches. Life was very slow and simple in the village, and the passing of the stranger would be the day's entertainment, to be discussed for a week.

A crowd began to gather around the group at the grave. The murmur of discussion grew louder, and faces began to appear in the ancient brown pueblo beneath beetling cliffs along the little canyon behind the village. Fray Marcos was vigorously refuting everyone who attributed the water to the stranger, while Aurelia claimed the credit for herself for making her worthless husband dig the hole. The stranger remained silent. His glaring steed seemed to make the priest nervous. "Bernardo!" he ordered. "Take the gentleman's horse to the hostler!" Bernardo winced. He was reluctant to leave the scene of all the activity and even more reluctant to go near that fiendish horse. He grabbed the reins and padded toward Antonio's stables, avoiding the eyes of the horse and hoping it would not bite him. The horse pranced and looked amused.

Antonio's little horse barn was dark and stifling in the noonday heat. "Antonio, Antonio!" he called. Antonio was short and wiry with enormous ears and suspicious eyes. He stared at the horse and seemed not to see Bernardo at all. Those red eyes, how they rolled and flashed, how the black mane flew! Bernardo clutched the jerking reins with both hands. "A stranger has come, a demon! He made water flow in the grave!" Shimmering muscles under glinting sable, high-stepping razor-sharp ebony hooves. Bernardo let go of the reins but the horse did not run away. It continued to dance on the floor of the barn, raising its knees and snorting, showing its immense white teeth in the gloom. Antonio stood transfixed. "I must tell everyone," said Bernardo and jogged out of the barn. The horse stood still and stared hard straight at Antonio. Antonio shuddered.

There was no need to tell anyone; Bernardo could see half the village gathered in a great circle at the side of the mesquite tree and the remainder emerging from the pueblo to join them. He could hear his wife Aurelia bellowing and some kind of heated argument going on. He elbowed his way up to the front. Fray Marcos still stood by the grave with the village circled around him. The stranger stood in the shade of the mesquite. The sides of the grave were already coated with lush green lichens and ferns which stretched and curled to new lengths before his very eyes, writhing in the now half-filled grave. Aurelia stood with her fists on her ample hips and tossed her braids as she ranted at the priest. Fray Marcos was ordering Juan the bricklayer to start bricking up the well, saying the sides would cave in and make a mud hole. Aurelia was bellowing at him not to tamper with it. That fool Juan would close up the spring again!

Fray Marcos knelt at the side of the well, leaned down and reached his hand into the water and tasted it. "It's bitter," he said, "but drinkable." No one was listening to him. "It is not a grave until there is a corpse in it." Clods of earth fell from the end of the grave and plopped into the water. The black roots of the mesquite were reaching out, digging deeper, writhing with growth . . .

* * *

The rat crouched in the shadow by Inez's foot as she cleaned the earthenware dishes with sand and a little water. Its eyes glittered at Antonio who sat picking his teeth with a straw, not listening to Inez's chatter. Inez, short and plump in spite of the near-famine, was chattering cheerfully about the great benefits the stranger's magic would bring to the village. Antonio did not hear the words at all. He stared into space, hearing every stamp and snuffle of the stallion in the adjacent horse barn. At length he got up very quietly and stepped through the tattered burlap curtain that walled off the stable from the house, stepped so quietly that his wife continued to chatter to the rat and the empty room.

As dusk neared the stable was in deep shadow. He moved softly across the dirty straw floor. He was near the stall before he saw glint of light in the stallion's eyes. It flicked its ears and grimaced, baring its powerful white teeth. It tossed its head, rolling its eyes as though in anger. Antonio stopped picking his teeth, dropped the straw and walked out into the waning daylight.

It was the mellow time when the heat of the day had abated but the chill of night was not yet upon the village. The towering mesa to the west hid the sun and cast a long shadow into the desolate sand and scrub, the luminous sky above flawless except for Venus and a gibbous moon. He heard the sound of a guitar from the direction of the town square and the murmur of sound as the people bustled about, preparing a celebration. Everyone was turning out to celebrate the good fortune of the village, even the Indians who lived in the crumbling pueblo under the beetling cliffs. The little valley cut into the mesa, which provided natural protection and made it hard to see the village except from up close.

It had been very green and nice at times when there was enough water, but now it was getting too arid and was a place to die, not a place to live. And they feared that such water as they had was turning bad; everyone said Pablo had died of bad water. The Indians were coming out of the pueblo, the ones who attended mass faithfully, knowing neither Spanish nor Latin, and cherished their adopted Spanish names like magic talismans. Now the mood of the village was telling them to accept the stranger and the wet gift of the earth. And in the street just off the dusty pathetic plaza Irena the Apache slave-girl of the trader Vargas was strumming the guitar in the melodramatic style taught her by a soldier of gypsy extraction. She was singing in the Spanish tongue, of which she understood little. But the passion and profound sadness of the music were very real and she understood them perfectly. She had been captured from her nomadic band and sold to the fat drunkard Vargas, who often beat her but was almost always too drunk to molest her in other ways.

He ran an establishment which traded goods and liquor to travelers, and was the only one in the village who had any money. This evening he had already lit the candle-lanterns hanging on each side of the door which marked off the center of night life and good living to the traders, miners and soldiers who passed through the town. Fray Marcos deplored this, though in fact it was the main financial basis of the town and the only connection with Spanish world which gave Fray Marcos his influence over the Indians.

As usual Señor Vargas had been drunk for many hours by this time, and just now he came lurching out of the swinging doors of his saloon and announced that there would be free drinks for everyone tonight. He was followed by a grinning Angelo, Angelo who supplied Vargas with cheap liquor and beer made from cactus. He was smiling and twirling his long mustaches and after Vargas reeled back into the saloon he came up to Antonio bragging of the great profit he would make from the impromptu fiesta. He stopped twisting his mustaches when Antonio asked if he were sure Señor Vargas was going to pay him for the stuff.

Antonio passed the saloon into the plaza, which was just a wide dusty space in the center of the village with a few threadbare trees growing in the middle. The trees had been festooned with decorations of turkey feathers amid figured wool in bizarre imitation of Spanish custom, and some of the people had begun a joyful Indian dance in counterpoint to Irena's wailing flamenco tonality. Juan the bricklayer cornered Antonio and began to speak of his great commission to brick in the new well, gesturing with his hairy arms and flashing his gap-toothed grin. Could none of these people sense the abysmal evil of the demon? Antonio felt a black dread, as though the demonic inhabitants of the inner earth were emerging slowly and imperceptibly into every shadow.

Around the erstwhile grave was another group, staring in awe at the demon who stood shadowed beneath the tree with gleaming eyes. The hapless Bernardo came running out of his little adobe house propelled by Aurelia's broom and was immediately collared by Fray Marcos, who had been fussing about looking for someone to give orders to. Now he was after Bernardo to dig another grave, without delay. Fat Aurelia with her tight pigtails came out waving her broom and countermanded Fray Marcos and another argument ensued.

At the rear of the crowd of Indians staring in awe at the demon stood Bartolomeo, the *curandero* and archenemy of Fray Marcos. He was as tall as the priest and as square as Bernardo, with his hair very long and very straight. The

Indians showed great deference to him and stepped aside whenever he moved. They had been watching him all afternoon waiting for a pronouncement on the demon. They all felt that the demon was more a subject for Bartolomeo's wisdom than that of Fray Marcos. To Fray Marcos, evil and hell and demons were things very far away and abstract. To Bartolomeo and the Indians, they were concrete living things that hid in every shadow, every peculiar landmark, every strange quirk of the weather. A demon that rode into town on a horse at noon was definitely a matter for Bartolomeo.

A sudden hush spread through the crowd, leaving the argument between Fray Marcos and Aurelia in bright relief. Bartolomeo was walking slowly and purposefully toward the demon. The others edged out of his way. Bartolomeo knelt and recited an ancient prayer in the Indian tongue. The others began to dance and chant a low wailing melody.

Fray Marcos stopped arguing with Aurelia, saw what was happening and became furious. He turned and seized the lapels of Bernardo's smock and demanded a new grave in the name of the Lord. The demon stepped forward from the shade of the tree and said "But you will need no grave—here is Pablo now." And indeed here he was, stepping stiffly out of the house where he had died, mouth open in a loose-lipped fatuous smile, glazed eyes seeing only the demon. The crowd was instantly silent. "You will never need a grave for Pablo," said the demon. A fly lit on Pablo's left eye and he did not blink.

* * *

A scuttling tumbleweed blew past Irena and on into the opaque night outside the village, where the desert lay like the maw of some great devouring beast. One of the lanterns flanking the doors of Vargas's saloon had burned out and the other one was flickering as it clattered in the night wind. The light inside the saloon had just gone out and Irena figured Vargas had passed out. Suddenly Vargas lurched through the swinging doors and staggered out into the street, bumping into another tumbleweed. He was followed by Angelo, who was beaming because Señor Vargas had promised him much money for the night's liquor. Irena saw Vargas stagger up to a stiff standing figure and start babbling with jocose drunken animation. It looked like . . . yes, it was Pablo! He seemed to have forgotten that Pablo had been dead that morning. Pablo just grinned foolishly. He was a good listener now.

Confident that Vargas was too drunk to notice, Irena moved on into the torch-lit plaza. Most of the Indians were hunkered down there in small groups, some talking desultorily, most just waiting for something to happen. Irena could hear the raucous voice of Aurelia, the gravedigger's wife. Her husband Bernardo had joined a group of men to one side of the plaza doing a sullen-looking Indian dance. It was getting cold and windy and the torches were blowing toward the east, barely able to stay lit, and one caught only rarely the scent of pitch before it blew away into the desert.

Ordinarily they would all have gone home long ago, but Bartolomeo had spread the word that the demon expected them to wait with him until midnight for something to happen. They rarely stayed up so long past the setting of the sun but tonight their eyes were intent, gleaming with awe and fear and the intoxication of evil, as though something amazing and terrible were about to happen.

Fray Marcos had brought them only hard work and ritual and tales of wonders far away. The demon brought pulsating, living evil that froze the noonday sun and seasoned the bitter midnight wind with fires of hell. They were the chosen ones of the dark gods of yore, and they would thrive. When Bartolomeo hinted that the gods demanded more than ritual and obeisance, they did not flinch. Many travelers disappeared in the desert; most of them were bandits and murderers anyway. And there were even a few among the village people whom everyone would be well rid of.

Beyond the little plaza, Irena saw a group of the biggest and strongest men in the village clustered around the graveside where Bartolomeo carried on a low conversation with the demon. Bartolomeo was a much more attractive man than Vargas, she thought. Surely Vargas could not live much longer, the way he drank.

Fray Marcos had given up on dissuading the Indians from trafficking with the demon, and was off to one side praying loudly on his knees for their souls. His prayers were blown away by the wild night-wind. There would soon be a terrible sandstorm and they would all have to go into their houses whether the demon liked it or not.

The water in the grave was bubbling and would not sit still as water should. Behind Bartolomeo and the demon the horse, which had broken loose from Antonio's stable, was prancing and snorting, dashing first one way then another. Vargas, evidently tired of Pablo's conversation, staggered into the plaza and started wandering from group to group, raving sententiously in a hoarse voice like a feudal don talking to his peasants. Bartolomeo and the demon looked at him and spoke, so low that no one could hear. Bartolomeo stepped over to the group of husky men and dispatched Juan the bricklayer and an equally big strong fellow from the pueblo who walked over to Vargas and quiet stood on either side of him, nodding and smiling and replying to his drunken inanities. They were the only Indians who spoke to him. He seemed to enjoy their company.

A word from Bartolomeo and two others moved forward purposefully toward Fray Marcos. He stopped praying momentarily and stared at the two men. They reached down and seized his arms. He started praying again more loudly than ever. They led him toward the ancient kiva, a round sunken building just outside the village itself. In it the timeless Indian rites had been held in the days before Fray Marcos came. He had insisted that they destroy it and not go near it again. The top was fallen in and the floor covered with drifting said.

The singing of the dancers and such talk as was still going on were silenced. The demon mounted his horse and began to chant in a low chilling voice. As Fray Marcos disappeared from view into the kiva something strange began to happen in the sky, something mysterious and incomprehensible that caused most of the villagers to avert their eyes.

Señor Vargas had begun to realize that things were not as usual. He made nervous remarks to the two men beside him. They did not answer. He did not see what came out of the sky but when Fray Marcos's loud prayers changed into guttural screams, he stopped talking. While the screaming continued, Juan and the other man placed their hands on Señor Vargas's arms and escorted him toward the kiva, his eyes bulging, his mouth open. They crossed the little sandy ridge that had been the kiva wall and descended into the pit; when he saw what was inside his knees buckled and they hoisted him by the armpits and the seat of his pants and hustled him right along.

Sitting against a wall across the plaza, huddled under a blanket, Antonio the hostler watched Vargas disappear into the kiva and wondered how his friends and relatives could embrace evil so easily. They showed no consternation at the fate of Fray Marcos and could only snicker obscenely at the unmistakable sound when, cold sober and blubbering, Vargas emptied his bowels.

II. The Last Harlequin

It was four miles from Stephen's apartment on the lower slope of Barkley Hill to his destination in the old residential center of Barrett. But he hesitated only a moment before walking away from his car, and descended on foot into the golden dusk where the sunset poured over the city. His long quiet strides led him down to the tree-shaded depths as surely as his restless curiosity had led him into the unseen underworld of cults and quacks and mysteries and the sinister haunts of forgotten knowledge.

There had been many disappointments along the way, 'cults' of gullible neurotics fattening cynical swindlers, 'sorcerers' training affluent disciples in the preposterous recipes of fraudulent nineteenth century grimoires. Yet he had persevered. He had drifted among the wealthy neurotics and the amorphous pool of rootless young people who held low-grade university and government jobs and lived in the sprawling poorly-built apartment complexes spreading northward from central Barrett. He had contacted many groups of evil seekers, and eventually, among the thrill-seeking, the elaborate phony rituals, the claptrap and the quackery, he had detected a darker undercurrent of solid belief.

Until then, the occult had merely been one of many subjects that interested him. He had been interested in extrasensory perception, eastern mysticism, the bizarre theories of von Daniken and de Gautier. Most of these he had found believable but unproven, and possibly improvable. He had come to be much influenced in judging them by his impression of the people who believed in them. They had been generally ignorant, neurotic, or just plain gullible.

They were very erratic in their belief. One week they would argue for something with irrational fanaticism, and the next they would jeer at it as they hared off after some new foolishness. They sought constant reassurance that their current fad was the real thing, the ultimate trip.

Then he had met Ramon, the young lawyer, stolid, practical, downright unimaginative. He had met him at a meeting of a wild group of Satan worshippers who seemed to be primarily interested in exotic sexual practices. Ramon had noticed that Stephen too seemed uninterested in the Satanists' shenanigans and the two naturally drifted together. They shared their negative impressions of the meeting and Ramon hinted that there were much more credible groups active in the city. But then he had not seen Ramon again.

The next solid believer he had met was Brian O'Herlihy, a sober scholarly university professor whose conversation had revealed him to be a careful and skeptical thinker. He had mentioned Ramon, and he too hinted that something more interesting might exist in Barrett. He left Stephen feeling that he might be contacted.

His interest in other realms of intellectual adventure first faded, then disappeared altogether as the feeling grew that he was near to something real, something that did indeed transcend the dreary emptiness of everyday life. He even found it a little unsettling; a real possibility that his too-comfortable world might not be wholly predictable and stable after all. He approached obviously preposterous meetings with a haunted sense of adventure.

Ramny had approached him at a meeting of medieval alchemists. The alchemists were insipid academic types in threadbare blazers or pre-faded jeans, and after a long-winded speech by one of them, based on a faulty translation of Albertus Magnus, the meeting fragmented into small circles devoted to cheap red wine and the problems of obtaining snow-white cockerels. Stephen managed to drift out of this and was progressing toward the door when he was approached by a tall man in an expensive business suit.

He introduced himself as Niles Ramny, and seemed to have some knowledge of Stephen. He shared Stephen's scorn for the alchemists, and spoke of darker things beneath the surface of Barrett, difficult but not impossible of access. It was then that Stephen first heard the name of 'Ymnar. A week later he attended his first meeting of the group known as the 'Brujos Escondidos.'

The 'Hidden Witches' of Barrett met in a musty old warehouse in the poorest part of town. The huge high-windowed hall had been carefully cleaned up and furnished with a rough circle of wooden bleachers. In the center was a square marked at the corners with braziers of Indian pottery. The crowd was larger than he had seen at the other cults, mainly Chicano, mainly working class, mainly middle-aged or older. It reminded him more of a backwoods Protestant sect than a freakish cult. The only thing out of the ordinary about the crowd was a scattering of individuals who appeared to be on drugs. The others seemed to be at pains to avoid their glassy unwinking stares.

There was little conversation and most of it was in Spanish. He felt very much out of place as the late summer evening faded and the braziers were lit, filling the hall with the pungent scent of pitch. A steady rhythm of guitars, tambourines and crotala began. There was no formal opening of the ceremony. The crowd merely fell silent by degrees until all attention was focused on the flame-lit square.

The ceremony was very simple. There was no chanting, no liturgy, just two dark men in ironed khaki carrying two big rattlesnakes, both very dead, one stiff and curled into an 'S,' one still twitching spasmodically. They were laid in the center of the square.

The bearers stepped outside the square and hunkered down. An incredibly aged man in a feathered Indian headdress came slowly from the back of the warehouse to the edge of the square and intoned a sentence in a tongue not English and not Spanish. The twitching snake lay still, the stiff one relaxed and went limp. They both began to move and curl and coil and Stephen could see the tongues flickering and hear the burr of the rattles echo through the hall.

It was simple but effective. It had no rational appeal, he presumed it could have been easily faked. But no one there was looking for a rational justification. The symbol was enough. The messengers of the underworld had been dead; now they lived.

He attended a half dozen such meetings and gradually learned that the people shared a deep faith based on past miracles beyond common memory. They attended the meetings, they asked the snake bearers and the man in the headdress who were both *curanderos* (healers) and *brujos* (sorcerers) for favors of both black and white magic, and they generally felt a little more secure in the shadowy enigmatic universe. Simple faith was what was expected. Novices were chosen by Indian rites predating the coming of the Spaniards and there seemed to be no way for Stephen to advance in knowledge.

When Ramny began to show up regularly at the meetings, Stephen learned that the occasional educated man who joined the group was given a quite different treatment.

There was a hidden place far to the west which was the center of the cult. There one could penetrate to the core of dark matters. He hinted that it was time for Stephen to make a decision. He felt strongly that what he was involved in was something evil, though Ramny said that 'Ymnar was beyond good and evil. Why was he drawn to this? He was not antisocial, he had no desire to work against the human race. But he had found nothing in ordinary life to satisfy his need for something beyond the workaday world, beyond our limited conventional wisdom. This most strange adventure was the only window he had found into the fascination and excitement of the unknown cosmos. Of course, he would not blindly embrace evil. But should he turn his back on it or experiment and explore? Ramny sensed his finely balanced indecision, and suggested an interview with another party, outside the cult, who might help him reach a decision: the individual known as the Last Harlequin.

It was dark now, and he had reached the oldest residential section of the town, the old area of high narrow two and three story brick and stone mansions just west of the center of town. These had been the homes of the elite in the days before the new oil money and what remained of the old had moved up the hill and out along the south bank of the river. Now the broad sidewalks were cracked, the fine shade trees untrimmed and too luxurious, the houses in need of small repairs. Many of the first story windows were lettered to advertise hairdressers and boutiques, others sported a dozen or more mailboxes for students and drifters. Here and there remnants of wealthy families lived out reclusive lives behind drawn curtains.

He had heard rumors of a hidden figure in Barrett, a figure monstrously knowledgeable about ancient and occult lore. The Last Harlequin had seemed so distant and inaccessible, the specific facts about him so completely absent that Stephen had written it off long ago as a point of local folklore. But Ramny knew otherwise. Ramny had directed him to the door of this three-story limestone with its small-paned windows and turreted bay. It sat back a little from its neighbors, silent in the shadows and surrounded by a chest-high wrought iron fence.

Stephen hesitated a moment outside the unlatched gate. There were glints of light showing through the curtained lower-story windows. The top floor was even more heavily curtained and no light showed at all. He proceeded to the door, found the doorbell in the gloom and rang it. He heard muffled footsteps and the clatter of a chain bolt. The door was opened by a small round man with an unruly fringe of white hair around a bald dome and staring eyes.

"He is waiting for you," the man said. Stephen was led down a dimly lit hallway and up two flights of narrow stairs. The stairs ended in a waiting room with several chairs around the walls. "Please be seated," the man said. "Wait until you hear a knock on that door, then wait sixty seconds and enter."

Stephen sat down. A light rattle; then three sharp raps that seemed to strike low down on the door; then the rattle again. Stephen waited the prescribed time and opened it. The rattle had come from a bamboo curtain through which shone a muted kaleidoscope of colored light. He pushed through.

The light came from the ceiling, which was lined with glowing trapezoids all the colors of the rainbow, blanketing the walls and floor with motley. There was an odor like ozone and a faint harmony of low drones which changed slowly and subtly. He imagined some alien machine; then he realized that it was music. The floor and walls were tiled with a crystalline mosaic in intricate designs that changed when viewed from different angles. He found that all of the top floor interior walls had been removed and a system of baffles or partitions installed to make one labyrinthine room, which began as a winding maze. There was no furniture other than shelves on which lay books, scrolls and oddly shaped objects of unknown purpose.

The windows had been sealed to form illuminated alcoves. In the first one he came to was a flower of opalescent coral, moving in time with the music. After that, curious objects alternated in the alcoves with plaques showing a very striking three-dimensional picture. As he passed each one, three different views succeeded one another. Approaching the first one he saw a panorama of a city of small white cubicles spreading up a lushly forested hill between a lake and a high cliff. There were cubicles built into the larger trees. The streets thronged with tarsier-like creatures in richly colored tunics. One was walking a small many-toed horse on a leash.

As he came abreast of the plaque, the city disappeared and he saw the head of a giant carnosaur, eyes glaring, jaws gaping, frozen in combat like an antediluvian hunting trophy. Past the far side of the plaque, the scene shifted to a design of glowing hues against a living velvet black, like a spiral galaxy with gas clouds of pulsating color and myriads of supernovae flashing diamond sparks.

The maze ended in a large chamber empty except for a frozen fountain of fluorescent crystal. Beyond that was a darkened room, lit only by a few of the motley panels at the back. He saw a silhouetted shape like a man in a wheel chair. The voice was a shock—a rich fluting ultra soprano speaking forcefully in English accentless except for a tendency to rise away toward the ultrasonic on the last word of a sentence. Stephen's scalp prickled.

"You must forgive the lack of suitable furniture," the voice warbled. "I have few visitors, and my bodily needs are different from yours. You are Mr. Ramny's friend, Stephen McLeod?"

Stephen assented. He asked why he had come and what he wished to know, gradually eliciting the story of Ramny's intrusion into Stephen's occult doings. He told how he was on the verge of joining the group in earnest, but Ramny could not quite persuade him.

"I will persuade you of nothing," said the Harlequin. "As for the decision to join forces with that of which you have learned, either you know or you don't. It is that simple. No one can decide for you." He paused. "I am no friend of Mr. Ramny's," he added. The heart-shaped head bobbed up and down as he spoke and the hands seemed to be gesturing, though Stephen could not see then clearly in the colorful gloom.

Stephen was momentarily taken aback by the Harlequin's response, but he quickly realized how well Ramny had calculated; it was not a matter of convincing him that the cult was good, but that it was real, significant, potent. The testimony of an enemy would be much more convincing than that of a friend.

"How old is this cult?" Stephen asked.

"Not old at all. It began in the early seventeenth century when 'Ymnar contacted a tiny Indian village in New Mexico."

"And was that the beginning of 'Ymnar?"

"Oh no!" tittered the Last Harlequin. "When my people came from   . . . the Trifid Nebula one hundred and eighty million years ago, he was here. He stalked the life of earth like the shadow of a menacing predator. Life had conquered the sea and overflowed onto the land. The amphibians, bound to the shores and marshes by their reproductive processes, had begat the reptiles who could expand inland. To each in turn had come that stroke of lightning whereby evolution takes a hyperbolic curve to intelligence and civilization. We found the peaceful Sanafyil in their marshes more to our taste, though we felt that they were already at the wane, that they had lost the lust for survival and triumph."

"We knew that they would soon be replaced by the aggressive reptilian Khitasz, who were populating the inland areas. But we ourselves had a limited time left to us. And we thought the Sanafyil would last a few million years anyway, long enough to provide a haven for us. We provided no technological aid against the reptilian hordes, they lacked the will to use it effectively anyway, and the reptiles did not really wish to overrun the marshes, just to encroach upon them. We did help them improve the esthetic quality of their cities, and while the technology involved could easily have been turned to warfare, characteristically the thought never occurred to them. They used it to build great marble steps reaching down into the sea, on which they gathered and followed the low tide into the depths as they chanted to the full moon.

"When their inland neighbors began to augment fangs with stone weapons and communicate in the hissing tongue Ghah-Khag, their first reaction was to encourage them. The Sanafyil showed great optimism as the lizard-men used the culture they acquired from the amphibians for more and more destructive purposes.

"It was easy for a few of us to join the serpent people in the wild, raw continental interior as cautious councilors. We were aware of events in Ghah-Khag as well as in the cities of the Sanafyil. The wretched Khitasz actually thought of us as superior mentors rather than spies, and displayed a certain pragmatic loyalty to us. We were very careful not to contribute to their destructive capabilities.

"We sensed the presence of 'Ymnar at about the time we found the records of the crystalline spiders, whose long narrow hieroglyphics recorded much of the history of your planet for the ten million years before we arrived, and the tower inscriptions of Tzechio Tzunnuq in their desert fastness where the ruins left by the frog-like parthenogenetic women of the Silurian were disappearing beneath the sands. According to their records, he was created 2.6 billion years ago and has been quietly but relentlessly active ever since.

"Of course the native life of Earth was still at a bacterial level at that time— 'Ymnar was created to work with and against life forms that originated outside. There were already many pockets of strange consciousness in the savage inorganic landscape, not only the primordial sparks of consciousness torn loose in the initial clash between Ngyr-Khorath and the fiery Paighon, but at least two civilized races, the fungoid 'Ithria and the ocean-dwelling Rloedha. The former soon fled, leaving the legacy of cosmic lore which still exists in the earliest portions of the *Chronicles of Thrang* and have provided a window on the wider cosmos to a few members of almost every intelligent race in the history of your planet.

"The Rloedha were incompatible with the ecosystem of native earth life and had planned to emigrate before that life could change the chemical composition of the oceans. But they failed to do so in time, probably because of internal conflicts generated by 'Ymnar's activities. As the sea water ceased to be a rich organic broth, they all died or became dormant. The records of the Rloedha would tell us much about the nature of 'Ymnar—the dormant survivors were reactivated one hundred and fifty-five million years ago, and improved their ancient records to a very complete account. But I've never been able to obtain them—they've remained in the hands of groups too close to 'Ymnar to deal with safely."

He was quite chatty, thought Stephen, like an elderly man reminiscing fondly about his youth. If this was a fake, it was an awfully elaborate one. Yet he clung to his reserve of skepticism.

"We soon detected the shadow of 'Ymnar over the fringes of both the Sanafyil and the serpent men of Khitasz. It would begin with a few curious individuals developing an obsessive interest in ancient matters, which to the uninitiated were indistinguishable from the superstitions of magic, religion and myth. It would then grow into obscure cult activity and the emergence of dangerous wizards. The most developed of these adepts would soon display symptoms of possession and evil strength, a lust for power—a more direct expression of the evil of 'Ymnar and Ngyr-Khorath, almost like a controlled, channeled form of the hideous phenomena of direct contact.

"Among the Sanafyil such individuals were shunned and, more rarely, suppressed by violent means. The Sanafyil simply lacked the drive to become potently evil. Among the reptiles, matters took a different course. The holders of political and military power recognized the danger and, though occasionally making attempts to use the dark power for their own ends, were careful and adroit enough not to let it get out of hand. The wizards would find their cults infiltrated and overwhelmed by military action, and they would be slaughtered."

"That sounds like his activities here in the Southwest," said Stephen.

"Yes, it's a very old pattern, one we saw repeated many times, though before that, in the Paleozoic era, he seemed more interested in experimenting with animal life, creating hybrid creatures.

"By the end of the Mesozoic my race had dwindled to few exceptionally long-lived survivors. We lived in seclusion as passive observers, yet we were often still aware of 'Ymnar's activities. At the beginning of the Cenozoic, when the charming little tarsioid creatures built their enchanted lakeside city—have you ever heard the recordings of the *Tarsioid Psalms?*"

"No."

The Harlequin stirred and a haunting sound came from somewhere near the ceiling, a harmonious chant which lulled and soared in an exotic mode, accompanied by softly tinkling and strumming instruments and exquisitely delicate percussion.

"Fortunately the wire medium they used to record is extremely resistant to corrosion and has survived. It is beautiful, is it not?"

"Profoundly so."

The lucid harmonies were lulling, hypnotic, yet also gripping, stirring. The music began to have a subtly evil cast which stirred tremors of dread in the cobwebbed corners of Stephen's brain. It was also palpably erotic. A chorus of high-pitched piping voices joined the instruments.

"Can you catch the words Moroka and Tyolaguru? They are the Tamaran words for Ngyr-Khorath and 'Ymnar. Moroka means 'The Great Shadow' and Tyolaguru is 'The Destroyer.' Yet in the end, they embraced them and were destroyed. Such beauty!" He paused, as though regretting a great loss.

"Yet it is possible to benefit, at least temporarily, from dealings with 'Ymnar. In the elfin civilization of the more humanoid descendants of the tarsioids, the high priestess commanded forces obtained from 'Ymnar, and in the oppressively religious feudal civilization that followed in the Miocene, dark wizardry flourished. I suppose they owed such prosperity as they had to the powers of evil."

The harlequin interrupted his own chain of thought—"I love this passage. Can you hear the beauty in it, even through the alien tongue?"

Stephen savored the clean consonants and clear warbling vowels of voices not unlike that of the Harlequin himself, ". . . *Moro-ri Düge-ye wura-dara Lara-ya keeme-we dana-mi taba-ma, Mööte-mee küüte-ree nyala-wa mooro-ma byelere-ye köle-wö Dyuka-ya Tomo-wa wuu nii-wo disi-mu da?*"

"It tells about the seduction of the lawgiver Tomo by the witch Lara—'Through the emerald trees of shadowy Düge the Princess Lara came dancing. Beautiful she was, her curving body shimmering among the darkling leaves. How could righteous Tomo resist her?"

The Harlequin had the ability of the skilled raconteur to hypnotize a listener with the flow of narrative, and Stephen realized that he had been too engrossed to ask the many questions that had filled his mind for weeks.

"'Ymnar seems at once immensely powerful and yet strangely limited in his ability." he commented.

"That is correct. He has very much the cleverness and the limitation of a computer bound by its programming. You see, creatures such as Ngyr-Khorath live and think on a cosmic time-scale, vastly slower than our own, and they comprehend ephemeral beings like ourselves but dimly. And while an artificial creation such as 'Ymnar may at times seem to be preternaturally intelligent, it can be only an imperfect tool. It is in the end limited by the nature of its central self, Ngyr-Khorath. Though his devotees often think of 'Ymnar as virtually omnipotent, he is far from it; a fluid constellation of forces, formed in reaction to the creatures with whom he deals. Like the human fist that disappears when one opens one's hand, when 'Ymnar is not functioning he does not exist. He is not even immune to fear; he was undoubtedly afraid of the extra-galactic Poseidon creature that settled in the ocean half a billion years ago and battled with Paighon.

"His strength lies in dealing with individuals, sensing their innermost yearnings and weaknesses, mirroring them and playing upon them. Thus he is always a subterranean influence, rarely known to more than a few individuals and rarely dominating an entire culture. When he does become dominant, he is invariably destructive—among the tarsioids, for instance, he functioned for millions of years as a mere vicious undercurrent within the sensual earth mother cult. But when he became the predominant influence among the wizards and priests, the Tamarans were first enslaved and then reduced to savagery and near-extinction."

"But if he is known to be so destructive, how can he continue to win recruits? Surely the most capable and knowledgeable members of every race, the individuals most valuable to 'Ymnar, would be likely to inform themselves about the danger?"

"That is not so easily done," said the Harlequin, "as you can see from your own experience. The information about such matters is not easily available; it is buried in rare records in dead tongues, often hidden away by secretive cult groups. Those who know the history of 'Ymnar may envision themselves as a ruling elite, immune to the general suffering and destruction, possibly even achieving immortality. And it is even possible that the intentions of Ngyr-Khorath (or at least of his organ, 'Ymnar) are ambivalent. There seems to be fascination as well as hate in their attitude toward earth life, and they may crave some form of dominance even more than destructions. Though destruction always seems to be the end result when 'Ymnar gains too much power.

"Thus it is easy to see how even the greatest minds are tempted to traffic with 'Ymnar. When his power can be kept in balance, it can be quite constructive. The great achievements of Duga-Luz came about in this way. Throughout the long dry Pliocene its spires and minarets of rose marble and turquoise flourished at the edge of the dusty savannah, in a great bend of the meandering Zurmak, and the last descendants of the Tamaran tarsioids lived in tranquility and plenty. For millions of years the queens of Duga-Luz were consummate adepts of all forms of spiritual discipline, and magic and the forces gotten from 'Ymnar, with their pitfalls and temptations, were always in balance with more benign influences. And in the universe of mortal creatures, there was no greater wisdom than in halcyon Duga-Luz.

"Being wise, the adepts and scholars and wizards of the river city valued knowledge above power, and thus were in little danger from their own power or from the lust to expand it. Even at the end, when proud Duga-Luz crumbled into the dust of the plains and the Kirmesh people scattered and died, it was not through 'Ymnar but through a thing of their own creation—a monstrous dreaming creature which they kept in perpetual sleep in a cavern below the city and used as a telepathic link or medium to travel, in their own dreams, to the distant past and future, as well as the farthest corners of space. In the end the dreaming became too sweet and they became careless; when a certain being from a dark planet orbiting a black hole detected their dream-presence, it used the dream-monster to invade the city; they had no defense.

"Fortunately their clever hominoid pets had grown capable enough to begin the chain of evolution leading to the development of your race. They were able to preserve almost none of the technology and wisdom of Duga-Luz, but they had learned the concept of making and using tools, and had begun to develop a crude speech and social organization. They were able to survive first as small-game hunters and carrion eaters, later as the savage hunters of the mammoth and bison. 'Ymnar was with them always, especially with those who became the ancestors of the modern mongoloid race. I was in seclusion until relatively recently, and I know rather little of the history of your own species."

Stephen felt fatigued by his bizarre surroundings, as though from an hallucinogenic drug trip that had gone stale, and one wished would go away. The dissonant strains of the *Tarsioid Psalms*, the slowly whirling kaleidoscopic lights, the brilliant sparkling of the crystalline fountain— individually they should each have been soothing, yet together they were not. His thoughts were chaotic and hard to focus. On an emotional level he was firmly convinced of the truth of the Harlequin's strange tales, yet something in his character stubbornly demanded logical proof.

"You must forgive me if I find all this difficult to believe," he said.

The Harlequin did not respond for a moment.

"I will perform no cheap tricks to convince you. As I said before, either you know or you don't."

"The immense knowledge you present is very appealing. I suppose by joining 'Ymnar I would come to have some of it."

"Yes, I suppose you would. Yet he is hardly a trustworthy source." Then abruptly, "I recommend that you have nothing to do with Ramny. I must rest now."

Clearly the interview was at an end.

Stephen got up and found his way back through the strangely lit labyrinth to the door. He paused just beyond the bamboo curtain. He heard the strange rattling from the general area of the ceiling again. He stooped and looked up and saw the outline of what might have been a great eight-legged worm. He left and walked out into the antique-jammed house. No one came to show him out.

He stepped out through the still open iron gate. The houses along the street were dark and forbidding now, he could see no lights in the windows. Far up the street a solitary figure stood silhouetted by a street light. Ramny had said Stephen would see him; he was free to go to him or to turn away. Stephen hesitated for a long moment, looking toward the figure in the street light's glare. The Harlequin had been utterly convincing; 'Ymnar was real, 'Ymnar was profoundly evil and dangerous. Yet it was possible to control the perilous relationship and to use it as a key to the most awesome vistas of time and space, though at great risk. There was an undercurrent of giddy fear in his excitement as he felt the skepticism weaken; the skepticism that anchored him to the dull and safe dimension of reality.

Stephen swung the gate closed on grating hinges and walked slowly toward the shadowed figure.

III. The Judgment

Outside the bus was an empty sea inhabited only by silent buttes and mesas. Stephen had been watching the solemn landscape since dawn, as it evolved through a languid shift of perspective. Now, at the base of an immense mesa where an eon-dry canyon disgorged into an arid void, the village of San Marcos expanded to visibility, a human presence both ruling the wasteland and beleaguered by it.

Only the three scruffy mercantile buildings along the highway belonged to the twentieth century, a run-down wooden building with a sign saying General Store along the top, a gas station with the pump rusted out and the roof fallen in, and a newer concrete block structure with a rusty but not decrepit gasoline pump. Behind them the scattered cubicles of brown adobe belonged to another time, though some seemed to be in use, and in the mouth of the canyon a cliff-shadowed pueblo recalled an era beyond living memory.

The bus stopped in front of the pump that looked like it might work and Stephen stepped down with his bag. He looked around with a sinking feeling, while behind him the bus hissed and moved on. He was worn out from the long trip and this looked more and more like a wild goose chase. It was hard to believe that anything of importance could be based in this wretched excuse for town. He felt an incipient dread of being alone in this immense fastness.

He watched the bus disappear and stepped into the block building. Then was no one between the old-fashioned counter running the length of one wall and the refrigerated cabinets behind it. The meticulously ordered racks of stale junk food were slightly dusty and a black scorpion scuttling between the rows only deepened the stillness.

The stony silence was broken by the tapping of shoes and the flapping of sandals on smooth concrete. The shoes belonged to a tallish man with an expensive sport shirt and broad Indian features, the sandals to a short one with the cruelly intelligent face of a conquistador wearing baggy Sears Roebuck khakis.

"Stephen McLeod. I believe I'm expected."

They appraised him with impassive stares that could have been predatory or merely uninterested. Then Indian-face's features moved into a bland benevolent smile.

"Welcome, Mr. McLeod. I am José and this is Porfirio. You are indeed expected. It will be a few hours before we leave. Before the sun goes down it is very hot up there where we are going, and of course no one is allowed in the inner caverns until he has met the Master."

"Will I see the Master tonight?" asked Stephen. He was stiff from the ride and slightly irritable. "I mean, I've waited a very long time for something more than just . . . talk."

There was a short tense silence before Porfirio laughed aloud and José's features moved back into his broad smile.

"Your desire to see things is quite understandable, Mr. McLeod. Please be assured that after tonight you will have no more need to be convinced. And you will have nothing to fear . . . no doubt the Master will find you acceptable for all of the tasks in which you may serve him."

Porfirio smirked. "That's right, either way you got no worries after tonight." This drew a scowl from José.

"Porfirio, please take Mr. McLeod's bag." The little imp picked up Stephen's bag and flapped toward the rear door.

José turned back to Stephen and spoke in the professional tone of a desk clerk in an expensive hotel. "We have prepared a room where you can rest from your journey. Surely you must be tired. Porfirio and myself will be engaged in certain preparations for the events this evening. Unfortunately there is at present no one else in the village who speaks English. Please accompany us."

The back room of the store was cool and dim. As Stephen's eyes adjusted slightly he saw with a thrill that machine guns were being transferred from heavy cases to lighter cartons. There was a stack of small boxes of various sizes by the back door. They filed past a dusty Scout and crossed the stretch of rock and hard dirt between the highway and the adobes, a procession of ants among the timeless mesas.

"Naturally we must be very circumspect in what we make visible in a place like Barrett," said José. "There are so many prying eyes, so many enemies. Here we have a secure retreat. You will see the full measure of what you are involved in. I can guarantee there will be no room for skepticism in your mind after today."

"Are we going up to the old pueblo?"

"Oh no. It would be much too dangerous to carry on our major activities so close to the highway. We are going to a most remarkable place."

"Will we have far to go?"

"It will take us the better part of an hour to drive there, mainly because the roads are not good."

José opened a door in the middle of a row of doors in a long adobe building and stood aside to let Stephen enter. The room was furnished with a table against the wall and a bed that looked hard but clean and comfortable. Porfirio deposited Stephen's bag by the bed and left.

Stephen followed Porfirio back outside and spoke to José. "I'm tired alright, but I doubt if I can sleep. Do you mind if I take a walk around the village?"

José's face froze for a moment, then he smiled. "Of course not. Be careful, though. It is easy to become lost in the desert, even over a short distance. And please stay away from the pueblo. It is in very poor condition and unsafe. Not safe at all."

His smile deepened momentarily. Stephen watched José and Porfirio walk away toward the Scout, then turned and walked down the adobe row. It was a cool spring day in spite of José's reference to the heat. A gusting breeze woofed in his hears. Several of the doors in the adobe were closed, but others stood ajar showing little drifts of sand inside the door. A few had no doors at all. There were about half a dozen rows of them. It must have been a good sized village in its time, but most of it was uninhabited now.

Most of the rows faced an open space in the center with a few threadbare trees, their sparse leaves twitching in the gusty breeze. He walked over to a double-width door with an arched top and hinges at the side. A scrap of wood hung from one of the hinges. The interior reminded him of an old-fashioned saloon. There was a rubble of rotted wood along one wall that might once have been a bar.

He walked out of the cluster of adobes. Toward the edge of the village he saw a clump of trees that looked like an oasis. There was a small oblong pool of water there, overgrown with lush vines, ferns and lichens. The water gurgled and the runoff from the pool formed a stream that disappeared into a shallow gully. Stephen didn't know why, but there was something repellent about it.

He saw a low mound perhaps a hundred yards from the village. He thought of José's warning about getting lost in the desert, and hesitated a moment before walking over to the side of it. Down inside there were charms made of turkey feathers fluttering in the freeze.

He marveled at how his initial love of cyclopean landscapes was turning to a queasy sense of dread, as though he might fall into the sky. He looked up at the pueblo, brooding under the beetling cliff. He thought of going to have a look, but knew he would be visible to José. He walked back through the silent village to his room. Inside he lay down on the solid little bed. A drowsy spring breeze moved through the room. He closed the door against the outer immensity but that made the room unbearably dark and stuffy. He opened the shuttered window next the door. And miraculously, as his mind retreated from vague dread into stillness, he slept.

José's knock aroused him from a dream of menacing shapes in a multi-colored mist. He opened the door and saw José smiling with Porfirio behind him.

"Time to go, Mr. McLeod." Stephen carried his own bag to the filthy but serviceable Scout behind the store. Porfirio hopped into the front seat and José took the wheel. Stephen climbed into the back among a jumble of boxes.

Porfirio giggled. "Now you'll see some of our spectacular New Mexican scenery, Mr. McLeod."

The Scout scurried through the village and up the gorge in a cloud of dust, bouncing along a rough desert track. Stephen held on for dear life.

"You see our natural defenses are as formidable as our contrived ones," shouted José. "We must be constantly on guard against persecution." They tore up the canyon for about ten miles. Once the Scout skidded and got stuck. José and Porfirio both turned to Stephen and grinned. José spun the wheels till they dug out, and took off to the right.

The road went up at a precipitous angle as they cut from gorge to gorge in a complex pattern. Eventually the way wound over a low spur beyond which rose an enormous mesa, towering thousands of feet, far more huge than any Stephen had seen. The topmost part must have been visible from the village, but would have appeared as a peak lost in the mountain mass in the background. José made for it across a sandy floor undisturbed except by the twin tracks of a few trips by the Scout. The sloping skirt of rock and earth girdling the lower reaches of the mesa looked too unstable to support a vehicle, but José drove up a rough track that only a knowing eye could have found. At the end the Scout plunged into a shadowed crevice hidden from most angles of view by a big vertical rock slab jutting out from the main mass at a contorted angle.

A terrific hairpin road had been carved out of its slopes by infinitely patient manual labor. Looking back out and down to the desert floor, Stephen was overcome by the height and vastness and awful loneliness of the place.

Porfirio seemed to sense his discomfort and grinned over his shoulder. "You'll get used to it! When the Master is certain that you will do whatever he needs you to, you will make the trip many times."

The road ended about half way up the mesa and below the top of the sheltering slab, on a narrow ledge just big enough to turn the Scout around on. The silence was eerie as he tore his eyes away from the awesome view behind and looked at the vultures circling above the cleft. Stephen sat puzzled for a moment in the silence. Then he heard a clattering and a wicker basket seat attached to a long rope came tumbling down the cliff face.

"Make yourself comfortable," said José.

Stephen seated himself in the basket. The rope went taut as unseen hands above hauled him away. Up and up he went, occasionally having to rappel himself from the cliff face, sheer though it was. An early evening breeze moaned in his ears and the infinitely distant abyss of the desert yawned whenever he took his eyes off the rock in front of him. After an interminable period dangling in space he was pulled onto a wide ledge by a team of three zombie-like Indians, glassy-eyed and listless. They reminded him of the cult members in Barrett whom he suspected of being on drugs.

It was only one step of a relay. He climbed into another basket and resumed the terrifying ascent. After five relays he was above the vultures and could see José being pulled up below him and Porfirio far below loading boxes onto the lowest basket. The rope men didn't speak to him and when José and Porfirio arrived at the top they didn't speak to them either.

It took Stephen several minutes to recover from his vertigo enough to notice his surroundings, and the vertigo never entirely left him in that high and terrible place. The top of the mesa was heavily wooded and sculptured into a labyrinth of green crags, mossy sinkholes and hidden corridors. There were several trails leading away from the rope hoist and along one of then in the evening shadows he saw a red-skirted and black-haired figure who turned and ran.

"How do you like our retreat, Mr. McLeod?" asked José.

"Magnificent," said Stephen sincerely.

"A beautiful place to spend one's life, Mr. McLeod. Here we think not in years but in centuries, millennia." He led the way up one of the twisted trails. Stephen saw the red-skirted woman again, flitting ahead just out of might. She seemed *older* than he had at first thought.

The path led into a bowl-shaped depression in the center of the mesa. From an airplane above, it would have been difficult to see any movement, any artificial element in the landscape. But from where Stephen stood, he could see lights twinkling in the twilight shadows, in cave-like openings whose distribution seemed unnatural. Near the center of the bowl was a large round opening going down into the rock. But there were no lights there.

Gazing around he made out indistinct figures moving in the shadows, many with the stiff motion of the rope men. Immediately in front of him was a flat grassy patch, protected by a ring of rugged shrubs. In the center a bare human skull sat on a vertebra in the black earth. "One who betrayed us," smiled José. A tarantula sat on the gleaming pate for a moment like a grotesque hairpiece, then crawled into an eye socket.

Moving down into the central depression Stephen realized that there must be hundreds of people living there, many in worse shape than the rope men, with livid faces and vacant eyes. There were also packs of hounds lying in the deeper shade. On the edge of the open space a nearly skeletal corpse slouched tied to a gnarled juniper. They passed close enough for Stephen to see tooth marks on the exposed bone. A few of the hounds trotted out into the light and sniffed at them tentatively; they had grinning baboon faces and a limited ability to walk erect.

"The mandrelones, a creation of 'Ymnar. They were created from baboons, with an infusion of human genetic material to make them more useful."

"Where do they all live?" said Stephen. "Looks like it would be pretty hard to camouflage all this activity from the air."

"We have an extensive network of caverns and tunnels here, extending far below the base of the mesa. We are very proud of it. It has taken many centuries to develop, even with the help provided by 'Ymnar."

"What do they eat? Can you really bring that much food up the rope hoist?"

José smiled proudly. "We grow most of our food in the caverns. 'Ymnar has given us convenient sources of light. We also grow edible fungi which need no light, and even a few animals for meat."

José led him to the mouth of a big cave. "We will enter the caverns through our business office. You will meet our administrator, Olga, who does so well taking care of our practical affairs in the outside world. Then we will go see Bartolomeo, one of our oldest members. He has gained much of the kind of knowledge you would like to have. After that, we will take you to an excellent place to watch the feast, until it is time for you to participate and meet 'Ymnar."

At the rear of the large but shallow alcove a stone-faced door stood ajar. An arc of light showed past it.

"We have no elaborate bureaucratic pyramid like most human organizations, but we still have some business needs. Olga takes care of most of them for us."

There were several desks and filing cabinets around the walls of a fair-sized room, and a bank of cabinets in a side chamber which was not lit. There were electric lights with exposed wires running along the edge of the wall at the floor. Olga was above medium height and big-boned, with wide designer glasses which did not make her look particularly intelligent.

"Olga, this is Stephen McLeod," said José.

"Welcome to the caverns, Stephen."

Stephen looked around, bemused. "Just what sort of business affairs would a group like this have?"

Olga lifted her chin and smiled officiously. "Well, to begin with, one needs money to do anything at all. We have quite a lot, but it's invested, and it takes planning to lay our hands on a sum when we need it. Of course, it must not be traceable in case anything goes wrong. Then there are passports and identification . . ."

"Olga knows where every penny is and sees that it is provided wherever it is needed," put in José. "Also, while 'Ymnar seems to be able to hold a vast array of knowledge in his own mind without technological aids, we find we need a record-keeping system to keep track of practical information about all our members, our enemies, our problems. We have thousands of members all over the world, you know. And we have enemies as well as friends. And then again, while 'Ymnar is a profound source of information about many things, there is much useful everyday information about our enemies and about what is going on in the world that we must gather and sift for ourselves. In the last few years Olga has talked us into starting a computerized intelligence database of our own, correlating information."

Olga beamed. "Before that," she said, "a few wise men kept it all in their heads."

"You will find that, when you are away from here, Olga sees that you have everything you need for the task at hand. From this day forth your hidden brothers in 'Ymnar will never be very far from you."

José turned toward a doorway in the rear.

"Now we will go see Bartolomeo."

José led the way down a sloping dimly-lit passage that ended in a stairwell with a stone handrail. Steep stairs went down at least a hundred feet. They passed through long corridors lit with torches in sconces. There were side passages turning off to the left and right. Once Stephen saw a rat scuttle across the floor. He lost all sense of direction. The network of passages within the mesa was truly fabulous, clearly the work of centuries.

At last a long straight corridor ended in a darkened archway; flickers of reflected firelight could be seen. José halted the group and spoke very softly to Stephen.

"You are about to meet Bartolomeo, our very oldest member and the one with the most intimate knowledge of 'Ymnar. He has vastly transcended the wisdom we humans can normally hope to attain. We take you to him in part because you wish to know more about us, but also because Bartolomeo needs to know about you. In the future, you will perform many acts mysterious to you. Many of them will originate in the mind of Bartolomeo, as he sits alone in his chambers pondering the goals and demands given him by 'Ymnar. When he speaks to us, his word is law."

They entered a wide high-vaulted chamber with many pillars. The only light came from the braziers on either side of Bartolomeo. He sat on a dais in a hooded robe, with his eyes slightly above those of Stephen. José led them up at a respectful pace and stopped before the sage, saying something in the Indian language which ended in Stephen's name.

Bartolomeo spoke, in a deep and hollow voice.

"Stephen McLeod . . . welcome to the Caverns of 'Ymnar. So you wish to become one of us."

"Yes," said Stephen.

Bartolomeo paused and lifted his head very slightly. The light caught his face; it was incredibly aged.

"Good, good. Though you are not of the ancient race of this continent, your people too once knew the Master, and have only forgotten him for a little while. In the long dark millennia before the deluge he haunted Hezur, the City of Bones, in southern Russia, and he dealt with your race openly until the beginnings of your known history. My own people first knew him only a hundred thousand years ago, when the first shamans made contact with him and other dark forces lurking on this planet. When my ancestors crossed from Asia to this continent, they brought the worship of 'Ymnar with them. And in the marvelous city of Beesh Bighan he was the shadowy force behind all activity. Then my ancestors handled the power wrongly, and met with disaster; that was twenty thousand years ago. By the time the Europeans came, few of us knew of the past glory of the Indian people, and almost none knew 'Ymnar. But now we Indians are coming to know him again . . . and among the whites, many join us. He will lead us to destroy most of your race, but those who have embraced him will survive."

"The cult grows . . . ?" said Stephen.

"Slowly, patiently. We have thousands of inhabitants here in our cavern city alone. Some are human, some are very ancient, some were quite recently created for 'Ymnar's own purposes."

"You mean the mandrelones?" said Stephen.

"Yes, those and others. Do I detect a hint of skepticism in your mind, Mr. McLeod?"

Stephen was startled and glanced aside to see José smiling. Porfirio smirked.

"Yes, Bartolomeo can hear your thoughts," said José.

"Not precisely," said Bartolomeo, "but I sense attitude and feeling clearly. Your reluctance to accept 'Ymnar's powers as rational truth does not concern us directly. Already in the back of your mind the realization grows that the mandrelones, for instance, could not be any charlatan's trick. By midnight you will have seen the Master and you will have no doubts about his power. But while you question, the faith, the total commitment which 'Ymnar demands cannot grow. And from the moment you came to our attention, your mind has been as open to 'Ymnar as the pages of a book. You are being judged, Mr. McLeod. 'Ymnar must know whether you would be a reliable strand of his web, or a troublesome weakness."

Stephen began to feel fear in the presence of this terribly old man.

"People join us for many reasons," he continued. "Some see advantage for themselves in our hidden power, and grasp at it thoughtlessly. Some seek escape from fear, through union with that which they fear most. Intelligent and curious minds like your own that crave the awe and wonder of things beyond mundane knowledge are very useful to 'Ymnar. They help him bridge the abyss between the alien sentience from which he comes and the mentality of earthly life. But there is potential weakness in such minds. Fear does not strengthen their bond with 'Ymnar, it weakens it. And there is indeed much to fear in what we know and do."

Stephen opened his mouth but did not speak. He sensed a tension in José and Porfirio, as the corner of his eye caught some sudden movement.

"As you leave, Mr. McLeod, you might look over the railing behind you and to your left." In the hooded face the eyes caught the gleam of firelight. "Perhaps it will help you find the confidence you need."

Stephen instinctively took a step backward before tearing his eyes away from the haunting figure and turning away. Behind him on the left side of the pillared room was a wide well with a stone railing around it. The three walked toward it. José and Porfirio stood back, an Stephen looked over the railing. He was looking down into a darkened pit of indistinct depth. A shadowy form moved below. Two glowing green eyes the size of plates turned upward toward him. He could not see any more details of the thing.

José led him in silence through another tour of the maze of caverns, this time gradually ascending. The caverns seemed deserted, the silence marred only by the three men's footsteps. At last, turning off of a main corridor and climbing a steep narrow stair, he saw deep blue sky appear in the doorway above. At the top he saw a mountainous horizon just above. They were in a niche in the cliff overlooking the flat grassy area across which they had entered. The only furniture was a heavy picnic table and two torches in a sconce. Stephen walked around the table and looked out over the sheer drop-off.

In front, about thirty feet, below was the clearing they had crossed approaching the cave. He saw the tree with the gnawed corpse. In front and to the left the space was bordered by a tangled mass of trees and rocks with many small cave openings. Beyond the skyline a few jagged peaks could be seen far in the distance. The sun had set, but the evening sky still glowed. To the right the grassy area descended across a layered stone terrace to a large pit with an oval cave mouth going down into the ground. A few Indians were bringing out picnic furniture like the table in the niche. At the edge of the clearing they were decorating the trees with gaily colored wool and feather ornaments.

"Very comfortable, Mr. McLeod," said José heartily. "Here we will have a fine place to spend the feast and a good view of everything that happens until it is time for you to participate." He saw Stephen looking at the oval sinkhole. "Yes, the Master always appears from that. We call it the pit. It will be quite a long feast— there will be a lot of singing and dancing. You will see many of our people and a few of those who live below."

"Will I see 'Ymnar up close?" said Stephen.

José smiled. "Yes, oh yes, you will see him as close as you could possibly wish to."

"And those from below? Will I see them closely?"

José grinned. "Perhaps, perhaps."

Stephen heard footsteps trudging up the stairs behind them. A figure arose from the darkness and stopped two steps below the head of the stairs. A tray with three drinks on it emerged into the light. The hands holding the tray were withered, almost mummified. The nails were dirty and broken.

"Ah, here is Pablo with our aperitif," said José in his heartiest tone.

"Pablo is also one of our oldest, and an intimate witness to 'Ymnar's earliest miracles among our people here."

The figure in the shadow stood motionless.

"Bring the drinks in and set them on the table, Pablo."

Pablo stepped up into the room and his face came out of the shadow. It was shriveled, shrunken, glassy eyed, livid, the mouth open in a foolish grin, like the rictus of death. He walked toward the table, set down the tray. Stephen was aghast in horror and total belief.

As Pablo returned the way he came the drone of an airplane grew in the distance. Stephen heard shouts in the Indian language. The picnic tables were quickly moved deeper into the shade, where they could not be seen from above, and blankets were used to mask the fires from the air. Every moving thing got under cover. Stephen scanned the sky for the black dot of the approaching plane. José stepped up to the edge by the wall, carefully inconspicuous, and looked out. He smiled and spoke in a business-like tone.

"It is not a helicopter. It is quite easy for a helicopter to land here. We use them ourselves as often as we can without attracting attention. But planes are no threat. They cannot fly too close because of the updrafts, and it is easy to hide things. But we still use the ancient Indian method of climbing the cliff as much as possible to avoid conspicuous air traffic."

Below the tables were being brought back out. Stephen heard a guitar fading in and out on the breeze, a driving rhythm in a wailing mode. Singing began in the shrill voice of a woman. Stephen looked around for the source.

"Irena is playing her guitar again," said José. "She is Apache, but that is gypsy music. She learned it from a soldier long ago, even before 'Ymnar came to us. She is the one you saw in the woods, on the path ahead of us."

Stephen looked among the trees until he spotted her. Even at this distance she had that ancient look. He thought of Pablo. More people came out into the clearing and began to do a stiff Indian dance. He heard the grating footsteps behind them again.

"Pablo again. Just put them right on the table in front of Mr. McLeod, Pablo." The second tray contained an assortment of fruits, some of them exotic ones that Stephen did not recognize.

"You are one of us now, Mr. McLeod. Or Stephen, if I may call you that." Stephen was startled by the idea of being accepted as an intimate of this group.

"Here you will share the sacraments with us and eat the food of 'Ymnar. When you are away our organization will take care of you. Olga is quite competent, she will remember to send you everything that you need, money, information, assistance. We will forget nothing. Of course, the Master himself has yet to judge you. There is still that. But there is no turning back now."

Stephen looked out at the zombie activities, at Irena with her moaning guitar. He stopped. He looked at Pablo, with his blank stare.

"You may go now, Pablo," said José.

Stephen began to eat.

The twilight had gone and a crescent moon hung over the landscape. From a cave opposite the pit came men with smooth energetic movements, unlike the zombies. They threw chunks of meat to the mandrelones in the shadows. A piece of meat fell short in the light and one charged out and picked it up. It raised its head and looked toward the niche, with a face both human and bestial. It scampered back into the shadows. Stephen heard Porfirio and José speaking together in the Indian tongue. They were standing with their arms folded looking sideways out of the niche. Stephen said with a touch of irritation, "You say 'Ymnar created those things?"

"You mean the mandrelones? Yes, from giant baboons now extinct. Mandrelon just means 'big baboon.' They are not so intelligent as men, but very dangerous. They can follow more complicated instructions than hounds."

Two men came out of the same cave gripping the arms of a third. He struggled and screamed in Spanish. He looked terrified. There was an uproar among the mandrelones. Some jumped out of the shadows and snarled at the prisoner.

"Another betrayer. He is very disgusting. He tried to escape and sell information to another cult, one hostile to 'Ymnar."

Stephen winced inwardly at the word 'escape.' Porfirio was staring down at the victim with a look of uninhibited cruelty, his mouth open, his eyes gleaming. Stephen sat rigidly and stared at the scene below. He sensed a movement, saw José and Porfirio look to the stairway. He turned to see eyes shining in the darkness and a figure like a mandrelon. He turned back to the terrible scene below. They were tying the victim to the same juniper as the ragged corpse. Stephen raised his hand slightly in a rigid gesture, then let it fall to the table. The men who had thrown the meat were herding the mandrelones back into the shadows. The victim stopped shrieking and all was silence except for the gusting wind. Everyone stared at the cave from which the victim had been dragged.

A thing appeared, shapeless, not human, slouching along in a loose-fitting cloak toward the victim. The guards turned from the mandrelones and watched the thing pass. As it reached the center of the grassy arena, the victim began to bawl hoarsely against the silence. When the thing got close, he fell silent but kept working his mouth like a fish. The shadow enveloped him. He let out a series of short moans, ending in one last sharp shriek. There was no sound or movement among the crowd as the thing returned slowly the way it had come.

A stiffly moving zombie, first one, then two, then a horde came out of the trees and clustered around the victim in a lurching mob. The crowd murmured and Irena began to play her guitar again. More food was brought to the tables. The mandrelones rushed out and pushed the zombies out of the way. Stephen stared at the plate of fruit as though hypnotized; he reached out and picked up an apple.

Soon Pablo entered again with a covered platter. He lifted the cover to reveal a portion of unidentifiable roast meat. Stephen picked up a knife and fork.

By the end of the feast the crescent moon was high above the arena. Porfirio and José sat casually at the end of the table chatting in Spanish. People were sitting at the tables below but there was no movement. A single sonorous voice began to chant in the Indian language. Others joined in. A droning voice in English began to repeat the chant to 'Ymnar. Stephen looked for the source. It was Brian O'Herlihy, dressed in rags and staring blankly. He stared in the direction of the pit as he chanted in the monotone of the stiff ones. Stephen began to join in the repetitive parts of the chant, repeating Dan's English words.

Everyone stared at the pit while the chant built in volume and intensity. Then it stopped abruptly. Dancing lights of many colors appeared in the pit against a steady red-orange glow. Stephen heard a clatter of hooves. A monstrous black stallion galloped out of the darkness. It faced the niche and rose with its front hooves pawing the air. It's red eyes flashed in the dim light, catching the reflection of the fires. He heard weird music emanating from the pit. Porfirio and José stepped toward Stephen with bland smiles. Stephen stood frozen, his eyes wide open, ecstatic with fear. Porfirio led the way down the stairs.

Through the web of passages and caverns they passed, emerging through a rough cave mouth. They walked past the guards and mandrelones, past Pablo with his mummified face, past the victims on the tree. They stepped up to the pit.

Out of the electric glow 'Ymnar appeared. He was very tall, with glowing, vaguely mongoloid eyes, huge, sunken. He had prominent flashing white teeth. He was richly dressed in ornate robes, black trimmed with gold. His size and shape were fluid and changing. Stephen came to a dull awareness that his food had been drugged.

"Praise 'Ymnar!" shouted Stephen, echoing the chants. His companions had stopped short, leaving Stephen alone before him.

'Ymnar's voice was deep and melodious, alternately sonorous and hollow, dropping to a grating base at the end of each sentence.

"Stephen McLeod . . . your thoughts have been as a tremor at the edge of my web . . . Your mind was mired in the empty boredom of rational mentality, confined to the limited spheres of what you call science and philosophy." At times his face focused into the likeness of Ramny. "You sought adventure in the distasteful and even dangerous fringe of the unknown."

Stephen raised his head slightly but did not speak. He was glassy-eyed, excited, frightened.

"Even the most drastic demonstrations could not overcome your skepticism. Reason can always deny what it cannot encompass."

Stephen struggled to stand erect and hold up his head.

"Half convinced," continued the demigod, "still propelled more by a hopeful romanticism than by belief, you sought to play the role of a dilettante, a dabbler, with a crafty eye to retreat and escape."

"Praise 'Ymnar!" babbled Stephen, "All power to 'Ymnar!" He felt the rapt stares of hundreds of eyes upon himself and the wavering figure before him, framed in the orange glow.

"Now, with your skepticism temporarily exhausted and thoughts of escape dashed, you seek to join with us. You wish to believe in order to feel safe, yet your fear is more of human fanaticism than of the powers beyond your comprehension. Your skepticism is ever ready to rebound, in the absence of immediate fear."

Tiny red and blue lights appeared in the sky above and beyond 'Ymnar's right shoulder, dancing in soft globular patterns against the velvet night. Black forms took shape within them and grew, great bat-like shapes with glaring red eyes of fire. They began to fly in vulturine circles in the abyss beyond the cliff.

"I need the capabilities of minds such as yours," continued 'Ymnar, "but I must wait for stronger minds, minds ready to seize wholeheartedly what they cannot comprehend."

José and Porfirio stepped forward and stood beside Stephen.

"You can be no more than a morsel for my servants," came the final judgment.

'Ymnar nodded his head toward Stephen. His erstwhile guides grasped him firmly him by the arms. He looked around wildly and struggled. They dragged him toward the edge of the cliff.

"Praise 'Ymnar!" he shouted. "I will be loyal to 'Ymnar!"

There came a sigh and murmur from the crowd. José and Porfirio approached the cliff. Gripping Stephen by the arms and the seat of the pants they heaved him over the edge. He was flying through the night in sickening free fall above the cyclopean shadowed landscape. He saw evil eyes and an enormous red maw with dagger teeth sweep toward him. He felt an ecstatic fulfillment and a grotesque pressure as he was devoured in midair; there was no pain at all before the black abyss consumed him.

The Feast

King Knesephon lay upon his bier, shrouded in royal purple, and listened gleefully to the sounds of his own funeral banquet. The noxious philtre obtained from Vlat the necromancer had worked to perfection and his royal frame lay still in feigned death while his mind, lucid and mercurial, conjured visions from the profusion of sounds and odors that wafted past him as he lay in state in the throne room. The oily smell of the candles was stifling and the smothering funeral incense tickled his nose from time to time but his drugged body made no response. He pictured the result of a window-rattling sneeze erupting from the bier and experienced the uncanny sensation of long, uncontrollable laughter with no sound, no motion.

When the aroma of roast meat from the adjacent hall cut through the incense it gave him little comfort; his macabre deception had lasted through a full day and a night now and the drug did nothing to dull his hunger. And the sounds of cheerful gluttony were hardly flattering under the circumstances. His subjects were observing the bizarre custom of his house, the feast hosted by the passing king, with unseemly gusto.

He could hear the click of knife on plate at a hearty rhythm; the provincial barons and the token representatives of the peasantry would be carving the fatted steers and sows and ewes whose toothsome smell rivaled the incense at times. The powerful dukes and earls would be slicing fine venison from the king's own forest, a fine pungent whiff that came his way from time to time. It would be in short supply; fortunately there had not been time for the king's huntsmen to deplete the game in preparation for the feast. And of course his queen and his brother and the three archdukes would be picking at freshly killed pheasant. He would be lucky to bag anything in the hunt this year. Knesephon wished he could have left orders for a more modest banquet in his memory. This mob would strip his larder to the bare walls.

His wine cellar would be no better off. The lower gentry pounded the long tables in a steady drumbeat as they guzzled the hearty red wine of his own provinces from his own brass cups. The dukes of course would be raiding his supply of imported vintages, swilled from jeweled goblets of gold, and Queen Fluorna and his brother Faermon would have that exquisite mead from Arafan, poured into crystal that glittered in the flickering light from the sconces.

His fury waxed as he thought of the treacherous queen and her lover, his brother and heir apparent. How they loved this opulent pageantry of symbolic grief and renewal! She would be discreet, not pretending a grief that no one believed but at least keeping a straight face, showing her intense joy in secret flashes of her green eyes to Faermon. He would be less discreet, looking bored and sullen and saying little until the wine took hold and then letting his unfettered happiness show more and more as he downed draught after draught of the golden mead.

Knesephon's volatile rage quickly evaporated to gloating again when old Woldemar, the senior retainer of the royal family, announced the end of the feast and the ceremonial paying of respects before Knesephon's descent into the family crypt beneath the palace. Woldemar's cracked and tremulous voice could hardly be heard above the chatter and scrape of dishes and wine cups but the guests would soon follow the old man in the line before the bier.

The disgracefully merry sounds of the banquet gave way to rustling and murmuring as the guests filed into the throne room for a final audience with their king. The royal orchestra struck up a dirge of horns and lutes, a melancholy piece of uncanny beauty. Knesephon wished wistfully that he could join them, plucking his fine inlaid lute of ebony as he had so many times in the past. If only fate had made him a minstrel instead of a king! He would be caressing a fine lute or a fine lady now, coaxing magical dreams out of the air instead of lying here in this grim charade, trying desperately to save his throne.

Woldemar's shuffling footsteps approached the bier and he began to murmur an obsequious tribute. He was sincere enough in his own way, the old fool. Though he was cautious with his tongue Knesephon knew full well that the old man thought him a knave and a weakling, but to Woldemar and hundreds, yes thousands, like him the royal house of Kondar was the stable force that ordered their world, gave them their place in society, guaranteed that the seed would be planted and the harvest gathered and the bread placed on their table. Little it mattered that the current occupant of the throne was neither warrior nor statesman, Woldemar would serve the younger brother Faermon Kondar as complacently as he had served Knesephon and his father before him.

And everyone knew that after a decent interval the strong-willed royal widow would once again occupy the royal chamber as Queen Fluorna, once again wield more real power behind the scenes than her husband, for Faermon, for all his fair good looks, was no stronger than Knesephon and rather less bright. Knesephon's rage ran through his motionless frame like an agony of fire at the thought and he pictured vividly, furiously the very different course of events he planned, a deep plan to break the power of his wife and his brother and their allies at court, a dark plan involving a lightless tomb, hot iron on stubborn flesh and a scaffold.

After old Woldemar shuffled off an endless succession of nobles and retainers padded up to the bier, knelt for a moment and padded off. Few spoke. Some of the women sobbed; those would be the professional mourners who never missed a funeral and cried equally for angel and rascal. A few of the younger mourners cried more convincingly, those to whom the vague legend of Death had suddenly become a new and terrifying reality in this still, pale form swathed in purple silk.

Out of all that procession past the bier only Violetta shed tears for Knesephon the man; plump and pretty little Violetta, his maidservant, who shared his bed in between his affairs with ladies of the court. Violetta squalled and hiccupped so inconsolably that no one could doubt her sincerity. Cheer up, Violetta! Your grief will be short lived . . . Knesephon was gloating again.

At last the monotonous rhythm of the mourners' tribute was broken. The crowded room grew suddenly quieter and there was a long pause before the sound of masculine footsteps approached the bier. Faermon! Of course! The two closest to the king, Faermon and Fluorna, would see him last before he was carried to his tomb. So his dear brother, Faermon the Fair, that obnoxious little wretch, was now kneeling beside him, making the obligatory show of respect. How fortunate that

Faermon's face was turned away from the crowd—his ability to hide his true feelings was limited. Was he still looking bored and sullen? Did he kneel before the bier with a secret grin of triumph? Or did his handsome face writhe with a hatred that even death could not end? Certainly Knesephon's fury would have contorted his face if the drug had allowed it. How he hated this nasty little mama's boy, the darling of their parents, who never saw him for the sneaking whelp that he was, the hero of the peasants who could not see through this shallow peacock who cared only for himself, the secret lover of his own wife who found him a more pliable tool than the king.

"May the tomb-rats gnaw your filthy bones tonight, brother Knesephon." The harsh grating whisper, muttering between teeth clenched in vicious hatred that matched his own, was a shock to Knesephon. His own fury flared anew; he could scarcely believe that Vlat's potion could suppress all outward signs of it, the bulging eyes, the swollen veins, the clenched fists, the gnashing teeth. Yet his body did not stir.

And then he heard it, at first so softly he could not be sure, heard it transmitted faintly through the stone floor of the palace and the wooden bier.

It was repeated, still faint but very clear.

A scream. A woman's scream. A raw, animal scream.

Could the others hear it? Probably not. There was still a steady murmur from the crowd and the torture chamber was deep beneath the throne room. He listened with unbearable intensity but the sound did not come again.

His rage turned to ecstatic joy. No doubt his wife's personal maid, Gretchen, the one with the full hips and the sharp fox-like nose, was talking very freely down there. She had screamed twice; she would not want to be made to scream again. She would be babbling of lover's trysts and midnight errands for her mistress and a tiny crystal vial. Yes, Faermon, your name is being mentioned! Even as you kneel before my corpse, smug in your position as king-to-be, your name is ringing in the torture chamber. Enjoy your gloating while you can! Knesephon's heart would have leaped with excitement without the quieting effect of the drug.

When Faermon returned to his place a deep hush fell over the crowd, the whispered gossip stopped. He could hear plainly the swish of Queen Fluorna's silken gown as she made her stately pilgrimage to the side of the bier, the rustle as she knelt beside him. He smelled her perfumed tresses, heliotrope and woman-smell, and thought of the softness of those raven locks, those green witch's eyes, that figure as full and ripe and sweet as a wine-grape of Ouros. He felt that pang of loss and envy and anger that he always felt near her, since they had became cold strangers.

When they married Knesephon thought her the most beautiful creature on the earth, and at first he found her the most passionate. The buxom serving wenches and plump peasants and daughters of minor court hangers-on were as the crude hearty ale of a country inn; Fluorna was a fine vintage from the eastern isles, darkling and resinous, never dull, a new delight in each sip. But in a few years' time their ardor cooled without producing an heir. And he found her to be no passive ninny to be set aside, but a brilliant schemer, a powerful political force to be reckoned with.

She was the daughter and the heiress of a duchy second only to the royal house in power and surpassing it in wealth. It became clear that her only interest was in binding the throne to her own house. Once she had tested Knesephon and found him wanting as a lover and political ally she became a focus for intrigue, attracting all the disgruntled elements of the realm to her side. When she took Knesephon's younger brother as her lover and ally he found the two too popular to strike down openly and he himself came to live under a constant fear of assassination. If Fluorna and Faermon didn't soon arrange his demise some ambitious ally would arrange it for them.

And in this dark time of intrigue fate had at last dealt him a good turn. Gretchen of the full hips and sharp nose had appeared in the bazaar in a flimsy disguise seeking the secret counsel of a wizard and had stumbled upon a hireling of Vlat the necromancer. And Vlat was bound to Knesephon by many evil secrets.

Fluorna knelt in silence for a long time, until Knesephon ached to hear her voice. And if she spoke, would there be any regret, any trace of the tenderness and affection and passion they had known in their first years together?

"Knesephon," she whispered at last. "You pathetic fool."

The blunt contempt in her voice stabbed like a knife.

"You lie there handsome but weak, as always. I needed a king and I found a minstrel. Play your lute in hell, Knesephon, while I try to make a real king of your brother. Be a vain fop in the devil's court. Charm the demon chambermaids of the underworld, dally with the corpses and tomb-ghouls in the catacombs, Knesephon. May demons shred your flesh tonight!"

The force and foulness of her hatred stunned him. The pain of her total rejection drowned his senses, his rage struggled slowly to the surface until another sound made him pulse with excitement. Booted footsteps, marching in step through the halls outside the throne room. As they drew near the crowd stirred with a buzz of wonder. The boots drummed into the great hall and stopped.

A voice boomed out, hoarse with tension.

"In the absence of a legally crowned king I, Kalispar, commander of the King's Guard, in the name of the royal house of Kondar, do on sound evidence accuse and arrest Faermon the crown prince and Fluorna the queen for the murder by poison of King Knesephon."

The crowd was breathless. He could hear Faermon's scuffling steps as he was dragged off, while two other pairs of boots marched down to the queen and stopped, waiting. He heard a rustle of silk as she turned to them. Would her nerve hold? Surely her black heart was pounding now, her throat dry, as she felt the first tug of Knesephon's web of intrigue.

He heard her take a few light but steady steps away from the bier, leaving the guards no excuse to seize and drag her. Would she resist, call for support from her political allies? So much the better—Kalispar would have his loyal guardsmen discreetly posted around the room, some in disguise, ready to slay anyone who came to the queen's aid. He heard her slow measured steps pass up the aisle accompanied by the clumsy boots of the two guardsmen. About halfway up the aisle she stopped.

"Kalispar!" Her voice was tense but strong, not loud but cutting. "Kalispar, you villain! With the king hardly cold on his bier you come with this treachery, gnawing his bones like a jackal! I'll see you hanged for this!"

"My queen, for still you be so, if I am wrong in this terrible accusation no doubt I shall die soon enough. You and the prince shall have a fair hearing and the evidence shall decide. No one is above the law and the law says that those who conspire to regicide shall hang."

Kalispar's blunt voice was as always simple and convincing. And the king's death had been sudden enough to make tongues wag. Surely the green-eyed witch knew that the shadow of the gallows was upon her. He could hardly hear the pat of her slippers amongst the guardsmen's clumping.

Yes, thought Knesephon. the hangman's ropes are the strands of my web, and already the flies are twitching helplessly. The vision of the gallows hung before him like a dream as the dizziness which had come and gone erratically since he took the drug took hold. He was dimly aware of the sound of the guardsmen coming to seal his coffin and carry him to the tomb. Then he swooned.

A squeak awoke him. He lay there straining to hear it repeated; when consciousness returned fully he realized how profound the silence had been. Rats? He shuddered, or rather he felt the electric thrill that would have been a shudder without the paralyzing drug. Of course the silence was deep, it was the silence of the tomb. It was the custom of the land to leave offerings of food in the tomb; that explained the "why" of the rats if not the "how." He heard a squealing and scampering, a quarrel over some especially choice morsel.

Thank heaven for the stout coffin of ebony. The air holes he and Kalispar had secretly drilled among the intricate carvings were much too small to admit even the smallest of the filthy scavengers. But he was surprised to find rats here. The palace was more than a thousand years old. The great cliff on which it perched had become a labyrinth of tunnel and masonry with depths and ramifications known to no living man. The royal catacomb lay in a deep level, below the dungeon. He and Kalispar had surreptitiously examined Knesephon's tomb and it had seemed in good shape, surrounded by brickwork and stone in excellent condition with a heavy door of bronze embossed with the royal crest. But then they had not checked every nook and crevice of the walls.

A skittering over the coffin lid reminded him of the closeness of his confinement. Without the drug he would surely suffocate, even with the tiny air holes. But Vlat had told him that the drug would slow his breathing to imperceptibility, giving the appearance of death and reducing the need for air. That was the mainspring of the deep plot to secure Knesephon's throne and destroy his enemies.

It had begun on a warm moonless night two weeks ago when a mysterious woman, wearing a hooded cloak and taking care to show her face as little as possible, had come to the dingy shop of an ill-regarded apothecary on the fringe of the bazaar. She asked for poison; for rats, she said. But when the apothecary offered a well-tried preparation, in great demand in the neighborhood of the bazaar, she showed an unwholesome interest in the hypothetical effects of the poison on a human being.

She seemed to disapprove of causing the little creatures such pain and felt that her mistress would be upset at seeing them in such violent convulsions. She would definitely prefer something more . . . refined. Think of the horror if, heaven forbid, a human being accidentally ingested the stuff and died so horribly. Could he not give her something that would give them a more . . . normal death?

The apothecary was not stupid. In fact, he had dealt with such matters before, more than once. For a small commission he directed the lady to a man named Merlikund who had a swarthy, pock-marked face and a permanent place at a table in a gloomy tavern. There he did business in a variety of illegal ways and prospered. He wasted no time discussing rats; he offered, for a handsome fee (part of which would go to the apothecary), a poison which would kill a human being painlessly with a semblance of natural death. She was to bring the money to the tavern two nights hence.

A shadow followed the lady at a discreet distance and traced her to the palace; then Merlikund hustled off to a more formidable creature of the night, a man powerful enough to make use of the knowledge of a murder plot within the palace: Vlat the necromancer. It took no time for Vlat to identify the mysterious woman as Gretchen, the queen's maid, and divine the intentions of the queen and her lover.

If fate had taken a different turn Vlat might have helped kill Knesephon and then blackmailed the new king and queen. But it happened that Vlat and Knesephon had a long and mutually profitable association based on the king's power and money and the necromancer's exotic methods of acquiring information and disposing of unpleasant people. So Vlat went immediately to Knesephon in secret and proposed a daring plan to dispose of the king's two most dangerous enemies and neutralize their allies. The plan was a godsend to the beleaguered Knesephon and Vlat would make sure that his gratitude knew no bounds. Two nights later the hapless Gretchen carried back, from a dark alley of the bazaar, a tiny vial of crystal containing the merest sip of an amber fluid.

For the next week Vlat, Knesephon and Kalispar planned together meticulously until Kalispar, Knesphon's most trusted friend at the court, knew exactly what steps to take when the king would appear to die. Careful timing was crucial; there was no room for error.

The suspense became almost unbearable, the long summer nights taut and endless. Then came the night Gretchen appeared in the high tower where the king was carousing with his cronies. She came on a flimsy pretext, inquiring for her mistress of Knesephon's plans for the next day. His eyes gleamed, his lips curled in a smile as he answered. When she hinted that a taste of wine would go well before her return and complimented the cool night breeze that wafted through the room he could hardly keep from laughing. He invited her to stay as long as she liked and watched out of the corner of his eye as she hovered around the sideboard where his personal jeweled decanter stood.

Kalispar worked his jaw and almost knocked over his goblet; Knesephon was afraid the fool would give their hidden knowledge away. At last Knesephon brought the gem-studded decanter to the table and, after a moment's hesitation, began to drink, steadily, almost solemnly. Gretchen was still in the room; good, that would be remembered. The last thing he saw before the black swoon overwhelmed him was Kalispar's face, eyes bulging, hands gripping the table. Then he knew no more.

He first came to consciousness as he was being prepared for the funeral. Through the funeral the plan had been fulfilled to perfection. Gretchen had been quietly abducted just as the funeral was beginning so that her absence would not be noted immediately. She had been made to incriminate the queen and the prince in time for Kalispar to arrest them at the funeral where his men had been posted and could easily control resistance.

He had no idea how long he had been unconscious this time. He wondered if he would be able to hear anything through the thick walls, anything but the rats. Would there be any activity near the tomb? The labyrinth beneath the palace was little known to him.

He heard footsteps, startlingly clear. They were above him and though they carried well through the stone he could tell that they were not near.

Muffled voices. A shout. Scuffling.

The dungeon was above him, he remembered that. In the dungeon was the room where Gretchen had screamed. A special room for punishing miscreants and questioning those who would prefer not to answer. It was well-equipped for that purpose.

A man screamed, far away through the stone. Prince Faermon. The plan must be going well. Kalispar would be attending to this detail personally. He was not a subtle man. Though Vlat had coached him at length on the art of torture Knesephon was afraid he would kill the prince before he confessed. It was essential that he be alive for the trial. He must not die in the depths of the palace—he must not become a martyr. He must be tried and, if not confess in court, at least acknowledge a confession made under torture.

The screams did not last long. Brother Faermon was not a brave man. From the sound of them Knesephon assumed that Kalispar had accomplished his mission without killing the prince.

Wonderful!. The trial had to be complete before Knesephon's resurrection. Gretchen had confessed. Faermon had confessed. Knesephon lay in the dark and listened to the munching rats.

He knew what the next act of the drama must be. He had been able to hear muffled voices in between the screams and he heard the tramp of boots as the prince was led—or perhaps dragged—away. Now the silence was maddening. Kalispar would waste no time before bringing the queen to meet her fate, yet the wait was agonizingly long.

Fluorna! Green-eyed enchantress! He had loved her above all women. Her words at the bier had slashed him like a hot knife. Now the thought of her coming ordeal at Kalispar's hands aroused both an exultant lust for vengeance and a deep pang of sorrow.

She would be magnificent at bay, he knew that. She would know that she was probably doomed anyway; Kalispar had been instructed to break Gretchen and Faermon first and to tell the queen of their confessions implicating her. But Knesephon knew that in spite of the desperation and numbing dread she would feel, isolated and vulnerable, she would hold out to the limit of her strength. If Kalispar wasn't cunning in his application of pain she would simply faint.

His straining ear caught the unmistakable tread of heavy boots, steady and purposeful. It was too distant and muffled to hear a daintier tread among them. After the tramping came voices, loud but not shouting. He could not make out words or identify a feminine tone. No, the queen did not deign to raise her voice. Or perhaps she did not speak at all in response to Kalispar's demands.

Was that a groan? Man or woman? Yes, there it was again. Definitely a woman. The plan was still on schedule. The groans came in a slow, relentless rhythm and gradually evolved into wild cries. Kalispar was wearing her down as Vlat had recommended. Be ruthless, Kalispar! Helpless as she appears, she is more dangerous than any enemy you have met on the battlefield!

The cries stopped. Bear down, Kalispar! Hammer at her with your questions. Would she try to win his sympathy, bring him over to her side?. Could they blame the "murder" of Knesephon on Faermon and rule together?

If Kalispar could destroy the necromancer it could work. Knesephon grew frantic at this imagined treachery! Only Kalispar and Vlat knew he was alive—with Vlat dead Kalispar could leave him to die horribly in this hideous black coffin!

A scream, deep, rising, ululating. A soul-wrenching howl of agony. Kalispar had not been dissuaded. Would he mark her too badly for the trial? No. of course not. Kalispar was not overly bright but he had been well coached. And he always followed orders.

The last scream ended with the word "Yes!"

When at last he heard boots again they were muddled and unrhythmic, as though the queen had to be carried carefully.

There was a difference in the swoon this time. Knesephon dreamed—perhaps a sign that the drug had almost run its course.

The dreams were black and sightless, dreams of disembodied sound. He remembered slitherings and hissings and murmurings and certain liquid gibberings and nasal cheepings. No doubt they had been inspired by the rats, though he could not hear them now. He supposed they had eaten all the food. Or all fled at some faint sound. If the swoon had lasted a full day the drug would be wearing off. Perhaps he had stirred in the coffin! At the moment he would have given almost anything short of his kingdom to see sunlight on flowers and breathe fresh air and move his limbs.

The drug should wear off late in the morning after the funeral. Funeral in the morning; interrogation of the culprits immediately after; trial in the evening; execution and resurrection early the following morning. As the story would be told later, Vlat would discover through occult omens the king still lived in his coffin. He would approach Kalispar secretly, out of consideration for the explosive political situation. The two would go to the tomb to investigate, hear the sounds of Knesephon's awakening and break into the tomb. Knesephon would return to power, with the stage set for Vlat and Kalispar to assume new roles of importance in the government. Those allies of Fluorna who seemed unreliable would be quietly dealt with one by one.

For the queen and her lover would no longer be in a position to make trouble for Knesephon. He lay in the dark gloating, seeing in his mind the three gallows ropes, a fat spider contemplating his web. Fluorna, Faermon and Gretchen would be led or dragged out in the gray morning light—perhaps at this very moment—to mount the scaffold. Kalispar's guards would again be posted to prevent resistance. He knew the maid and his wretched brother could not conceal their terror at the brutal fate awaiting them. Fluorna was made of sterner stuff but surely she would feel the same numbing horror and despair, the same bowel-wrenching panic at the fearsome finality of the gallows. And the strands of Knesephon's web would twitch for a time and then sway slowly in the morning breeze.

Stone grated on stone.

At last! The thrill that ran through him was like a bolt of lightning! Vlat and Kalispar were come to deliver him from the black awfulness of the tomb and return him to the world of the blue sky and fresh bread and sweet wine. Even more—he realized that his right hand had moved at the sound! It had nudged the silken lining of the coffin lid. The drug was at last wearing off, after a full three days or this grotesque disembodied existence of sensation without movement, without the power to act or to respond.

He, Knesephon, had offered himself as all men must do in the end, as a carrion feast for the dark shades of the nether world, and now he would arise in time to see his own murderers dangling from the gallows. Surely he would live in legend forever. He must give another feast—this time he himself would be the wildest reveler. He felt like he could eat a roast stag and down a barrel of red wine all by himself. Let there be color and gay music and bright merriment around him—not least because of the strange emptiness he felt at the vision of the pale gray world without the brother with whom he had fought since the cradle and the haunting woman who had dominated his adult life.

The sound came again, furtively.

But the door to the tomb was not made of stone. He remembered the great clang it made when they slammed it shut on him. Could it possibly grate like that, when it opened slowly? He had heard no footsteps. If he could hear the rats gnawing why not the footsteps of Vlat and Kalispar?

His hand brushed silk again. Suddenly it was very important to him to be able to move. If not the door, what then? The great cliff beneath the palace was honeycombed with the capricious burrowings of a thousand years, a great warren of unknown extent. There were rats here who knew secret ways to a toothsome morsel.

There were, in fact, legends. It was, in fact, rumored among the ignorant servants that certain parts of these nether regions were not safe for the living. There were, in fact, even more ghastly tales that whispered that this black underworld was not safe—for the dead.

Legends! Peasant foolishness!

A block of stone was smoothly slid out of the wall of the tomb and, a moment later, set upon a stone floor. Something made a meeping sound, quite near the coffin. There was no solid stone wall between that meeping and the flesh of King Knesephon.

GOD! KALISPAR, COME NOW! The involuntary attempt to cry out resulted in a faint inarticulate moan and this time both hands brushed silk.

Unseen hands stealthily removed one block after another from the rear wall of the crypt and placed them gently on the floor of the passage behind. There was scarcely a rustle as several of the creatures climbed though the opening. A luckless rat scurried then squealed in a crescendo that ended with a crunching of gristle and tiny bones. The latches of the coffin clicked open and the lid hit the floor with a deafening crash as Knesephon felt a touch of cool air and smelled a faint nastiness, a breath of death and decay. The tomb-ghouls of the house of Kondar had come to the funeral feast, and they did not care whether death was feigned or not.

They were in no hurry. Three pairs of paws methodically explored the king's writhing body in the dark. The one that caressed his face was armed with stout sharp claws and had been in something rancid. Four of the hands began to shred his shroud and clothing as matter-of-factly as a hunter skins a rabbit.

His mindless moaning and squirming gave cause for certain meepings and glibberings but no hesitation. Jaws that devoured a squeaking rat would not balk at a moaning king. The hands were incredibly strong: one grasped his face firmly while another ripped off an ear. Blackness gave way to a vision of blood-red as filthy claws tore a chunk of flesh from his thigh and iron jaws gnawed his foot. A foul steaming stench blasted his nostrils as a surprisingly wide set of fangs chewed off his face.

The torch flickered in the draft from some hidden source and made the long shadows of the two men dance and sway. The short, hooded figure of the necromancer hung back almost comically behind the great blond warrior. Vlat had crept through many evil places but he did not relish this one. Many of the house of Kondar had been powerful witches and warlocks and who knew what unclean traces and revenants one might meet in these deep catacombs?

For his part the stolid Kalispar had too little imagination to wonder what lay beyond the shadows in the damp tunnels about them or whether the odd rustlings might be something worse than rats, though the torch picked out the red pinpoints of their eyes and sometimes they were disturbingly far above the floor of stone. But Kalispar, who had never blanched at battlefield gore, was badly unnerved from the spectacle on the scaffold. Gretchen and Faermon had broken down appallingly and from the platform he could see even the queen quiver in terror before she was hoisted kicking above the gasping crowd.

They were both relieved to reach the massive bronze door to the king's crypt. A moment's inspection showed that the tomb was undisturbed, the brazed seal intact. Kalispar bade the swarthy little magician hold the torch while he struck off the seal with his shortsword. The heavy bronze door yielded slowly with a sly creaking sound. The widening wedge of light stretched across the floor to cut the lidless coffin.

Something was horribly wrong. Could the king have awakened prematurely and thrown off the lid? The ritual offerings of food were scattered and trampled. They crept toward the coffin one step at a time, Vlat peering around the tall warrior.

Kalispar mumbled and almost tripped when he stepped on something. A shoe. It seemed to have something in it. His blonde hair stood out on end.

The king's hand dangled over the side of the coffin, a signet ring catching the torchlight. When Kalispar reached out and touched it, it fell to the floor. It had been gnawed off at the wrist. They leaned over the coffin and peered with bulging eyes at King Knesephon.

The sturdy soldier retched and retched and the necromancer fainted dead away.

When Kalispar could control himself he carried Vlat out into the corridor and pulled the bronze door to. The royal house of Kondar was at an end.

Control

It was to be a controlled experiment, you see. That was the whole point of it. A controlled venture into the unknown, proving at once that the known laws of space and time could be breached by the immemorially old black arts, and that the processes could be so controlled that the influence of each factor could be thoroughly determined, and the whole experiment made absolutely reproducible. And she was to be my right arm, my protégé, in science and scholarship; my meticulously trained assistant, my independent observer—and my loyal companion. It was she who found at last the moldering fragment of that medieval grimoire, that echo from a distant past that put success within our grasp.

I met her while the project was maturing in my mind, after decades of patient scholarship, fruitless experimentation. Again and again my practical efforts had fallen just short of success, my research papers denied publication as fanciful. Again and again I had slaved in low-paying positions in mediocre colleges, only to have tenure and the prestige that went with it denied. I migrated downward from post to post, eventually hitting bottom at this wretched institution in a teaching status little better than that of a graduate student.

But the years had not been completely wasted, not by any mean. My bookish research had discovered for me the faint and hidden traces of those dark eras and haunted cities and mysterious individuals who had indeed preserved the real tradition of black magic; real, working processes that terrified the faint-hearted. And I had convincing proof that some of these explorers of the dark had in their megalomania left written accounts of their work. I knew what I must do; I must find one of these records, however fragmentary, and apply the ancient methods, guessing and experimenting where necessary, until the magic worked beyond dispute, and do it all in a controlled, impeccably scientific manner.

And Marika would be my companion and most trusted associate. I met her in my seminar on medieval history, an enchanting pixie with a keen and flexible mind, amidst a pack of prize boneheads. It's true that I was physically attracted to her: the little heart-shaped face with the green tilted eyes, framed in dark blond hair; the lithe, exquisitely curved dancer's figure; she never failed to excite me. Her buoyant, coquettish personality was unforgettable. But it was above all for her *mind* and her *spirit* that I loved her. In my stale little campus world, only she had the imagination and intelligence to follow out my arguments and see, as I did, that there was an awesome truth beneath the layers of legend surrounding the dark arts. Indeed, she had the courage to dare the unknown and experiment with things that had terrified the faint of heart since the infancy of the human race.

She responded to me as a combination of father, mentor and lover. No one paid any attention when I leased the old two-storied bay-windowed pile on a shady side street a half mile from the campus, and no one noticed when Marika quietly moved in with me. Those first few weeks together were a golden idyll of delicious and uninhibited love, of shared enthusiasm, of resonant dreams. During that Edenic time I taught her carefully what must be done, how to keep every last detail controlled and meticulously recorded, while together we prowled the libraries and rare book dealers of the nearby metropolis.

It was Marika who found the book.

"Rod!" she gasped in a loud whisper, "Come look at this! I can't believe . . ." An explosive sneeze cut her short. The mold and dust of these rooms full of ancient books always got to her after a long exposure. I touched my forefinger to my lips to remind her not to betray our enthusiasm to the hard-dealing little bookseller buried in his accounts on the other side of the room.

She had opened a cardboard book box with a catalog number penciled on it, and was staring with wild-eyed delight at a tattered fragment of a medieval book. She was fairly bouncing with excitement (in between stifled sneezes), looking, I noted, comical and sexy at the same time, as though the intensity of our quest held an erotic quality for her.

It was in rather peculiar Latin, in a variant of black letter, quite difficult to follow. It appeared to be the back portion of a much longer book, sans cover and with many of the pages torn or dog-eared. The paper was yellowed and almost too brittle to touch. It looked like the kind of item sold mainly for scientific tests on paper and ink, or to help round out someone's thesis on paleography. As I adjusted to the script, it became apparent that it was indeed a grimoire, a dark record of arcane methods. Interspersed among the Latin were occasional words of what I recognized as very archaic Dutch. The fascination of forbidden things gripped me as it became clear that it was no less than a treatise on demonology—the careful record of a vain and brilliant man who had trafficked with evil, with malignant things, things hidden away in darkling spheres of dimensionality mercifully concealed from our own. His pedantic prose left no doubt that he was recording his own experiences. By the time I glanced at the last page I didn't really need the confirmation; the phrase, "I, Nicholas van den Poel . . ." I had long since identified the author of these midnight horrors.

I sent Marika out of the store and managed to conceal my burning interest well enough to make the purchase at a bargain price. As soon as we were out of earshot and driving home with our treasure, Marika let out an unrestrained whoop of delight. That night we pored feverishly together over the black letter pages till it was long after midnight and we knew what we would have to do to fulfill our dream. Then we made love until dawn.

The next two weeks were taut with suspense and anticipation. I insisted on absolute precision in all details, checking and rechecking our translation of the ceremony to raise the obscure demon-creature Meliog, making careful notes of our sources as we verified the corrupt Latin and colloquial Dutch words. We scoured the city for garden fresh spices, live bats and salamanders; we compromised nothing in the details of our preparation. I think the suspense worked badly on Marika; again and again she tried to cajole me into a premature experiment. I realize now that she was talking to her friends, hinting of great things to come. She was of the 'instant gratification' generation; patience was painful to her.

The thurible sits before me now; a three-legged brass brazier, decorated with the letters of the cryptic Enochian script. The subtle aroma of spices is cold and faint. I remembered how it filled the upper-story room that night, the night our preparations bore fruit and we first peered into the very face of the unknown. We wore the rich robes Marika had sewn for us (she wore nothing else, I found afterwards). The thurible sat smoldering on the sideboard, by the brass chalice with its carefully brewed infusion. We moved solemnly about the room, consecrating the space, erecting the barriers against psychic interference. We outlined the circles of protection for ourselves with the special chalk and retraced them with the black-handled knife, the athame. With each movement and with every syllable we intoned, with every touch of the cold steel or warm brass I could feel the power of the occult tradition; everything we did was an echo of what had been done beneath the full moon since the Paleolithic age.

We took our places within our circles and began the chant in unison, in low penetrating tones. Marika was not bouncing that time; her eyes were huge and riveted to the space within the pentacle which would contain the . . . thing. There was no long, heart-sinking wait wondering if it were, after all, a fiasco. Before twenty syllables had sounded in the stillness there was an unmistakable change to the very *space* in the room. The yellow candle light seemed to become a tangible entity, giving solidity to every shape it filled, creating a sphere of golden mystery where the laws of nature could not be trusted. The candles themselves seemed to flicker almost imperceptibly, though there was no movement of air.

The sound came first, at first formless, like the ocean-sound in a conch held to the ear; then an emerging rhythm, a rolling of eerily low tones sculpting the formless rush into syllables too faint to distinguish. I had to remind Marika to continue chanting; she was gaping open-mouthed at the pentacle. Then came a shapeless cloud of purple, shimmering and writhing in the pentacle, like black light illuminating an invisible fog.

As we strained to pick out some recognizable detail in the cloud, Marika chanted louder and strained forward with her toes right at the edge of her circle. I motioned her back wordlessly while I kept up the droning chant; later I would remind her forcefully that we must at all times keep all parts of ourselves within the circles, and above all, never interrupt the chant or speak to any being that came, before it spoke to us.

We could hardly be certain of the dim form that congealed out of the violet cloud, in the exact center of the pentacle, but there was no doubt about the preternatural chill that raised visible goose bumps on both of us and made my hair rise away from my scalp, or the sudden darkness as though the candles had been magically turned down, or the *ruby eyes that glared at us*. I could see from the bookshelves behind it that the eyes were a bit below the height of my shoulders.

And then the voice, that low, grating, abominably *cold* voice clarified into a horribly toneless chant, "I AM MELIOG, I AM MELIOG, I . . ." and there emerged from the violet cloud, clutching spasmodically and groping toward the edge of the pentacle, a foul, hairy, taloned claw.

I'm quite sure that almost no one but us could ever have repeated the experiment after hearing that voice, seeing those eyes and that hand. As well prepared as we were, we both froze with horror and stopped our chant. Immediately all of the phenomena receded; within thirty seconds the room felt warm, the candle light looked like normal candle light, the pentacle was an empty figure on the hardwood floor.

It took another ten seconds for Marika's stunned silence to turn into manic jubilation. "Rod! Rod! We did it . . . did you see that *thing?* It . . ." It was all I could do to get her back to our essential procedure of writing down all of our impressions before comparing notes.

After a sleepless night of intoxicating speculation and self-congratulation, she was ready to do it again, right then, in broad daylight, at eight in the morning. Of course she understood as well as I the need to be methodical, planning carefully, conducting a *controlled* experiment. Finally I agreed to do it again in three days, even though the moon wouldn't be in the proper phase. I wanted to go over our notes and look for any clue as to how to enhance the ceremony or eliminate anything that didn't seem to help. I also wanted to compare our experience with what was said in the van den Poel book. Of course we had to get fresh materials again, too.

Again I could see the strain of waiting in a state of almost hypnotic excitement. But she worked devotedly on her notes and the meticulously scholarly debriefing process which I had prescribed. Underneath her bubbling impatience, she was a true scholar. It was a joy to see that I had succeeded in teaching her a professionalism that is almost impossible to find in students these days.

But we never held that second session. Nemesis can take bizarre, even ludicrous and clownish forms. Disaster struck Marika and I in the form of a burnt out electric generator. The campus had generated its own electricity since it was built seventy years ago, when the small town's facilities couldn't supply them. Over the years the campus had continued to operate its decrepit machines long after it ceased to make sense financially. The day we were to plunge again into the unknown, generator number 3 finally destroyed itself beyond repair. It was connected in an obsolete form of network that allowed it to damage all the others badly.

The college was paralyzed. There was no light. They couldn't even pump water to the restrooms. The administration erupted into civil war, with platoons of ambitious mediocrities squaring off to tattle over who was to be blamed and who would be appointed to save the situation.

I was appointed to one emergency committee after another, attending endless meetings till all hours of the might. As the lowest-ranking least-prestigious lowest-paid member I invariably got tagged to draft the long, dull, perfectly stupid, ultimately unread, report, which each committee issued. For two weeks I hardly had time to shave and shower, much less cushion Marika's rage and frustration at the delay in fulfilling our work. Only now, in retrospect, do I see in my mind's eye how her frustration turned to anger, how a dull glaze grew in her green eyes and her mouth turned down as rage soured to bitter disappointment. She simply had too much energy to contain like that, day after agonizing day. I finished typing my last report at 2.00 a. m., on a foggy night. It was All Hallows Eve.

For the first few steps I plodded, my exhausted feet pounding the hard pavement, the clammy air an irritant. And then the magic of the night grew upon me; the halos of light mysteriously hanging in white, wispy space. My hearing intensified. I was a fish at the bottom of an echoing ocean, the sounds whispering clearly, intimately of mysteries just beyond sight. My footsteps became cat-soft, marking the time, as time hung heavy in the dripping air. The fall of each glistening drop from every brooding tree was answered by a dozen more, in answer to its little gasp.

Space took on substance, as it had under the demon spell. How could it be? I stopped; I listened even more intently. The darkness clasped its secrets to its damp and muffling bosom while each isolated light ruled its own vault of glistening treasures; the streets before me were a labyrinth of black-arched rooms where long-forgotten treasures sang their whispering songs.

There had been a padding out there, beneath the rustling drips. I strained to see. Did something move out there? I waited, my night vision coming quickly, my heart pounding.

There! By that clump of juniper. No shape, just a slow oily movement, as though the rightmost tree had surreptitiously grown a new bulge in the darkness.

It did not move; it was the growing clarity of my straining eye that separated it from the tree. Silent it stood; did it sway slightly? No; my eye made it seem to. It had the silhouette of a man against the gloom, though I could not see the legs.

The street became a jungle of dank pavement and hovering trees, the sidewalk a dim-lit path from lighted glade to glade. I would not need to come near the man, or whatever it was. My footfalls seemed even louder in the long tunnels between the haloed lights.

I stopped again; and for one elusive moment I heard it padding, so soft, so near; my blood was ice. My heart pounded, my breath was forced and shallow. Once again I stopped in the false safety of a globe of misty light. It was so far to the next, so far. I broke into a forced pace and did not stop again; in the interstices between my own footsteps I could hear, now halting, now scurrying, a soft padding counterpoint. At times I couldn't be sure whether it was behind me or in front of me. I ran the last block to our house.

The street was pitch black here; there were lights upstairs, in the study where we raised the demon and in the right-hand bay window of the room where we slept. I rushed up on the front porch and pressed my back to the front door, gasping. I strained to hear that sinister padding; between the drips, the panting breaths, the booming heartbeats. Nothing; the foggy night was pristine, innocent, enigmatic. Was that a sound within the house? I couldn't be sure. I turned and tried the door knob. It was unlocked. We often left it that way. I pushed in, slowly. The ground floor was pitch dark except for a few stray dim shafts from distant streetlights through the windows.

"Marika?"

Silence. I realized I had called out in a loud whisper.

"Marika!" Not a shout, but she should have heard me upstairs. The hackles rose on my neck. I moved in tiny, silent steps to the foot of the stairs, stopping at each point where I could see into a ground floor room.

"Marika!" It was a frightened plea.

A tiny glint of light caught my eye. It came from the kitchen at the rear of the house. There was something wrong about it. I held my breath as I inched toward the kitchen door. The tiniest glint of reflected light from a lighted window far away was reflected by the window in the back door. It had seemed wrong because of the angle; the back door was ajar.

I stood frozen for a long time. Nothing stirred, no shadow oozed with oily movement, the house was as silent as the bottom of the sea except for the barely audible creaking of old wood, swollen by the damp air. I moved back to the foot of the stairs, still silent. The second stair creaked as I eased my weight onto it, as did the seventh. Light shone out the door of the study into the hallway, a dim, steady yellow light. Candle light. At the top of the stair I could smell the spices in the thurible. When I looked into the room I saw instantly what she had done, and my heart screamed silently in pain and rage and irretrievable, inconsolable loss.

She could not endure the waiting. The patience of the professional, the dedicated scholar and investigator had been too much to demand of her.

Night after deadening night, alone in the old house, the bright enthusiasm turning bitter, finally drinking in a defiant insult to the fates—there was an almost empty wine bottle on the sideboard by the chalice and the still-smoking thurible— she had finally done the unforgivable; she had indulged in a childish prank, a fatuous, undisciplined, bungled parody of our work, certain to discredit us as investigators if the merest hint of this ever got out. And I knew in the pit of my stomach that it would, must come out. For the chalk marks on the floor told the story, the scuff marks where she had inched out of her circle toward the pentacle, no doubt cajoling the thing in her drunken excitement. Perhaps she lurched past the border of the pentacle; perhaps her ceremonial controls were defective in some way we could never have foreseen. There had been a struggle which had obliterated one entire side of the pentacle, and an end table with a lamp on it had been overturned. There were a few dark spats on the floor, like blood . . . I picked up the long black-handled athame from where it had fallen.

The thing was loose and I had little idea of how to regain control of it. In her impatience she had betrayed us. My career must end, not in triumph, but in a humiliating fiasco—if not a tragedy! The thing was loose . . .

"Marika!" I cried, and this time I heard light footsteps tripping down the hall! I rushed out into the hall aid called again, "Marika!"

But it was not Marika. It was a thing with crimson eyes and a muzzle like a wolf's and a lolling tongue, a thing that rolled its eyes and bayed in a sepulchral moaning voice and crouched on goat-like haunches before it sprang at me with outstretched hairy claws and a stench of death in its hot breath.

Foul claws ripped my face, my chest, the powerful talons of the hind paws dug into the flesh of my thighs, gripping me as the head twisted and the open jaws went for my throat. My hands went up instinctively to push the thing away; the blade of the athame sliced its cheek.

It howled with pain and fury and backed away, still pawing at me, trying to reach past the knife. I staggered backwards down the hall, holding the knife in front of me. It followed, alternately lunging and cringing, whining and snarling.

I sensed the door to the bedroom beside me. I thrust at the demon with the knife, and as it pulled back I opened the door and jumped in and slammed it, dropping the knife and clutching the doorknob with both hands. A fraction of a second later it crashed into the door, visibly bowing it inward. Again and again it crashed, taking no notice of the doorknob. I held on with one hand and turned to pick up the athame and then, through the bloody haze over one eye and the maddening clarity of the other, I saw her, eyes bulging, mouth gaping, sprawled in the tatters of her robe, her fine soft figure raked and bloodied, dead. Her childish betrayal had led her to final tragedy.

I crouched frozen while the door behind me boomed a dozen, two dozen times. My grief paralyzed my mind; there was time and space for nothing but the hideous reality of my beloved's death, her pitiful, ravaged corpse, the end of all our brilliant hopes and dreams, our tender loving moments, our future of marvels and success and happiness . . . then, for the last time, that agony left me. I rose in an ecstasy of hate and fury and yanked open the door.

I leaped at it, thrusting the consecrated knife into the shadow-thing's face. It jumped backward in surprise, cowering back stepwise down the hall before my heedless thrusts. It seemed to shrink each time the consecrated knife touched it. It leapt sideways into the study, seeking the broken pentacle as a haven. I followed it to the edge as it bayed and shrank and faded away in a purple haze to whatever vale of horror it had come from.

It was to be a *controlled* experiment, you see. But now my beloved, my fair, my faithless, my tragic Marika is dead, and I must follow. To you who have followed my work and believed in me I leave this tape, that you may know that all our years of search were not in fruitless delusion. But the cost, the cost . . .

I will drop the tape in the mailbox at the corner, so that it will not burn with the house, and my hopes and dreams, and my Marika.

That Which Devours

I felt a pang of nostalgia when I turned from the sidewalk down the dark walkway to the old Haemlich place. The tall elms were in full leaf and the streetlight at the corner did not penetrate far into the gloom. Edgar had let the skirt of willowy shrubs grow long and unkempt and the line of the roof was obscured by the trees; the few scattered window lights only emphasized the dark bulk of it. But I remembered from childhood long ago the beautiful limestone Victorian edifice with the long wooden porches upstairs and down. It was the seat of my mother's family, rich in wistful memories. After my grandmother's death my older brother Edgar, the wild brother, the unpredictable one, had moved into it.

That was natural. He had always taken after that side of the family with their wildness and imagination and touch of madness, while I had adopted, or, perhaps, been forced into, the stodgy conservative mold of our father's clan, stolid bourgeoisie all. A business degree at the state university, a tranquil apprenticeship in Father's business, the president's desk at Father's death—a career heartily approved of by every member of the Armstrong family. Except for Edgar, that is. He thought it an appalling waste of life and taunted me endlessly with the dullness of it. For Edgar life was one escapade, one scandal, one dreamy quest after another. In adolescence it was girls and liquor and cars. In young manhood it was traveling to remote corners of the earth, often in trouble with the authorities and frequently wiring for money. I envied and despised him at the same time.

I was glad to have him take the old house under the elms when Grandfather Haemlich died. It divided up part of the family estate fairly without disturbing my household in the big white house eight blocks away. And after all, Edgar was more of a Haemlich than an Armstrong. He certainly had more than a bit of the strangeness that had culminated in our mother's death in a mental institution when we were children. His adventures were reminiscent of Grandfather Haemlich himself, and now he was repeating Grandfather's black magic scandal. In Grandfather's time it had been scandalously evil: now it was scandalously foolish. I was afraid Edgar would make us a laughing stock.

Yet at the same I was jealous. More and more as I entered middle age I felt the stifling monotony of my life and the secret fear grew that Edgar had been right all along. I had been a fool and would grow old and die knowing that all adventure and excitement had passed me by. It grated on me more and more the way Edgar boasted of his inheritance, Grandfather's memorabilia from the four corners of the earth and above all the treasure trove of magical and alchemical manuscripts and the paraphernalia he had amassed to use them.

He had alternately ignored and mocked my protestations that they were legally as much mine as his, that no division had been agreed upon, and countered saying that he was better equipped to make use of them. So now I had come to confront him, armed with an impressive legal document drawn up by the firm's lawyers stating my claim and intention to sue.

There were lights in at least four rooms, upstairs and down. That was unusual for him. In the past when I had driven by there had never been more than one and that usually upstairs. I stepped up on the porch and rang the doorbell beside the oval-paned door.

I listened for his footsteps but could hear nothing stir within.

I rang again. This time I thought I heard a board creak upstairs but no footsteps. The light was on in the hallway behind the front door but I could see no sign of Edgar. The doors to the parlor on the left and the den on the right were open, as was the door to the kitchen at the rear. The stairs were visible on the left side of the hall but nothing stirred. I remembered that there was a landing at the top of the stairs but I could not see it from where I stood.

"Edgar!" I called, irritated at the wait. Of course! He had seen me coming up the walk and decided to amuse himself at my expense. I tried the doorknob gently. It was unlocked. I stepped into the hall. The parlor was unlit but the light from the hallway showed me that he was not in there, unless he was playing a really childish game of hide and seek. There was nothing at the top of the stairs.

I looked into the den. The light was on in there but I didn't see Edgar. I remembered the big old room, with its great fireplace and leather couch and armchairs, its walls decorated with Indian swords, Masai shields and spears, ancient muskets and daggers. Edgar shared Grandfather's outlandish tastes enough to leave it as it had been.

The last time I had been here he had sat smirking in a sumptuous leather armchair in the middle of the room as I labored to persuade him to the common sense step of selling some land we owned jointly. During his long-winded and asinine rebuttals I found myself staring at the remarkable volume on the table by his right hand, it was a huge folio, as thick as a big dictionary, with an intricately decorated leather binding and tarnished silver clasps. The spine was split at the top showing the ends of the gatherings and if there had ever been a title there it was no longer discernible. Closed it took up the whole table. He must have been gloating over it rather than reading it. He noticed my attention.

"No, little brother, its not from Grandfather's collection. I bought it myself." That in reference to our longstanding dispute over the ownership of Grandfather Haemlich's collection and quite likely a lie. And he knew how I hated being referred to that way. I began to fidget and move aimlessly around the room while he blathered an interminable monologue of childish heckling and fatuous argument. There was no lamp on, only a bit of sunlight from one undraped window. That's why I didn't notice what was on the bookshelf until he infuriated me further with some juvenile taunt and I spun on one heel to turn my back on him.

There on a partially cleared shelf a foot in front of my nose was a cage containing a large plump rat. Not a white or jet black or calico laboratory rat but a filthy brown whisker-twitching glitter-eyed barn rat with stained teeth.

I actually let out a little squeal and jumped back. Edgar cackled uproariously.

"I forgot you're not *familiar* with my pet." He articulated the word "familiar" archly as though it held some secret joke; then he burst into laughter again. "A delicate creature, you see. I must take great pains with its care and feeding." He was still laughing when I slammed the front door and stomped down the walkway and I was still paying taxes on that worthless dab of pasture.

This time I was certain I had heard the floor creak upstairs, followed by light muffled footsteps, as of stockinged feet. He was up there all right, barely able to stifle his laughter I'd say. I climbed the stairs soundlessly, easing each foot gently onto the old threadbare run-ner, hoping to catch him at his own game.

At the top I looked both ways down the dimly lit upstairs hall. I wasn't sure where the footsteps had been. There was a lighted doorway to my right. I tiptoed down to it and looked in. It was the big upstairs study, the one Grandfather had never let us enter.

It was a long high-ceilinged room, dark from the ancient figured wallpaper and heavy drapes and dark hardwood floorboards showing between the worn oriental carpets. It was lined with endless bookshelves, many glassed in, all filled to overflowing, and yet an open chest by the lamp in the middle of the room was full of more books. There were few chairs. Grandfather had rarely allowed visitors, but many tables. They were of all sizes and descriptions and cluttered the floor, making it difficult to walk around. Scattered haphazardly on their surfaces, covering them completely and threatening to spill over onto the floor, was a phantasmagoria of evil: all the symbols and accoutrements of black magic and necromancy were there, braziers inscribed in unknown alphabets, bottles and vials of unidentifiable substances, obscure talismans and parchments covered with cryptic formulae and diagrams. A large crystal ball sat on a stand in the midst of a table full of human skulls in various states of deterioration. On a table near a window was a collection of archaic chemical ware, a long-necked retort, alcohol burners and primitive distillation apparatus. A blackened spot of wallpaper marked the failure of one of Grandfather's experiments.

The chest by the lamp revealed an incredible collection of manuscripts and early books on magic and the occult that I judged would outclass most of the museums and private collections of the world. On the table in the lamplight a great tome lay open revealing long columns of Latin in a richly textured medieval Gothic hand. I shuddered when I recognized it as the same volume I had seen downstairs on that earlier occasion. I looked carefully around the room for a rat cage but saw none.

Next to the manuscript was a reference work on medieval Latin and a pile of notes on yellow legal size paper, apparently an attempt to translate the ancient Latin. It looked like Edgar had been re-evaluating his earlier work, for there were a number of notations evidently made with the red felt-tipped pen lying across the top sheet.

". . . most fearsome familiar spirit . . . tempts the (necromancer) with (its) uncanny power and fierceness."

Here there was an interlineation in red: . . . turn on (master?) . . . devour . . . body and soul." Then the older notes continued.

". . . created from earthly creature. Beast in womb or reptile in egg exposed to . . . influenced from the darkling spheres . . . at birth not wholly of earth . . . if fed upon unclean spirits of the earth and (relics?) of the brilliant and terrible among men . . ."

I drew back, repelled and fascinated. I looked around, appalled at the accumulated evidence of my Grandfather's and brother's aberration. Had Mother's premature dementia overtaken my brother? I didn't like the look of some of the skulls—they were too white, too fresh. In the dim lamplight they appeared oddly scratched. There was another chest next to the one full of books, at an angle as though it had been pulled there hastily. I lifted the lid with some trepidation. There was a charnel smell. It was full of bones, old and new, large and small. They appeared to be human, and they had been gnawed.

The soft thump-thump scampered down the stairs this time, there was no mistake about it. I rushed out on the lending but he had already disappeared again. I descended the stairs, watching carefully. I had the idea that Edgar was going to jump out and try to scare me. The door to the kitchen was standing at a different angle than before. There was a raw smell. When I looked inside I gagged. *My God, what had he been doing there?* There was blood everywhere. I tiptoed around the dark red splatters on the floor. There was no sign of the source of the blood. I had no more doubts that Edgar should and must be institutionalized.

The cellar door was standing ajar. My skin was crawling and I couldn't avoid the blood on the floor but I had to look, it was dark down there, pitch black at the bottom of the narrow stair. There was a sharp animal stench that cut through the rank smell of blood. Something moved in the darkness.

Behind me a hinge creaked. I turned and saw a waist-high cupboard door swinging slowly open. A limp and bloody arm flopped out. Edgar had been stuffed in there, what was left of him. The blood was his. He stared at me open-mouthed but saw nothing. He was past seeing. He dropped forward slightly and I could see that the back of his skull had been gnawed away.

It squealed with fury as it scampered up the stairs; it would have had me if I had taken time to turn and look at it. I jumped toward the door and swung around just in time to block its lunge for my throat.

It was the size of a collie. It looked like a rat except for the evil intelligence in its eyes and the human expressiveness of its mouth. And it stood on its hind legs and grappled with the chair with its filthy paws in a way no rat could do.

I doubled up my legs and kicked the chair away as hard as I could. The chair and the rat-thing went sprawling halfway across the kitchen while I rolled out the door and sprang up and grabbed the knob. I got it closed in time to feel a loathsome thud when it slammed into the lower panel. Three times came the muffled boom and the bulge in the panel, then a second's silence. I felt the knob turn against my hand, its paws were amazingly strong. The knob slowly twisted backward. I heard the latch click out of the socket. All the force I could exert pulling every tendon in my body could barely hold back that door as it pushed me back a millimeter at a time. Then abruptly the force was gone, the door banged to, the lock clicked back into place.

A trick? I held on desperately, sweating. There was a nauseating scurry in the kitchen. I twisted my head around and looked behind me. I stared at the door again and listened hard. No sound.

I let go the door and ran to the foot of the stairs. I grabbed the small telephone table, letting the phone fall with a clatter. Still no sound from the kitchen. I ran for the front door.

My hand was almost on the knob when I heard the scampering thumps on the porch in front of me. I dropped the telephone table and grabbed the doorknob with both hands.

It whammed against the door twice. I could see the dark shape bobbing around in the dark below the oval window. It jumped up twice so that I could see the sharp discolored gnawing incisors and the baleful glare in its manlike eyes. When it backed up to the edge of the porch I knew what was going to happen and jumped back into the doorway of the study before it came crashing through the glass oval squealing with rage.

Before it could change direction I grabbed a big armchair and heaved it into the doorway. It only covered the opening waist high but at least it was too low for the thing to get under. I knocked a lamp to the floor and picked up the end table under it by one leg.

When it tried to scramble over the back of the chair I slammed the table into it with a sickening thud. But it was too strong and heavy to be knocked back, it grasped the top of the table with its fore-paws and pulled.

I stood with one knee on the chair fencing with the thing as it squirmed and twisted, trying alternately to shake my grip on the table and to get around it. It got up on its hind legs on the back of the chair, I could see its scaly tail lashing behind it. A sudden unexpected thrust of the legs sent me reeling backward with table and clinging beast rising over my head as I bent backward to keep my balance. The clumsy tail whipped forward around my left wrist, I could see the whiskers twitching around the wrinkling muzzle and dark yellow incisors as it squealed and chattered in its fury. I screamed and ran forward against the weight and heaved the table with its unwholesome burden through the doorway above the chair.

My mind was paralyzed with terror, knowing only the frantic need for action in each glaring moment. I instinctively ran for the windows but behind me I could hear the thumping scamper of its run and the powerful thrust of both hind legs and the interval as it flew over the chair. In wordless panic I jumped up on the long couch and ran its length, then scrambled up the back of it onto the wide mantelpiece, smashing a ceramic demon and an ormolu clock to the hearth below. Crouching, I swung my arm back and caught the monster behind me in midair, sending it twisting to the floor. The incisors slashed my arm; my blood splattered the hearth.

I grabbed up the Masai spear from the wall beside me and turned it around with the point toward the floor. The thing glared at me past the point, grimacing and snarling and twitching its hideous whiskers. In ultimate desperation I thrust forward and down with my full weight, feeling the spear splinter ribs and pass through its rubbery guts and pin it to the floor. I hung in midair with my feet on the mantelpiece, clinging to the spear while the rat-thing shrieked and wailed in its death agony.

And as I hung there in space, sickened by the stench of its urine and bowels and feeling its writhing death throes, the siren-like squeals formed themselves into words, a furious string of curses and obscenities, and with its last gasp it shrieked, quite clearly, "I'll be back, little brother!"

The Bookseller's Second Wife

A. MACLACHLAN & CO., Bookseller said the gold letters on the big panes on either side of the door. The old book dealer was in an ancient brick building with a cement facade, just off the center of town in an area not slum, not prime territory to be propped up by subsidies. Not a place for an aggressive new business to get started; a place where the solid profit-makers of the past clung precariously to the present, each hoping to retire its band of proprietors and old hands gracefully before some random surge of economic change or new technological gadget made them obsolete. Nathan looked up and saw a dark figure move away from a dusty window on the fourth and top story; he thought he saw a rat jump back from a cornice.

A dreadful place to spend a youthful summer; his father's judgment upon him for graduating in art instead of engineering. His graduate fellowship did not begin until the fall three months away and the job market was just awful that summer. But he would have been content to live impecuniously at home and could have painted there, at least. There could be nothing but malice behind his father's insistence that he spend the summer assisting his great-uncle Alistair MacLachlan, a distant figure whom neither he nor his father knew well. The wages would consist of little above room, board and Greyhound fare.

Nathan set down his suitcases and knocked loudly on the door. The great glass panes, so vulnerable in this rough-looking neighborhood, were bleary with the grime of decades. He could see endless rows of tables piled high with disorderly stacks of books. Nothing stirred for a minute and he knocked again, rattling the long-paned door. He tried the door latch. It was unlocked. He maneuvered his bags through the doorway.

He was in a cavernous room with a ceiling almost twenty feet high. Most of the floor was occupied with books, with many of the stacks high enough to block his view. The walls were lined with bookshelves reaching almost to the ceiling, reached by tall ladders on rollers. Across the back of the room and half of the left-hand wall was a wide iron catwalk reached by a stair that appeared to be retractable like a fire escape.

Scurrying footsteps with a noticeable limp heralded a very short man with curly white hair and a seamed face with the startled eyes of the perpetual worrier. Instead of speaking to Nathan he turned and called, "It's him, Miz' MacLachlan, he's here!" and hared off like a bystander fleeing someone else's accident, leaving Nathan openmouthed with a stillborn question.

Fiona MacLachlan appeared on the catwalk. He had seen her once years ago, at a big family funeral. She had been 'one of the grownups' then, introduced and immediately forgotten, too old to be interesting. Now he guessed that she was in her thirties (a mature eye would have judged forty) and, in spite of this advanced age, strikingly attractive. She was tall and blond and her green dress clung to curves that were full but not plump as she descended the stair. She did not yell at him across the room but waited until they met at the foot of the stair.

"Welcome, Nathan," she said. "We are so glad that you could come." She had a trace of a foreign accent. "We are desperate for help, even though you have no business experience." The words stung him. His father was always taunting him with his economic uselessness.

"Well, I'll help you as well as I can. I guess even a painter can pack boxes and shuffle paperwork."

"Painter? Oh yes—your father said something about that." Her eyes twinkled a bit; they were dark brown and appraising him as boldly as a coach eyeing a rookie. She made him quite uncomfortable.

"Let's go back to the downstairs office. We can have a drink while I tell you what's going on. You must be tired—surely you didn't carry those bags all the way from the bus station?"

He blushed slightly. "It's only eight blocks. I thought I'd save the cab fare." Actually he was broke.

"Well, it's just as well you didn't call us. We don't have a car."

He left his bags at the foot of the stair and followed her through the maze of books to a large alcove at the rear. It was furnished with the dark heavy furniture of the 19th century, all recently dusted. There were a few small piles of the inevitable books but the place had obviously been tidied up. Fiona opened the roll top desk against the back wall revealing several bottles of liquor.

"Do you like Irish whiskey? That's my favorite. And we also have Scotch."

"I'll try Irish," he said. He would have referred a cold beer or a soft drink. He was thirsty after the stultifying bus ride and the long walk in the heat. The air in the alcove was fresh and moving, though it was quite warm. He guessed that they controlled the humidity for the sake of the books but not the temperature for the people. She mixed weak highballs from a pitcher of ice water and eat down at a big mahogany table with a cloth cover. He sat opposite her.

The little white haired man appeared abruptly. "Miz' MacLachlan, I can't find that 1892 Golden State Encyclopedia, it's not where you said and . . ."

"Don't worry, Pumphrey, we'll find it later. Nathan can help us look for it. Just go on to the next item on the list."

"Yes, Miz' MacLachlan," he said and vanished again into the maze.

"Pumphrey's the only help we've been able to keep for many years." She was eyeing him again, this time with an unreadable intentness. "We have to have somebody reasonably intelligent and also able to do a certain amount of physical work. Pumphrey's really good at handling the rare books that need special treatment but he's not so young any more. And now we have a huge order in, a big contract that we need desperately to get on our feet financially, and he and I just can't handle it by ourselves."

She was gazing out at the book-lined cavern now and there was a touch of weariness in her expression. She had strong clean features, he noticed, with none of the tell-tale flabbiness that so often marks the onset of middle age.

"Alistair doesn't do any physical work any more," she added. "Though he is completely alert mentally and handles all the special museum items personally except for the actual shipping. Actually that sort of business has really kept us going for a long time now. But we need this big book order to get in good shape financially. Alistair landed the contract through an old friend at the University of

Montana. They're expanding their library system and we were lucky to get a piece of it."

"I don't understand," he said with a sinking feeling, "You mean you want me to stuff all this in boxes? Is that it?"

She smiled. "Not all of it. We need to start shipping the things we already have in stock right away and send out requests for the rest to other dealers. That way they can start cataloguing right away. The only way they can get it all done in time for the fall semester is to get shipments from us regularly throughout the summer. Unfortunately the first part is the hardest."

"You mean shipping the things you already have? How *do* you find them?"

"Unfortunately—sometimes we can't. It comes down to a lot of digging through stacks of old books."

"You mean you don't have records of the locations of all this stuff?" He looked out incredulously at the endless piles of books on the tables, on the floor in the aisles between the tables, on their side on the lower shelves, in neater rows higher up, in piles again on top, nearly touching the ceiling . . .

"You mean you just dumped them as they came in without making any records? Even an artist would know better than that!"

"Well of course we keep records!" she bristled. She took a pull on her drink. "Or at least we did . . . Then Alistair became less active, Pumphrey got more and more scatterbrained, a lot would come in and something else would come up before we could log it properly. When an order had to be filled we were always in a desperate rush, we moved things around and didn't have time to put them back. And then some of the log books were destroyed in an accident. Our catalog got so out of date we haven't mailed it in years. Our best stock isn't in it, half of what *is* in it is gone and we can barely locate the rest," The sharp tone had trailed off into despair.

"So," he said, and savored a sip of his whiskey, "you hired me to spend the summer scampering up and down the ladders like a squirrel and packing boxes."

She smiled and cocked her head. "That's about it. Not what you would call an artistic job. But you look able enough, even if you don't know a thing about the business. We can't pay you much but with room and meals furnished you can save most of it."

He stared gloomily out at the appalling chaos throughout the room and felt the whiskey spread through his veins. He wanted to be somewhere else, anywhere. He wanted to reject his father and his father's judgment on him. He could drag out the summer, playing the idiot she thought him, surviving somehow to flee back to the world of art and intellect that had beckoned to him. But—

He also wanted to show this woman, so irritating yet so appealing, that he was not a nincompoop at all.

Fight or flight—

He chose to fight. "Why don't you put it all on a computer? It's not that hard, you know."

"A computer?" Her eyebrows went up in surprise. "But they cost thousands of dollars. And I don't know anything about them and neither does Pumphrey. Or Alistair. We can hardly afford ledgers."

"You could get one for about five hundred that would handle this mess for you. I could show you how to get started. My roommate had one and I learned a bit. By the time we get on top of this order we'll have looked in just about every nook and cranny of the place. If we start making notes and buy a machine as soon as the University makes a payment—they are paying something before fall aren't they?"

"Yes, of course. But are you certain—?"

"Well, we've got plenty of time to talk about it," he said, enjoying a secret glee. "It won't hurt to start making notes on where things are located, will it? Whether they wind up on a computer or not. Well, when do I start?"

"I'll show you your room upstairs. Then if you're ready we've got plenty of lists . . ."

An hour later Nathan sat perched atop one of the high ladders where he had climbed in pursuit of a 17th century grimoire looking out giddily over the vast room. The gilt-lettered panes that had seemed so tall from the street were below him now, a myriad of runnels streaking their length from the evening thundershower outside. The air had gotten gradually cooler. He felt Alistair's presence behind him as a sudden chill, almost an electric tingle on his skin, even before he heard the dry cough. When he turned his uncle was on the catwalk, behind and a little below him.

He stood motionless, peering intently at Nathan and, after the little cough, made no sound. He wore a black suit of old-fashioned cut and leaned on a stick whose golden head was cast in the shape of a gargoyle. His wispy white hair bushed out as though electrified and his intense expression might have been a smile.

Although he was no more than twenty-five feet from Nathan and the silence was marred only by the patter of rain he felt it would be somehow inappropriate to hail the old man across the room. He made his way gingerly down the ladder, threaded the piles of books and climbed the iron stair to meet his silent host and patron. When he finally faced him he found himself tongue-tied.

"Hello, Nathan," came the voice at last, exceedingly thin and dry yet resonant, like the whisper of an operatic baritone. "I have needed you for a long time." The mouth was small and pursed, the teeth tiny and sharp. "Your youth will be of great benefit to us here. Your strength, your intelligence. This place has seen no youth for much too long."

Still Nathan's tongue was dry and still. Alistair was definitely smiling, not so much in the mouth as in the eyes, which were of a feline yellow. Of every feature of the ancient's appearance, only the eyes did not tell of age; they were timeless.

"We will make good use of your youthful vigor here, Nephew," he said and then he turned and moved slowly and deliberately back into the hall that led from the catwalk into the warren of old rooms and corridors, apparently unconcerned that Nathan had never spoken. And ever after Nathan felt his presence there, permeating every stone of that place.

Later, when Nathan fell asleep in his tiny second floor room to the distant roll of thunder and the spatter of rain in the alley outside his window, he dreamed of great yellow eyes, and falling, and of a strange sickness that made him feel weak and old.

For the next two weeks Nathan swam in a sea of first editions and 'half morocco binding' and 'slightly foxed pages.' The faint dusty smell of the books, mild and not unpleasant, was always with him day and night. In a surprisingly short time he began to find his way through the endless stacks confidently, acquiring a vast amorphous knowledge of the untidy book-trove. Alistair he rarely saw; he took his meals in his room and only rarely appeared on the catwalk to look out over the work, a presence more felt than seen. Pumphrey was always quietly scurrying among the piles of books, almost never speaking more than a few words at a time and all of them to Fiona. Nathan genuinely enjoyed the quiet and the solitude of the work but after a stretch of an hour or two he would find himself looking for an excuse to talk to Fiona.

She seemed to welcome his conversation, like someone rediscovering the joy of companionship after a long enforced loneliness. She soon found that Nathan was an asset in filling the big university order and treated him with a new respect. Like Nathan she spent long days hunting books, even climbing the great ladders (Pumphrey was afraid of heights), typing lists, packing boxes. She wore jeans which looked fine on her firm ripe figure; it became apparent that she had dressed up especially for his arrival that day. Pumphrey lived near the shop but off the premises so the two of them ate together and talked about the order and the computer project, which Alistair had half assented to, and of Nathan's youthful enthusiasms which seemed to stir her oddly. At his suggestion they ate out twice, at nearby restaurants. They left almost furtively, after Alistair had been served in his room (Fiona slept in her own room) and she seemed delighted with this simple pleasure. There was no television set in the place and Nathan finally enticed her out to a movie where she seemed to rediscover the basic experience of laughter.

It was the night after the first big shipment had gone out that she came to his room. The excitement of meeting the goal and proving his worth had vanished like a bubble, the vision of the long stifling summer lay upon him like a shroud. He had showered off the dust of the books and lay on his narrow bed, listening to the first drops of rain.

She did not knock. She opened the door silently and held a finger to her lips, cutting short the blurted greeting on his startled tongue. She closed the door soundlessly behind her and came to him. She wore a diaphanous peignoir; she untied the sash and let it fall open. Firm breasts, flat stomach, a profusion of blond body hair; no words, no proposals, no assent, their bodies entwined and explored with rapt abandon. Soft eyelashes, mobile lips, hard nipples, hips both muscular and downy-soft, all as new and amazing as if he had never touched or imagined a woman before in any dream or incarnation. The college girls he had known, with their coquetry and self-conscious sophistication seemed like spoiled children playing doctor. For an awful moment his own self-consciousness surged up and he wondered in panic if he would be able to respond to this fierce, knowing, *total* woman but when she mounted him on that narrow little bed and took him deep and hot he found that his own body knew precisely what to do and when and it mattered not what he thought or felt. He willed nothing and all was perfect. When she left him the rain had stopped and there was dawn-glow in the sky.

For Nathan the weeks of that endless summer crept on in dreamlike slow motion. On the one hand the work in the labyrinth of books became less oppressive and more interesting as the old bookseller's became the one place in space and time where he wished to be; on the other, time hung in the air about him like stagnant smoke as he waited for the next time of passion in his little room. Only then, in embrace with her flesh and hair and musk and whispered voice, did time swirl and rush with abandon.

Fortunately the peculiar arrangements of the old bookseller's household made it possible for her to come to him more nights than not. Although Alistair did not seem at all feeble and obviously dominated Fiona and Pumphrey completely he lived the life of a recluse, appearing rarely and speaking little, taking all of his meals alone in his room. Fiona slept in an adjacent bedroom on the fourth story so that, even though her husband's room had been lined with cork in the distant past and was largely soundproof, it was out of the question for Nathan to go there. But it was safe enough for her to tiptoe down to him after the shop had been locked for the night. Pumphrey lived off the premises nearby and was gone by seven each evening. Once the work was done for the day and Pumphrey let out like a pet cat the doors would be locked and, unless Nathan was going out for the evening, the stair to the catwalk pulled up. The city had more than its share of violent crime and this unusual security precaution didn't surprise Nathan as much as the survival of the great glass panes of the windows on the street. Thus their trysts were almost nightly.

Those delicious, summer nights were long and sultry and in their murmured conversations he learned as much about his exotic lover as she was willing to tell him. She had been married before and had come to Alistair as a mature and forceful personality, attracted to him by his knowledge and power in the eldritch lore of subterranean magic. Fiona had been steeped in such things herself before she met him, as had his first wife, Cordelia. In reply to his timid hinted questions she discussed the physical passions of the first years of their marriage frankly, mischievously amused at Nathan's embarrassment. Yes, Alistair had been an attractive lover in those days. Though no longer young he was physically vigorous and his powerful personality had been fascinating to her. Their lovemaking had been enhanced by the atmosphere of ritual magic and the use of esoteric drugs. But for many years now Alistair, though still physically strong in most ways, had shown no interest in her as a woman. He remained strong, she said, but not youthful. Now she feared him but feared more to leave. His first wife had disappeared under mysterious circumstances. Alistair had given out that she had first gone on a long trip, then decided not to come back. The fear in Fiona's voice and expression when she whispered of this convinced Nathan that she knew (or suspected) more than she would tell him.

At first Nathan was too infatuated and fulfilled and flattered to question their relationship; like a naughty child he felt exhilarated to be breaking all the rules and the rewards were too overwhelming even to consider turning down. But as the summer went on he began to chafe at the deception of the old man. It was his pride more than his morality that prickled; he began to feel sneaky and cheap. He felt trapped as she did, oppressed by his surroundings but having no money and no job prospects elsewhere. He assumed her trap was the same as his; her references to the black arts and her subtle signs of physical fear puzzled him briefly and passed from his mind. And so Fiona began in her own oblique way to educate Nathan in the realities of their enclosed world.

Fiona made out the lists of books for he and Pumphrey to retrieve, as well as for herself. At first he thought she was just giving him the most strenuous assignments, most of the ladder work and the corners of the room. But soon he noticed a pattern to the spaces he was sent to comb and a distinct trend to the titles he sought. On the tables in one of the less accessible corners and in the lower glassed-in cases was an enormous cache of modern authorities on mythology, folklore, witchcraft, ritual magic and kindred subjects in frayed dust jackets and sturdy uninspired 19th edition bindings. Margaret Murray's *The God of the Witches* was there in multiple copies, as was her *Witch-Cult in Western Europe*, Montague Summers' *History of Witchcraft and Demonology* and many others. The complete works of the bizarre magician Aleister Crowley had pride of place there.

The first cases high enough to need a ladder contained 18th and 19th century treatises and translations of older sources, many privately printed, with leather corners and gilt-lettered spines and yellow-spotted pages: *Maleus Maleficarum*, the Ashwin translation of Remigius' *Demonolatria* and the rare *A Warning to Those Who Delve* of the mysterious Squire Philip Howard . . . works of similar vintage were stocked in depth. Another category here that puzzled Nathan was a profusion of titles concerning Indian religion and yogic practices.

But when he mounted the rickety ladder to the topmost cases and the dusty individual boxes on top of them he began to realize the full extent of the old wizard's store of infamous lore. Indeed, this had been the object of Fiona's lesson, for she often directed him in furtive tones to 'inventory' just these regions, when nothing had been ordered from them. There, as he perched on the flimsy ladder glancing frequently at the door where Alistair might appear, he found nothing newer than von Könnenberg's *Uralte Schrecken* with its plain black leather binding and silver lock. Dr. Dee in a great Elizabethan folio with the royal imprint and a Latin title in gold on the front edge; Ludwig Prinn in brooding black-letter; the much-debated Count Cagliostro in a magnificent private edition full of engraved diagrams, decorated in gold filigree echoed on the edges; a manuscript in Hebrew on parchment enclosed in heavy wooden boards covered with plain leather, with an inscription in French on the front end-paper containing the words 'Abra-Melin' and 'originale' . . . every dark soul who had dared the forbidden arts for centuries was there, in the original or in translation. And the old man's trove did not stop there. The boxes on the top contained manuscripts and incised clay tablets at which Nathan could only shudder. Fiona referred to these as Alistair's trading stock; in his unseen chambers he had copies of everything here that he considered of value and more that he would never sell to any public institution.

As the outlines of the bookseller's monstrous collection became clear to him Nathan was shocked; yet he could only see it in terms of hysterical gullibility, the common delusion of a group of frail old men. He was amazed to see that Fiona did not react in the same way as himself; she was always tense and deadly serious when she spoke or hinted at Alistair's strange predilections. She in turn seemed puzzled at his casual attitude. Her hints and subtle pointers began to direct him toward the side of Alistair's business which they referred to euphemistically as 'special museum items.'

He was aware that these objects were an important part of the business and had often seen Fiona and Pumphrey carrying packages out to the parcel service truck in the alley behind the business. Now Fiona began to leave the special account books for these items under Nathan's nose when he visited her alcove office. The titles and descriptions told him little; 'fragment of a statue,' 'probable South Pacific origin,' and 'dimensions . . .' What struck him immediately was that the prices were always quoted ridiculously high and that the finished deals almost always showed the prices reduced drastically because of items taken in trade. Too, the items almost never went to museums; the buyers and traders were individuals, often residing in foreign countries. The prices asked and sometimes paid were enough to convince him that Alistair and his kindred spirits were morbidly serious about their eccentric pursuits.

He suspected she would soon show him more and sure enough, one day she asked him to ship a museum item. The invoice said 'dagger' with the usual uninformative description. She led him quietly through the books to an alcove in a side wall. There were many of these alcoves, all populated with books, and all of them contained at least one locked door. He had assumed these led only to closets but that day Fiona produced a key of antique design and opened a heavy door to reveal a rickety wooden stair leading down. An old ceramic switch clicked and an unshaded bulb glared at the bottom of the stair.

She descended slowly, her bead cocked slightly as though listening for some faint sound. Nathan followed gingerly, wincing at each tiny creak of the stair. At the bottom she turned to him with a finger to her lips. Her eyes were wide and dark and once she licked her lips nervously as she looked left and right down long hallways and peered ahead into the gloom of a third. She led him off to the right in a direction he knew must lead under the neighboring building. Later she would tell him that Alistair owned most of the buildings on the street and that there were many ramifications to the bookselling establishment, more than she cared to explore. The neighbors were afraid of Alistair and usually only too glad to sell out and move on; they knew they would be lucky to get anything for a property in this area and it was rumored that those who fell foul of the old bookseller encountered bad luck and ill health.

The door she chose was on the left, so far down the gloomy passageway that Nathan wished they had brought a flashlight. There was a second key for this room and another of the old style switches and she took the odd precaution of closing the door behind them. The walls were lined with rough wooden shelves, all loaded with wooden boxes of various sizes and shapes. There was a deal table in the center of the floor. With silent gestures she showed him the catalog number on the invoice and a matching number penciled on the outside of one of the boxes.

He brought it to the table. The top had been unfastened, opened, and inspected on arrival and never resealed. Inside was an object of a powerful, morbid beauty. It was a dagger fifteen inches long. The blade, of tempered steel, was only slightly marred with pinpoints of corrosion. For a few inches near the point it was discolored with a faint bronze cast that was iridescent in the light. The haft was decorated with bloodstone; the ebony handle intricately carved with a filigreed inscription, from his recent browsing Nathan recognized it as the Enochian script used in the rituals of witchcraft.

Before carrying the box upstairs they silently viewed the contents of a dozen or so of the boxes on the shelves. Brass censers, pottery vessels of primordial design, a polished ceremonial bowl crusted with an unknown material, all in perfect condition, effigies of demons and maleficent gods—the worst of these was a figure in malachite, a thing with wings and claws and tentacles for a face. Here for the first time Nathan's body, if not his conscious mind, realized that there was something to fear in this place.

The treading tension was broken by a scampering rustle somewhere outside the room. Nathan jumped, then almost laughed till he saw that Fiona was standing rigid with her mouth open and her eyes wide with terror. He placed a warm hand on her shoulder in a gesture of comfort and to his surprise she turned and clasped him in a desperate passionate embrace and kissed him long and hard.

When she relaxed he asked, "What . . . ?" in the lowest of whispers.

"Rats," she murmured, "just . . . rats. Let's get out of here." And they did, taking the dagger in its box and locking the doors behind them. But Nathan found it hard to believe that this woman, so strong and intelligent, could be terrified by mere rats.

She gave him no more assignments handling the 'museum items.' Apparently that would not please Alistair; and Pumphrey, who was curious and resentful of Nathan, was likely to tattle. She did tell him that there many rooms full of such objects in the closets and cellars and that the most important ones were on the fourth floor with Alistair's rooms.

It was after the incident of the rats that she began to direct him to certain passages in the more arcane books in Alistair's collection. She would send him to get something in an obscure alcove and there next to it or underneath it would lie a book he recognized as especially rare, something that certainly did not belong on a table in a humble alcove, something she must have fetched surreptitiously from a high shelf or a locked room. In it would be some innocuous scrap of paper unobtrusively directing him to a particular passage. An hour after he had read it the book would be gone from the alcove.

The first dozen or so were in books on Indian mysticism, originals or reprints from the early days of British imperial control of India. They told of a secret teaching of southern Indian origin which combined certain forbidden yogic practices with ritual magic. Orthodox religionists had despised and condemned it because of its aggressive nature and because its primary goal was prolongation of one's own life by preying on others, all in total opposition to both Hinduism and Buddhism.

Like Buddhism the teaching had traveled north to Tibet and China where it had both influenced and been influenced by Taoism, with its ancient herbal lore and obsession with immortality. A darker strain of Neolithic shamanism from northern Asia also made its mark, and the cult was linked with the names of Yidhra and 'Ymnar. Nathan had seen those names, in crumbling leather-bound manuscripts on the highest shelves and inscribed on objects of doubtful purpose in the locked room below. As he read on in the works of fabled 19th century scholars of the occult he found that the cult had indeed invaded European culture and spread worldwide in an underground network of wizardry. He began to sense a direction in Fiona's clues.

Von Könnenberg's 1854 *Uralte Schrecken* (in Crowley's London translation) was the most modern source to shed new light on the cult. In his time its practitioners were known as the 'Masters of the Life Force' and were profoundly feared by the occultists who knew of them. Although having little power in the areas outside their special interest, they were known as deadly vampire-like beings who destroyed others in order to live to abnormal ages, although even von Könnenberg with all of his erudition did not know precisely how they harmed their victims. Their control of the life force was so great that they could actually bring about physical transformations in all orders of life forms, which may account for the recurrent stories of keeping demons or familiars on their premises. The mad lama of Prithom-Yang may have hinted at this when he wrote of a mysterious ascetic who kept about him, ". . . that which walks but cannot speak, and that which speaks but cannot walk."

The implications of a group of fanatics, intelligent, amoral, obsessed with prolonging their own lives at any cost, believing every word of these ancient horrors and prepared to act on them . . . Nathan began to feel menace in the air, to become watchful and wary, to listen for faint sounds. Pumphrey's rabbit-like nervousness was no longer ludicrous and Fiona's quiet fear no longer seemed meaningless.

Yet their apparent entrapment, both his and Fiona's, still seemed unreal, and their deception wrong. She sensed this, in the sultry closeness of their evening trysts, and continued to try to convey the depth of her fear and the gravity of their jeopardy.

His attention was directed to a particular item in an account book he had not seen before, one normally kept out of sight of any casual visitor to the shop. A folio-sized leather-bound tome of a design he was sure had not been seen since the turn of the century, it contained accounts going back to 1864, only a few items per year, usually quoted at fabulous sums. The descriptions of the items were innocuous and uninformative, those taken in trade for them equally so. The item she evidently wished him to see was the latest entry, first listed in March of that same year. It was styled *Elizabethan diary. Folio. 99 pp 1 blank leaf. Contemporary undecorated pigskin over wooden boards, some wormholes, two clasps; London, 1580.* with some vague comments suggesting a dreary picture of country life in a largely illegible non-professional hand, and there was no record of its acquisition. Nathan could hardly imagine a less intriguing description. It was listed for a quarter of a million dollars and there was a list of six sets of initials of individuals to whom it had been offered. Beside four of them were small marks which he took to mean they had rejected the item. There was a set of coded entries that seemed to indicate that the other two had made offers considerably below Alistair's asking price. These entries had covered the period of Nathan's presence in the shop and entries continued to be added as offer and counteroffer were made. Then one day Fiona, taking care that Pumphrey was not within earshot, showed him a new entry. The 'diary' had been exchanged for $10,000 and a *chest, carved and inlaid, medieval, prob. Flemish origin* which item, presumably, was worth to Alistair approximately $240,000.

As usual, Fiona refused to discuss the matter openly but she did tell him, in careful murmurs, that the initials '*K.v.S.*' stood for Klaus von Schleiwitz, that he was the most feared man in Vienna, and that under no circumstances would the diary be shipped until the chest arrived.

During the two weeks it took to arrive she gave him no more clues or readings, leaving him to build his curiosity with speculation and ponder his distressing situation, his seeming helplessness in the face of his frustrating trap. He was not the only one affected; there was a tension in the air and Fiona and Pumphrey were both even more taciturn than usual. When the United Freight truck pulled up in the alley and a voice announced a package from Vienna it was as though an electric charge had galvanized every molecule in the building.

Nathan wheeled a heavy dolly out behind the truck. The rough wooden crate, fully six feet long and one and a half wide and deep, sat alone in the center of the truck. The usually helpful driver pushed it out to Nathan, touching it as little as possible. It was a bit lighter than it looked and no help was asked or offered in loading it onto the dolly. Seconds later Fiona scribbled a signature on the driver's clipboard the truck roared off down the alley leaving Nathan and Fiona alone with Alistair's sinister prize.

Pumphrey disappeared completely and it was Nathan's back at risk when Fiona directed that the thing be taken downstairs. She had to move books here and there to clear a path for it as she led him back to the alcove that led to the basement storerooms. The rickety stair groaned ominously under the weight. Nathan glanced back once and saw Pumphrey's frightened face peering around the door frame and again to see Alistair looking down with shining yellow eyes and a leer of triumph. Fiona directed him to a room to the left, where another dingy bulb illuminated a litter of empty shipping crates and excelsior and Styrofoam packing. Then, with his curiosity at fever pitch, she thanked him, picked up a pry bar and sent him to cool his heels upstairs. He passed Alistair on his way to the stairs; Nathan might have been invisible for all the notice the old man paid him. He heard the screech of nails pried out of dried wood before he reached the top of the stairs. Furious, he stamped out the front door and walked energetically and aimlessly for two hours.

When he returned Fiona was working as usual in her alcove office. She was tense and not too taut to be sympathetically amused at his frustration. She quickly shushed his questions and asked him to help ship the 'diary.' It was in another room below, this time to the right of the stair. He noticed that the air of listening was back, though he could hear no rustlings or scurryings in the labyrinthine undercellars.

He saw immediately that he was not really needed; she had brought him for his own education. The small crate sat in the middle of a work table along one wall. It had been carefully prepared for the long trip to Vienna and nothing remained to do but nail it shut. She motioned to him and he carefully lifted the wooden lid, then the lid of the stout cardboard carton inside.

It was huge; wide, long, thick, between heavy boards clad in black calfskin. The heavy leather covers were cracked and rubbed and their was no title on the outside—a plain book for its time. Inside the text was easily legible, in a graceful Roman typeface, though the Elizabethan English was difficult for Nathan to follow. It was not a diary at all but a printed book, attributed to Dr. John Dee and purporting to be an English translation of a medieval Arab work entitled *Al Azif*, which Dr. Dee translated as 'Ye Horrors cried by ye insects in ye night.' The colophon at the back was in French; it contained no names and indicated that a mere 169 copies had been printed, a puzzling number.

Hesitantly Nathan turned the pages and saw again and again the most dreaded names of his earlier readings, the most appalling horrors of the earth's immortal past and precarious present and unknown future faintly echoed in the tones of human speech and the runes of human writing, names like Nyarlathotep and 'Ymnar, Yog-Sothoth and Ngyr-Khorath, Mlandoth and Azathoth. There were awesome assertions about the course of history on this planet as the primordial life-force created in the chaos of the universal beginning unfolded, often in the most hideous forms, and chilling speculations on man's ephemeral role in the awful pageant.

Nathan paled and closed the book of his own volition. They carefully sealed the crate and together carried it by taxi to the shipping office, a most unusual measure in the frugal MacLachlan household.

That night when it was time for Fiona to come pull up the stair Nathan heard two sets of footsteps pass his door. The sound of the stair rolling up on its runners didn't come. He turned off the lamp and waited silently in the dark. About half an hour later he heard uncertain steps faltering up the stair. He silently went to the door and opened the latch, holding the knob but not opening the door. The soft shuffling footsteps that crept past him would have been inaudible from the bed. He eased the door in enough to open a hairline crack.

Fiona and Alistair, silhouetted by the light from the stairwell at he end of the hall, were carrying a short stretcher. Fiona, at the front of the stretcher, was walking backwards but did not see Nathan's door move. Alistair's back was no more than four feet from the door.

The object on the stretcher was over five feet long and covered with a blanket. It was lumpy, its shape indeterminate. A fold of the blanket had fallen away to reveal a rigid claw-like mummified human hand.

For the next few weeks Alistair was abnormally active. He was queerly energized, appearing at unpredictable times on the catwalk to summon Fiona for some special task or just to look around aimlessly and pace mechanically as though in a frenzy of wordless mental activity. He often sent Fiona up the ladders to the highest treasures and there gave her gestured directions, always unspoken. When he did speak above a whisper it was often to tease poor Pumphrey, who was palpably afraid of him, with cryptic references to 'finding new uses' for him. Nathan often heard noises from the floor above his bedroom and higher late into the night. It was after one of these marathon fits of activity when the old man was sleeping exhausted till noon that Fiona took Nathan up to the fourth floor to see the erstwhile contents of the 'chest, carved and inlaid.'

In mid-morning she gave him whispered instructions to slip up to his room. After five minutes of suspense came the soft footsteps down the tall and a barely audible pat on the door. When he opened it she signaled for silence. She led the way to the stairway at the end of the hall and set the style for their slow catlike ascent. They crept past the featureless third floor hall and on to the top of the stair.

Here the silence was thick and turgid, the two lovers could hear every breath. There were no footfalls as they crept through the old wizard's lair, only the faint creakings of the floorboards. It was a very long hall, extending across the width of the book room below with many doors on each aide, lit only by a small bulb in a sconce halfway down. There was a mangy carpet runner on the floor, a few decorations on the walls, prints of Aubrey Beardsley, a copy of a Goya. As they moved past the lamp he could tell from her manner that it marked the door to the old man's cork-lined room.

At the second door from the end on the left she stopped and produced a key from her jeans. The well-oiled hinges made no telltale sound. It was a long room with three windows overlooking the alley below. The heavy curtains were tightly drawn except for a narrow strip in the middle window which gave the room its only light. Fiona turned on a small table lamp. The room was a study finished in the dark heavy style of the 1890's. There was a faint smell of incense and the paraphernalia of ritual magic and witchcraft lay about as though casually discarded in the middle of a game—censers, herbs, vials of curiously colored infusions, cabalistic diagrams on parchment. On a long table near the windows lay the blanket-covered object he had seen in the hall.

She waited for him to come stand at the head of the thing before she touched the blanket. She pulled it back delicately, disturbing nothing. The mummy was a pale gray-black color where the skin remained. In many places it did not. Someone had cut an oval hole in the skull, a long time ago by the look of it. Yellow-gray bone, cable-like tendon, hard blackened muscle were all visible on the man from the chest, 'medieval, prob. Flemish origin.' The blackened lips remained drawn back from carnosaurian teeth and the great black hollows where the eyes had been stared up with hypnotic power. It took an effort to break eye contact with those sinister hollows.

The thing was shrouded in the tatters of a garment with many gathers like a judge's robe. It had obviously been explored thoroughly since exhumation, as though he had taken some object of great value or power to the grave with him, though the neat incisions and minimal disturbance of the shroud did not show the random vandalism of the typical grave robber. Alistair had done some work here; some of the cut edges were too crisp to be very old.

When she finally replaced the blanket she made sure it held no new fold that might alert the necromancer. She gestured Nathan to another table that held two open books and an amulet made of polished bloodstone. The amulet was intricately inlaid with a design in gold; through the ornate whorls and filigree Nathan recognized the sign of 'Ymnar. One book was a tattered but complete copy of von Könnenberg's *Uralte Schrecken* in the original German edition. Nathan could not read German but the name 'Nicholas van den Poel' occurred repeatedly in the text. The other book he recognized immediately as another copy of the dreaded volume that had been exchanged for the ancient sorcerer's remains.

They disturbed nothing as they left and locked the door as silently as they had entered. To Nathan's surprise she led him to the left, to the last room on the end. It was unlocked. Again a small lamp lit up an old-fashioned sitting room, this one smaller and lined with glassed-in bookcases. But on close inspection he saw that they contained row upon row of little doll's heads. A museum-type placard, looking almost silly in a private home, labeled them South American Curios. Looking more closely he saw that they were shrunken human heads, with the lips and eye sockets sewn shut in the Jivaro manner. All of them had long white or gray-white hair and in spite of the distortion caused by shrinkage of the skin after the skull was removed, he could see that all belonged to very aged individuals, with Caucasoid features. She led him back out as soon as he had seen this.

Their cautious retreat downstairs was maddeningly slow. She was even more tense as they passed Alistair's room. She seemed to be listening intently for the faintest sound from within.

When they reached Nathan's room she led them both inside and went almost limp with relief. At her urging they took the unusual risk of making love in the daytime, with Pumphrey on the premises and Alistair likely to stir at any time. He had noticed the aphrodisiac effect of fear on her before and this time it was overwhelming. Afterwards she began, in haunted whispers, to complete his education.

"He is a kind of vampire, you know. A vampire and a necromancer and many other horrible things. Legend has only the palest names for the hideous things an evil man can conjure up. He sucks the life force like a vampire drinks blood, leaving his victims drained in body and spirit. If the transfer does not kill them he murders them himself to keep them from talking. You have seen his trophies. Only rarely does he leave them alive. Pumphrey is thirty-one years old."

"But now he is desperate. He has done it too many times. The methods he knows no longer work for him, and he is aging. There are more powerful methods, but the Masters of the Life Force are selfish, evil creatures. They share nothing willingly, give nothing for no return. He has driven a hard bargain to get the unholy relic of Nicholas van den Poel, but the reward will be centuries more of Alistair's evil life."

"But how?" he gasped. "The amulet? Was it in the chest? Any grave robber would have taken it."

She gave him a peculiar smile. "I don't think any ordinary grave robber could molest the remains of the likes of van den Poel and live to tell about it. The amulet was hidden within the corpse. I don't know how it got there, any more than I know how or why he died in spite of his power, but I know that the remains of the great sorcerers are prized by those who still live. Religionists speak of a soul, mystics of Akashic records, scientists of memory molecules—I don't know how it can happen but I have seen it happen—soon Alistair will succeed and raise the dead shade of Nicholas van den Poel and torment it until it teaches him new ways to prey on others to keep his evil self alive for many, many centuries.

"And when he learns this, Nathan, you and I will be very close at hand. We will be tempting and convenient."

That evening Nathan was encouraged to go out to a movie alone and after his return the faint sounds from the fourth floor continued almost till dawn. He never saw Pumphrey again. Pumphrey had evidently been even more convenient than Nathan or Fiona. The change in Alistair was immediately apparent. He came downstairs more often during the day, there was a new spring to his step, he actually showed an interest in the day to day workings of A. MacLachlan & Co., Bookseller. Coupled with the abrupt disappearance of Pumphrey, who was said to have resigned quite suddenly, the effect was terrifying. And yet it took two more incidents to convince Nathan that he and Fiona must strike for freedom.

The first was the cancellation of Nathan's fellowship. The college was on the brink of bankruptcy and had cancelled their graduate program altogether. Nathan had been lucky to find financial support even from a small college on its last legs. He would be lucky to get another chance, even in a year. He had no illusions about the value of his Bachelor of Fine Arts in the job market. Suddenly the gray moment of the present was no longer finite; unless he did something be hadn't thought of yet he would not be leaving at the end of the summer. The thought of Pumphrey scurrying among the books year after year made his stomach feel like cold lead.

The second was the occasion of Fiona's punishment for falling behind on the library order in the unnerving days following the arrival of the chest. It was a sultry evening, a week or so after the departure of Pumphrey. The stifling days of early August were upon them. An after-noon shower had turned the city into a steam bath without lowering the temperature at all. He showered for the second time that day and lay on the bed in his shorts waiting for his lover to feed the old man and steal down for the tryst they had both hungered for all day. As the late summer light waned with eerie slowness he smoked cigarettes (a new habit) and tried to interest himself in a novel he had started a month earlier. When her usual time to appear came and went he thought nothing of it, knowing how she shared his anticipation the wait would only make the consummation more delicious. But as the minutes dragged on toward an hour he began to worry. Could something have gone wrong? Could the old sorcerer have claimed his long-neglected conjugal rights? Nathan's hearing, grown morbidly keen in that quiet place, heard faint muffled sounds from within Alistair's sound-proofed lair; he was sure he heard Fiona's voice raised in what might have been an argument. He gave up on the novel, did pushups, sponged himself with a cool damp cloth, smoked more cigarettes, fiddled with the electric fan to clear the air . . .

When she finally came he was lying on the bed again. She wore the peignoir and slipped in without knocking as on their first night together. When he jumped up she motioned him back with an outstretched hand. Her eyes were red and puffy. She moved stiffly over to the window and stood looking out at the alley, body taut and erect. Nathan stood still behind her, not sure what to do. Once she threw back her head slightly and her body shuddered from head to toe.

Without turning she unfastened the peignoir and let it drop to the floor. A row of fiery red welts ran from her neck all the way to her knees. The stripes had been fiercely, methodically laid on; they were almost perfectly parallel and evenly spaced except for her bottom, which had been crisscrossed at least three times. Alistair had been very thorough.

Nathan was paralyzed; he felt horror, he felt shame, he felt anger in a bewildering vortex of emotion. She turned and spoke.

"It is time now," she said. "We must kill him, before he destroys us." And after they had exhausted each other with consoling passion she explained what they must do.

They waited a week. During the punishment Alistair had taunted her with her interest in "the boy" and Alistair had hidden ways of finding things out. It seemed wise to stay completely away from each other for a while to lull his suspicions. Too, they were both shaken, as much by their own decision as by the brutalization of Fiona, and needed time to steel their nerves for the deed. So for a week they hardly spoke to each other and did not meet at night. Nathan tried to look bored and sullen, an easy task as Fiona and Alistair gave him more and more work to do. Fiona looked cowed and listless as she pressed the work to meet Alistair's demands, but after three days the stiffness had gone out of her movements and Nathan could see, when Alistair was out of sight, a panther-like energy growing in her.

On the appointed day he did not speak to Fiona at all. He went out alone for an early supper. When he returned in the twilight and let himself in he heard the chink of a dish in the downstairs kitchen. He made his way through the books and into the narrow hallway that led to it. Their eyes met; the spark that passed between them would have been obvious to any observer. Alistair's dinner, which was to be his last, was on a lacquered tray, ready to be placed in the dumbwaiter. A breaded cutlet, peas, corn . . . and a cup of hot chocolate, sweet enough to mask the taste of the powder which would tranquilize him into a drowsy, vulnerable torpor.

"I'm back," Nathan said, and went up to his room.

Minutes later he beard the clang and whirr of the stair being pulled up on its rollers. Fiona padded by his door, moving quickly. She slowed on the stair, peering carefully down the unlit third floor hallway, mounting the last flight of stairs a step at a time, listening, looking. The shadows held more terrors for her than for her young lover; to him she had only hinted at the powers at Alistair's disposal, at the weapons he could command, at the unnatural means of acquiring information, at the allies he might summon . . . like those below in the cellars. She had to force herself to move at her normal pace down the corridor toward the lamp ensconced between the dumbwaiter and Alistair's door, all the while listening, imagining shadows where there were none, so totally conscious of her own sound and movement that she could hardly walk. She slid up the door of the dumbwaiter and began pulling on the rope. As Alistair's final meal floated up out of the darkness she quailed for a moment, wondering if she could go through with it, thinking of the consequences of failure, at the hands of Alistair or the law. She could say she forgot the chocolate and go on as before. But she was too stiff with fear to change her plan now. As she lifted the tray and faced the door the strength was running out of her legs and she wished she had gone to the bathroom. She held the tray with one hand and opened the door with the other. She realized that her cotton-dry mouth was open and her eyes bulging and fought for control of her face while she fumbled through the doorway and closed the door behind her.

The only light was from the little opaque-shaded table lamp next to his armchair across the room. He sat there looking very small, shrouded in a voluminous robe with a hood. He did not speak or move. She stood for a moment screwing herself up to approach him. Something warm and furry embraced her ankle and nuzzled her with sharp little teeth. She made a hoarse gasping sound and dropped the tray.

Nathan heard nothing after the rattle of the dumbwaiter. Even the usual distant traffic sounds of the city seemed hushed on that sultry August evening. He sat up on the bed fully dressed and tried to distract his mind from the anticipation that tried to overwhelm it. It was impossible of course not to think about the coming crisis but at least he could stifle the compulsion to go over and over every detail in his mind's eye. Alistair had ways unknown of learning other's thoughts, true, but some thoughts were more dangerous than others. Imagining one's own movements was the worst; that was why the sullen-looking little automatic lay on the bedside table. His entire nervous system itched to pick it up and fondle it and uncock and unload it, load and cock again. Guns were strange to him, he could not be sure of the processes so new to him. Ease off the safety, point the barrel, squeeze the trigger—that was all that mattered now, he told himself. When the old sorcerer's heart and brain stopped all the evil conjured by his will would surely cease.

When the time came he stood up and felt his heart race. He took the gun off safety and managed the door with only the subtlest of sounds. Unlike Fiona he must move silently and his fear, more physical and less uncanny, made him want to rush to be done with it. Movement was a release that calmed him and cleared his mind; he remembered which steps creaked. Faltering or failure never crossed his mind.

On the fourth floor the lamp by Alistair's door was on as usual. The shadows did not stir; the way was clear. As he approached the door with exquisite stealth he felt a first shock of surprise—the sliding door to the dumbwaiter shaft was still open. She must have forgotten it in her excitement. He stood squarely before the door and took deep quiet breaths. Alistair would be sitting in an armchair directly in front of him, about twenty-five feet away. He felt his gun hand trembling as he reached across with his left to grasp the knob.

He flung the door aside and rushed across the threshold, bringing his left hand up to the gun pointing at the shadowed blur in the chair. The first roar and flash were stunning, the second more so. The blurred thing jerked twice like a straw man. The third roar toppled it with half the face in the lamplight; half the eternal grimace of Nicholas van den Poel.

Nathan's knees turned to water as his comprehension reeled. In the chair the folds of the rotted shroud were moving. The thing that rose out of its folds resembled a hooded cobra, yet it had a face, a tiny, evil face with piercing ruby eyes and a pig-like nose and a mouthful of needle-like fangs and it laughed a high-pitched sneering laugh.

Run. His body made the instant decision, impulses rushed to every muscle—then he heard a muffled squawk and lurched. There was an alcove to his left and in the dim light he saw Fiona's face, eyes enormous with terror. She had been gagged, stripped and her hands tied to some fixture depending from the ceiling. She was stamping her feet in a parody of sprinting. A small agile thing was clinging to her leg, easily riding her wild gyrations, Alistair had thoughtfully placed cushions under her feet to spare Nathan the sound of her stamping during his long wait.

He ran to her and jerked the thing off her and flung it across the room. It clung tenaciously, like a tick. Fiona shrieked when it came free and blood ran down her leg from the point where its mouth had been. The rope was knotted to an open hook. He heaved and raised her enough to clear the point. He pulled her into the room, toward the door. She had been thrashed again, this time haphazardly, desultorily; Alistair too had passed a long hour waiting. And there were smears of blood where his monstrous pets had nibbled at her.

The creature was staying a couple of paces in front of them, scuttling back and forth sideways as though at bay and tittering. Two more swarmed out from under the chair and scrambled toward them. They were furry with short tails, about the size of weasels and equally vicious. They ran low on all fours but stopped to dance in front of the terrified pair on hind legs with arms out like wrestlers. The faces were short and much too human, except for the long pointed teeth that grinned in deadly mirth. There was a musky smell like a tomcat but worse. More emerged from the shadows around the room. More of the serpent things were appearing too.

One made a dash at Nathan and retreated at a reflexive swipe of his foot. Another darted at Fiona, who moaned and ducked behind him. He pointed the gun at it and closed his eyes as it roared. Its head was a red pulpy bulb but still it groped for him, pressing the bloody remains of its head against his leg, then cavorting off aimlessly like a waltzing mouse. Nathan shuddered and moaned too. He panicked and fired at the row of grinning teeth until the slide of the automatic stayed back and the trigger didn't click when his finger jerked on it.

Then the tittering and the sneering laughter ceased and they heard a dry cough. The foul menagerie fidgeted and looked from their quarry to their master and back again.

Alistair stood in the archway at the back of the room and leaned on his cane. He looked more alive than Nathan had ever met him, an evil Einstein with the glowing eyes of a tiger. He was certainly smiling now, mostly in the eyes.

'Well, well," he said, in that dry hollow voice of his. "It seems that your plan has failed. And mine has succeeded."

"Did you think me too feeble to observe your fatuous passion? Or too stupid? I have watched you at your work many more times than you have seen me. And my little friends have been very busy indeed, watching and tattling. Did you know they could speak, Fiona? I commanded them all to hold their vile little tongues in your presence of course, I have never been foolish enough to trust you, my dear. But their brains, though small, are more human than otherwise.

"You, Nathan, are more forgivable in your foolishness. You could not know how a powerful will can command the eternal life force, how the life force can transform matter. If your lover told you, you could never accept it. Yet it is the plain truth, as you see.

"You see here the dregs of the biosphere salvaged and combined into the most enchanting companions and helpmates." The weasel things were starting to titter again, softly.

"Stray cats and dogs, ferrets, rats, human derelicts and criminals—I wasted nothing, you see. The human specimens are quite lucky to be alive in any form. I had drained them. Like Pumphrey.

"Did she tell you about that? About what you faced when your plan failed?"

Fiona whimpered and Nathan's fear took on a new dimension.

"I used to drain them, like a glass of sherry. The method was simple, I won't bore you with details. I would become strong, vital. They would wither. I could see it first in their faces, their carriage. After a week or two the physical signs became unmistakable—the hair white at the roots, the sagging flesh, the doddering walk. I could have taken it all, all their life force, and left them dead. Yet I did not. I combined the remains of their human psyche with the vitality of wild and feral beasts, leaving them enough brain to be useful to me. And the results you see before you, hungering for your flesh. But have no fear; they are completely under my control, and I hunger for something less tangible."

The hollow timbre of the ancient's insidious voice held Nathan in trance-like fascination.

"The methods I used to drain these souls will no longer work for me, you see. That is why it was necessary far me to . . . consult a colleague. About more sophisticated methods."

At that obscure witticism the necromancer burst into cackling laughter, ending only when he had to catch his breath.

"And old Nicholas, you see, had no desire to help me. None at all. And no gratitude for letting his shade come into the world of the living, if only for a brief hour or so. But I was persuasive. Yes, very persuasive. I can be very persuasive, can't I, my dear Fiona?"

Nathan felt her shudder behind him.

"At last I was able to make him be reasonable, and tell me, in Latin, that which he had known centuries before my birth. And now I have the means to continue my most agreeable life for quite a long time. Even longer than poor Nicholas, who died untimely of his own errors. I do not make errors. And that is how I came by my new toy. It is beautiful, is it not?"

With that he held out his cane, pointing it at Nathan, and for the first time Nathan saw that it was not his usual gold-headed cane but a darkly beautiful rod of murky crystal, inlaid with a filigreed inscription entwined around the sign of 'Ymnar. He felt Fiona let go of him and retreat from Alistair's thrust and instinctively did the same. Alistair moved slowly forward behind the enigmatic staff, savoring the moment.

"Not a mere walking stick you see, but a funnel. For the life force, from you to me."

And he advanced unhurriedly toward the hapless pair, the grinning beasts scattering to make his passage, the rod thrust out like a rapier. Nathan felt Fiona shivering behind; he was beyond rational thought, seeing only the rod and the image of Pumphrey, hopeless Pumphrey with his grizzled hair and his seamed face and his limp. There was no decision made, no conscious thought before he hurled the empty gun at Alistair and it was only luck that jabbed the pointed corner of the slide squarely into his left eye.

He dropped the rod and clutched his face, reeling backward and roaring with pain. The beasts all stared at him stupefied. Nathan was out the door in an instant, pulling Fiona by the wrist and slamming the door after them. It took him a moment to free her hands from the rope. They started toward the stair then stopped when they saw the shadows move there. The horde of snake-things that came crawling up into the hall looked dazed and clumsy but they still glared balefully at the fugitives.

"The fangs," cried Fiona in a quavering voice, "venom . . ." She clutched him and trembled again.

The dumbwaiter next to them was still open. "Quick! In here!" he blurted and grasped the pulley rope. "Let yourself down. It's the only way past them!"

She needed no urging. Alistair's groans were fainter and more intermittent through the cork-lined door. She swung her legs over the sill, sat on the platform and took the rope. Nathan closed the sliding door leaving her in total darkness.

He looked at the squirming mass creeping toward him. Behind the door the muffled groaning stopped. He took a deep breath and ran for the stairs. Beady eyes and needle-fangs caught the lamplight as he ran and his first great leap carried him twelve feet over a hissing chorus. He landed on something that squashed and cursed him in a squeaky parody of a human voice before it died. The second leap took him to the top of the stairs where he stumbled and rolled down over a dozen wriggling bodies. The hissing and squealing behind him were furious.

He landed with his eyes a foot from a tiny face that reared back to strike. He scrambled back and felt fangs graze his hand; he felt two thumps against his pants leg before he got to his feet and went pounding down the stairs clear of the serpents. His hand and two spots on his left leg were needle points of pain, spreading like slow fire. He was limping by the time he reached the second floor and heard Fiona screaming in the dumbwaiter shaft.

When Nathan closed the door on her the darkness was total. She sat huddled on the little platform, bowed in the center with her weight, and let the rope up hand over hand while the platform jerked and slid a few inches at a time down the seemingly endless shaft. Her mind was frozen in wordless fear, the inky blackness a threatening ocean around her, the distant vibrations of Nathan's progress a cryptic rumor of disaster. She had no sense of how far she had descended when suddenly the blackness was not total. She puzzled for an instant then looked up at the bright trapezoid of the fourth floor door far above. A small shape clambered over the sill, then another. The rope quivered in her hand. She let go and plunged three feet before grasping it again, searing her palms. She screamed hoarsely, methodically, rhythmically, her entire organism enthralled by the primordial function of the trapped animal, flight gone, fight gone, waiting to be devoured.

When Nathan opened the second floor door she was a foot below him. He dragged her out limp and screaming with four of the horrors gnawing at her like leeches. He himself was badly bitten pulling them off and throwing them down the shaft. He had to drag her to her feet and pull her down the hall.

He had never lowered the stair before and the mechanism baffled him. He shouted for her to help but she stood at the rail staring open-mouthed at the darkness below. He looked down and saw movement. Something, no, many things, were jumping up and down as though eager to get at the pair on the catwalk. The largest of the lot was as large as a Doberman; their shapes reminded him of rats. They began to chatter like monkeys.

"He let them out! He sent one of them to let them out!" she gasped. Then with a scurrying rush the catwalk was full of squeaking and hissing forms pouring out of the hallway onto the catwalk and he and Fiona were climbing up on the rail. Nathan leaped for a ladder eight feet away, barely saving himself from a long fall; he had forgotten the pain of the serpent bites but now his left leg and arm were numb and hard to control. Fiona lost her footing and fell with her hands gripping the rail and flailing her legs wildly as the great rat-thing leaped at her and the others crept within a foot of her face.

And then the squeaking and gibbering and thumping died away to a low rustle and the things on the catwalk drew back as their master appeared.

He held his left hand over his left eye and in his right he held the rod inlaid with the sign of 'Ymnar. The urbanity, the cat and mouse teasing were gone; he glowered at her with his good eye, hatred undisguised and uncontrolled. His voice was a foul hissing shriek.

"Whore! You FILTH! You PIG! You came crawling to me begging for life and youth, begging to learn how to suck the life from others to prolong your filthy existence, you ignorant slimy pathetic little WITCH! And after fifteen years of youth that I gave you, not yourself, not your own power but mine, you betray me with this CHILD and then try to destroy ME! Did you think me blind and deaf, did you think me an imbecile?

"Very well—life you shall have. Life, like Cordelia before you. You shall join her! But—not too much life. I shall have the best of you. He advanced holding the rod before him, aimed at her heart.

"You shall nourish me, and then you shall join her and her friends and you shall help them guard my treasures at night. I shall leave you enough of the life force to live for many years and to remember who you are and what you once were. But very little of your body—you shall have plenty of vigorous new bodily material, most of it rodent. I find that very fitting. But for now I want Cordelia and her companions to have most of your flesh. His voice rose to a bellow. "Do you hear me Cordelia?" And the great rat-thing began again to leap up to snap at Fiona's heels.

Hypnotized by the scene before him Nathan was unaware that his left leg and arm were completely numb or that he was drooling from the slack left side of his mouth. When the rod of 'Ymnar pressed against Fiona's chest there was a sensation like a subsonic hum and a crimson glow that enveloped the wizard and the rod and its victim. She gaped at the necromancer, wide-eyed and open-mouthed, her thrashing legs slowing, her horrified face growing seamed and withered, her hands weakening. There was no strength left for a final scream as her hands began to slip, and when Nathan finally lost his balance there was no response to his reflexes and they both plunged to the floor below.

When Nathan finally came to full consciousness he knew that he had been out for a very long time, that he had been drugged, that he had dreamed long, that there had been much pain but that it had quiesced to a dull ache that pervaded his whole body. The face before him was one that he had seen before in dream, a beautiful heart-shaped face framed in raven hair over emerald green eyes, beautiful but cruel, passionate but cold.

"Who . . . ?" he stammered, "Who . . . ?"

"I am Firenza," she said.

"I am the bookseller's third wife," she added.

There is a permanent economic recession in that city and now and then a young man desperate for employment answers the uninspired ad deep in the classifieds and reads the gold lettering on the big panes on either side of the front door. He may be repelled by the gloomy aspect of the place and leave immediately, or he may knock. The creature that confronts him through the glass, the seamed face beneath grizzled hair, the limping gait, the frightened visage curiously scarred about the neck and face, may drive him away forthwith.

Or he may enter.

Solar Pons & the Cthulhu Mythos

Dr. Eric von Könnenberg and Dr. Pierre de Hammais

In August Derleth's thumbnail biography of Solar Pons, it was stated that he had written six monographs, two of which concern us, as they deal with the "Cthulhu Mythos." The first monograph, published in 1905, was entitled *An Inquiry into the Nan-Matal Ruins of Ponape*, and the second, published in 1931, was entitled *An Examination of the Cthulhu Cult and Others*.

In going through the adventures that were written up by Dr. Lyndon Parker, there is only one adventure which touched upon the "Cthulhu Mythos." This adventure was entitled "The Adventure of the Six Silver Spiders" upon its publication in the public press. In examining a catalogue for the sale of a private collection of twenty volumes, Parker mentioned some of the titles therein: *Necronomicon, Unaussprechlichen Kulten, Cultes des Goules, De Vermis Mysteriis*, and *Liber Ivonis*. It is obvious to the student of the "Cthulhu Mythos" that these are titles of books which are integral to the understanding of the threat from this mythology, if everything about it can be taken as absolute truth.

Pons told Parker that "All these books have a precarious existence only in the writings of certain minor authors of American origin, all apparently followers, in a remote sense, of the work of Edgar Allan Poe. The catalogue is, in short, a hoax."

There would seem to be a discrepancy here, for if Pons firmly believed that these books were spurious, then what do we make of the two monographs which he published? To rectify this discrepancy, and to give some justification for the rectification, we need to backtrack a little.

Solar Pons was born in 1880 and graduated from Oxford in 1899. His first monograph, *An Inquiry into the Nan-Matal Ruins of Ponape*, was published in 1905. He established his private inquiry practice in 1907, which was only interrupted by his service with British Intelligence during World War I. Dr. Lyndon Parker moved in with Pons at 7B Praed Street and began writing up the adventures of Solar Pons in January 1928, moving out in January 1933 when he married. "The Adventure of the Six Silver Spiders" occurred in January of 1930. And the second monograph, *An Examination of the Cthulhu Cult and Others*, was published in 1931.

In this day and age, the 1990's, the two monographs are exceedingly rare, whereas Parker's write-ups of Solar Pons's adventures are kept in print almost continuously. To give some feeling to the conclusions which will follow, we will quote from both monographs.

The following excerpts were deleted from Solar Pons's monograph *An Inquiry into the Nan-Matal Ruins of Ponape* before its publication in 1905 and were recently discovered among his notes. He is known to have commented to Dr. Lyndon Parker that he had found it necessary to omit several striking incidents because of a request from the Admiralty in one case, an obligation to protect the reputation of a certain noble family in another, and in all a fear that their outré nature would work against acceptance of his conclusions.

Of course hearsay abounds concerning strange happenings in the area, but there is one well-documented incident, the episode of the sloop *Naples* near Ponape. The account released to the press said only that the crew had been lost in a storm, but certain additional details were made known to me privately. Several shells of molluscs, pierced as though for use in jewellery, were found aboard. They were identified as belonging to a species of clam thought to exist only at great depths. There were peculiar scratches on the decks, arranged in star-shaped groups of five and suggesting nothing so much as the claw marks of some strange beast. But the most bizarre point did not appear until the ship was towed to New Zealand and placed in dry dock. There was found jammed in the rudder hinge the limb of an unknown sea creature, resembling the arm of a frog the size of a man.

I was reminded of those star-shaped scratches during the Adventure of the Abandoned Lighthouse, where a man went mad after following up a hint in a forbidden book. I was unable to shed any light on the young man's death and was obliged to record the case in my files as an inconclusive failure. He had locked himself into the beacon chamber and collapsed into gibbering imbecility, leaving no testimony to his experience. On the stairs leading up to the chamber I found minute traces of scratches arranged like those on the *Naples*. There were also traces of a slimy substance which was definitely organic, though I could not match it with any known marine or terrestrial organism. Considering our limited knowledge of sea life and the chemistry of living things this is not surprising; but I did succeed in matching it with traces found on the outside surface of the beacon room window, a place so difficult of access that my companion professed fear of heart failure while watching me obtain the samples.

The second excerpt is as follows:

There exists in the files of Scotland Yard another case with a thread leading to Ponape. It is officially labelled "unsolved," as is the humane custom when the murderer is known to be dead. In my own files it is labelled the Adventure of the Eye of Lapis Lazuli. The murderer was the educated and widely travelled son of a highly placed family and showed no outward sign of any morbid, vicious or unbalanced qualities either before or during the period when he committed some of the most atrocious deeds in the history of crime. Indeed so wholesome did he seem that the police, convinced that the murders must be the work of a raving lunatic, never considered him suspect until I entered the case. He ultimately took his own life, leaving a handful of crushed fragments of lapis lazuli and a diary which recounted his acquisition on Ponape of a device in the form of an eye of inlaid gemstone and his gradual enslavement, through the stone, by some malignant intelligence from beyond the visible world.

And the third fragment:

I have had one other case in which a connection with Ponape appeared: the case of the Doom among the Standing Stones. The connection was indeed tenuous; my quarry had spent two years there in his youth and made a cryptic reference to it in a letter, which I contrived to inspect, to a mysterious and untraceable associate on the continent. But the case itself, or rather the end of it, was quite worthy of the reader's attention.

My client had been for some time subject to harassment, at once terrifying and yet so subtle that the police could do nothing with the object of forcing him to hand over certain books and artefacts of great antiquity which had been carefully guarded by his family for generations, even though their significance had been lost and was now unknown to him. The perpetrator was an evil man with a reputation for dabbling in black magic. At my suggestion the client had agreed to his demands in order to trap him with proof of extortion. Possibly suspecting a trap, the villain had dictated a meeting at night in a circle of megalithic tors and arches in the midst of a desolate moor.

Early on the day of the meeting I went there alone to scout out the terrain. I soon observed that the place had been very recently visited, though the indications were inadequate to deduce their purpose. There was a circular smudge from the base of a bull's eye lantern, there were coloured wax drippings as from candles, and a foul smelling oil substance had been poured on the ground at four points around the central altar stone. I was able to identify this as a mixture of herbal distillates combined with unidentifiable animal material.

There was an even more peculiar trace just outside the circle. It had been completely surrounded with a series of rough stones in the shape of five-pointed stars, very evenly spaced at intervals of three feet, four inches. Upon picking one up I felt such a strong tingling sensation in my hand that I dropped it, smashing it into four parts. I reassembled the broken star as inconspicuously as possible, picked up another and placed it in my pocket for later examination and made a substitute of pebbles and clay that would keep my man from noticing any change in the arrangement.

I returned that evening, a half hour before sunset and an hour and a half before my client had agreed to meet him, approaching the circle cautiously by a devious route from the village where I was lodging. My intention was to arrive well before either of them and find a hidden vantage point but as I made my wary approach I descried the blackmailer proceeding alone along the main path. This slowed my progress considerably and I was unable to reach the circle before darkness had fallen and a mist was rolling in from the direction of the sea. By then I could see that he was performing some sort of ritual by the light of a number of small candles, declaiming to the empty night in the harsh syllables of some alien tongue.

I have never been able to explain what happened next in terms of our normal concepts of reality, and shall leave it for the reader to form his own speculation, bearing in mind that I am a trained observer of unimaginative temperament.

The mist now formed a solid grey background across the candle-lit circle of great stones, while the circle itself appeared filled with low curls of the drifting vapour. I have had much experience with fogs of all kinds and am quite certain of the preternaturally dense blackness which began to form within the fog outside the circle and move in oily billows as the ritual proceeded. It appeared on the side opposite my position, but gradually drifted around the circle, sometimes seeming more dense and sometimes less. As it neared me I could discern minute pinpoints of light within it, like a swarm of radiant bees.

The blackmailer had completed his ritual and now stood quietly in an attitude of watchfulness, alternately looking toward the black cloud and staring blankly as though listening for some faint sound. I heard the distant crunch of a footstep on the gravelly path from the village and knew that my client was approaching. The blackmailer seemed to hear it too and smiled.

By now the black cloud had reached the point to my right and behind the man where I had smashed one star-stone and removed another, which I carried in an inside pocket of my coat. I could see the cloud bulge inward, as though purposefully probing against some unseen barrier. The man was staring intently in the direction of my client and did not see the great tendril of star-flecked blackness move toward him through the gap I had made in his carefully arranged circle of star-stones, and began screaming only when it reached and engulfed him. Before my eyes he disappeared into the thing, though I could still hear his hoarse animal cries. As the blackness withdrew

from the circle and disappeared the voice receded and seemed
to be coming from above, though whether this was some strange
acoustical effect of the fog I cannot say.

Naturally I returned and went over the site meticulously in
daylight, but I found no trace, no clue to what had happened.
The man never reappeared, alive or dead, and my client and his
peculiar heirlooms were never troubled again.

These excerpts were written in, or prior to, 1905. At that time, if Pons was not
writing his monograph with tongue firmly lodged in cheek, he believed in what his
researches had revealed concerning the "Cthulhu Mythos."

By January of 1930, Pons has seemed to have done a complete reversal
concerning his knowledge of the "Cthulhu Mythos." He tells Parker that the
catalogue is a hoax, meaning the books themselves are a hoax, and, in effect, that
there is no basis in fact to substantiate the "Cthulhu Mythos."

Then, in 1931, Pons's second monograph was published, of which the preface is
hereby appended:

In the annals of crime, cases involving magic, witchcraft and
traffic with supernatural powers are by no means rare; to the
connoisseur of crime one need only mention the schemes of
"Count Cagliostro" or the scandalous affairs of Aleister
Crowley. The great majority of these are easily explained in
terms of ordinary fraud and of the unbalanced mentality
naturally attracted to such things. But there remains a residue
which teases the intellect and haunts the imagination.

The cases I have encountered in my own career may all be
dismissed as the result of mundane human criminality except
for a small number. The disturbing feature of these, however, is
that they all have a common link in a body of lore known in
occult and scholarly circles as the "Cthulhu Mythos."

I first became aware of these apparently outlandish ideas in
the wake of the hideous case of Threadgill, the notorious
necrophile, whose fiendish activities were conducted with such
maniacal cunning as to elude the official police for many years.
At his death the case was treated with circumspection by the
press, and his crimes described only vaguely as the most
repulsive results of mental aberration. But I had learned that the
man had combined the sort of insanity documented by Krafft-
Ebing with attempts at necromancy, guided by a collection of
recherché books. Unfortunately his library was destroyed in the
fire in which he perished, save only a handful of notes which I
carried out with me. They consisted of copies of lengthy
inscriptions in an unknown tongue, labelled "Eltdown Shards,"
together with a partial translation. They purported to be the
records of visitors from beyond this planet who visited the earth

long eons ago. The earth had by that time a long history of contact with extra-planetary life, in particular a group of fearsome creatures referred to as the "Old Ones." Naturally I dismissed this at the time as a ludicrous imposture.

My next inkling of the "Mythos" came in the affair of the murderous astrologer Hawthorne. His criminal depredations were all too real and all too human, but like many of his kind he combined blatant chicanery with a genuine belief in the supernatural. Three days before his execution he wrote a will leaving me his library. It consisted for the most part of preposterous quackery, but there were two books which did not share the hysterical gullibility of the others. They were *Cultes des Goules* by the Comte d'Erlette and *Unaussprechlichen Kulten* by the Baron von Junzt. They were obscurely written and difficult to interpret but undoubtedly shared many concepts with the "Eltdown Shards."

My next and most important exposure to the "Cthulhu Mythos" again proved nothing; but this time the documentary evidence was more impressive. I encountered it while pursuing a criminal genius whose exploits have been substantially recorded by my loyal biographer, but about whom a great deal more may be told someday, and about whom a very great deal may never be known. In the course of an unauthorized visit to his quarters during the small hours of the morning I discovered an ancient manuscript written in Arabic. I have made a special study of documents of all ages with regard to identification and authenticity, and can vouch for the age and Arabian peninsular origin of the book. This genius among criminals had translated the bulk of it into English. I was deeply impressed by this, for aside from his strange compulsive inclination toward criminality the man was a logician and scholar of the first water. From the time and effort he had expended one could safely deduce that he knew of additional facts which made the book of more importance than legend or fraud. In the brief moments at my disposal, I read of the Great Old Ones, including great Cthulhu of the ocean deeps, Hastur of the starry void and the formidable Yog-Sothoth among others, who once ruled the earth and waited with malign patience to rule again. The treatise included rituals of magic for contacting these creatures and creating the necessary conditions for their return. Sandwiched in among the pages of translation was an apparently unrelated item, several pages of mathematical calculations, in the man's own hand, based on the existence of more than three spatial dimensions.

The translations were labelled "Necronomicon," which intrigued me because I had heard of this rare book before and believed, on seemingly good evidence, that it was a fictional invention. But this formidably ancient book was quite real, and its translator was no gull or fantasist.

It was many years before I found the leisure to follow out these threads and track down the obscure sources which detail the Cthulhu Mythos. I found with monotonous regularity that books had been stolen or destroyed, and often had to exercise the greatest ingenuity in gaining access to carefully guarded copies. This monograph is the result of that investigation, and I trust that it will stimulate interest, if not acceptance, and point the way to further research. I believe that I have demonstrated, at the very least, that subterranean groups of dangerously fanatic cultists do exist, and that enough hints exist to warrant re-examining our limited concept of the earth's vast and awesome history.

And a short quotation from the body of the monograph:

It is said that the middle American town of Harkness is populated by the spawn of Othuyeg, the doom-walker who was imprisoned by the Elder Ones. It is also said that J'Cak Iggarthan, author of the *Black Book of the Skull* lives here, and has done so ever since Quy vanished except when he must take off for some esoteric journey.

It is obvious from the preface to his second monograph, that Pons did, indeed, believe the truth of his researches into the "Cthulhu Mythos." It is believed that the two monographs were intended for students of the "Cthulhu Mythos," whereas "The Adventure of the Six Silver Spiders" was intended for a wider audience, it was best to put forth the "truth" that the "Cthulhu Mythos" was a complete hoax, in order to protect mankind from the horrors masked by that terminology. In effect, there is no discrepancy between the monographs and the written-up adventure. Parker had been living with Pons for at least a year when this adventure occurred. There is no doubt that Parker went along with the facade in order to protect humanity from his own bumbling naiveté.

As an afterthought, it should be noted that the quotations from both monographs point out adventures that Dr. Lyndon Parker never got around to writing up. A pity that these adventures will never be seen in the public press!

EDITORIAL NOTE: When it was pointed out to the good doctors that the first and second excerpts from Pons's first monograph mention adventures that occurred after he started his private inquiry practice, they stated that they had erred in thinking the three extracts had been deleted from the monograph and now assume that Pons had been proposing a revised monograph for subsequent publication, which never came about. Or, if it did, no copies are known to exist.

Lament

It was near midnight when he heard her knock. He looked through the fisheye lens in the heavy door and saw her face and his emotions surged like a breaking wave, as though some momentous, long-awaited event had finally materialized. Yet anger and fear tore at him and he hesitated to open the door; anger at the pain she had caused, and fear that she would bring more. There were no lights on in the apartment. He had been sitting alone, brooding before the embers in the fireplace, among his beloved books and the exotic objects that helped him feel the vastnesses of space and time; he could pretend no one was home. But in the end, he opened the door.

"Hello, Alifair. So you're back."

"Justin . . ." Her voice was thick with emotion. "Justin." She repeated it, as if just saying the name brought her comfort. He didn't invite her in. "I need you, desperately. You've got to help me," she said. "Please, let me in."

He led her to the comfortable well-worn armchair he used for guests. He looked at her in the firelight. She hadn't aged; it was only been five years since she left him for Aaron. But her blond hair was disheveled, there were worry lines around her deep blue eyes. She collapsed into the chair, lay her head back and closed her eyes while she composed herself.

"You might at least offer an old flame a drink," she said without opening her eyes.

"Still scotch and water, no ice?" he said.

"Make it a double."

"How is Aaron?" he said when he returned with the drinks. Aaron with the quick smile women couldn't resist, with the air of mystery and secretive excitement. Justin had ignored the tell-tale signs, her boredom, the way her eyes flashed around Aaron, the coolness toward himself: then she was gone. And now that he was just getting past the pain, here she was again. He tingled with hope, and at the same time ached because he was almost certain he was just going to get hurt again. Almost; but he couldn't bring himself to cut off the last spark of possibility.

She took a long time to answer, and when she did, she gave him a boldly curious look as though gauging his reaction.

"Aaron is dead."

She waited for that to sink in.

"He died because of the book," she said. "Our whole life together revolved around it. You know how he was always half hinting that he was onto something tremendous, something beyond anyone's mundane dreams—that book was what it was about. He already had it then. What he had was a complete version of *The Lamentations of Sheol*. Not the fragmentary remnant in Sumerian cuneiform, the complete phonetic version in Devanagari script, from central Asia."

Justin was stunned. The *Lamentations*—the revelations of the trans-human world of Sheol, obtained from the creatures of the dark side of nature by Queen Shub-Ad of Ur at the cost of the many lives, lives of her sacrificed courtesans. Other books of mystery told of the dark worlds—only a few provided the means to reach out to

223

those worlds and touch them. The *Necronomicon* of the mad Arab Abdul Al Hazred was one. The *Lamentations* might be even more potent. No one really knew; the pronunciation of the Sumerian language was not known with precision, and few of the chants were complete. But there had been rumors of an occult oral tradition that preserved the sound of the chants, and of a 1,600-year-old version in that most phonetic of scripts, the Devanagari used for Sanskrit.

"It was intoxicating, Justin. Just to know we were on the edge of the deepest mysteries, hidden away for thousands of years. On the brink of adventures undreamed of . . ."

He was sick with envy. Aaron had stolen away the most haunting, magical woman Justin had ever known, and had possessed the key to mysteries Justin could only glimpse from a tantalizing distance. Then he remembered what she had said: he envied a man who would love no more and go no more adventuring.

"He couldn't use the book, you see. He could read the script, and he understood the Sumerian language, but the sound wasn't right, not right enough anyway. We had partial successes, when we could see the shimmering boundary of known and unknown, when the smell of the dark worlds made our hair stand on end and we could sense alien voices trying to speak from beyond the veil . . . but nothing quite worked—until they found him."

"They never identified themselves, but Aaron always called them the Black Druids, right from the start. They were from Europe—they must have spotted Aaron when he was investigating the *Lamentations* at the British Museum in London. Of course he didn't look like he did here—he used a false name and dressed like a professor. When it disappeared from there, they realized who had smuggled it out and traced him back to the United States.

"We guessed someone was searching our apartment. Once the letters in a desk drawer looked like they had been moved, another time a book on the couch wasn't exactly where I'd left it. Two days after that they came to the door.

"There were two of them, Ian and Seamus. They wore American clothes, jeans, but they were always hooded. At first they tried to buy the *Lamentations* outright. Aaron kept saying no and getting more nervous about the whole thing. He told me he was afraid that if they got it they would kill us. When he turned down $1,000,000 even I wondered if he was crazy. That's when they made the final offer.

"Aaron couldn't refuse this one. We would give them the complete phonetic manuscript they needed, making a copy for ourselves; they would teach us the correct pronunciation, and give us $100,000 to boot."

"Sounds dangerous," Justin said. "Wouldn't that give them a chance to get close to you and figure out how to steal what they wanted?"

"That's what I thought, too, but you know what Aaron was like. He was sure he could outsmart them. He had it hidden, away from our apartment. He didn't even tell me where it was till later, when things were getting out of control. He brought copies of a few pages, specific chants that they requested, to each session.

"We had to meet them in a place they had set up, a dangerous-looking place we didn't like at all. It was deep under an abandoned building in the warehouse district, down by the tracks. I think they must have rigged a pretty substantial hideout there. But the only part they let us see was this one big room in the second basement. You know I'm not afraid of adventure, Justin, but I was really terrified every time we went down there, about ten times altogether. They had rough benches, like picnic furniture, and it smelled musty like a basement and oily from the Coleman lamps and heaters. Ian and Seamus were there, but the third man, a much older man they called 'Master', he was always in control. I think his English wasn't too good, Ian did most of the talking, but he kept talking to Ian in a foreign language, telling him what to say to us and demonstrating the sounds.

"They kept their part of the bargain scrupulously. First they would look over the chant Aaron had brought, all three of them, with a lot of nodding and muttering in that language which Aaron said was Celtic. Then they would all agree and start teaching us how to pronounce it. We went very slowly, in short phrases. They were afraid we would call up more than they wanted to deal with.

"The last meeting was tense. They must have been afraid we'd skip out on it and disappear, because they'd carefully avoided teaching certain key phonetic patterns up till then. Aaron had done a lot of analysis to make sure they covered every possible combination of letters, and at that last meeting he kept prodding them till they hit them all. On their side I could see they were upset when we didn't bring the manuscript, and when he told them he'd take them to it afterwards they were pretty sullen about the teaching. They obviously hadn't prepared the 'lesson' carefully like they had before but Aaron had shrewdly brought along chants that used the combinations he needed to learn.

"He made his move while the Master was voicing the last verse, before he even finished. I swear I didn't know what he planned to do. He had one of those automatics made out of non-metallic parts. He was afraid they would smell the gun. Before anyone could react he put a hole in the Master's forehead. He flopped over backwards like a rag doll and his head hit the floor like a melon. Aaron took out Seamus and Ian while they were still staring open-mouthed. I didn't know blood stank so."

She took a minute to get her poise back.

"Did he really think he could away with it?" he said.

"Oh, yes. He always thought he could do anything. He was like a bright, precocious kid, not understanding that he could get hurt, that he could lose everything. We changed apartments, careful not to leave a trail. Didn't even move to another city. He kept the book away from the apartment in case they tracked us, even though he was sure they couldn't."

"He used to play chess with me," said Justin. "He was a hell of an attacking player, but not much good at defense. How long did it take them to find you?"

"Not long at all. It was only a couple of weeks before we felt like we were being followed. Both of us. And we found little things out of place around the apartment, like before. Aaron assumed they wanted the book more than they wanted us. They must have wanted it awfully bad to hold back, when they could have killed us so easily. I was scared, really scared, but Aaron just didn't sense how much they hated us. It was all just a thrilling game to him.

"I was afraid to go out at night, did everything in the daytime when the streets were crowded. But Aaron wouldn't live that way, and he put off leaving the city. He still went out at night, but he started to act worried. He quit cutting through the park across from us, said the trees seemed to move sometimes. Just before the end he thought he heard footsteps following him, quick tapping footsteps, 'like little hooves' he said.

"It happened in that park. The police found blood there, and signs of a scuffle. Maybe they dragged him in there. They probably left him for dead, but he crawled across the street and rang the doorbell to our apartment before he died. There were bruises and little cuts all over him; his face was unrecognizable. The police figured it for a gang attack, in spite of those strange marks like the hooves of a goat.

"I was out of that apartment ten minutes after the police left and never went back. I've been hiding for three days now. Today I went to the place where the *Lamentations* is hidden. It's still there. He must not have told them where he hid it. I have to use it to save myself. They want to kill me, they know I was Aaron's partner and I know too much about them. It wouldn't be enough to give them the book."

"What do you mean? What else is there to do?"

She stared into the fire. She closed her eyes and took a deep breath.

"I have to give it back to the—entities—it came from. I have to take it to one of the hidden places where our world touches theirs, and offer it to the Horned One who walks on goat feet; I have to beg the forgiveness of Shub-Niggurath."

Justin hesitated. He had assumed she wanted help hiding, or running.

"And just how would you do that?"

She looked at him intently, secretively.

"We learned things, you know. Before they got him. If he had gotten away with it there's no telling where it would have ended. I know what I have to do. The Black Druids hate me too much, because we killed the Master. He was important to them. He was centuries old. Nothing I could do would placate them. But if I can supplicate Shub-Niggurath, and his servant on Earth, the Horned One, return the book to them so it can be used for their hidden purposes here, I will come under their protection. The Druids will have to let me alone.

"I know how to summon them, how to speak to them. There's a place near here, where the spheres impinge. Go there with me. Please."

"What do you need me for?"

He was deeply suspicious. He knew she could never care for him as she once had. If she didn't need his protection, what could she be after? As much as he cared for her, he knew she always had an angle.

"I need your powers of concentration. We'll be surrounded by evil forces, trying to drown us in our own fear. I know how powerfully you've developed your mental focus through the bhatranj practices, how you can keep your mind steady in the face of threats. Better than Aaron, even. I need your help."

She stared at him questioningly. When he refused to respond she lay back in the chair and closed her eyes, her hand still around her glass.

Justin looked around the room, at the comfortable refuge he had made for himself these last five years, the familiar books and recherché objects that fascinated him without threatening him. The he looked at her face again, beautiful in the firelight, calm and innocent in repose. Could it possibly work with her again? Could he ever trust her?

"I'll do it," he said.

"I knew that you would," she murmured, softly but distinctly. Before he could speak again she was asleep.

* * *

Twenty-four hours later they stood in the moonlight on a rocky hilltop an hour's drive outside the city. They had left the car on a dirt track far from the highway and walked for half an hour under the dark and silent trees, unnaturally large and regular. She carried the heavy tome cradled in both arms, refusing to let Justin help her with it.

"Here," she said simply. "Sit there and focus your mind, say nothing, think nothing while I build the messenger fire and chant the summons. Don't let yourself be distracted by anything, no matter what happens."

"But how will I know when you want me to intervene? What if it goes nasty?"

"It won't. Not here, not at the beginning. If trouble starts it will be later. Whenever trouble happens, your role is to stay steady, be a rock for me to lean on, something fixed to cling to. Anything else you do will probably backfire."

Still puzzled, he took up an erect sitting position facing her. He opened up his mind to the darkness, the soft night space around them, stilling his mind to a clear mirror of the events in front of him. Alifair laid the book on the ground and fumbled in the moonlight with the little backpack she had carried there. She built a tiny fire, heating charcoal blocks to an orange glow. She sprinkled a coarse powder over the fire and whisked the smoke to the four cardinal directions with a black feather. The fragrance of juniper reached him; at the scent his clear mind expanded still more, taking in her slim figure, the flat stony hilltop, the black circle of trees, the enigmatic vault of the heavens, glimmering with stars even in the brilliant moonlight.

She did not need to open the book to voice the chant. She sat by the fire, cross-legged and erect like him, with the book beside her. As the words filled the air he sensed an awesome meaning, touching his mind through the strangeness of the ancient words. He held himself in a timeless stillness; he had no feeling for the passage of seconds and minutes as she droned the arcane syllables.

But in the long monotony of the chanting he grew tense; at length his own anxious thoughts began to break in. He brushed them aside, returning to the open readiness of the mirror-mind that is the starting point of all bhatranj, until gnawing uncertainty grew into a major distraction.

Only when she turned and stared away from the fire into the darkness did he loosen his concentration enough to turn his head, and by then the movement of the trees was complete and they had parted to open a path leading down the far side of the hill, away from the direction of their arrival. They rose slowly and carefully, maintaining the balance and clarity of their minds as they approached the open way. It led steeply downward into the blackness, rough and lit only by the hovering moon. They had to walk carefully, with total awareness of each stone beneath their feet. At the bottom the path was level again and though the way grew even darker, their feet found the way without effort, as though the path were made smooth for them by unseen powers.

He saw with an uncanny clarity the trees that surrounded them. There was movement, though there was no breeze to interrupt the quiet: silent, sporadic, short movements that he detected only with his peripheral vision. The trunks seemed abnormally straight and thick for this part of the country. He trod the open path before them with care, instinctively dreading to stray among those solemn sentries in that mysterious glade.

Ahead of them a faint blue light appeared between the trees. They reached the bank of a pool, littered with big stones and boulders, lit by the quicksilver reflection of the moon and by a glow like foxfire from the stones and bushes around it. Across the water was a cliff face and the black mouth of a huge cave, an evil maw gaping in the night. Justin was filled with courage and determination to save Alifair from her own fate, but fear radiated from that gaping blue-lit cavern like an unseen cloud, a keening overtone to his resolve.

A rustling began deep within the cave, resolving into a clicking, rattling tumult, and a reddish glow swelled from the back outward. Out trotted a short, bald man dressed in an ordinary business suit, moving with a fidgeting, prancing gait. Behind him surged an army of shadowy forms, unidentifiable in the gloom, each no larger than a sheep dog. The man skirted the pond and came before the two supplicants.

The minion of Shub-Niggurath was superficially ordinary, plump, smooth-skinned, with a fringe of sandy hair like a monk. But his movements suggested hooves rather than feet, and he tossed his head and rolled his eyes like a crazed stallion as he took in the couple before him. When he spoke his voice was shrill and lilting.

"You bring the book, you foolish thing," he mocked. "Whatever are you thinking of?"

"I seek the forgiveness of Shub-Niggurath, the all-mother, for my error. I didn't know what Aaron would do to the Master. I only sought to learn. Now I seek to abase myself before the power of earth and life and find peace and safety. I bring the book as an act of atonement."

She knelt before the preposterous yet terrifying creature. Yet she clung tightly to the book and did not offer it.

"If you seek atonement, give me the book now, you wretched creature," he bleated. "I can take it, you know. I sense your friend's shield, but his sorcery is feeble. Give it to me, or we will overwhelm you and trample you to a bloody ruin like your lover Aaron."

The clatter of the little shadow creatures swelled, grew frantic and menacing. Justin centered his consciousness in his abdomen, mentally reached out to the cardinal directions and the stars overhead and the firm earth under his feet, making himself a firm center of power unswayed by the flickering glow, the clattering of tiny hooves, the leering threats.

The bald man advanced toward Alifair and the shadows rushed to join him. Then he stopped and stared at Justin. The clattering diminished. The feeling of menace seemed to ground itself against the shield of power created by Justin's bhatranj yoga.

"I see your new friend is stronger than I thought. Not such a weakling as the one we caught in the park. Perhaps you must see the Horned One after all. I am not empowered to give absolution. Will you go further?"

"I must," she wailed. "If you cannot absolve me, I must seek a higher power."

His braying laughter echoed from the stone and the black water.

"So you must see the Horned One! Such hope, such courage, such dismal foolishness. He will devour you. Follow me, if you must!"

The grinning demon did not turn but moved backwards, with an inhuman jittering step, and receded into the glowing cavern. She advanced hesitantly. Justin followed closely behind her, careful to keep her within the edge of his small envelope of power. He wanted to reach out and touch her, to reassure her, but kept rigidly to the erect bhatranj posture, arms crossed over his chest in a mudra of defense. When they came within the cave the glow became a glare, and the clattering of the dark beasts intensified to a frenzy. Yet their shapes remained indistinct, a blur of small sharp horns, stamping hooves, yellow pinpoint eyes, covering the floor in an undulating mass, scampering up the walls. They surrounded the two supplicants but did not come closer.

A dim form took shape before them, a black vortex growing and clarifying in the rear of the cave. A wave of dread washed over both of them. Justin broke posture to take five star-shaped stones from his jacket pocket and quickly place them in a pentacle around himself. He made it large enough to hold both himself and Alifair.

"Alifair! Step back into the pentacle!" he called out. But she was already frozen with fear at the sight taking shape before her.

At first it was only a black spot in the orange glare of the cave; but it swelled quickly to a swirling cloud. Then features grew distinct, like an out of focus image sharpening on a screen. The emerging entity was much taller than a man, with glaring eyes set wide across the enormous goat-like head, gleaming yellow with vertical pupils. Heavy ebony horns curled like tentacles, sharp points forward. The towering body was dead black, hairy from the waist down. It walked on cloven hooves. When it advanced Alifair involuntarily stepped back, cringing and hugging the *Lamentations of Sheol*.

"Give it to me," it snarled in a bass voice like distant thunder.

"I beg forgiveness, mighty one! I will do anything you ask," she cried, trembling and buckling at the knees.

"I will have the book and I will have blood," roared the avatar. "You are helpless now."

It strode toward her, its head rolling slightly from side to side. Alifair fell to her knees in limp terror.

"Alifair! The pentacle! You must get inside the pentacle of star stones!" Fear shook his mind, rocking his consciousness like an earthquake. He had to center his mind, to let go of the panicky thoughts of escape and despair, and regain the steady power of bhatranj consciousness which was his shield against the avatar of Shub-Niggurath. Without the energizing power of mind the star stones alone could not prevail against such power.

She turned her head to look back at Justin but did not move toward him. She stared up at the Horned One.

"Great One! I have brought sacrifice to atone for my crime against the druids! I have brought flesh and blood to satisfy the hunger of Shub-Niggurath!"

Justin was startled and confused. His consciousness wavered, and the mob of sinister creatures surrounding them grew agitated and pressed closer to the pentacle. He summoned the power developed through long hours of practice and opened his mind even more; the creatures receded. He strove to expand his sphere of protection, to reach out toward Alifair and help her get to the protection of the stones.

"Take him! Crush his power, trample the star stones, offer him to Shub-Niggurath as the price of the druid master!"

A horrified comprehension clutched him. She half turned and pointed directly at Justin, not letting her eyes meet his. The beast turned its head deliberately to glare at him. Numbed by the brutal betrayal, he raged against the abyss of despair; painfully he strove to let the violent tugs of emotion pass. He centered his consciousness in the eye of the storm, with the clarity and symmetry of the bhatranj state. Fifteen years of practice had trained him for this—the powerful emotions swept through him, but he strengthened into an unmovable tranquility.

He saw her proffer the book to the thing, head down, arms extended. It turned its head toward her, then tossed its head and neighed in triumph. The bald man scampered out from behind it, giggling and whinnying, and seized the book, dancing back into the darkness.

The thing approached with powerful, purposeful strides, ebony hooves thudding on the rocky floor. As it passed her Justin saw her kneeling upright, slack-jawed, eyes grotesquely wide in her terror. It bore down on him; his mind ceased to touch anything but the motionless center of his consciousness and the snorting evil that towered only a pace away from him. He sensed the storm of uncanny malevolence that poured from the thing and washed over his shield. But it could not penetrate; it flowed all around Justin, short-circuiting in the mind-field and reflecting back to its source with redoubled intensity. The beast staggered back, bellowing its rage, then rushed toward Justin in fury. But again its own vile power reflected back against it, and again it staggered, almost falling. This time it roared in disgust and turned back toward Alifair.

Justin heard her high-pitched screaming, saw the sweat of fear run down her face like rain. She ran, away from the terror toward the depths of the cave, beyond reasoning, beyond anything but screaming and running. It overtook her in a few long strides and stooped to catch her with a sweeping horn. It tossed her against the cavern wall like a limp doll. She jumped up, blood seeping from her forehead, ran screaming again, now toward the cavern entrance. This time the horns took her from behind, one razor point slicing a huge wound across her back, the other passing through her abdomen. Justin smelled the rank, raw stench of blood and the biting ammoniac odor of urine an instant before the screaming stopped.

Then his tortured mind imploded into a full trance state, leaving behind his rigid, barely breathing body and the horror of Shub-Niggurath. He would remember the trance-wanderings of his soul vividly, and what he learned in those supra-human realms would haunt him for the rest of his life; but consciousness of earthly events returned only as he stumbled out of the woods in the gray cold light of dawn. The events of that night, leading to his second and permanent loss of Alifair, he would remember only rarely, painfully, and never willingly.

How Nohoch Koos Met the Xtaaby

The aged priestess rose from the altar and turned to face the novice. The torches cast her shadow large against the cramped stone walls of the shrine, magnifying her feathered headdress, making her jade collar and armlets glitter like the stars of deepest night.

"Go now, Nohoch Koos, before the sunlight fails. Forget not the way to the consecrated field, and choose only the best plants of each kind. Ya'ax Naay must be satisfied, in every way. The herbs, the potions, the jewels must please him as completely as the hearts of the sacrifices."

Nohoch Koos touched his breast in salute and rose. He stepped outside the shrine and stood atop the pyramid facing the setting sun and the fire star already glistening above it. The face of the pyramid plunged so precipitously that he could not see the steep narrow steps; he felt suspended in space, between the earth and the heavens, in the magical space where gods spoke to men, whispering their inconceivable mysteries. The sacred city of Mixba'al spread below him, the great temples and the mansions of the high priests and nobles announcing their stone mastery over the tangled green of the forest. His breast swelled with pride; he had been chosen to go out to the consecrated fields and select the precious herbs and aromatic spices for the ceremony of supplication to great Ya'ax Naay, the Green Dreamer. The fate of Mixba'al had been entrusted to him, the outsider, the child of another city, adopted in a new alliance.

He descended the pyramid in a serpentine path, stepping sideways down the deep narrow steps. The city was still at this hour, few moving out of doors. He passed between the great stone buildings, each surfaced with intricate patterns and glyphs to chorus man's power and wisdom through the good will of the gods of the Maya.

He stepped quickly, for he had been dispatched late in the day. It would not be good to be alone in the forest at night, even for a priestly novice of Ya'ax Naay.

Near the city the sacbe, the road of stone, was built on a high causeway where he could easily see the tall buildings of Mixba'al behind him. But the sacred fields consecrated to the priesthood were far from the city, in locations determined by intricate calculations and prophecy. Nohoch Koos felt a tightness in his stomach. He loved the brilliance of the tropical sunlight, the dark jade forest under the sky of crystalline blue. The starry velvet of night was full of mystery and menace, when any black tangled thicket could hold a jaguar or a demon. And this was not the forest of his native land. This forest was a strange place he had never seen under the moon, the stars, never probed with a child's curiosity. When the high causeway dipped to a flat ribbon between walls of dense thicket, he lit a pitch torch even before the last sunset gold faded away.

Something rustled the brush to the left of the sacbe. Something bigger than a dog or a rabbit, more stealthy than a peccary. He stepped a little faster. The jaguars who guard the forest are not friends of Ya'ax Naay: they belong to Chac Mool, whom the people of Mixba'al worshipped before the coming of Ya'ax Naay.

With the sun down the sacbe was a dark tunnel through the forest. When it forked, he tried hard to remember what the priestess had told him about the route. The directions had seemed simple, but now it was hard to think in this tiny bubble of yellow light within the inky labyrinth.

The brush rustled with an ominous rhythm, now before him, now behind him, always to the left of the road. There was more than one stalker. The tightness in his stomach had become a thrill tingling throughout his body, the thrill he felt when the gods came out of the sky and the earth and entered the shrines to accept the sacrifices. Surely the creatures that stalked him were demons; a priest of Mixba'al, even a novice, could not fear a mere brute. He grasped his ceremonial dagger of obsidian in his right hand and with his left raised the torch high, scanning the wall of vegetation all around him. He hurried down the right fork.

The stalkers crashed through the brush on both sides. But it was the soft slap, slap on the stones behind him that made his hair stand up and the still night air rush by, flickering the torch as his legs pumped furiously into the darkness ahead. The jaguar that landed on the road in front of him was huge, eyes greener than sacred jade, teeth like sabers, its growl summer thunder.

With death ahead and behind Nohoch Koos did not think, was hardly aware, as he turned down the dirt path to the right of the road. He did not notice when the torch blew out, or when the ominous sounds behind him stopped. Only when he stumbled among corn stalks did he stop. With the eerie vividness of dream he knew that the night was still except for the chanting of crickets and cicadas; that the only light was from the dazzling half moon.

The path had ended in a corn field surrounded by black jungle. On the left under a huge ceiba tree was a thatch-roofed choza, the doorway flickering with soft firelight. The stalks in the right-hand part of the field were flattened, as the farmers did after picking the corn from each stalk and the beans from the vines around them and the squash from the ground. Not only food grew here; he smelled aromatic herbs, bay leaf and demon's breath and purple snake-root, the magical plants he was sent to gather. Yet the scent was oddly different, and certainly this was not the consecrated field he was sent to find. There was no altar.

A shadow moved under the ceiba tree; something passed behind the choza. He heard a song, faint, sweet, a woman's song. It fluted in his head, not in the air, like a dream remembered as one wakes. Of the words, he understood none, except for his own name. He was sure it was an unearthly creature calling him, not of earth and water and sunlight, blood and bone. It must be, because Nohoch Koos felt his scalp tingle and his knees tremble as they did only in the presence of the god, in the awful resonance of the ceremonies. He remembered the tales of the Xtaabay, the demon spirit who came to men in the shape of a woman to lure them to their doom. He must turn back and face the jaguars of the forest, but his feet would not obey. The dream-song in his brain pulled him like a fish on a line. His feet shuffled toward the fire-lit doorway.

In the choza she stood by the fire, smiling. She wore the short skirt of a peasant, but her necklace of green jade and the gold bands on her arms and legs belonged to no woman of the corn fields. Her small breasts were those of a young woman, but her eyes were ancient, pools of black light that swirled in the shadow and flashed yellow when the light flickered across them.

The song changed, and told of him and his mission in the forest. It sang that his mission was benighted with the curse of the ancient gods. It told how he had been driven away from the herb garden of Ya'ax Naay, drawn to another sacred place, to the garden of the ancient gods who had protected the city before the coming of Ya'ax Naay. Nohoch Koos trembled, eyes wide with fear of the gods. He wanted to run but his heavy feet rooted him to the ground.

And Naxkul the Xtaabay came to him and her eyes wrapped him like the night sky, her hot soft hands touching his arms, his neck, his face, drawing him to the hammock in the shadows. She bound him with her arms, fierce and probing, with her legs, powerful beyond denial.

Only the senior priests took wives, and the novices lived apart from the young women who preened and flirted in the marketplace. In the dark sweetness of the Xtaabay, he came to a thrill that ran through his body like sudden lightning out of a storm; he convulsed and shuddered, then he slept, and he dreamed.

In dream he rose high above the jungle. He had the keen sight of the eagle. The world below was pale under a waning moon, yet he could see every detail in every corn field and every city. Yucatan was checked with corn fields, webbed with the roads that linked the great cities of stone. He saw the stone pyramids and temples and palaces of Mixba'al, starred with the yellow fire of braziers and torches. He saw the Xtaabay hovering next to him. She turned her head, twisting slowly on her neck like an owl, smiling. Swiftly, with no sense of falling, they were low over Mixba'al, soaring softly in the night air. He could see people walking among the hallowed stone monuments. Through doorways he could see the rich and powerful of mighty Mixba'al taking their ease in the silken tropical evening. They rose to the top of the great pyramid, and into the shrine at the top. The ancient priestess was still there, speaking in hushed tones with Xaank'an, one of the high priests of Ya'ax Nay, in secretive whispers. They did not move when Nohoch Koos and the Xtaabay floated silently into the room. The intruders were invisible to ordinary minds.

"You sent him late, very late," said Xaank'an. "The jungle night can be very dangerous."

"There are many paths in the dark," she crooned. "Many lead to death. Ya'ax Nay may not get his herbs tonight."

"And we will no longer need to trust the outsider in the priesthood. We could never trust Nohoch Koos. His heart could never submit to the Green Dream. You have done wisely, ancient lady."

Nohoch Koos felt a hollowness in his soul. He had no body to feel this blow, but pain stormed his mind. He had striven with all the strength of his soul and every fiber of his body to serve Ya'ax Nay and Mixba'al, and still the highest ones of Mixba'al called him outsider and conspired to destroy him, like an enemy.

The Xtaabay smiled and turned her head again and again they soared high, higher than eagles. Beyond the shores of Yucatan he could see black ocean and a reflection of the crescent moon. She drew them west, far out over the unknown ocean. Long they flew, the watery murk below marred only by the tiniest crumbs of land. He stared and stared until his mind was one with the vast space below and above and all around him. The mystery of this truest of dreams made him drunk and fearful and still thrilled him like a glare of lightning in a jungle storm.

He felt the place of death below; the surface of ocean showed no sign, yet the cold evil of the Deep Place crept into him like the howl of a beast far away in the jungle, strengthening as Naxkul brought him near to it. The vision of the city beneath the sea came to him, unsought, like a creeping nightmare from which one struggles to awake. The city spread across the ocean floor, wider than any city of the Maya. Huge blocks of stone, far heavier than men could move, filled a deep fissure with mile after mile of buildings, a honeycomb of rooms and halls and tunnels. Here and there life stirred in the darkness, but only the brute life of fish and squid and other strange denizens of the ocean depths, though he gasped at the size and strangeness of many of them.

But Naxkul did not linger in the vacant upper levels of the city. Ever deeper she brought him, passing through stone as through the water itself, for it was their souls that traveled, not bodies. Below the city was a layer of cavernous galleries where lay row after row of sarcophagi, strangely proportioned. Something about those shapes made him glad that Naxkul did not show him their inhabitants. Tombs, he thought, until he sensed the current of life, fainter than dreamless sleep, that informed this deathly army.

Nohoch Koos was a brave man, strong with the warrior-courage of his birth city, awed but not terrified in the eerie presence of the gods. But there was a cold evil about this place that penetrated his soul; a chill menace of beckoning death that intensified as they glided deeper into this lightless hell. As they passed below the deepest chamber he knew the evil he felt was no echo of his own fear but a presence; a living shadow that underlay the city from end to end, a life that was to the dreamless army as the full moon to the dimmest stars.

Down she led him, down to a place of monstrous slabs of stone, more massive than any pyramid or temple of Yucatan and laid at strange angles that tortured his mind, refusing to resolve into a sane space or straight-flowing time. They entered the tomb of the entity, as long and broad as the city. Even in this vision he dared not look upon the creature that lay here. Yet he touched its dream; the dream of Ya'ax Naay.

The dream charged him, like the eel that could stun a man; it froze him, like cold rain in the wind. Ya'ax Naay dreamed a dark and formless world, a world where life and warmth and intelligence had no place. Even in dream-death Ya'ax Naay was hostile to living energy; Nohoch Koos drew back lest his own life enrage the monster. Touching him even so faintly, he felt his life-force being sucked out and devoured. Even Naxkul was alarmed, and they fled.

High above the midnight sea and on they flew, till he thought they must come to the end of the world. But instead they came to another land, where jungles and mountains and deserts such has he had never seen slept in darkness. They must be nearing the magic world where the sun sleeps through the day, for the horizon ahead was rimmed with golden light.

Out of that dark land grew a column like a sea-spout, stretching up to the starry vault. It had no color; he saw it not with his eyes but with his soul. Touching it filled him with awe and energy, a joy of pure life. When they immersed themselves in its stream all fearing and believing and wanting were dissolved, washed away in pure energy and the colorless light of pure intelligence, till nothing remained of mind but a pure knowing, open and unobstructed.

She bore him along the stream, whether up or down he could never be sure. Through worlds they passed, whether hells or heavens he could not know; a world of dark stone towers, a black watery world, a world of golden light, a world of fire. At last they reached the uttermost of worlds. In this last world he needed no guide to teach him. He knew; he was the knowing and the knowing was he. He saw the brilliance of life, a light-like energy that spread through all the worlds in an unquenchable fire of awareness, dimmest in the primitive creatures of young worlds among the stars, glowing like campfires in man and manlike life, most effulgent in titan minds that reached near this ultimate center.

And he saw the dark shadow that intertwined with life wherever life reached. A blackness, a tortured energy that sought to thwart and corrupt life, to neutralize the brilliance of pure awareness with a vicious evil. Life could not exist without conflict; the evil was created by the very existence of life. Ya'ax Nay was one tentacle of that cosmic evil.

He saw how Ya'ax Nay hovered over the earth, working against life, especially intelligent life, as it arose from the lifeless primordial world and arrived again and again from other worlds. Ya'ax Nay strove to corrupt and destroy, ensnarling intelligence in dark knots of struggle so that it thrashed like a fish in a net, instead of fulfilling its glorious promise of growth and wisdom. It ensnared unsuspecting allies, used them in its mad destructive writhings and destroyed them in turn. Thus Ya'ax Nay had snared the priesthood of Mixba'al and would use them to destroy all of the Maya civilization of Nohoch Koos's beloved Yucatan.

The dreamed collapsed like the wind after a hurricane, dwindling to a sigh and a dreamless sleep.

When Nohoch Koos awoke, he was lying on his back on the hard stone road, staring up at the gray sky before the jungle dawn. He remembered the shamanic flight. It was no fleeting dream, melting in the light. It did not leave him. The world had a new resonance; the earth beneath throbbed with sleeping power, the sky above echoed silent wisdom and mystery. He knew he was no longer the novice dispatched into betrayal. He wondered if the Xtaabay was near. She was not; he was sure. He knew he would feel her if she were.

He sat up. He felt the pouch bulging at his belt. He opened the flap. The tangled fragrance tugged at his mind. He knew the neat bundles of herbs and aromatic stalks were like those for which he had been sent. He knew they were not the same. He knew that Ya'ax Naay would not be pleased, and the results would be violent. He would take them to the priestess and say nothing.

His sandals tapped on the stones of the road, making no echo against the greening forest. Ahead a bush rustled. A jaguar padded onto the road and looked at him, a bright-eyed swirl of beauty and terror. It sensed the power of the shaman and fled into the shadows.

Natty

"Rob! Get the door!" sang Natty over the babble of conversation. "That heavy touch on the doorbell could only be Adelaide."

Rob Carlton elbowed his way through the guests and opened the antique glass-paned door for Mrs. Adelaide Hackberry, reigning matron of Huddleston and chief broker of the town's gossip.

"Evening, Mrs. Hackberry, so glad you could come," he recited timidly.

"Wouldn't miss it for anything!" bellowed the statuesque dowager, with a straightforward sincerity rare for her. "It's so . . . bold of Natty to give a party so soon after your parents' untimely passing. One really must admire her ability to deal with her grief so quickly. Especially after the cloud of . . . uncertainty surrounding the circumstances."

Over the sculpted smile her brazenly curious stare fixed him like a wooden stake. Rob tugged at his collar and murmured, "So happy to have you." He knew he looked like a deer caught in the headlights of a speeding truck. It had been just two months since the horrible deaths, by food poisoning, of their mother and father and Natty's third husband, George. Maybe Natty was ready to move on from the horror, but Rob could hardly step out into the sunlight again, much less deal with this mob of critical and suspicious townspeople. The deaths had shocked the quiet little town. The sheriff had inexplicably declined to investigate, beyond taking statements from Natty and Rob. He hadn't even ordered autopsies. His behavior had astounded everyone in town, everyone but Natty. Natty's party was a gesture of defiance.

"Of course, your sister has always been so strong, so independent. It must be very difficult to be the man in the family. Is your sister older or younger than you, Rob? I've never been able to tell."

"Younger," he blurted, resisting the impulse to lie. "Come in, please. I'm sure she's anxious to see you."

Adelaide made a sound like "hmff" without relaxing the smile or the glare and pushed through the door like a pirate ship sailing out to attack. Rob stared at her back and tried to disarm her image by visualizing Adelaide naked, her huge limp buttocks jiggling away across the room. It helped.

Natty turned to meet the challenge.

"Adelaide! Darling . . . ," cooed his sister, her firm alto resonant above the prattle of the guests. They parted liked the waters of the Red Sea as she fastened her dark eyes on the formidable dowager, gliding across the room to meet her. Some found Natty's eyes hypnotically beautiful; others thought them aggressive and repellent. Few could ignore them. Even the redoubtable Adelaide was momentarily speechless as Natty held her in a steady gaze. "So good of you to come, Adelaide. Rob, be a dear and get the Reverend another drink. It's disrespectful for us to leave him dry, and Adelaide and I need to get to know each other better. Don't we, Adelaide?"

If the other guests expected some entertaining fireworks between the two, they were disappointed. Rob knew better.

"Naturally, I couldn't miss it . . . your courage to . . . so soon . . ." Adelaide's babbling trailed off into a murmur, as Natty's eyes fixed her with the cool steadiness of a predator contemplating its prey.

"Our family tragedy . . . it's been terrible, Adelaide." Natty's low, vibrant voice could soothe a hungry tiger, or a scared rabbit. Her eyes, large and still, the irises almost black, rested on her adversary's. "So sudden, so unexpected. A normal, happy life, and then . . ."

"You poor dear . . ." Adelaide's voice was losing it's sarcastic edge.

"Food poisoning: who would have thought it, in this day and age?" Natty's tone was calm, wistful. "I was in such shock I couldn't think; it took Sheriff Powell to figure out what had happened to them."

"I can never forget that day," said Natty. "We were all gathered around the dining table: Rob and I, George, my husband, our parents— you knew Mother and Father didn't you?"

"Oh yes, I saw them often, at the country club. Your father played golf, didn't he?"

"Yes, he did. There was no course in Carlton Cove, where we lived before, and he took it up with a passion after we moved here. He and George were going to play that afternoon. I gather they weren't terribly good at it, but they spent every moment they could on the course. Till Mother's mutton put a stop to it."

"Mutton?" asked Adelaide.

"Mother prepared a highly spiced mutton dish that day. It seems the mutton had matured a bit too long."

Natty's smile had a wry twist that most found unsympathetic. But Adelaide didn't notice.

"Were they popular, at the club?" asked Natty.

"I suppose so," said Adelaide. "Most people knew them, at least by sight. And your mother played bridge. You and your brother, on the other hand, were something of a mystery."

"Rob and I are more like the rest of our clan, in South Carolina. Stay-at-homes, almost reclusive, devoted to ancient things, the mysteries of the past, the forgotten lore of antiquity. Not that we had much choice. If we'd wanted to broaden ourselves with outside activities or travel, we hadn't the money. Father and Mother held the purse strings very tightly. But then, death loosens anyone's grip, doesn't it?"

Adelaide cooed sympathetically, oblivious to Natty's subtle irony.

Natty recounted the whole story, patiently and deliberately, as though to fix each detail in the mind of a trusting child. Rob had seen this tableau many times. An adversary would stand before her as though hypnotized, while she told them precisely what to believe, a story they would never again challenge. Others stood by in amazement, unaffected by her spell. He remembered Sheriff Powell standing in front of her on that terrible day two months before. His deputy stood behind him, fuming at Powell's passive handling of Natty. Rob had been glad of her power that day, and of her strength. He had been devoted to their parents, and he could never have dealt with the aftermath of their hideous death. Dear Natty, what would he do without her!

"Horrible, horrible," said Natty. "But you can't stay mired in tragedy for the rest of your life. It's time to get back into the swing of things, don't you think?"

"Of course, of course . . ." said Adelaide, her broad head bobbing up and down in sympathetic assent. Her eyes, so recently curious and insolent, radiated sympathy under turned-up brows, her lips pursed as thought to chide fate for their imposition on the innocent who stood before her. Rob had never seen anyone stand up to a one-on-one confrontation with his sister. And she made it looked so easy. She simply told her side of the story, with the other fixed in her gaze, and resistance melted.

Rob fled in relief from the invisible tension between the two dominant women. The Reverend Burnside was a mousy young man with thinning sandy hair. Even Rob could intimidate him, if he were so inclined. His glass was indeed empty but still he clutched it with both hands as though to defend himself against Nadine Foreman. Nadine was a voluptuous red-haired divorcee. She simpered at the Reverend with predatory intensity.

"Rob!" she gushed. "Do get the Reverend—May I call you Bruce? Get Bruce another glass of red wine. And another for me, too, please."

"Of course, Mrs. Foreman," said Rob. "Was that the Burgundy?" Her third or fourth, he guessed.

"Oh, call me Nadine! And you too, Bruce. I've been Nadine a lot longer than I was Mrs. Foreman, and enjoyed it more, to tell the truth. Have you ever been married, Bruce?" The Reverend blushed and fingered his white collar. She didn't wait for a reply. "Yes, that scrumptious Burgundy. What -*is* that wonderful stuff, Rob?"

"It's a French vintage, part of the family stock we brought from Carlton Cove. We Carltons were traders, you know, from the days of wooden ships and sails, even way back in New England, before we came to South Carolina. We collected things from all over the world. I'll get you some more."

Rob listened through the crowd noise as he went to the bar and filled the glasses, but all he could catch was the word "Carlton Cove." When he returned they interrupted a sentence and both looked at him. The preacher spoke first.

"Actually, Rob, I was surprised when Natty invited me. I don't think you ever joined a congregation here. What is your religion, Rob?"

Rob improvised.

"I believe the Carltons, my father's family, were originally Episcopalian. I don't know about the Coopers." Actually the last clergyman had disappeared from Carlton Cove fifty years ago, under mysterious circumstances. Conventional religion no longer had a foothold there.

"Of course, everyone in town knew about your tragedy," said the Reverend. "I'm sorry I didn't reach out to her at that time. I'm sorry to admit I don't even know Natty's full name–Natty is a nickname, isn't it?"

"It's short for Asenath. It's an old family name."

"Rob!" called Natty.

"Excuse me," said Rob with relief. He pushed his way back to his sister.

"I'm going to announce a toast, Rob," she said. "Get ready to top up everyone's glass"

"Better wait till I fetch a few more bottles," he said. "The Burgundy's almost gone and the Chablis isn't far behind."

"Then do it quickly. I want to raise the toast while the energy's still climbing, before they have too much time to gossip." Her eyes roamed the room with a calculating look.

Rob exited the big parlor and followed the long gloomy hall back to the kitchen. The house was a hulking Edwardian relic, complete with turrets, bay windows and a widow's walk atop a partial third story. It had been much too big even for the Coopers and their two adult offspring. Many rooms lay unopened and unexplored. They had inherited it from an ill-fated offshoot of the Carlton Cove Coopers who, like themselves, had wished to escape the brooding spell of the ancient seaport.

The kitchen was scaled like the house, with long counters and tables and rows of hooks for utensils to serve a small army. The previous family of Coopers, with their brood of curiously deformed children, must have been hearty eaters. The Chardonnay was in one of three large refrigerators. The Burgundy was below in the cellar. The cellar door was wide enough and heavy enough to honor a royal mortuary. It opened on a similarly solid wooden stairway built of heavy timbers. The cellar was much deeper than any modern basement, divided into a maze by the stout beams and archways which supported the house above, as though modeled on the bowels of a medieval castle. The scattered electric bulbs created islands of yellow light, besieged by shadow.

The wine racks were in a dim alcove far from the stairs. The prize Burgundy had been brought by the previous Coopers and stored in the rearmost racks. Something scampered across the floor in the gloom. Rob wished he had brought a flashlight. He fumbled with the bottles, trying to read the faded labels, inadvertently nudging a brick in the wall beside him, one that protruded slightly beyond its fellows. He heard a click and the wall moved back a finger's width. He touched it tentatively; it swung back on oiled hinges. The space beyond was dark. Rob groped for a light switch and found one on the inner wall. He flicked it.

The hidden door opened on a small room lined with shelves, empty except for a few books and wine bottles. The only light came from a shaded lamp hanging from the ceiling, over a rough wooden table and a chair. Arranged neatly in the lamplight were two bottles of wine, an ancient ledger, a modern book and a paper tablet.

On the exposed page of the tablet were notes in Natty's tiny, neat hand: "32 invited. est. 25 show up." was one. There were notes on hors d'oeuvres and drinks, worked out for 25 people. He recognized the preparations for the party going on above. She had taken special pains to plan the wine and doubly underlined the fine old French Burgundy, adding the comment "the Cooper house specialty!" The two corked bottles were of that vintage.

He was not surprised she had kept this secret from him, though he resented it. Natty was always secretive. At the party she would talk and talk, but the guests would learn exactly what she wished them to learn, no more. He wondered how long she had known about the room, without giving him the slightest hint. Well, if she could conceal, he could pry. That was only fair. He could peep into her secret mind.

Several pages of the tablet had been used and folded back. Most of the notes were an inscrutable jumble of fragments and abbreviations with a lot of question marks. One seemed to be a series of calculations for mixing "str." with "Bur.", with the first walter c. debill, jnr.

measured in grams and teaspoons and the second in ounces depending on a weight in pounds. She did calculations for 4 weights: 110, 140, 150 and 170. 140 pounds was Rob's own body weight. Could the others be their parents and her husband?

A giddy chill crept through his entrails, even before he looked at the book: *The Author's Guide to Poisons*. He picked it up. It fell open naturally, to the chapter on strychnine. He saw why: a little scrap of tablet paper was inserted there as a bookmark. In a crawling nightmare he forced himself to follow the bland, cheerful text that described, in clinical detail, the awful death that so resembled a form of food poisoning. He felt each word in his bones, felt the agony and the writhing in his own body, saw the convulsions on familiar figures, the rictus on beloved faces.

She had done it with the wine, of course. The scene at the dinner table, so meticulously suppressed, flamed in his mind with the clarity of deepest dream. Father had proposed a toast to their fresh start in Huddleston, far from the ancient rumors whispered about the accursed Cooper and Carlton clans. Natty had poured the traditional family Burgundy. Rob had taken only a sip, and had lived. Natty had drained her glass in one triumphant tilt; it must have come from an untainted bottle.

Natty, Natty, how could she do it? Everyone knew was strong-willed. She had quarreled with their parents, had wanted more freedom and control over her life. She had asked for her future legacy from the family fortune and father had refused. But how could it come to this? Rob had loved her, as he loved all of his haunted and even sinister family. And now he lost her too, in that terrible vision of her monstrous nature. Murder must be avenged. She must be destroyed.

The memories came back, in strange distorted flashes, as of an unremembered dream. It all seemed so obvious now. As the scales fell from his eyes, he was amazed at his own naiveté. And at that of the authorities: three people had died with symptoms of a well-known poison, yet there had been no autopsies, no real investigation. He realized that had been the sheriff's doing, and no one else's. It came back to him that the deputies had been angry and hostile, almost mutinous in the face of the sheriff's acceptance of Natty's story. The people in town had been suspicious and unfriendly up until today, when the party began a new face to face relationship with Rob and Natty. Before that, only the sheriff had accepted the status quo, he and Rob himself.

He remembered her talking to him, in her strange calm way, as the three victims lay dying. And he remembered her, later, speaking to the sheriff. After that, all of her dealings were through Rob or the sheriff, one or the other of them, never through the deputies or anyone else.

That calm voice. A hazy memory from his childhood: Uncle Elkanah teaching he and Natty that special way of talking to people, "the Power of One" he called it. Natty had caught on quickly; Rob couldn't get the knack. But Elkanah Cooper thought that was natural, because girls were better at some things and boys at others. The Power of One could take three forms. In the weakest, the patterns in one mind would induce currents in the Powerful one. It was a form of telepathy, and sex didn't matter. In the strongest, one mind could occupy and preempt another: boys were better for that, according to Elkanah. But girls excelled at the third. In the third, the object mind remained intact, but the stronger, the one with the Power,

240

could plant it's patterns in the weaker. The weaker mind would believe the thoughts were their own, and never question their authenticity.

Natty had used the Power of One to control Rob and the Sheriff, heading off any real investigation. If Rob tried to expose her, she would do that again and again. But Rob remembered something else about the Power: it had limitations. It could only be exerted over one target at a time. He must expose her in a situation where the Power would not work. Only then would people see her as she was, a lethal monstrosity. He saw a solution. And he saw a resolution of his own pain and despair. An icy resolve grew in him.

He carefully selected one of the still sealed poison bottles, clearly focused as he gathered up the wine bottles from the racks. Each movement was careful, precise. He knew he could do anything now; his will, always scattered and divided, full of contradiction, was now a calm, transparent reality, an unmistakable path down which fate propelled him with no possibility of hesitation. All the pain, the fear, the guilt of the past months was transmuted into a smooth force, making even his cold anger at Natty irrelevant. He carried six bottles. There was never a possibility of dropping one, or of forgetting which held the fate she had prepared for herself.

She was working on George Hasdell, the town lawyer and insurance agent, when he entered the crowded room. She appeared to have him hypnotized.

"I'm going to pop these corks and spread this Burgundy around now," he said. "I'll tell them to save some for a toast, so be ready."

"Excellent, dear brother," she purred. "Don't forget to bring me a refill, too."

"You needn't worry," he said dryly. "I'll bring you the first glass."

The guests were getting relaxed and talkative and the refills were refused by none. The wine was good enough to impress even the most ignorant palate. Their faces were frankly curious when he told them that Natty was going to speak. At Rob's signal she tapped the side of her crystal wine glass with a spoon.

Asenath Cooper Carlton Braxton Graham Post prepared to taste her triumph.

"May I have your attention, please," she said. She paused dramatically while the conversation muttered to a halt.

"I want to thank all of you *loyal* friends for coming here to help me celebrate my freedom. Freedom, yes, from a dark and unhappy past. And of course, for all of your support during these past months of dark personal crisis."

Rob saw a lot of blank looks at this obscure remark. As Rob well knew, they had carefully avoided her.

"Although few of you have had occasion to speak with me since our family tragedy, your sympathy was completely . . . *predictable.* I never had any doubts about how you felt."

Suspicious, thought Rob. That's how they felt. Even the sheriff, so completely in her power. All but he himself. He alone had believed in her completely.

"I've been so terribly confined by the shackles of the past. But it's time to move on, to free myself and go forward, out of the shadows."

The family wouldn't confine her any more, he thought. Clearly she hadn't considered him a hindrance, or he wouldn't be alive. He looked around at the faces of the guests, with their bland smiles. They were taken in by Natty's charming public façade.

"I must *act* to free myself from that confinement. In the end, one has the life one makes for oneself, isn't that true?"

Agreeable nods rippled around the room. Rob thought about the action she had taken three months ago and smiled bitterly.

"Now we can see our way through to happiness and freedom from the past. To a future without constraint."

Most of them had had enough wine not to notice the oddness of her wording. So bland they all looked, he thought, like sheep in a pen. He positioned himself in the middle of the crowd opposite Natty. He had handled the poisoned wine very carefully, knowing exactly where each glass was at every moment. Not until now did he look up from the extra glass and meet Natty's eyes, hypnotic and glowing in her triumph.

"To freedom!" she sang out, and glasses upturned all across the room. Rob took a deep breath and drank deeply. He felt nothing, no change, no liberation.

"And because there is no freedom without it, to action!" Her voice trumpeted over the rustle of the crowd. She left wine for another toast. Many of the guests didn't. It was very good wine, he thought with ironic mirth that he could barely contain. His throat was suddenly dry, impossibly dry. His glass was almost empty.

"And most of all, now that action has brought freedom, to the future!" It was a trumpet of triumph, a defiant fanfare to all the world. Rob turned to take the second glass of death. It was gone! Nadine Foreman was standing there, hoisting a full glass. She tipped it slightly and winked at him mischievously, before downing half of it in one gulp. He opened his mouth to shout a warning, but just then a red hot sword passed through his bowels. He lurched into the coffee table between him and Nadine, alarming her without conveying any message. He tried again, then realized how little time he had. He turned as he fell and shouted at his sister. He heard his own voice distantly, a ghastly croaking stage-whisper that could be heard throughout the room.

"Natty!" came the rasping hiss of death. Natty stared fiercely, unblinking, her upper lip curled as though at some intruding rodent.

"Natty! You poisoned me! You switched the bottles, in the cellar. You poisoned me like others!"

Witnesses disagreed as to whether any other articulate speech passed his lips. The consensus was that he said something like, "Urrrkh," and doubled up on the floor.

"Rob! You lying bastard . . ." was her startled rebuttal. Through the sudden hubbub in the room and the pain and the dense awareness of impending death, certain events stood out in resonant clarity.

Nadine Foreman was flopping around like a landed fish.

Natty was trying to fix the sheriff with the voice of Power, her low alto strangely grating, intoning. "No! He's lying. Don't listen to this craziness . . ."

A pair of deputies barked at the sheriff from both sides and dragged him away, out of her range.

"Seal off the basement, Sheriff, before anybody tampers with it," said one. "Mike, you get on the radio and get an ambulance out from Ashton, quick."

"Natty . . . Mike . . . ," sputtered the sheriff, "I . . . we need to . . ."

"Don't listen," rasped Natty's sepulchral alto. "He's sick, his mind's not . . ."

"Haley, find the door to the basement and block it off. I think it's in the kitchen," called Deputy Mike.

"Right, Jordan!" barked the sheriff. "Mike, make the call."

"John, please . . ." pleaded Natty.

The sheriff drew himself up and braced himself to face her.

"Natty, I'm sorry. This time we've got to investigate," he said stiffly. And then he turned away from her. No one had ever done that to the Voice, never.

"George!" she pleaded to the mayor.

"No, Natty, I've got to talk to John," came the voice of the mayor.

Her voice was cracking as she tried one shocked guest after another, breaking between the controlled alto and a panicky shriek.

Rob was fading. The room was frozen in a bright light, voices echoed far away. Words rippled across the room, cackling again and again, "thorough investigation," "murder," "murders," "murdered," and a rumbling "exhume", "exhume."

She was finished. The last Cooper witch would die in a prison cell, fat and gray, or perhaps even strapped down in the big oaken chair in the state prison. Rob felt no peace, only an empty relief as blackness filled the scene, forever.

What Sort of Man

"Ricky! It's marvelous!" purred Roberta Willingham. "It's the most drop-dead gorgeous thing I've seen since the King Tut exhibit. Someday you've got to break down and tell us where you get these things. Mustn't he, Virginia?" she said to the elegantly dressed and coiffured older woman standing next to her. Virginia Eddings was fifteen years older than Roberta and a good deal less voluptuous. Both were women who enjoyed owning things. Special things.

"Yes, of course. You'll just have to worm it out of him," said Virginia, smiling demurely with her immaculate dentures. Like Roberta, everything about her advertised wealth. In a tasteful way, of course.

Purvis Rix, Jr. tugged at his lapel unconsciously and blushed. No one but Roberta had ever called him Ricky. Since his extremely sheltered childhood, no one had called him anything but Mr. Rix. Except for his father. Father called him "Junior," or, when he was in the doghouse over some imagined shortcoming, "Sonny."

"Someday, perhaps," he murmured. "I don't know how long I can hold out against your charming persistence."

Virginia simpered. Roberta seemed hypnotized by the object lying between them on top of the glass display case.

It was a ceremonial dagger, about twelve inches long. The blade was of a color lighter than bronze, darker than copper, with a rich patina of greenish cast. It had a slight back curve. The slender handle suggested ivory, but was more coarsely grained, and of a pale golden color. It was inlaid with tiny cabochons of red, amber and green in an intricate filigree suggesting curling waves. There was no hilt, but a curved thumb rest integral with the handle was inscribed with a single mysterious rune.

"That character," said Roberta in a lower and huskier voice, "what does it mean?"

Purvis smiled.

"I must confess I don't know. Though I've seen the script before, on other items."

"And you won't tell us what kind of writing that is, naturally," she said. Her nostrils flared slightly as she gazed at it, eyes gliding sensuously along lines of the inlay.

"No. We're very firm about that," he said, trading smiles with Virginia Eddings. "We maintain a monopoly on this line of imports, and secrecy is absolutely essential to our business." Roberta knew all this; he was talking for Virginia's sake.

"But Ricky, if I may call you that," said Virginia, "how can you provide proof of authenticity, without telling where it came from?"

"Unfortunately, we can't provide a pedigree," said Purvis. "But any customer is welcome to have an item examined by his own experts, or subjected to any test, as long as the object isn't marred or taken away from the shop. One lady, from Dallas, actually had a van come here with all sorts of microscopes and spectroscopic equipment. The answer's always the same; they don't know where it came from, and aren't sure about the materials, but the quality is exquisite. I think you can see that, if the provenance of this material ever does come to light, you won't be disappointed."

He smiled and tried to look mysterious.

"No one's ever asked to return anything," he said.

His father was so much better at this. It didn't matter; the special imports sold themselves, for fabulous prices. Roberta was holding the dagger in one hand, caressing it with the other, like a lover's face.

"But Ricky," Roberta looked at him coquettishly, "this piece is so masculine—so macho. Don't you have something more feminine?"

"Well, ah," he stammered, "I don't think . . ."

She fluttered her eyelashes. To a different flutteree, that might have looked odd on a statuesque salon blond of forty-odd years. But then no one had ever fluttered at Purvis Rix, Jr. before.

"Oh please," chimed Virginia, "won't you show us more of these fabulous 'special imports'?"

"Please?" echoed Roberta. "Do it for me, and I'll make it up to you later."

Now Virginia fluttered, looking discretely away.

"We're going out this evening, you see," Roberta confided to her friend.

"I'll see what I can do," said Purvis, turning to leave them alone in the cramped showroom, cluttered with art and antiques, trying not to run toward the stairs at the back of the shop. He knew he shouldn't do this. He should show them a lot of mediocre stuff, a little selection of good stuff, then just one special import: that's what his father always said. Then you can name your price. Besides, they hadn't set a price on any of the other items yet. Father liked to do that one item at a time, after the preceding piece sold. He flushed again, sweating a little, with a sudden perception of himself as a forty-year-old virgin worrying about what his father would think. When he glanced back down the stairs, the women were looking up at him and speaking in low tones. He caught the word "cute," and ". . . what sort of man he'd be, without his father . . ."

The second floor wasn't large and two thirds of it was taken up by the open loft at the head of the stairs, which served as Purvis's bedroom. The rest was a closed room over the showroom. The lock would only respond to a big brass key on Purvis's key ring. He continued up the next flight of stairs to a cramped landing and knocked on the door. He heard an inarticulate grunt from the other side and entered.

Purvis Rix, Sr. was propped up with pillows in his big brass bed. On the muted television set at the foot of the bed, a grinning host pantomimed a game show. The hawkish eyes under thick curling eyebrows and an explosion of frizzy white hair didn't deign to rise from the calf-bound folio in black letter lying in his lap.

"Well, Sonny?" he said without moving his head. "What is it now?"

Purvis Jr. always felt tongue-tied when his father called him "Sonny." He cleared his throat.

"It's about the . . . special imports," he said, stammering a little.

"What about them? Speak up, Sonny!"

"We haven't set any prices since we sold the bracelet. I think I have a good prospect. Can we quote something now, a loose figure maybe?"

Sr. snorted and looked at his son with disdain.

"A good prospect, you say. And just who might that be, pray tell?"

"Virginia Eddings is downstairs. And Roberta Willingham."

"Humph," said Sr. "I know Virginia. She's from the old Ulrich money. She's a moron. Worse, she's a fool. Rich. But not as rich as she thinks. Any business you do with her, you check her credit before you make any commitment, Junior, and don't forget it. Can of worms. Fools bidding more than they can afford, that's a can of worms. The other one? What's her name again?"

"Roberta Willingham. She has money, but I don't know how . . ."

"Don't know her," sniffed Sr. "Must be one of the new people." The "new people" meant anyone who had moved into Ulrich in the last twenty years. All of them made their livings in Barrett, and spent most of it there. Few got to know the old-time locals. "You find out what she's worth, before you talk business with her, you hear? And don't let her twist you around your finger, like that Manning creature five years ago. You're a fool about women. You'd give away the whole store if I let you."

Purvis Jr. ignored the abuse, as was his habit.

"Do you suppose we could set some kind of loose talking figure, to draw her out? Or just quote a date when we'll have prices? I'm kind of thinking of the tiara."

"Don't want to set prices right now. Almost out of stock, time to trade for more. Then we'll look at the new lot and the old stuff at the same time and bracket them. Next week will be a good time, to trade I mean. October 31st. You need to get busy. We'll need the usual trading stock."

Purvis Jr. stepped out on the landing and closed the door, without saying another word. He paused a moment to take a deep breath and straighten his posture. The interview had ended in total frustration, which was the normal outcome of any attempt to influence his father. He returned to his sleeping area below and entered the back room.

The furnishings of the room were sparse: a central table with two chairs, of very old and dark wood smoothed with use; simple wooden shelves lined with parcels, cartons, crates and their scattered documents; and a man-high combination safe of antique design. Purvis went directly to the safe and dialed the combination from memory.

The safe was almost empty. In a square compartment at the upper left were three worn ledgers: these contained nothing but a minute description of each special import item handled by Rix Art and Import over the last forty-eight years, each dated, with no figures, no information on provenance. The most recent twenty pages were in Purvis Jr.'s hand. On the shelves below were five objects resembling the dagger downstairs. One was a small double-edged hatchet, about the size of a claw hammer, another ceremonial weapon. Nothing feminine about that. There were two decorated goblets, a jeweled tray. Then there was a sort of tiara. Did anyone still wear them? And below, almost filling an entire shelf . . . no, it would never do to show her that. He remembered how he had gasped and held his breath when he first saw the thing.

Slim pickings, altogether. It was time to bring in another shipment. For Roberta, the tiara would have to do.

He descended the stairs carrying a teakwood box attentively in two hands, like an offering to some demanding god. Both women fastened their eyes on it and followed it shamelessly as he moved behind the glass case and lay it before them. Both were breathing a little fast. When he raised the lid their mouths opened and little sighs slipped out.

He had posed the tiara to be facing them. The high-fronted band was of the same golden ivory as the handle of the knife, lustrous and warm. He wished he could show it by candlelight. Around the band wove a pattern of subtly lined cabochons of smoky hues, while across the high front faceted stones dazzled like a fireworks display. Naturally a buyer would have them examined to see if they were synthetic. They were not. All of the ivory not covered by stones was inlaid with incredibly fine threads of silver-gold metal that glittered even in the poor light of the shop. Close inspection showed they were arranged in a wave pattern, like the carving on the dagger. He couldn't imagine how such tiny patterns could be executed.

The tiara was a little small for an adult woman's head. But it wasn't going to be worn on anybody's head. Whoever paid for it would keep it on a cushion in a glass case with a sensitive burglar alarm, and only take it out to allow a select few, whom he wished to impress, to fondle it. Roberta eyes smoldered the question and Purvis nodded. She picked it up. Virginia was visibly jealous. But Purvis wasn't worried about Virginia. There was never a dearth of buyers for something like this. Eventually she took it, reverently. And appraisingly.

"So," said Roberta after a long interval, "you haven't set a price yet?"

"No, not yet," said Purvis. "It takes a lot of thought. It's not like the ordinary things we carry, where we can research other items like it and see what they sold for. Not only is each piece unique, the whole line is unique. We have to look at the materials, the amounts of them, the complexity of the workmanship. We look at what our other special imports went for in the past. But we almost never have information about resales. People don't like to part with them."

"I really would like to talk seriously about purchasing it," said Virginia, putting the tiara back in the box. "When do you think you'll know? I assume we're talking six figures."

Roberta stiffened almost imperceptibly and her eyes got colder. A bidding war wasn't what she wanted. Purvis guessed that six figures was beyond her resources.

"I think we can have something in about a week," he said. "May I call you?"

"Here's my calling card," she said. "And now, Roberta, I really need to get home."

Roberta took a long last look at the tiara and reluctantly closed the box.

"See you at seven, Ricky?" she said.

"At seven o'clock sharp," said Purvis.

* * *

Dinner didn't last long. Both ordered light meals and ate quickly. It had to do with Roberta's stockinged foot sliding up and down his leg under the table. At first contact he thought the table was too small and apologized. When she just smiled and persisted, he found he liked the sensation. But it was hard to concentrate on the menu. When the food came he couldn't remember if it was what he had ordered. It didn't matter. He ate without paying attention to it.

They had planned on a movie, but dinner conversation steered them away from that.

"I've wanted to invite you over, to my place, for the longest time, Ricky," she said. "But with my daughter and her baby there, it wouldn't be much fun for you, would it?"

He flushed, ever so slightly.

"We could go to my place. I mean, my room upstairs." He had fantasized many times about having her there alone. "I have some wine," he said. He felt very naughty.

Did she actually purr, like a cat? He thought he detected a low throaty sound. He leaned forward conspiratorially.

"I've always wanted to show you the special imports by candlelight," he said.

Her foot became tense and muscular, more massage than caress.

"But your father . . ."

"You don't have to worry," he said, with a mischievous smile. "I gave him a double dose of sleeping medication. I've done it before. He won't hear a thing. We can even play music."

"I'll teach you to dance," said Roberta.

They drove up to Purvis's tall narrow home, tower-like, backlit by brilliant moonlight, the front dark save for a small bulb above the door. It had been built on a hilltop to watch for Comanches from a circular observation deck above the third floor. The ten acres of Purvis land around it guaranteed privacy. The small town of Ulrich, now a bedroom community for the affluent professionals who worked in Barrett, had never encroached upon it's rural isolation. They entered under the light, giggling a little with excitement, careful not to jingle the bell over the door. He led her gently by the arm as they threaded the glass cases and tables and display stands he knew so well. They crept up the stairs together, warmed by the closeness and the dark and quiet. He smelled her perfume, a sultry jasmine.

At the top he moved away to the table against one wall and lit a candle. When he turned she as sitting on his little bed, legs crossed. Above them Purvis Sr. snored softly and evenly. She looked up at the ceiling and grinned. He lit two more candles and went to her to offer wine, a fine red he had opened earlier to avoid a pop in the nighttime. She pulled him to her and kissed him full on the mouth. She kissed long, exploring, experimenting, involving a lot more anatomy than their two mouths. Finally he pulled away and stood up, his knees oddly liquid.

"Would you like some wine?" said Purvis Rix, Jr.

"Why, yes, I'd like that," she said. Her breath was deep and slow. When he brought her the glass, she drank deliberately, staring boldly into his eyes. He felt it was a cue for him to do something. He couldn't kiss her again, they had done that. He could sit down next to her; would that be too bold? Things would have been simpler if she had sat in the chair by his desk.

"Would you like to see all the special imports now?" he said.

That got the glass out of her face with half the wine left in it.

"Ooooh, yes," she said in that low, throaty tone he was learning to like. It did funny things to his lower abdominal region.

He brought them in three trips, all but the largest, arranging them artistically in the light of the two candles on the side table. Roberta was off the bed and at the table as soon as he placed the first two. In the yellow candlelight the ivory luster was creamy white, luminous. The thread-like inlay swirled with the wavering flame. Even Purvis had never seen them like this.

Roberta leaned over the table, enchanted. He watched her eyes move sensually over the display, wide and moist with wonder. She licked her lower lip. She touched a goblet, tracing the patter of the stones with her finger. He couldn't resist touching her. At first he put his hand on the lower part of her back, tentatively, as though testing her reality. She smiled sidelong, with heavy-lidded eyes, then looked back to the unearthly beauty before them. His hand pressed into the depression along her spine, moved upward. Her eyes and her hands moved over the warm ivory, the cool stones and cooler metal, while his hand moved all over her back and his eyes hung obsessively on her rapt face. After a long time he reached out, almost unconsciously, to caress her earlobe between his thumb and his forefinger. She turned to him and cupped his face in her hands and kissed him till he felt it down to his toes. His hands came, quite accidentally, to rest on her hips. The soft globes bucked and ground against his palms and fingers while his eyes widened with ecstatic alarm and his entire body turned to seething liquid.

Undressing was one long miracle of discovery. Roberta manipulated the fabric and the buttons and the zippers, while one wave of revelation after another washed over Purvis Rix, Jr. Magnificent breasts clad only in a beige brassier. Hot sweet breath on his neck. A woman's hot belly pressed against his. A statuesque figure in bra and skirt. The quick, graceful departure of the skirt. A woman beyond all dreams in a beige brassier, transparent panties, hose dark in the candlelight. Shoes scattered across the floor. The bra loosened, lowered, tossed away, revealing . . . the quick, graceful departure of the panties, revealing . . . and somehow, unnoticed, he too had become naked.

He quit wondering what he should do, what action he should take. There was nothing to do but lie on his back with the erotic current tingling his entire length and all his extremities, equally it seemed, while Roberta's soft warm moist body executed a complex rhythmic motion in three dimensions, centered somewhere in her pelvis. No one had ever dangled long blond hair in Purvis's face before. He had never seen full breasts dance like that, except on video of course, swinging inches from his face. He reached out and touched them. It was not a calculated act to please his partner. It was just what his hands wanted to do at that moment. A little later they chose to grasp her bottom, which was soft, firm and muscular all at the same time, and swiveling wildly.

When it was over, for him and for her, he had barely caught his breath when a limp embrace metamorphosed into something wildly active and it was happening again, a little slower, a little more purposeful. Once his father snorted and snored very loudly for several minutes. The lovers froze, stopping the faint creaking of the sturdy little bed. Roberta smiled and gyrated in slow motion till the snoring attenuated. It was she who got up and blew out the candles before they slept.

He woke in a room drowned in moonlight. The harvest moon was low, passing straight through the windows at the ends of the bed, onto the table where ivory luminesced and metal inlay swarmed lazily, as though sated, like the two lovers. Overhead Purvis Sr.'s snoring was choppy, less comatose. Roberta, sprawled in guileless abandon, moved in small twitches, muffled murmurs escaping every minute or so. Deep night could not last much longer.

He still felt weightless, suspended in a field of erotic energy. Knowing the night must end, he regressed to wondering what he should do, should have done, should be doing. She had done so much, done it all really, he had been so passive. How to take the initiative, show her his passion, equal to hers. She awoke, unblinking, and smiled at him. Had she felt his eyes on her sleeping face?

He was who he was. He knew what to do. He signed her to silence with a finger across his lips, and took her arm gently and raised her up and gestured for her to follow him, through the moonlight into the back room, to the safe. He worked the combination in the dim magical light, making two mistakes because she had her arms around his waist, rubbing her magnificent bush against him. He took out the grandest piece of all, that had been in the safe since he first saw it open as boy of seven, and turned to her and held it up before her to catch the full light streaming in the window behind her. It was twelve by twelve inches, twenty separate pieces of the mysterious ivory, held together by a mail of the bronze-like metal fashioned into tiny rings. The stones were reflective beyond any earthly gems, easily flouting their colors in the mystical light of the moon. She drew herself up and breathed deeply. He reversed the thing and fastened the broad collar around her neck.

Roberta did not teach him to dance that night. Instead, she danced before him, to a silent music they could both hear plainly, in the pectoral of Vityalpa, the Vampire Queen of Carcosa, which the raiders of her tomb had traded to Purvis Jr.'s grandfather long ago. When he moved to light the candles, she shook her head no, and he watched her until an orange glow shattered the last of the moonlight and Purvis Sr.'s snorting became unpredictable. He drove her home before some encounter could ruin the night.

Outside her home she kissed him again, thoroughly and sensually. She sat a moment, hesitating to speak.

"Ricky," she said. "The . . . that incredible thing . . ."

"Don't worry," he said. "We'll keep that one in the family."

She squeezed his thigh appreciatively and went inside, just in time for the baby's first squall of the day.

* * *

The hardest part of trading for the special imports was getting his father up the stairs from his room to the observation deck. The elder Rix seemed especially heavy on this occasion, being quite limp and unable to help raise himself. After Purvis Jr. got him set up in his chair, he stood a while panting at the waist-high stone wall.

Few streetlights illuminated the hamlet of Ulrich, but the lights and tall buildings of Barrett painted a glowing mural across the horizon, temples and monuments to high tech business. The world outside frightened him, but he yearned for it, too. He read newspapers and magazines, watched television; he understood that there was a panorama of sights and sensations and activities beyond this isolated tower and the secretive activities of the Rix business: people to meet, things to eat, sounds to hear, art that didn't live in a glass case or drool out of a television set. And since last week, he understood that there were real women out there, many women, not just flat pictures or hollow fantasies, women who could transport him to paradise. The wider world frightened him, but did not intimidate him. He could join that world, he could be a player. The Rix business made a lot of money, he knew that, he kept the books. It needn't be so furtive and exclusive. Off his father's leash, he could make a much larger enterprise out of the trade and still keep their essential secrets. He could be a wealthy and mysterious art dealer, exclusive and admired, mingling with the jet set. Barrett had more than two thousand millionaires, all looking for special things to spend their money on.

He glanced at his watch. It was time to get on with it. He went back down the stairs and retrieved an antique cylindrical carpet bag, smoothed by handling, its flowered pattern faded by a century of sunlight. He set it down by the seven-tiered pyramidal stone altar which stood against the north wall of the enclosure. Once he had surreptitiously brought a compass up here and confirmed that it was aligned precisely with magnetic north. His father had no curiosity about such things.

After his eyes adjusted, the Barrett sky glow provided enough light to guide his hands. It took half an hour to remove the twenty-eight objects from the bag, carefully peeling back the chamois skin wrap from each one, carefully placing it on its mark on the appropriate stone shelf. He had watched his father do it many times, learning to match object to mark, memorizing the precise alignment of each one on the shelf. The bottom three shelves took flat objects of metal, seven, six and five respectively, circles, ovals, pentagons, triangles. He had never seen them in strong light, but the hues differed slightly even in the sky glow. There were inscriptions reminiscent of the rune on the dagger.

The objects for the upper tiers were all large gem stones, some opaque, a few completely transparent, set in bases of carved ivory. There were ovoids, pyramids, cubes, and, alone at the top, a translucent bluish sphere the size of a billiard ball. Two were faceted, with too many facets to count easily. He smiled; the time would come when he could count, measure, investigate and experiment without interference. Who knew what he might discover?

His father was stirring in the chair, and making little sighing sounds sporadically. The medication was wearing off sooner than Purvis Jr. had anticipated. But the timing was near perfect. He had ample experience with the sedative. He brought the bag around behind the chair, removing the last object and snapping it shut. He took his place sitting cross-legged on the black cushion next to the chair, facing the altar. The object was a flute, not of ivory but of bone, bearing a suspicious resemblance to a human femur. He began the low monotonous dirge he knew so well, more chant than melody, sultry and ominous, like the cooing of some crepuscular bird that one would rather not see.

Along the bottom row of the altar metal talismans began to glow and shimmer, successive waves of illumination passing through each and continuing on to the next until the whole row throbbed with coppery light. The next row took up the pulsing glow, with light of a pale greenish cast, and the next, surging with deepest indigo whose intensity was more felt than seen.

The first row of gemstones were opaque cabochons, ovoid, marbled with sinuous seams that sparkled when the wave motion overtook them, showing the dark hues

251

of their main matrix. As the motion touched the next row, lighting an intricately faceted crystal of vermilion, the image of the altar wavered, then shimmered, until it danced like a mirage in the desert. A current of distortion stretched between the two men and the altar. Just when the topmost sphere flashed like blue lightning the altar vanished. Purvis put the flute down. The Traders were here.

Where the altar should have been, he saw another world. There was an altar there, but it was vastly larger than the one on this side, in Purvis's world, and carved from smoky obsidian. The objects arrayed and glowing on its seven tiers resembled those he had placed so meticulously, though larger. But the traders were not so solemn as he. The cadaverously thin black figures, so human yet so alien, leaned and draped over the lower shelves, sat on the higher ones, squatted on the ground before it around a black wooden chest carved with the runes of Carcosa. Or so his father had named them. He wondered if his father or his grandfather had really known, or only guessed, at the identity of the city of ebon spires that he could see in the distance. Was it truly the Lake of Hali that lay mirror-like beside the city, reflecting the enormous globe of dark gold sinking beneath the horizon? He did not like to think about what might lie beneath that waveless surface.

The Traders could definitely see him now. He saw their agitation, heard the sharp barking calls which he interpreted as whoops of enthusiasm. The ones around the chest jumped up and crowded against the shimmering interface. A tear in the fabric of space-time, a shortcut across folded space—perhaps someday he could figure that out, with enough freedom to explore and experiment. The Traders loafing around the altar rushed forward to join the others. He could see them very clearly, better than ever before. Their skin, if that is what it was, was dead black. They had the outline of men, but the arms and legs were too long, too thin. The eyes suggested an oriental humanity, but they were too long, too narrow for any earthly race, and the pupils fluctuated in size in shape in response to unknown stimuli, at times diagonally slitted in a field of china blue, at others filling the width and most of the height of the eye socket. They wore crude kilts of hairy animal hide and nothing else. The three toes were long, flexible and clawed. The hands too had claws, which seemed to be retractable, and more digits than he could ever quite count, and two opposed thumbs. He would not like to be grasped by those hands.

They stared at him and his father in apparent puzzlement. Articulate sounds emerged that must have been speech, and too-long fingers pointed at his father. He stepped behind the chair. The Traders all stood still as though dumbfounded. His father was fully alert now and would certainly have liked to comment on the situation. No doubt he would have filled the air with his hateful sarcasm, if it hadn't been for the duct tape stretched tightly across his mouth.

Purvis Jr. pushed the chair forward, sliding roughly over the stone floor, till it was only a foot from the undulating interface with the other world. The traders signaled consternation with abrupt gestures of hands and head, crowding around opposite the chair. They peered and gestured till recognition struck them. Then a wave of their alien homologue of laughter spread through the crowd. The leaders nearest the chair waved in assent.

Further back, two of them lifted the lid of the chest, lay it on the ground and began stacking it with baubles and trinkets worth millions on earth—properly marketed, of course. When the lid was suitably loaded, they carried it over the interface, to the left of the chair, then looked at the younger man expectantly. Purvis nodded his acceptance; his opposites nodded in agreement. They pushed the lid through the barrier an inch at a time, while Purvis Jr. pushed the chair, and his father, into the world of Carcosa. They preferred younger stock, but evidently the irony of taking their old trading partner in the bargain appealed to them.

Purvis Sr. was wide awake and quite frantic now, contributing as much sound to the conversation as the tape would permit, struggling to move his extremities. But Purvis Jr. had done the job well. He had plenty of past experience restraining the "trading stock" they recruited from among the hitchhikers and runaways so plentiful along highways and in bus depots. Though drugs were a necessity for managing the stock before the trade, the Traders insisted on a conscious piece that did not look drugged or ill. His father had originally used clothesline rope, which was tricky to tie and sometimes worked loose. He had read about duct tape in a book about serial murderers, and it had worked out very well. Who could know what his father and grandfather might have accomplished, if they had only looked around for ways to improve their methods?

He spread a cloth and transferred the precious loot onto it. A splendid haul—the Traders must have felt that a better than average price was in order, in keeping with the irony of the occasion. Returning the lid of the chest was a standard part of the deal. He wondered if they would return the chair. It was a rather nice one, dense hard wood with curved armrests, a type common in old-time saloons.

He soon found out. His trading counterparts wasted no time in "unwrapping" the merchandise, leaving the tape across the mouth till the last. Sure enough, here came the chair. So that was what a Carcosan grin looked like. Purvis was learning fast. A fresh point of view and a desire to learn, that's what the Rix business needed. Across the way the Traders were proceeding, as they always did, to process their acquisition. There was always a frantic quality to the action that made him doubt that they were sophisticated representatives of an evolved society. Probably they were barbarians living among the bones of a dead civilization. If the trade-goods were tomb loot of little significance to them, that would explain why they traded such quantities of it for something they would consume immediately themselves, with no thought of further profit.

Normally he would quickly close the barrier. It was done with the same flute, playing an inversion of the opening melody in a different key. But this time he sat a while and watched the activity on the other side. No one was going to chide him for doing that. They were butchering the new stock, while it was still alive. They always began by cutting thin strips from the long skeletal muscles and eating them right away. Further back they were building a fire for the larger cuts. The tape gag came loose while the elder Rix was still conscious, but there was no sarcasm, no recrimination. Purvis Rix, Sr. was done with articulate speech. There was nothing left for him now but screaming. But not for long. The Traders noticed Purvis Jr. watching and produced a flute like his. They played the same inverted melody that he expected, but in a higher key. Interesting. It produced the same effect, and he was left alone with the trade goods. The objects on the altar were almost completely dark.

He took down the altar first, wrapping each object in its chamois skin, placing it carefully in the carpet bag. He carried it down to its accustomed place in the third floor room. He left the lights on before bringing down the trade artifacts, slung in the cloth with the four corners tied loosely together. He looked around the room before switching off the lights. It had a lot of potential. He would get rid of all the useless old junk, and make a splendid bachelor pad out of it. So much to do, now. When the new items were safely locked in the safe, he lit a candle and poured himself a glass of wine. Everything had gone so smoothly. Tense, to be sure, but he had never broken a sweat. He picked up the phone and dialed Roberta's number.

"Wait till you see what I've got," said Purvis "Ricky" Rix. He would have new business cards made up that way, leaving off the "Jr." It was no longer necessary.

The Changeling

Matt followed the intricate directions from the state highway off onto two-lane blacktop and then onto a frequently patched county road overhung by ancient oaks. The Heinrich farm was somewhere past the end of county maintenance, and the rain-gullied clay surface threatened Matt's wheel alignment. The farmhouse belonged in another era, simpler, more solid; stout wooden timbers wedded to blocks of limestone cut from the surrounding hills. Beyond it he could see plowed fields wedged in a narrow valley between steep wooded slopes. Night was coming, and the forest seemed to wait for the cover of darkness to creep up on the house and overwhelm it. He parked in the yard next to a dusty pickup and trudged reluctantly up to the door. He didn't understand why his boss, Kazimerz Grodek, had sent him here. It seemed even less promising than the other situations the Observers had sent him to report on.

The woman who opened the door was about forty and pretty in a rawboned, no-makeup way. She had not let her appearance go, though her eyes looked like she had gone beyond anxiety into terror and then on to grief.

"Mr. Rourdan?" she said. "Mr. Grodek said you'd come tonight."

Her eyes lowered with embarrassment.

"He said he'd pay us a little money." She raised her eyes and challenged his. "He said you had nothing to do with those awful tabloids in the supermarket. That whatever we told you wouldn't be sold to them. Is that right?"

"We can assure you of that, Mrs. Heinrich, absolutely. The Observers of the Unknown is a very small organization that publishes a newsletter for its members only. It's sent only to members, who pay dues because they're interested in unusual phenomena that may point to the unknown. We believe your child's case could be one of those. We'll be glad to pay a little money, which may help with the medical bills, but not the huge sums the tabloids pay. If I take pictures, you're not going to see them in the checkout line."

He smiled gently and she smiled back, mostly with her eyes.

"How much?" she said, without losing the smile.

"A thousand dollars, today," he said. "More if you'll keep in touch with us and let us come back as things develop."

She relaxed a little and led him into the gloomy living room. It was impeccably neat, furnished with big comfortable pieces and lit by a single floor lamp. She sat in a threadbare armchair and he sat at one end of the couch, close to her.

"I guess you already know about Gretchen," she said.

"Mr. Grodek told me something about it, but I'd like you to tell me all of it again in your own words, if you don't mind. Start at the beginning, please."

"Gretchen never had any problems before, not a one. Never even got sick, except for the measles once. She's eleven now, the nicest little girl anyone could want. She was a little lonesome, out here on the farm, but once she started school she was happy as could be. She'd go play with her friends after school and I'd come pick her up and bring her home. There was nothing unusual about her. Here, see how pretty she is?"

She picked up a small framed picture from the table beside her and leaned to hand it to Matt. He saw a lanky girl in a blue jumper holding a cat and smiling, an innocent face with bland regular features framed by blond hair. When he passed the picture back to her, she smiled at it for a moment before putting it down. Her face turned drawn and worried again.

"She did seem a little nervous for a couple of months before it happened. Sometimes the animals, the farm animals you know, would make noise at night, like maybe a fox was sneaking around, and she'd wake up scared and come get us. A couple of times she had nightmares, dreamed something was creeping into the house and trying to get her. But that's all.

"The first we knew there was any problem was when the chickens all got killed."

Mrs. Heinrich's eyes widened as she began to relive her daughter's transformation. Her hands gripped the arms of the chair.

"I remember we had heard noises earlier in the night. That's because Hank, my husband, went down and put the chain on the front door, locked the side door too, because he heard something outside. The only door he didn't lock was the one to the back yard, because that's fenced in. We can get to the chickens and the pigs and even the barn. And it was later that same night we heard a racket in the chicken pen. We didn't think much of it because they're fenced in, so usually nothing can get in. Animals just come sniffing around on the outside and the chickens make a racket but that's all there is to it, so we didn't go check. But the noise went on and on and just got worse. Hank finally went down to look, and that's when he found Gretchen sleepwalking. It was the first she'd ever done it. She didn't even walk in her sleep when she was little. Well, there she was, just staring at him in that weird way. We never saw her do that before either. Wouldn't say anything but 'No!' and 'Don't!', like she'd forgotten how talk. Now she won't even say that.

"But that wasn't the worst," she said. She dropped her eyes again and paused a little. It clearly hurt her to talk about it. They must have needed that money, thought Matt. She was earning her thousand by enduring pain. He didn't pressure her to go on.

"She wouldn't talk to Hank and wouldn't come to him, just hunkered down like a little animal, with that look. I call it scared, but Hank thinks its plain mean. When he tried to pick her up, to bring her upstairs, at first she snapped at him, like she was going to bite. But she stopped that and went limp, let him take her in his arms. That's when he saw the blood.

"She was smeared with blood, her hands, her face, all over her little pajamas. Of course we were terrified. Almost jumped in the truck and took her to the hospital in Barrett. But we couldn't find where she was hurt. We bathed her and put clean pajamas on her, but we couldn't find a single scratch. She let us do what we had to, didn't put up a struggle. We decided to put her to bed and take her to a doctor in the morning. She tried to get out of the house that night. We heard her rattling the chains and went down and got her. Been locking her room at night ever since. Nailed her window shut, so she couldn't climb out. My poor baby!" she sobbed, losing her composure altogether.

"Mrs. Heinrich, I could come back later, if that's better for you," he offered, a little unnerved. He hadn't run into anything like this before, reporting for the society. He heard heavy footsteps and Hank Heinrich barged into the room. His movements were unsteady, not quite staggering.

"Is this man upsetting you, Betty? We don't have to put up with anything now, just because . . ." His speech was a little slurred. He was paunchy and not very tall, and most of his brown hair was gone.

"It's alright, Hank, he's been very polite. They're helping us with the bills, a thousand dollars to start with, and who knows, they might even find out something that could help. Lord knows the doctors haven't. Why don't you sit down now?"

Hank softened and collapsed into an overstuffed chair just outside the lamplight. He faced Matt with a wary stare.

"I think I can go on now," she said. She took a deep breath. "We didn't find out about the chickens till the next day. They were all dead. Not eaten or anything, just choked, crushed, some of them had their necks wrung. They tested her pajamas and found nothing but chicken blood. So they claim she did it, but I don't believe it. There was something evil out there that night. I'm sure of it."

"To make a long story short, the doctors couldn't find anything wrong with her. Not physically, anyway, except for ups and downs in her temperature. So they call it a mental problem. They use a lot of medical terms to describe what she does, but it's all just a fancy way to say what I already told you—she doesn't talk, she doesn't behave like she used to, she gets violent, she tries to get out. I'm afraid she'd run away if we let her get out of the house. It's a good thing this house is so well built, she's a strong little thing, I don't think we could keep her in. And she's smart, always was; she figured out how to pick the old room lock. We had to replace it. Now she keeps trying to pry the bedroom door open, or scratch through it with one thing or another. The door's ruined."

"Mr. Grodek said you had experienced poltergeist activity—that is, noises or objects being moved outside her room?" This was one of the things that had aroused Grodek's interest.

"That only started about a month ago. Noises on the outside. Things broken in the kitchen. Always at night. In the dark. I just don't believe she's doing it, no matter what they say. Something's outside, trying to get in. I know it. It's gotten into the house, and into the chicken yard, and onto the roof. It just doesn't make sense that Gretchen could make these things happen. There have always been strange tales about these woods. I've heard about them ever since we moved here, twelve years ago."

Matt's ears pricked up. If Grodek knew about this, he hadn't passed it on.

"What kind of stories?" He tried to conceal his excitement. "Who told you about them?"

"Well, they say people hear voices whispering, when there's no one around. And people who camp out have strange dreams. Then there's the problems with the livestock. Foxes or weasels or something that seem to get through fences and gates and walls that an animal shouldn't. But the hardest to believe are the ghost stories."

"Ghost stories, Mrs. Heinrich? You mean the woods are haunted?"

"Not exactly. People seen out there who are really some where else, or dead."

"Betty!" blurted her husband. "You know those old stories are just foolishness!

Just crazy gossip. Don't go and embarrass us like that."

"I know those stories sound crazy, Hank, but then what happened to Gretchen was crazy too. It's true that these woods have always been weird. The Indians told stories to the first settlers who came here."

"Please," said Matt, "tell me more about the ghosts. It's most unusual, I haven't heard anything about it till now."

"Well, the story I know the most about is the one about Harry Willows. He was taken strange, nobody knew what to make of it. But then he died. After that two different people said they saw him in the woods."

He heard the front door open. A man and a woman in their thirties appeared in the archway to the entry hall. They stopped short and looked startled.

"This is my cousin Helen Guidreaux and her husband Armand," said Mrs. Heinrich. "They live with us. Helen, Armand, this is Mr. Rourdan. He's from the Observers of the Unknown society. I agreed to talk to him about Gretchen's case."

Armand had black hair and narrow shoulders and a weak chin. Helen's hair was auburn and her face was a heavily made-up version of Betty Heinrich's. They looked uncomfortable, like kids slipping in ten minutes after curfew. Both gave shallow nods and went upstairs without speaking.

"Were they living here when the change happened to Gretchen?" asked Matt.

"Oh yes, they've been here since Gretchen was born. She came to help out, and they wound up staying."

"Is there anyone else living here, besides you and your husband and the Guidreauxs?"

"Just Aunt Jane. She's Helen's aunt on her mother's side. I'm not sure about her last name. I think it's Taylor."

"About how old is she?"

"I'd guess at least eighty-five."

"Can't you see she's getting worn out now?" Hank Heinrich interrupted. "I think we've talked enough."

"I understand, Mr. Heinrich. Would it be possible for me to see Gretchen tonight? That would save me having to trouble you another time."

"I guess I did promise Mr. Grodek. We might as well do it now. She isn't getting any better; one time's no worse than another."

She got up walked out of the room wordlessly. Matt went behind her, followed by a glaring Hank. It was already dark outside and light sockets were few in the old farmhouse. The stairway was dimly lit, the narrow corridor upstairs more so. Betty walked very softly up to the first door on the right. She stopped, her head cocked slightly, listening for the slightest sound from within. The girl must have known someone was coming, Hank's footsteps were not particularly quiet. Matt moved up close to her as quietly as he could. They stood motionless for at least a minute. Then Betty took a key out of her apron and carefully inserted it into the shiny brass lock.

The door opened a crack. A light was on in the room. Matt could see furniture in disarray. A dresser was turned over, chairs strewn in strange positions, some broken; toys were strewn about at random. An open door at the rear showed a bathroom, decorated in pink. There was no movement in the room. Betty pushed the door wider, scraping the floor with something that had been propped against it.

She pushed it again. A small pale hand flicked out from behind the door and grabbed her wrist.

The wild-haired gargoyle trying to rush past Betty Heinrich bore little resemblance to the pretty thing in the picture downstairs. It was half-dressed in underpants and a tee-shirt, both filthy. The eyes were beady and staring, the mouth curled in a vicious snarl. When it's mother blocked it, it bit her arm. It took both parents to push it back into the room.

They all stood breathing hard, Betty squalling in despair and Hank swearing and sobbing at the same time. Matt was shaken to the core. He had seen the mysterious, even the awesome, but never this tragedy, this evil intrusion on commonplace life.

"I'll write the check now," he blurted, anxious to leave them alone in their private grief. By the time he left, she had calmed down enough to voice a heartfelt "Thank you" for the money, which made him feel even worse about it all. He almost ran off the road rushing to get clear of those dark woods.

* * *

It was after eight when he drove up to the big stone mansion, deep in a residential neighborhood full of old money, where the Observers of the Unknown carried on unobtrusively. Matt hoped that the Society would be closed by the time he got back, but there still were lights on inside. He was duty-bound to report to Grodek. He parked in the circular gravel driveway in front and went in.

The two huge downstairs rooms off the oval entryway, which might have been a ballroom and a study at one time, had been converted into something that looked like a library with rows of books going all the way to the ceiling. Both rooms had lofts where more books and file cabinets were reached by spiral iron stairs. There were at least two employees still around, the kind that brought things to his boss on demand no matter how much work it took.

Grodek's personal office and study opened on the left-hand room. His desk was very heavy and old-fashioned, incongruously topped with a computer. Grodek sat behind the desk, scowling at the computer. He looked big behind the desk, and he looked huge whenever he got up from it, which wasn't often. His mane of white hair looked both too long and freshly cut. His gray tweed coat looked neatly pressed, though he apparently lived in it.

When he saw Matt he put down a large magnifying glass and sat motionless, staring blandly at him, while Matt approached the desk and sat down opposite him. He continued staring until Matt spoke.

"Well, aren't you going to ask me how Shallowford was?"

"Why? You're going to tell me momentarily. It's your job, is it not?"

"It was a different kind of job, today. Not so good. The Heinrich's are unhappy people."

Grodek studied his face carefully, while Matt tried to look distressed enough to quit. The big man folded his hands over his paunch and gave an inaudible sigh.

"I suppose I should have warned you. The false leads aren't usually upsetting. When we run into something real, people are affected differently; scared, hurt. But it's just those cases that we care about the most. Now give me the details." He relaxed and, without moving more than a half an inch, slumped in his chair, his eyes pointed at a spot in middle of Matt's tie.

"There aren't any UFO sightings, abductions, crop circles, or anything like that. Some dead farm animals but it's pretty clear the girl killed them. The parents . . ."

"Please," the large man interrupted without rancor, "from the beginning. What did the farm look like? What was the surrounding countryside like? I know what Shallowford looks like, I've been there. Are they far from town?"

Now Matt sighed, accepting his appointed role as observer and reporter, not analyst. A quick, pithy summary just wasn't going to do.

"It's five miles outside of town. Back in the hills, off of county roads in a maze of hills."

"How about the surroundings? Open fields, other farmsteads?"

"No, it's kind of isolated, in fact. In a narrow valley between two steep hills. The road in stops at their house. Plowed fields in back of the house. Along the road and the sides of the house the woods are thick, they come pretty close to the walls."

Kazimerz Grodek nodded in approval and pointed his eyes at Matt's tie again. Matt decided that was a signal for him to go on. This time he recited the exact sequence of events that had occurred at the Heinrich farm, mentioning every detail he could remember, quoting the Heinriches verbatim wherever he could, as Grodek had trained him to do over the six months he had worked for the Observers. Throughout the recitation Grodek's head never moved, but after a while his eyes closed. When Matt finished he opened his eyes but didn't move them. After a long minute he raised them and spoke.

"Well, I think you've finally found a real one. A real case, I mean. We told you that the Observers investigate situations that apparently involve the paranormal. I don't think we told you whether we found any that actually do. We have. I think this may be one of them."

He didn't exactly stare, but Matt felt that his reactions were being closely watched. He tried to look imperturbable. Grodek went on, still watching.

"We are involved with a lot of phenomena that most people would consider paranormal. Most of them don't show up in the tabloid press. Many of them have been known to a few men for a very long time. Centuries. Many centuries. But they've never entered the mainstream of knowledge. We research them, in ancient lore, in laboratories, in covert agendas within conventional archaeological digs. We track them, sifting news services and other media. In some cases, rarely, we intervene. I'm going to introduce you to one of those phenomena. This will constitute your next level of initiation into the Observers. You may consider it a promotion. Have you ever heard of the Dlyrion Tharkos? Or the *Chthonic Revelations* of Thanang Phram?"

"The *Revelations*, yes. But I thought they were a myth, or a hoax."

"There have been hoaxes, it's true. But the texts do exist. There are three known manuscripts. One of them is here, in this building. I could show it to you, if you like. But only a few scholars can read that ancient form of the Thai language. It will be more to the point to show you something in translation. I've copied a few pages from the English translation of von Könnenberg's nineteenth century version. You can read them here, while I attend to another matter."

Grodek passed him a new brown folder, rose and walked away toward the corridor in the back of the big room, leaving him baffled and frustrated. The folder contained three pages Xeroxed from a book printed in large type in an old-fashioned font. Grodek had marked the beginning of a paragraph on the first page with a heavy black arrow. Even in English the text was hard to follow.

The Dlyrion Tharkos, or Dark Ghosts, had existed long before mankind. The author of the *Chthonic Revelations* took pains to give their story a credible genealogy, citing earlier prehuman works such as the *Records of the Rloedha* as sources for their history, as well as hinting at more direct communications, with non-human intelligent creatures alive in Thanang Phram's time.

The Dlyrion Tharkos had originated elsewhere in the galaxy, on a dark planet on the periphery of a dying star. They sought a more hospitable home, beginning the migration by diffusing their disembodied minds across the veil of time and space to Earth. It was not clear whether their intention was to bring their own physical shells later, after establishing a beachhead on Earth, or build new bodies here, or even usurp new hosts from the bodies of the Earth life of that time. Though the wording was ambiguous, it suggested that large creatures native to Earth, some of them intelligent, already inhabited the terrestrial continents and seas. The Dlyrion Tharkos were not the first arrivals from space. Other star-creatures had preceded them, and were aware of them.

But something went horribly wrong with their plan. The new bodies never appeared. The records were unclear about the reason: perhaps the old planet was destroyed, or communications were permanently interrupted. On Earth, they could communicate mentally with other sentient creatures, but could take no action. Thus had begun an eon-long quest: the quest for a physical body to walk the Earth.

The other star-travelers had been unwilling to help them. The Rloedha, in their dark metropolis deep beneath the sea, had rebuffed them, and would have destroyed them had they possessed the means. The *Records of the Rloedha* refer to them as vicious spirits prowling after tangible prey. The 'Ithria paint a more sympathetic portrait of them, one of lost souls, deprived of their corporeal existence, sensing the physical world as a ghostly dream, elusive and hauntingly seductive to them. Only after age upon age of their ghostly outcast existence had they turned bitter and envious.

As the fragile flame of civilization flickered through the eons, lit sometimes by the native life of Earth, sometimes by cosmic travelers, the Ghosts had tried to obtain bodies advanced enough to support their own intelligence. Animals were too primitive to support the complex patterns of sentience and intelligence, textured with emotion and sensual perception. As the primordial life force inducted coarse matter into myriad living forms, the Dark Ghosts tried again and again to find their place in the space of green vegetation, rain and sky. Attempts to co-opt the bodies of lower forms led to horrible degradations and entrapment, in the form of things less intelligent than a man, yet more aware than any beast.

Whenever a civilization emerged, the natural targets for the invading Ghosts were the wizards. Every era had its special knowing ones, who came to understand the world in terms that led them to the Dark Ghosts. It was inevitable that their attempts to understand the cryptic intelligences that haunt our planet should meet the probing of the Dark ones, seeking rapport with intelligence housed in the physical organisms they so desperately craved. But again and again the invaders failed. Sometimes the result was death to both participants, sometimes an earthly intelligence that survived in tormented madness, sometimes a Dark Ghost intelligence trapped in a body it could not control and manipulate in even the most primitive way. Von Könnenberg had learned of many such accounts, and after much study speculated that the failure lay in the attempt to overlay a mature earthly mind with the contents of the alien Dark Ghost. For the Dark Ghosts to successfully invade our world corporeally, it would, theoretically, be necessary for the host body to be imprinted with both the natural growth experiences of the hosting species, and also the mature mind of the invader: an impossibility.

Grodek returned as Matt sat coming to grips with the new vistas opening to him.

"I don't get it," Matt announced. "In the first place, how do you know there's anything to these old books? There were all sorts of screwy theories kicking around in von Könnenberg's time, as there are now. There were any number of fraudulent books, fake grimoires and others. And fake artifacts—the archaeologists weren't much better than grave robbers then, at least as far as their ethics, and fakes could be sold for high prices. What do you and the Observers know that makes you take this stuff seriously? Have you ever encountered the Dark Ghosts first hand?"

Grodek eased into the big leather swivel chair and sighed.

"No, not the Dlyrion Tharkos, the Dark Ghosts. But I've met things just as bizarre, things that convinced me there is something to the ancient lore. The ancient prehuman civilizations left traces—physical as well as documentary. The whole point behind the Observers is that we can learn from those, and be prepared for what may come in the future.

"The experience I have in mind was an encounter with a bodiless vortex of pure life energy, a thing called a Black Eddy. Most religions posit that life—that is, mind, intelligence—can exist apart from any physical body. Life is a separate energy in the universe, like gravity or electromagnetism. When it forms matter around it, it exists in creatures like ourselves. When it doesn't, you have something like a Black Eddy, or a Dark Ghost. The process that forms a solar system always interacts with life energy. The Black Eddies are small currents of life that were created in the cosmic struggles of formation, when titan life forms fought to possess the solar system. There were no chemical life forms for them to inhabit then, and they aren't intelligent enough to seek bodies now, as the Dark Ghosts do. Science hasn't incorporated a separate life force into its picture yet, though there are clues like Kirlian photography. You could probably photograph a Black Eddy with that technique; I don't know what shape you would see. I only saw it's effect on physical objects. They can throw things around, like a poltergeist. And set fires. I saw one set fire to a car once. It looked as though the driver burst into flame first. You could say that the Dark Eddies have a mean streak. The Ghosts can only affect matter on the electronic level. They use that to communicate, and try to seduce intelligent creatures with bodies into helping them."

"Alright, assuming things like the Dark Ghosts exist, what makes you think that's what's happening at the Heinriches'? The dead animals sound like a poltergeist phenomenon. The little girl doesn't sound like a likely target for them. This looks like a medical problem to me, a family tragedy."

Grodek furrowed his massive brow.

"We couldn't tell much from the Heinrich incident alone. But we've collected a bit of information about Shallowford over the years. That whole area of the Hill Country has always been strange. Shallowford is near Milando, where the most appalling cult activity was discovered some years ago. We screen news items from that area routinely here. When we heard about people disappearing from the Shallowford area, we thought of the Milando cult. But we couldn't find any connection. The Milando bunch stick to themselves and don't bother outsiders.

"We started monitoring news from Shallowford and finding out all we could about the history of the place. It was considered to be haunted by the Indians. It's not far from Enchanted Rock, a unique place of power. There were some pretty suggestive tales of medicine men going insane or acting as though possessed. We thought of the Black Eddies first, but there wasn't really enough information to be sure of anything, much less distinguish between the Eddies and the Ghosts. Then there were the sightings of people thought to be dead, always in hilly, wooded places. We don't know what to make of that, but it doesn't look like the Eddies at least. We sent you there hoping you would get a line on something. I still think you will. Tomorrow we'll brief you on everything we know about that whole area of the Hill County. Then you can go back and look for any possible connection or parallel with the Heinrich situation."

Matt wasn't at all pleased with this. He liked his job with the Observers of the Unknown, and was intrigued by what he had just learned. But he was still skeptical of a connection with the Heinriches.

"I get the idea, I think. I just wish you had told me more up front."

"My apologies. We watch people pretty carefully for a long time before we start confiding these controversial matters. We don't want a lot of ex-employees starting wild rumors. Next time you go out on a case, you'll know all the background that will help you. In fact, we'll begin educating you systematically in what we know. And don't know, and would like to know."

"But these people are really upset. Aren't you afraid to intrude into a painful mess like that? Besides adding to their pain, they could turn on us and cause a public relations disaster."

Grodek thought about this for a moment.

"You've made good points on both counts. We're not inhumane, and we don't want any publicity, nasty or otherwise. But I'm genuinely worried about this one. If the Eddies are invading the little girl, or the Dark Ghosts have some kind of scheme to use her, then she's in a lot of danger and we're the only ones that might know enough to help her out."

He looked at his watch.

"It's almost nine. Come back tomorrow at eight and we'll go over all the files on the area around Shallowford, and some information about the activities of the Dark Ghosts and the Black Eddies in the twentieth century. You'll still be able to get out there by lunch time and start digging."

The phone on Kazimerz Grodek's desk buzzed. He picked it up and spoke curtly.

"Grodek. Yes?"

Matt saw his pupils dilate and his eyes open another millimeter. He thanked whoever it was and hung up. He looked at Matt with that peculiar look of someone about to conduct an experiment and curious about the result.

"Well, well. It seems it won't wait till tomorrow. We just picked up a police band call from Milando County. There's been a break-in at the Heinrich place. The girl's gone. You'll have to go back tonight."

* * *

Matt was miserable on the long drive back to Shallowford. He was shocked and saddened by the violence to the people he had just spoken with a few hours ago. He was tired from driving all day. He was irritated at Kazimerz Grodek and the Observers for sending him right back to intrude again. He was still not convinced that the Heinrich tragedy involved anything paranormal, and he knew he would arrive in the middle of a police investigation where he would be as welcome as poison ivy.

The radio report was puzzling as well as shocking. It said the little girl had been kidnapped and Hank was attacked. Other members of the family were also missing, but their car was still there. He couldn't figure all that out. It looked more complicated than a sick little girl, but he still couldn't see anything pointing to the supernatural. It was going to be hard to find out what was going on. He would have to be careful not to antagonize the police. Probably his best bet would be to get past them to Mrs. Heinrich and try to get a coherent story from her.

There were four County Sheriff's patrol cars pulled up on the lawn with lights flashing when he arrived at the Heinrich place. Two of them left, driving out past him before he came to a stop. The scene was spookily quiet except for the sporadic bark of the police radios. A flashlight moved along the edge of the woods to the left of the house. An officer in a brown uniform and a Smoky the Bear hat stepped up to him immediately.

"I'm Chief Deputy Mallory, sir. There's been a serious incident here tonight. Are you a friend of the family?"

Chief Deputy Mallory didn't look like someone you would want to lie to, or at least get caught lying to. Matt swallowed and said, "Yes," hoping his nose wouldn't grow any longer, then added, "I'm an investigator for an organization that's trying to help them find out what's been wrong with their daughter. I interviewed Hank and Betty this afternoon. As soon as I heard, I came right back."

Matt almost choked when he realized exactly what he had said. He hoped that Mallory wouldn't stop to think about how he knew about tonight's incident. At this point, probably nobody but the police knew. Mallory's eyes narrowed.

"Investigator? What kind of investigator?"

"We look into incidents that look like they might be outside the normal, you might say the paranormal, and we give the families a little money if they need it."

"Are you some kind of reporter?" said Deputy Mallory.

"No," he said with sincerity. "We try to find out what's happening in these kind of cases, and we don't publish anything about it. We don't exploit it for money in any way. We're strictly a research organization."

"Well sir, this is a crime scene now, and we're concerned about protecting evidence."

The flashlight had been moving closer to them and now a tall beefy man in the same uniform as the deputy intruded.

"Who is this, Mallory?"

"He says he's a friend of the family, Sheriff. He's an investigator for some kind of research organization. He talked to the Heinriches this afternoon. He thinks they might want to see him now. He's helping them out."

"Investigator? You mean like a private detective?"

"No sir," said Matt. "My organization investigates unusual situations like Gretchen's. We try to help out, if we can."

"Are you some kind of damn reporter?" he said with a downright mean look on his face.

"No," said Matt quickly.

None of them noticed Betty Heinrich quietly appearing on the porch.

"Sheriff Roby?" she called. She peered into the chaotic scene and recognized Matt.

"Oh, Mr. Rourdan. This is terrible, terrible! Gretchen's gone, Hank's dead. Helen and Armand and Aunt Jane are all missing. We don't know what's going on."

"I'm terribly sorry to hear that," Matt said. Her sad face looked like a disaster victim in shock, dazed and terrified.

"Please come in," she said. Sheriff Roby said, "Alright, but don't you dare touch a damn thing. This is a crime scene and if you cause any problems we'll throw your ass in jail." He used a low voice so Mrs. Heinrich wouldn't hear.

"Thank you," said Matt with unintended irony.

Mrs. Heinrich burst into tears and stepped up onto the porch. Matt followed and they went inside. By the time they got indoors her tears were a flood. Matt put his arm around her hesitantly. She welcomed it and quieted a bit. He felt awful about asking her questions. Finally he said, "It must have been horrible. They said Hank is dead." This brought on a fresh flood of tears and Matt felt even worse about questioning her. But when she finally ran out of tears, she seemed to want to talk.

"It's been awful," she said.

"What happened?" said Matt.

"A noise woke me up. Hank wasn't in the room. I went out into the hall. There was Hank on the floor. His shotgun was there next to him. He was hurt. There was blood on his head and his face. Gretchen's door was open; she was gone. I went and tried to wake up Helen and Armand but when I knocked on the door and they didn't answer, and I went in and they were gone. I was afraid; I went to the front door, thinking they might have gone outside. But their car was still here, and so was our truck. I thought I saw a light out in the woods, just for a second. But then it was gone and I couldn't be sure. That's when I called the police."

She sat back in her chair and sobbed quietly. She seemed to find a little relief in telling her tale, as she had that afternoon. Matt was puzzled by the vehicles. He felt strongly that Helen and Armand had been the actors in this and thought it unlikely that intruders had come in and taken them and the girl away. If all the vehicles were still there, what could have happened to them?

"Mrs. Heinrich," he said, "is there anywhere to go from here besides out on the road? I mean, are there trails that go anywhere or anything like that?"

"The deputies asked me that too. There isn't much. When we were kids we used to go through the woods to cross the hill to Armand's old home on the other side of that ridge, but I'm sure it's all overgrown now. The deputies have been looking all around the woods and haven't been able to find any trace where anybody went through there."

Helen and Armand; his suspicions became more and more focused on them. "Would you mind if I looked in the rooms? I'm sure the deputies have looked there, but I just might spot something new."

"Yes. They said not to touch anything in there, but I guess it's okay. Anyway I don't like them very much. That Sheriff, Roby, he's so rude and thoughtless. I trust you more."

Matt felt embarrassed. At least he wasn't a reporter. He didn't exactly trust the Observers of the Unknown, but he knew they weren't in this for money. She looked guiltily out the door and the windows, then led him quietly up the stairs.

Gretchen's room was between the head of the stairs and the Heinriches' bedroom. He could see bloodstains on the floor. Hank's shotgun had been taken away. He was mildly surprised that there wasn't a chalk outline like in the movies. He entered Gretchen's room with certain amount of trepidation, remembering her violence that afternoon. What surprised him was the absence of the usual things he would expect to see in a little girl's room: no rows of stuffed animals, no dolls on the bed, no children's books. The furniture had been tossed around and broken. He turned to Mrs. Heinrich.

"There isn't much in here. Did you remove some of it?"

"Yes, we had to take most of it out. She was so destructive. All we could do was try to save it for her to have after she got better." It might have been the lair of a wild animal. The child had made a nest out of a mattress piled in the corner and some bedclothes and cushions and articles of clothing. She had slept on that. He went back out into the hall.

"Could I see Armand and Helen's room?"

"You might as well. The police have been all over it like ants. There's no privacy left here now."

He looked inside. It was a strange haven: fantasy art posters, crystals and rocks, a crystal ball, rows of herbs in little bottles, a lot of books on UFO's, crop circles and kindred phenomena. There were books by New Age gurus and a print of a painting by Nicholas Roerich showing wise men in turbans around a campfire in an awesome mountain landscape. There was fiction by H. P. Lovecraft and Stephen King, books on ancient history, art and religion.

"Helen's stuff," said Betty. "She always had a wild imagination as a kid. I see she's no different now."

Armand's personality had left no imprint at all on the room. A thought occurred to Matt.

"What about Aunt Jane?" he asked. "Is she alright?"

"She's gone too," said Betty. "I didn't even think of her at first, she's so old and weak. When the police came they asked about her and we knocked on her door. She was gone like the others."

This made no sense at all. There was plenty of precedent for kidnapping a child, but for kidnappers to take an elderly woman with no value as a hostage was bizarre. She was too feeble to be considered as a conspirator.

"Here, I'll show you her room," Betty volunteered.

Matt stepped inside. Again he was astonished. He had expected something like a sterile hospital room. Here he saw vase after vase of fresh flowers, a box of chocolates, a half dozen bottles exotic liqueurs. There was a small but expensive stereo. Among the CD's he saw Rachmaninoff, Stravinsky, Webern and Philip Glass next to John Coltrane, R.E.M. and Metallica. The walls were covered with prints of van Gogh, Picasso, Dali and Jackson Pollock. For all the rich variety of sensations and details, the room was extremely neat and tidy. He moved in, drawn by curiosity. He heard heavy steps on the stairway and Sheriff Roby barked, "Alright you, that's enough. Mrs. Heinrich, we just can't have anybody messing around with a crime scene like this. Mr. what's-his-name's got to leave now. Sorry."

He didn't look sorry. He looked like he felt very good about throwing his weight around. Matt pressed Betty Heinrich's hand.

"I'll be back," Matt promised. "I hope everything turns out for the best." It sounded hollow to him even as he mouthed the words.

He went outside. He looked at the woods. Trying to find anything in there at night was probably a waste of time. He got in his car and drove between the crowding trees toward the paved county road, feeling baffled and frustrated. There didn't seem to be anything useful he could do here, but he couldn't just go back to Barrett empty handed. He thought about Armand's house over the hill. If Armand and Helen didn't want to be seen there, a quick look by a deputy might not have spotted them. The place could be worth another look, perhaps a more subtle one than the deputies' drive-by. He turned right and headed around the hill.

The first mailbox on the other side of the hill was overgrown with weeds, and Matt could barely make out the letters "Koeh". But the lane into the farm was clear enough to suggest recent use. Armand could have leased the land for pasture, or driven over to check on the place regularly, but the surface looked pretty clear for that sort of infrequent traffic. Weeds grew like brush fire in these fertile hills. Matt guessed that the farmhouse would be at least as far from the county road as the Heinrich place, pulled to the side, dowsed his headlights and stopped the car when he thought he was about half way. He took a small penlight flash masked with amber-colored cellophane and used it sparingly until his eyes adjusted well enough to walk in the dark. The lane went on further than he expected, and he stumbled a few times before coming to an open space. A sliver of moon showed him the dim shapes of several buildings.

The high-roofed barn was to his left. The single-storied farm house was to the right. Between them and farther away was a small shed. Twin ribbons of white clay led to the house; they forked toward the barn, but that branch was spotty with weeds. Matt stood still in the shadowy lane for a long time, watching and listening. He heard a sound, an indistinct disturbance of the silence, and sensed a movement in deep shadow by the barn. Minutes later another movement blurred the blackness between the barn and shed.

If he followed the clay ruts leading to the house, whatever or whoever had moved by the shed would probably see him in the moonlight. He moved to his right, following the tree line around to the house. He hoped he wasn't conspicuous against the trees. He had to go slow to keep from rustling the high weeds.

Up close he saw that the house was faced with light-colored stone. He could see casement windows with empty window boxes. The front porch was recessed under an overhang, in deep shadow. He couldn't see the front door clearly. If there were anyone in there, entry from the front was sure to alarm them. They would be on the alert for that. He crept around to the back of the house.

The weeds were not as high on that side of the house. Either someone had trimmed there or it had gotten some recent use. There was a door near the rear of the house. Matt stepped up and tried the doorknob gently. It was unlocked. Inside his penlight showed a big kitchen, bare except for a dishwasher and a refrigerator. The refrigerator was humming, or so he thought. But when he opened it there was nothing inside and no light. The hum was coming from somewhere else. He felt it more than heard it; it came through the floor. He looked around the room. There was a dark passage leading toward the front of the house. Next to the refrigerator was a closed door. There was a simple hook and eye latch, unfastened. He tried the door cautiously. He eased it open, an inch at a time.

Dim light, indirect, lit a stair leading down. The hum was louder there. He heard a muffled word, in a woman's voice. He crept down three steps before one made a barely audible squeak. His heart jumped, but there was no reaction from the space below. I really ought to turn around and go get the law, he thought. There was definitely something going on here, that was what he had come to find out. He didn't need to get involved. His curiosity pulled him down two more steps before the decision was taken out of his hands.

"Get your hands up or I'll blow your head off," said the voice behind him. He recognized Armand's voice; it sounded nervous. He raised his hands and looked carefully over his shoulder. Armand was sweating and licked his lips. He was holding an Uzi, a shiny semi-auto civilian model. He held it awkwardly, way out in front of him like he wasn't sure just how it worked. Matt wasn't sure whether Armand was desperate enough to shoot him deliberately, but getting shot by accident looked like a real possibility. "Downstairs, real slow," said Armand. Matt didn't argue.

The stairs ended in a big room lit by a shaded bulb hanging from the middle of the ceiling. Helen was there, dressed in jeans and pointing a revolver at him. Aunt Jane sat in a rocking chair, outside the circle of light. And on the floor, laying on a blanket with another pulled up to her chin, was Gretchen. She lay still, breathing rapidly and shallowly but apparently unconscious. A kind of harness around her head connected her to a bundle of wires running up to an electronic device on a workbench against the wall behind her, a long low black box with knobs and switches and a couple of illuminated meters with twitching needles. The box was in turn connected to a two-foot antenna-like device standing next to it, shaped like an Egyptian ankh and glowing softly with a flickering iridescence. Next to Gretchen, just outside the light, was another child, on its side with it's back toward Matt. It too was connected to the apparatus on the workbench.

"All right, who are you?" said Helen. She jabbed the gun at him. Her voice was tight and edgy, but not shaky like Armand's. If she shot him, it would be on purpose.

"I told you before," said Matt. "I'm an investigator for the Observers of the Unknown."

"Whatever that is," she said. "You're not a reporter. You're not a cop. So why are you breaking into this house in the middle of the night?"

"We heard that Gretchen had disappeared," he said. "My boss sent me back to investigate. There wasn't much I could do. I decided to look this place over."

"Didn't they tell you they had been here?" she said.

"Yeah, but I figured they were in a hurry," he said. "I had all night. No place to stay."

"Now you have," she said. "You're not going anywhere till we're through here. Sit down in that chair." She waved the gun at an empty folding chair against the left wall. "Armand, tie him up. Do a good job of it."

Armand prodded him and he sat. His wrists were pulled behind him and he felt a shaky fumbling and something like nylon clothesline. He kept moving slightly, trying to get some slack into the knots. He suspected Armand wasn't highly skilled at this.

Helen looked at the girl. Her eyes went dreamy again, like they had been that afternoon. She looked back at him again.

"You clowns have about as much chance of figuring out what's going on in these woods as you do of landing on Mars," she said. "These woods were here before Columbus. Before Egypt. Before man existed. And they've never stopped brooding, never stopped dreaming. I've been here, dreaming with them, sensing them, listening to them, since I was a child."

"And what do they dream about?" he prompted.

"Never mind. It's none of your business," she said. She turned away to look at the electronic box, turning a knob very slightly. She looked over the two children carefully.

"Armand," she said. "Get back outside and watch for the deputies." Then, to Matt, "Do they know you're here?"

He almost said no.

"Yes, of course." He caught himself about to lick his lips. She stared at him suspiciously.

"What is all this? Who is the other child?" he asked quietly.

Her smile came back, slow and contemptuous.

"You still don't get it, do you?" she said. "Let's make a trade. I'll tell you what you want to know, after you tell me exactly what you and the deputies said when you told them you were coming here."

"Don't bother, Helen," said a soft, dry voice from the shadowed rear of the room. Aunt Jane leaned forward slightly and moved the rocker gently. "They certainly don't know he's here. They would never have let him come."

Helen opened her mouth slightly with an irritated look that said "I knew that." Matt looked to the figure now rocking slowly, rhythmically in the deep shadow.

The hairs rose on the back of his neck. None of this was what he expected. Nothing made sense. He had to get some information out of these people, quick.

"Isn't that right, Mr. Rourdan?" said Aunt Jane. "I'm sure we have plenty of time before he's missed."

"Time for what? A ransom demand?" he said.

She made a gurgling sound that might have been a chuckle.

"Time to complete our project," she said. "Then we can release you, and return the child."

"Don't you mean children?" he said. He glanced toward the little blanketed figure next to Gretchen. He kept squirming in the chair to cover up the movement of his hands behind his back. The figure moved. A twitch of the head; a shudder; then a half-turn toward Matt. At first he stared uncomprehending. Then he looked at Gretchen, then back to the other. They were identical. Either one could have been the child he saw that afternoon.

"A twin?" he asked.

"Not a twin," said Aunt Jane. "A clone. Armand created her, with a little technical advice from me. We raised her here, with periodic sessions like this to develop the neural patterns she would have gotten from a normal childhood. Tonight she is completing the neural connections needed to support a fully developed ego."

"Such as yours?" he said.

"No, unfortunately," she said. "I can never be translated out of this body. I will die with it. Soon, if I'm not mistaken."

Matt grappled with the implications of this.

"Who are you?" he said at last.

"I am Jayyeen. That is a good approximation for your language. The right rhythm, the right contour. Jane is not so evocative. It is merely convenient. Colorless, not exotic, not likely to attract attention. Just how much do you know about us?"

And Matt felt her mind blow through his consciousness like a gust before a thunderstorm, swirling through his own thoughts, evoking his recent experiences, probing at his deeper memories. It made him giddy; his body and mind were out of control. Her mind touched his, mingled with it. With it came an emotional timbre, one of humor and sadness, not threatening. Her intelligence was luminous, thrilling; strangely tranquil.

"I see," she said. "You know more than I thought, and less. I should like to meet your Mr. Grodek, but I don't think that will be possible. Dark Ghosts—I like that. Dlyrion Tharkos is a fragment from a language of Earth, of men, a language dead for a very long time. Yes, we have become like ghosts, haunting your planet and your race. It is not what we wished for."

The sadness throbbed; and then her mind withdrew from his, leaving him looking at the bent figure rocking gently outside the light. His mind felt so dry and hollow by contrast that he wondered if he could have imagined it, the telepathic contact, even the words. She seemed to need to tell her story; he tried to be an attractive listener.

"So what did you wish for?" he said.

"A new home for our minds, in bodies of our own, nothing more. Our old home was much like yours once, though, to our specialized sensory array, even more beautiful. Our sun was green, our moon was bigger. We had a sense of smell, and our world was perfume to us. There is a name for that world in your language, a name that has crept down the eons through many alien tongues to a few knowing ones; the name of Yith. But Yith was doomed. I will not trouble you with the intricacies of our history, the tortuous path that led us here, to this age. We lost and won and lost again our beloved Yith; we took refuge here on earth more than once, in more than one epoch, in more than one kind of body.

"At the last we few, a final pathetic remnant of our great race, sent our minds here for the last time. We planned to grow new bodies here, from native terrestrial materials. Of course we tested the plan before all of us came over, before abandoning our old bodies. But the test project hadn't been thorough enough. The new bodies all succumbed to terrestrial microorganisms after a year or so, the mind dying with the body. Many of us died that way, having lived only a few short centuries. The rest of us were stranded. Eventually we even lost the ability to create the new bodies. All of us who knew how to make the bodies had migrated and died in them.

"Nothing had prepared us for this. It was a time when we all tested every aspect of our new noncorporeal existence. The amazing freedom that came with not being bound by a physical body was not without charm. We have a tradition that our remote ancestors lived that way, before they found their first bodies. Telepathic communication had been limited and tiring among us; and now it was the norm. But there was a dimness of sensation, as though seeing the Earth through cloudy glass, that frustrated us. Our lifelong physical needs were never satisfied. I think your kind would say we lacked sensory gratification.

"At first we studied the creatures of Earth with frantic desperation. We could reach telepathically into the minds of the earthly life forms of that time, and flitted nervously from mind to mind, looking for any shred of hope. None of us believed that we could be trapped in this limbo forever. We tried everything we could think of. The smaller bipedal carnivores were the most intelligent, but none of them were intelligent enough to match our thought processes. The few of us who succeeded in embodying themselves suffered horribly, torn by the claws and teeth of ferocious reptiles because they could not operate their new bodies well enough to compete and survive.

"Sooner or later each of us came to a hideous realization. We were doomed to haunt this planet as a ghostly presence, one that could sense the world but dimly and act in it in only the faintest ways. Some of us went quite mad—those still roam the earth, raging in the shadows. Others tried to voyage through space, away from this prison. But they found they could only travel very slowly, and year after year drifting through the void was worse than existing here. A few actually managed to extinguish themselves through an act of will. But most of us were unable to do that.

"You see, without bodies to age, we seem to go on indefinitely, no matter how mad or miserable we might be. Our old bodies lasted longer than yours, sometimes several thousand of your years. But my mind has now existed here for about one hundred and twenty million years. And only now, in your time, do we find a new hope. But there are still major problems to overcome.

"Your nervous system is complex, not too different from our original one but not a perfect match. Like ours, its physical development follows genetically determined lines, shaped by experience. We cannot take over an infant body; our mind reverts to an embryonic state in which it can't survive. Yet we can't take on a fully developed brain; it is already imprinted too thoroughly with human patterns. That is what I attempted seventy years ago; you see the result. Humans have always taken me for the victim of some pathological condition, such as a stroke. I have never had full control over this body, or experienced it's senses as fully as you do every day of your life, Mr. Rourdan."

"Can't you leave it, to try again?" asked Matt.

"Probably not," said the creature called Jayyeen. "But then I would never choose to. A clumsy body and dulled senses are still better than the dim nightmare I endured for millions of years."

"But won't you die when that body—Jane's body—finishes it's normal span?" he said.

"Yes," she said. "Of course. But I couldn't go back to that existence. I couldn't bear it. I would become like those who became distorted by it, half mad with suffering and rage. Better to enjoy every day that I can feel the soft air on my skin, feel hunger and satisfy it with rich flavors and textures, thrill with music . . ."

She paused, moving the rocking chair gently. Helen stopped fidgeting and tinkered with the apparatus on the bench. Behind him he felt the rope loosening around his wrists. He was sure he could free himself any time now. But Armand was pointing the gun directly at his chest. He would have to wait for a diversion.

"So—the clone?" he said. "How do you get around that with the clone?"

"We created her right after Gretchen was born, accelerating her growth until she was as mature as Gretchen," said Jayyeen. "We kept her comatose most of the time, to minimize the development of any individuality. We took necessary precautions to protect her from intruding influences; the brain is vulnerable in that unformed state. We gave her the basic physical exercise she needed, speaking as little as possible. As frequently as we could, we connected the two of them as you see them now. The device on the bench is systematically picking up the patterns of Gretchen's neural networks and imprinting them on the clone's brain. It causes the clone's neurons to develop in ways similar Gretchen's—she will be able to speak as well as Gretchen, for instance. She will have the neural infrastructure to support an ego. But she will not be Gretchen. We tuned that out."

"Who will she be, then?" asked Matt. "You haven't mentioned a name."

In the dim light around her Matt could barely see Jayyeen smile, a lopsided grimace in a poorly controlled body.

"Now, she is no one. She is at her most malleable, and could be imprinted by any strong mind with a knack for the technique. But by morning she will have a name," said Jayyeen. "She will be Deighan."

"And who is Deighan?" said Matt.

"A friend," she said. "An old, old friend."

"Jane," said Helen. "REM's stopped. Her eyes aren't moving at all now."

She stared expectantly at Jayyeen. At last the whispery voice came.

"Then the imprinting has gone as far as it can. Make the adjustments now, just as we practiced them. It is time for Deighan to inhabit her brain. He is near—I've felt his presence for the last hour. Be still, and I will summon him. Mr. Rourdan—you must remember that the mind you are about to encounter has been through an ordeal that no human being can imagine. Do not expect him to be pleasant, or gentle."

The room was silent except for a hum from the electronic device. The rocking chair stopped moving. Helen stood very still, keeping even her breath soundless.

Matt felt Deighan's mind; it expanded into the space of the room. It penetrated his mind like a searchlight, coloring his perception of the scene before him. He felt it examining each area of the room, each sentient creature. When it focused on him in turn, he felt paralyzed, like a nocturnal creature caught in a spotlight. Jayyeen had probed his mind, delicately. Deighan invaded it. Matt could not think, only observe the glare of Deighan's energy. The color of the glare was rage. It came to rest on the still form of the clone.

He felt the intrusion of Jayyeen's mind as clearly as a voice. Her serenity was a stark contrast to Deighan's brutal rage and desire. Without words she reminded him of better times, when they had been lovers, hopeful of life on this new planet. In her presence he gentled somewhat, grew cautious.

The third presence had been growing for some time before Matt, Jayyeen or Deighan noticed it. Matt recognized it and remembered a growing feeling of dread, an ominous low hum, at first faint, increasing so gradually that no one was alarmed till cold psychic viciousness erupted into swirling conflict with the two Dark Ghosts. A name came to him: a Black Eddy.

Matt could grasp but dimly the nature of that conflict; moving, flashing sparks of rage and pain, space-bound, yet unconfined by the constraints of corporeal creatures. Each mind was everywhere, but there were concentrations. One entity could force expansion into a focal space of another and cause painful psychic damage.

Matt closed his eyes to suppress the instinct to picture the three combatants. To his mind, they seemed entangled like clouds of colored vapor. Deighan and Jayyeen were barely able hold the monstrous sentience at bay with their combined force. They were forming a shield between the Black Eddy and the two young bodies on the blanket. Matt opened his eyes.

All attention now circled the still figure under the light. The clone was breathing slowly, shallowly. Matt could barely see the blanket rise and fall. Deighan's mental presence withdrew from the space of the room, like an ominous noise fading, leaving Jayyeen alone to keep out the Black Eddy. Suddenly Matt sensed only the still, partially lit space of the room, uninspired by the ancient ghost-minds. Then the clone moved.

The clear blue eyes opened, staring intently at the ceiling. They rolled around for several seconds before the head moved, twisting slowly to view the room without moving the body. It sat upright, dropping the blanket and bringing its head into the light. The face was without movement or tension, expressionless.

It got up and explored the room. They had dressed it to be identical with Gretchen, but the difference was obvious. It's movements were quite odd, now eerily slow, now quick like the pounce of a predator. The limbs often went beyond a natural range of motion into alien postures. The facial muscles took on tone, widening the eyes slightly into a drilling stare and baring the teeth in a bestial grimace. Matt realized that it was not Gretchen he had seen in the Heinrich house. An imprinting session had gone wrong; they had taken the clone into Gretchen's room and Hank had surprised them; he had unwittingly locked them out with the real Gretchen. They had been caught with the clone trapped in Gretchen's room and Gretchen outside.

Matt struggled to comprehend what he saw—an ancient soul turned evil, now inhabiting a small energetic body with sun-blond hair. The creature moved toward its double and leaned over her, as though curious. A small fist poked the unconscious child through the blanket. Deighan grabbed Gretchen's arm through the blanket and shook it violently. Matt felt the disembodied hatred again. Deighan's right hand went to Gretchen's throat.

Again the solemn beauty of Jayyeen's mind was present in the room, pleading with Deighan to protect the child who had brought new physical life to a ghost. Matt felt the rage anew, saw the small hand tighten on the pale little throat. Matt was alarmed. He freed his hands behind him. But Armand was glancing around the room nervously, his finger on the trigger.

There was a sound from the stairs. Heads snapped toward the door. Armand pointed the gun at the door and emitted a strangled squawk. Matt sprang up from the chair and rushed at the clone. He grabbed both arms above the elbow. The slim little creature thrashed like a wild animal, throwing him off balance. Helen came at him with a shriek. Armand turned in panic. And then the Uzi was exploding in an irregular rhythm as Armand jerked the trigger as fast as he could, bullets rattling off the walls around him, the sound hammering his skull and ringing off the cement. Stunned, Matt whipped his head around to see Armand, eyes wide, mouth agape, blasting away in his general direction.

"Police!" barked Deputy Mallory. Armand whirled, again pointing the gun toward the door. The deputy didn't wait to give another warning. His shotgun barked and Armand flew backward. Matt heard the back of his skull hit the concrete. The Uzi skittered across the room and stopped. It was quiet again.

A short blond blur rushed the door. Matt heard a startled exclamation from Mallory.

"Lohman! Stop her! The little girl's running away!" shouted Mallory. But Deputy Lohman wasn't quick enough.

Matt surveyed the room. Armand stared at the ceiling, not blinking. Helen was sitting on the floor, legs splayed, leaning against a cabinet. She was looking down at a dark stain spreading from the center of her blouse. She looked up at Matt as though to ask him about it. Then her face went blank and gray and she fell over sideways. Aunt Jane was slumped in the rocking chair. She bled so little that it would take an autopsy to find the nine millimeter bullet. Careful examination convinced Matt that he was unhurt. Armand really was a lousy shot.

Deputy Mallory had entered the room. He was watching Gretchen stirring under the blanket.

"Who . . . ?" he was saying when Gretchen sat up and started to scream.

* * *

The air is deliciously cool on her skin, sparking her to move quickly through the dark woods. The exertion makes warmth flow throughout her skin. The coolness of the air and the warmth of the blood under the skin mingle in a sensuous turbulence that envelopes her. Breathing the air is another delight, cold and warmth mingling, the smells of the woods teasing her nose. It is good to have a body.

The alien mind is already shaped by the physical body and brain around it, creating a She, a being of Yin energy and resonance with the moon, albeit an immature one. It is rapidly imprinting it's own memories on that brain, while sharing the memories it found there. There is no strong ego here to vie for control, unlike the other body. It had been much easier to penetrate this one.

She can sense that other, away across the woods. She follows that sense. Now she glimpses window lights from the house. Her movement slows, gains stealth. She knows how to hunt. She has haunted the minds of earth's predators through the millennia, and brings those memories into her new body.

Near the edge of the woods she sees a different light; a tiny orange glow above the ground, it brightens, then dims again. Sniffing the acrid cigarette smoke, her nose more than her eyes tells her that this is one of the big men who came with the sheriff. A leaf rustles under her foot. The light flicks away toward the house and lands on the ground. His big black silhouette moves cautiously toward her. She crouches low, not moving a hair. He comes almost close enough to reach out and touch her. He leans over and peers into the dark.

The child was wolfing down cookies and milk at the kitchen table. Betty still hadn't gotten her to speak. Since the deputies brought her into the house, she had alternated between clinging to Betty, sobbing loudly the whole time, and pulling away from everyone who came near her. During the pulling-away periods she would retreat with her back to a wall and warily study her surroundings, making no sounds at all. During a cling-and-cry period Betty had maneuvered her into the kitchen and offered the cookies. She was ravenous the way only a growing child can be, and the act of eating seemed to stabilize her. Betty kept trying to soothe her.

"There, Honey, you're safe now," said Betty. "Nothing's going to hurt you now."

Gretchen stopped in mid-cookie and looked up at her.

"The other one," she said.

"What other one?" said Betty.

"The other one wants me," she said, and started bawling again.

Betty cuddled her for a few minutes and she fell asleep in her arms. She lifted her gently and carried her upstairs, with Matt following on tiptoes. She paused in front of Gretchen's bedroom, remembered the mess in there, and took the girl down the hall to her own bed. The child didn't wake up when Betty tucked her in and kissed her on the forehead.

This would clear the way for the sheriff to talk to them some more. Matt wasn't looking forward to it. Crammed in a patrol car with poor Gretchen squalling her head off, he'd only been able to communicate that he went over there on a hunch and stumbled onto the kidnapping scene. If Mallory hadn't insisted that he saw Matt jump Armand, Matt would surely have been locked up in the Shallowford jail at this point. And the night wasn't over yet.

None of the lawmen had seen the clone well enough to spot the resemblance to

Gretchen. But the presence of another child, one not in custody yet, had the sheriff thoroughly shaken up. For reasons known only to himself, he thought that meant Betty Heinrich knew more than she was telling. She and Matt could both become guests of the county if they weren't careful about what they said.

Patiently explaining the role of Jayyeen and Deighan to Sheriff Roby was not an option.

Deputy Mallory came in the front door just as Matt was descending the stairs. Matt followed him into the kitchen and helped him find a glass to drink water from.

"Any word on the other girl?" asked Matt. There had been a constant crackle of radio messages between Mallory and Lohman at the farm and their colleagues back at the Guidreaux scene.

"No," said the deputy. "They figure she's hiding in the woods near the house, scared to death. Can't say I blame her. They're walking around the edge of the woods calling to her, telling her it's safe to come out. But it's a zoo over there, with the Coroner's people, the ambulances, the state troopers we called in to help us search. All flashing lights and noise."

"What's the plan if she doesn't come out?" said Matt.

"Tomorrow we'll get a Ranger out here to help us figure things out. We're just a rural county force, we know we're in over our heads. But my guess is we'll try dogs first."

"Dogs? Like bloodhounds?" said Matt. "Isn't that kind of extreme?"

"Not as bad as it sounds," said the deputy. "They're trained for rescue as well as fugitives. They won't hurt anybody either way. It'll be terrifying for her, of course, that's why we haven't got the dogs out here already. But an army of troopers and volunteers would be about as bad. And any evidence outside the house would get stomped."

"Anybody have a clue about what kind of electronic gear that was over there?" said Matt, feeling dishonest.

"We were hoping you would," said Mallory. "But I was waiting for Sheriff Roby to ask the questions. He'll be pissed if I don't."

"They had both kids hooked up to it with wires," said Matt. He would say only true things; commit only sins of omission. He could handle that. Unless they put him on a polygraph. Damn. They could ask him if he knew anything more, and the needles would fly off the machine. Matt decided to keep the conversation short.

"Some kind of experiment maybe?" he offered innocently.

Mallory chuckled.

"Mad scientists in the Texas Hill Country? That's too much for a country cop like me."

Matt let the conversation stall for a couple of minutes. They were both tired, underneath the tension.

"Mind if I step outside and breathe a little fresh air?" said Matt. "It's been pretty intense, and you can almost smell the sadness in here."

"Yeah, crime scenes get like that. Just don't touch anything. Need to catch a smoke? That's what Lohman's doing out there."

"Nope, that's one bad habit I missed. I'll help Lohman look for clues."

"He's not going to find anything out there in the dark," said Mallory. "If he does, he'll probably step in it."

They had turned off the lights on the patrol car and the fragment of moon had gone down. The starry abyss twinkled in infinite mystery. He stood on the porch in silence, struggling for equilibrium among the dizzying events of the long, long day. The air was still and textured with the faint sounds of nocturnal life, rustlings, whisperings, a drone of insects, a coyote in the distance.

After a while, the present reality ensnared him again. He wondered where Lohman was. There was a pinpoint of orange light on the ground to his right, near the trees. He walked to it carefully in the starlight. Near it Lohman was spread-eagled on the ground. An incongruous image flitted through his mind, the deputy lying on his back looking up at the stars. But closer he saw that Lohman lay face down, in a dark pool that had spread as far as his shoulders.

The one she seeks is in the house, upstairs, sleeping. She can sense the others, less clearly. They are downstairs, two in the kitchen below the sleeping one, the mother in the room next to them; all far from the hated one. The fleshy memories are very clear, those that came with the body, though the feelings attached to them are sometimes alien to the dominant mind. The more ancient entity has it's own memories, stretching back far into the past, dark and misty memories, malevolent passions. She knows a way to get to the sleeping one without alerting the others.

She creeps to the left around the side of the house. The chicken house is back there, empty now. The fence around the chicken pen is nailed to the corner of a tool shed attached to the house. With practiced dexterity she climbs up the fence to get on top of the tool shed. It comes easily. It feels good, using the small but strong musculature to move the little body in space, against gravity. From the roof of the shed she can stand on tiptoe and look into Aunt Jane's room, dark and empty. A big oak, even with the center of the house, needs trimming; it's lower branches brush the shed, one of the highest brushes the roof. The branches are plenty strong enough for her willowy little body. She swarms up the tree like a monkey, lands on the roof with a light pat. No chance of being heard on the ground floor, through the half-attic and the second floor.

The front door slams. A car approaches down the dirt drive. She scampers over the ridgepole, to the side away from the car. The car door opens and closes. A knock at the front door. She senses them, all four of them, hears muffled words, sharp, excited voices. The door opens again. The three men are running across the yard, to the smoking man.

There are small dormer windows on the front side of the roof, but now she is afraid to use them because of the men. But she knows another way, one she found last year. It will be more fun anyway. She loves to climb. She crawls back to the end of the house, by the tree. She grips the branch, turns around to face the house, finds the window sill with her feet. She has no fear of falling. She lets go of the branch, grips the window frame. With one hand she tests the window. It is still unlocked. It slides up easily.

She is in the attic. It has no floor, she has to find each cross beam with her foot. But she can hold on to the rafters above. She can't see them but she knows there are boxes, chairs, parts of an old bed. She doesn't have far to go. She finds the trap door. She opens it with exquisite caution, making almost no sound at all. She sees the floor below, the floor of the hall near the end, by Aunt Jane's room.

Sheriff Roby stared slack-jawed at Deputy Lohman.

"Damn," he said. "What's going on around here?" He turned his stare on Matt, right in the eyes, unblinking. "Mister, if you know any more than you're telling us I'm going to find that out. And you'll need a hell of a lawyer just to mop up the mess. That's my deputy there on the ground."

"I swear, Sheriff, I don't know who or what did that," said Matt. It was perfectly true. "But whatever it is, don't you think we need to make damn sure it doesn't get in the house? We don't know what it wants, but Mrs. Heinrich and the girl are in there alone right now, and the front door's wide open."

The Sheriff was taken aback by this.

"You've got a point, whoever you are. Mallory, I need to call the other site and get backup and crime scene personnel over here. I'll stay with Lohman, you and . . ."

"Rourdan," murmured Matt.

". . . him go in the house. Get Mrs. Heinrich to check all the doors and windows. Keep somebody in sight of the front door at all times. I don't want to lock it, with a possible emergency going down. And check on the girl. She's the one was kidnapped; could be she's the target again."

"That's a lot of jobs to go around, with just us," said Mallory. "And it leaves you out here alone with whatever got Lohman."

"I got a gun," said the sheriff, "and right about now I'd love to use it."

On his way to the door Matt saw the sheriff standing outside the patrol car with a shotgun in one hand and microphone in the other, barking orders to the other site.

Mallory broke the news to Betty.

"A deputy's been hurt, ma'am, and there seems to be something dangerous on the loose."

"Oh my God, Gretchen!" she said. "I've got to make sure she's safe."

"Before you go up, are there any doors or windows down here that could be open? Besides the front door?" said Mallory.

"There's just the back door, I think it's locked. All the windows are."

"I'll check them anyway," he said. "Matt, you check the front windows, but make sure the door's never out of your sight. Close it so you'll hear anybody trying to get in, but don't lock it."

Betty hurried up the stairs and the deputy moved to the back part of the house. Matt checked each window carefully. They were all locked and the latches finely coated with undisturbed dust. He had to let the door just out of sight a couple of times, but only for a second at most.

Mallory reappeared.

"I should check upstairs, too," he said "Not likely anything would come in that way, but I ought to make sure. I'm going to talk to the sheriff for a minute first. Go on up there and stay with Mrs. Heinrich. I'll keep an eye on the door."

Once Mallory was out the door Matt picked up a poker from the fireplace. For once he wished he had a gun. He took the stairs three at a time. He paused at the top, suddenly wary. He thought he had heard a subtle sound to his left. He listened hard; he heard nothing more. He went right to the room where Betty was comforting her daughter. Gretchen was clinging to her mother and sobbing softly, but she was unhurt. Matt met Betty's eyes without speaking, afraid of setting off another torrent of crying. He turned back to check the other upstairs rooms.

He skipped Gretchen's room, dreading to see the pathetic mess again. All seemed secure till he reached the end of the all. He felt a draft on his neck and looked up. The hatch to the attic was open.

Instantly his world changed. Hackles rose. His pulse throbbed. He raised the poker to a striking position. He instinctively moved his back to the wall at the end of the hall. His attention focused on the one door he hadn't entered. It seemed to take minutes to reach the door. It was painful to leave an open space behind himself, a space an unknown predator could occupy. But logic told him the menace was in the child's bedroom.

He stood outside the door holding the poker ready. He wished he had the key to lock the door. He realized he needed to protect Betty and Gretchen and get the armed lawmen up here. He turned around and shuffled backwards to the bedroom, never turning his back to Gretchen's room.

When he reached the doorway Gretchen looked at him, making no sound. She pulled away from her mother and got out of the bed. There was a stiffness to her movement, a clumsiness unexpected in a healthy eleven-year-old. She turned her back to the wall, moving backwards as Matt had. She spoke, in a voice high-pitched yet husky, coarse.

"It is here," she said. "The other one."

Matt tautened, like an overstretched wire. A terrible understanding was dawning.

"Who is the other one?" he said.

"The earth thing, the black swirling one. The—what do you men call it? The Eddy."

"Then you are . . ."

"I am Deighan. When the Black Eddy seized on the clone, I couldn't push it out, couldn't enter. I had to take the girl Gretchen. But she is nearly mature, too thoroughly formed. I can't hold on here, not as Jayyeen did with the woman. Jayyeen entered by a better process. Soon I'll be gone from this body. I have no control now."

"What about the girl?" asked Matt. "Does she still exist? Have you destroyed her with this invasion?"

"She is still here. Sometimes she is in control, and I can only watch her."

"Will she be damaged, or die, when you leave?"

"I don't think so," said Deighan/Gretchen. "But the other one will kill this body if it can."

The front door slammed. Matt looked down the hall. The other one had crept within six feet of him. It's entire face was smeared with blood. The hair was tangled, the blue pajamas ragged. Crouched low it looked hardly human. Matt thrust the poker without thinking, just as it launched itself at him without warning. Repelled by the poker it scampered back and forth, feinting, ducking, trying to get around the poker. It's teeth were bared in a predator's grin and it snorted and snarled.

Matt was yelling. Sheriff Roby appeared at the top of the stairs midway down the hall, handgun drawn. The creature turned and rushed him. The sheriff would later report that the shot was involuntary. The thing staggered and bounced off the wall before leaping for his throat. He dropped the gun and went down like timber with it clinging to him and biting his face, trying to get to his throat. He pushed it away and let go and it scurried down the stairs. Mallory was just coming through the open door and it rushed past him, for the second time that night. It left behind bright red spots of blood turning dark. The little body that should never have existed, that could never have housed a fully human spirit, was never again seen by a human being.

Gretchen was clinging and crying "Mama, mama," while Betty hugged her tight. Was Deighan still there? Matt didn't know and didn't try to find out. If anybody was going to come between mother and child again that night, it wasn't going to be Matt Rourdan.

* * *

When Matt finished his report, Kazimerz Grodek sat staring into space for a moment, hands folded across his stomach.

"Mrs. Heinrich," said Grodek. "She heard the creature Deighan speak through the girl? Clearly?"

"Yes," said Matt, "but she seemed to be in denial about it. Just before I left, I asked her if Gretchen had spoken again 'like she did back in the bedroom'. She said no, she hadn't been 'babbling' like that any more. If Deighan's gone, I don't think Betty will bring it up again. She wants desperately to believe Gretchen's back to normal."

"And the police found no trace of the clone?"

"In the morning they found a few more spots of blood in the woods," said Matt. "The hounds followed the scent to the bank of the Atascosa River, then lost it. They were saving samples of the blood. Won't DNA tests show her identical to Gretchen? Then all hell will break loose. The sheriff will be sure Betty Heinrich and I are conspiring in some hellish scheme involving a twin."

"No doubt," said Grodek. "But they won't run tests unless they have something to compare it with. They might want to check against some children from their missing persons file, but why should they compare it with Gretchen Heinrich? No one but you got a good enough look to see the resemblance. No, I'm more concerned about you. Do you really think the Sheriff's satisfied with your story?"

"No," said Matt. "He'll never be my biggest fan. But everything I told him will check out. They're already coming around to the idea that the Guidreauxs were operating some kind of illegal enterprise with children, long before I showed up on the scene."

"So we are left with the conundrum of the missing clone," said Grodek. "If she drowned in the river, we may never know for certain."

"True. The police believe she did."

"And you, Matt," he said. "What do you believe?"

"That's a tough one. I think I saw two one hundred and twenty million-year-old souls in human bodies. Every other possibility makes even less sense. But can I accept that? Take what I've believed about man's place in the universe and turn it upside down? Because of what I saw in one night, in a poorly lit basement with adrenaline running out of my ears?"

Grodek smiled.

"It is a problem, isn't it? It would be so much nicer if proof came in a neat, definitive package, with a platoon of credible witnesses and plenty of physical evidence. Unfortunately, this is what we get, most of the time. The ancient relics can always be challenged, new tests demanded and the ambiguous results given more weight than the clear ones. But I've seen a lot of it. Here at the observers, we live in a haunted universe." He lit the pipe and stared into space some more.

"So," said Grodek after a while, "now that you know what the job is about, do you still want to work for the Observers of the Unknown?"

Matt smiled.

"Of course," he said.

* * *

The Black Eddy soars over the water, sensing the last flickers of the life force in the small body drifting downstream. It had been so easy to enter the body, with its half-formed unconscious mind. It senses that the animals feeding, hunting, scurrying in the night, would be easier. Especially when they sleep. There are deer in the woods, possum, armadillo, javelina, but they are not attractive to the Black Eddy. It prefers the coyote, the bobcat, the rattlesnake. It picks out a mountain lion prowling alone. It follows easily, waiting for dawn, when the lion will sleep. It will be even more exciting than the little girl.

It is good to have a body.

The Taint of Lovecraft

by Stanley C. Sargent
Robert M. Price, Editor

DH

The second collection from the author of *Ancient Exhumations,*
Stanley C. Sargent, with wonderful illustrations and
featuring his novella, *Nyarlatophis, a Fable of Ancient Egypt.*
$20